DAWN

MY CHILDREN FROM ANOTHER WORLD

BOOK 1: DAWN

PAYTON FLETCHER
AKA _GLASSES

Podium

Podium

DAWN

1

It was with little gentleness that I wrenched the door open, toppling inside with a dry mouth and a heavy heart. The room was well lit, warm, with the viridian-green blankets of the midwife laid out across the end of the bed.

On the bed, her pale skin wracked with sweat and a weak, gentle smile upon her lips, was Lydia, my darling, beautiful wife. In her arms, swaddled by emerald ruffles of cloth, were our children.

They were quiet. Sleeping?

I dared not utter a word as she looked up at me, a peaceful resignation in her eyes. The peace dug into me, into my heart, and even during this dire time, I felt relief.

A relief I cherished while my Lydia was still here to stoke it.

"They're beautiful." Her words were like the last chimes of wind that preceded the calm before the storm.

You're beautiful, I wanted to say. There were a thousand things I wanted to say. Why now, of all times, did I have to be cursed with such a difficult tongue?

I walked over to the bedside, sitting down in the ornate chair that I had kept vigil in for hours before she had truly gone into labor and my presence would have been only a detriment.

Lydia shifted the cloth bundled in her arms, showing me the faces of the children, my children. The children that Lydia and I had dreamed about in our years together, and yet I would have to cherish them alone after today.

Gazing upon them for the first time, I was almost startled at the three sets of eyes staring back at me. I had thought they were sleeping, the quietness fooling me, but no. They were awake and well aware.

Truly, perhaps, more aware than children of such freshness should be, certainly. Something itched at the back of my head, but I ignored it. These were my children, and this precious moment had no room for tedious feelings.

I swallowed, my tongue struggling to find the words. "They . . . They look so much like you."

For such early intelligence could hardly be attributed to me.

My wife smiled. "I think they favor you more."

Perhaps, she had a point. Even now, I could tell that the three children favored the darker-brown skin of the Ruskans, although nowhere near my own.

Perhaps it was the cerulean eyes of the infant held in Lydia's left hand, the soft, budding hints of silver hair, glimmering in the candlelight, of the middle child, or the paler skin, more like her mother's than my own, of the last little girl.

"Names . . ."

I looked over to Lydia, my wife's form beginning to buckle under its own weight more and more as every second passed, and nodded, "Names."

Settling in beside my wife, taking up as little space on the restorative cushions as I could, I gently took the first child from her, a girl from the looks of it. The one with the dazzling sky-blue eyes of her mother.

I glanced at Lydia, suddenly realizing the enormity of this impossible task. "I'm . . . terrible with names. You should name her."

With a soft shake of her head, my wife was stalwart. "I'll name the others."

I looked down at the small child in my hands, my daughter, and . . . she was so small in my grip. She gazed up at me, as if questioning why her small form was now in the warmth of my hands, her father's hands.

And I was scared of her, of hurting her, more scared than I had ever been fighting the demons and monsters of my land. Terrified of the idea that one day I might damage the innocence before me.

To inspire such fear within me, to already have such a grip upon my heart within moments, this child was strong. So unimaginably strong.

A strength that I could only hope she carried with her throughout her entire life.

I uttered the first name that came to mind, "Daka, a name for one who inspires fear and love."

Tentatively, I looked over to my wife and felt relieved as I was met with her approving smile. It was similar to my own name, I knew, but . . .

"I think it's beautiful."

You're beautiful, I thought. How could I have been blessed with such a kind soul? For a moment, the tragedy of the situation tugged at my resolve as my wife's breath stuttered, what might have been a cough if she were stronger, but her gaze calmed my heart.

This is how it is. Her resolute eyes gave my heart no space to doubt the words within them.

I swallowed, turning to meeting the eyes of Daka once more, before smiling as much as the bittersweet moment would allow, and placed her back alongside her siblings.

Lydia sighed, as if drawing strength from the return of her young, before she looked down at the palest child. "My daughter, your name is Natakia."

I let out a breath I had not realized I was holding; there was no way I would not recognize the name. "Lydia . . ."

She gave me a look. "You named for the future, Rakta, but I must respect our past. Perhaps our mistakes can be cleansed through them."

A part of me felt like she was much more qualified to name for the future than I, but my grievance at the choice of name stood strong for a moment longer.

"They should not be laden with such a burden as mere infants."

Lydia smiled down at the eerily silent children. "I have faith."

I said nothing at that, my protests dying in the back of my throat. Religion was one of the few subjects that I did not wish to linger on with my wife. The faith of the Ruskans was far different from that of Lydia's people, I knew.

Paying no heed to my silence, thankfully, my wife met the gaze of the last child, the small one with silver hair that nestled in the middle of his sisters. "My son, you . . . shall be Dalton."

I said nothing, but the unsteady way she bequeathed the name gave away how uncertain she was about her own choice.

She had obviously been planning this, my wife the schemer, but . . . I would not take away her right as a mother. Not on this, her first and final day with her children.

For as the minutes stretched on, I could see the strain on my wife worsening. I comforted her, laying one of my large hands upon the small of her back, the surface slick with her sweat from the hard labor.

She looked at me, distress building in her once-solid demeanor. ". . . I should be here, Rakta. How can I even think of myself as a mother after abandoning them this soon?"

Tears raced down her cheeks, her eyes practically shining with the Mana she was burning to keep herself alive long enough to say goodbye.

I leaned forward and felt her forehead touch against mine, feeling her ragged breath crash against my lips. "You will always be here with us. In the stories I tell, in the stories they weave."

The freest my tongue had allowed me to speak since I'd entered the room, a true gift from the spirits and gods of the land.

"I love you, Rakta Velbrun."

"I love you too, Lydia Velbrun."

Her feathery-light kiss tickled my lips, scarring it in her final moments with her tenderness, before she broke off, her shining eyes looking down at her children, our children.

My wife tenderly gave them each a kiss on the head, her body shaking at the effort to do so. "Listen . . . listen closely, children. The world is not always safe, it is not always easy, but know that I shall love each of you with all my being from the Great Beyond."

She held them close to her, and I wrapped her up within our final embrace.

Moments later, I pulled away, taking the children from the cooling clutches of their mother. One of them, the pale one, began to cry, and I was relieved when the others soon followed.

Emotion, my children had it. The gazes of confusion and curiosity were novel, but for them to finally express themselves as I had seen from so many other infants . . .

The door to the room creaked open, breaking me from my thoughts.

A man dressed in fine red clothing, dotted with the gold-and-green embroidery of House Velbrun.

Lydia's brother Markus Velbrun. His dark hair was nothing like his sister's silvery locks, and his eyes were similarly darkened, in both hue and emotion. He moved with a grace befitting his title, a practiced air of knowing following him as he stepped inside.

Markus looked at my children, as one might look at a hound lightly nipping at their heel. "So there they are."

His voice was clipped with anger, and a quick peek into his eyes only revealed the pain and hatred that enunciated his speech. Was such anger for the children? For me?

I nodded, experienced in ignoring such distaste. "Daka, Natakia, and Dalton Velbrun."

As I spoke their names, I calmed them down, gently caressing the head of each mewling infant until they began to quiet.

Lydia's brother flinched at the last name. "You . . . cannot be serious, can you? My sister allowed you to name th—"

"It was her idea."

He stopped, instantly more respectful. It had always been like that. It probably always would be. Markus had been the biggest opponent to our marriage, but never openly.

He seemed to consider the children again, a familiar detached veil beginning to stretch across his expression, until his voice came again, more measured than last time. "The heads of House Velbrun have already decided. You won't be allowed to stay here."

"Expulsion?" My question wasn't a surprised one.

Lydia and I had always thought it possible in the aftermath of something happening to her, albeit we thought such a thing unlikely. It was only her influence within the family that had allowed me to use the house's name, much less their abode.

Surprisingly, Markus shook his head. "No, you'll be going to the border of the Velbruns' interests. There is a small town that you've been given lordship over, effective immediately."

He didn't sound entirely pleased by the decision, but I hummed thoughtfully at the news.

Lordship was better than I had been preparing for. My things were already half packed, and a wagon had been purchased in my name months ago. If Lydia had survived, she'd made it clear that she desired our children to grow up traveling on the road, like she had.

I would make the most of the journey to wherever I was going.

"The town's name?"

"Gelvurt."

I waited for more details, but with nothing forthcoming, I gave one last look to the body that once housed the love of my life, before I stepped past Markus and into the hallway with my children.

It was hours later, the early-morning sun rising, that I had finished preparing my faithful wagon, looking up to the large stone structure of House Velbrun. It's tall spires and high walls were meant to keep the noble family safe, but it had never felt safe to me.

I would not miss the atmosphere of the place—neither the suffocating politics nor the judging gazes upon my Ruskan skin had ever made me feel welcome—but I would miss the view that Lydia had me fall in love with.

Lydia . . . and I would miss Lydia.

A soft cooing noise broke me of my thoughts, my eyes drifting to Daka in her wagon seat, a small wooden fixture filled with soft hay to keep her and her siblings safe from bumps along the road.

Her eyes were . . . understanding. Murky, unfocused, like that of a child, but alight in a way they should not be. A spark of something beyond me.

Three souls from beyond.

The ancient lisp of long-forgotten words flitted through my mind, but I paid them no heed for the moment.

I was no longer an adventurer searching for evil to fight or glory to attain, just a father. My only goal was to keep my children safe and guide them.

I could not have known at the time that such a goal would be the difference between an era of peace and prosperity marked down in history for ages to come or an apocalypse the world would never recover from.

2

The Certillian Empire, the larger nation that House Velbrun, and other noble houses, were bound to, had once had a bandit problem, denizens with ill hearts or empty stomachs selling their morals for scraps of food and coin.

Lydia and I, alongside our allies, had cleaned out many such roaming bandits, but after she became pregnant, we had taken a step back from such responsibilities.

"Did ya fucking hear me or what!?"

Perhaps I should have kept a better eye on such matters.

There were four of them, each of them dressed in heavy, dirt-stained clothing made to withstand the elements, with coarse bits of leather strapped over some of the more vital areas. Crude, but more protective than simple clothing.

Two carried blades, short and sharp, with heavy hilts that one had a harder time carrying than the other. The other two held sickles, more akin to farming tools than weapons of war, even their stances looking more akin to reaping wheat than cutting flesh.

I looked at the lead bandit, my gaze lazily falling to the sickle held toward me with hostility, "My children are with me. I don't want any trouble."

Perhaps another day I would have attempted to stop them outright, cleanse the land of threats to future families, but my children were sleeping, and a struggle could wake them.

The bandit's teeth were yellow, but straight. "Hey, I get ya, we all just want what's best for our families, yeah? Hand over ya goods, and we don't have to get ugly in front of the kiddies."

While the others with him had discomfort in their stances, obviously not used to kids being involved, the apparent leader had no hesitation. It was disheartening, but not unexpected. Some took to banditry concerningly well.

I closed my eyes, sending a quick, subtle pulse of Vitae through the area, feeling only seven pings come back. My children and the four bandits.

There were no hidden assailants flanking my wagon, meaning I was still in front of any danger to the triplets. Although Fretz, my ox for this journey, was still in danger.

If a fight broke out and she ended up being injured, I would have to pull the wagon myself.

"I can spare five silver sils." It was my first and final offer, generous, I'd say, for the group of bandits. Even so, I was reticent to part with it.

Most of my personal riches had gone to making sure I would have all the supplies the monthlong trip to Gelvert would require. The milk substitute offered by Velbrun's alchemists had not been cheap nor freely provided by any of the other lords.

The bandit's eyes furrowed. "This ain't the time for negotiating, duster. All of it."

Duster, another word for Ruskan. Not a kind word, but one I'd become accustomed to within the empire.

The others shifted in their spots, all of them looking tense. They had readied themselves for a fight, but they really weren't. Not with their unsteady stances and ill-fitting equipment. I'd seen fresh recruits with more mettle and skill than them.

One of the men, the one having trouble with his ill-weighted sword, looked like he'd recently twisted his ankle, but was trying to tough it out.

"I will give you one more chance to take the money and leave." It was the greatest kindness I could offer.

The lead bandit's face turned sour. "Ya—"

I continued, cutting him off before he foolishly declined. "The next river is an hour away. That means, if we come to arms, I will have to ride for an hour before I am able to wash your blood off my fists."

I would kill the leader only if I had to. The other men were misguided and hungry, not malevolent. This kind of leadership would only lead the others to an early grave.

The clearing was quiet, the brigands glancing to one another as they digested my words. The lead bandit's sickle had dropped closer to his side at my words, his reckless confidence fading.

Lydia would have been able to handle this better. She had always said that words were meant for peace, a Beyond-given gift to humanity to communicate and compromise.

"We're not given tongues to threaten," she would often say.

One by one, the bandits withdrew from the wagon, the lead brigand lingering with a fearful, but determined gleam in his eye. ". . . The silver."

"Thank you for not causing any trouble."

I nodded, rifling through my belt pouch before tossing him a single golden sil.

Twice as much as I had initially offered, yes, but perhaps the charity would make amends for the threat. And perhaps, they would not seek out other travelers for more coin quite so soon.

The bandit caught the coin, mumbling a quick, bitter word of thanks, before leaving to catch up with the others. Perhaps they were all from the same struggling village?

I watched them leave, before looking back to check on my children, still sleeping except for one pair of eyes staring at me.

Dalton's gaze was even, a glint of interest shining in his eyes. Had he seen what just occurred? Did he understand?

Perhaps I should have been comforted by him being just an infant, still in the fever dream of a youngling's first few weeks, but the intensity of my son's gaze gave no such comfort.

I smiled, taking solace in my children's lack of harm, before returning to the road and pushing Fretz to move again.

We had no more troubles with banditry for the rest of the day.

The gazes of my children were not the only thing one might consider odd about them, although I had no other infants on hand while traveling to truly compare them to.

Daka would regularly awaken in the middle of the night, with cries that bordered on terror. My sleepless vigils would often be filled with comforting her back to sleep, her body shaking in my grip as I surveyed the area for unseen predators.

On the other hand, Natakia would cry if I tried to feed her as Lydia's midwife had instructed me, even as her stomach growled and begged for food. Not keen on starving my daughter, I often had to deal with her tantrums after making sure she drank her milk, no matter how foul she thought it was.

And Dalton, my son, was counting.

"Dalton, are you playing with my sil?"

I'd just put Natakia and Daka to sleep after feeding, to discover that my coin pouch, which I had left on the wagon while bathing in a nearby brook, had been knocked over and spilled.

Gold and silver sil were scattered across the wood of the wagon, Dalton making small *buh* noises as he pulled and pushed the coins around with his arms while on his belly. He'd made a fuss when I'd tried to feed him a moment ago, but it seemed he was in a much better mood now.

I sat beside him, the wagon slightly shifting under my weight. "You are interested in the coins?"

Dalton looked up at me, momentarily, before returning to the coins, pushing and pulling, before repeating his actions, his movements sluggish and uncoordinated as all infants' were. Although my children were certainly active for their age, even by Ruskan standards.

Perhaps just the play of a youngling, but I knew, to some degree, how inspired my children were. They very rarely mindlessly played.

I tapped one of the gold sils, getting Dalton's attention, before counting out ten of the silver sils. "One gold sil is equal to ten silver sils. As decreed by the Donns of Neve."

I took out a few copper sils from the pouch as Dalton watched on, showing him the engraved markings of the global merchants, the stylized *D* that was difficult to perfectly imitate.

"And one silver sil is equal to ten copper sils."

I tapped out the amount, demonstrating for the baby. With a soft *buh* noise, Dalton turned back to the coins and began playing again.

And yet, as he began to group the different kinds of coins into rough piles of gold and silver, ignoring the copper, and grouping them into collections of ten, I once again found myself longing for Lydia's guidance.

Soon, Dalton had exhausted himself playing with the coins, and I put him away to sleep alongside his sisters. I'd feed him later when he inevitably woke up hungry.

It was a day later that I arrived at my first stop on the way to Gelvurt.

Jonsten was a small town within House Velbrun's influence, as denoted by their flags whipping above the garrison and other civil buildings.

Criers on every corner, yelling about some new threat to the empire's safety or scandal by one of the houses, although never the Velbruns, and shops on either side of the main road, their large windows filled with product.

Natakia suddenly cried out from the wagon seat, my head snapping to her. Her hand was held aloft to one of the passing stores, her eyes shining with interest.

I followed her gaze to a large establishment, brilliantly white with blue accents around its doors and windows and the words *Madame Wyott's* emblazoned above the door.

And yet, the fanciful script had not caught Natakia's eye as I had quickly assumed. No, upon second glance, I saw her eyes focused on the dresses beyond the store's large window. Beautiful, even to my uncultured eye, silken dresses that would have practically smothered the infant if she was given the chance to wear them.

I pulled on Fretz's reins. "Hold on, girl."

Letting the wagon come to a stop, I gently pulled Natakia out of the wagon seat, giving Daka and Dalton gentle smiles, before carrying the excited baby over to the window.

Natakia smiled, staring up at the dresses, and placed an awkward hand on the glass, cooing at the sights. It was the happiest I'd ever seen my delicate, picky daughter. I always thought my children to be precious, but they were truly at their best when they were happy.

And then she burst into tears.

I ignored the looks I got from passing townspeople as I returned to the wagon, gently rocking her in my arms as I grabbed up Fretz's reins and pushed the ox onward.

"Calm, Natakia, calm. You are okay, my desert flower, you are okay." It was something my mother used to do for Natakia, a different Natakia, and the words came easily. Her cries eventually faded, but I could see the misery floating in her eyes.

Whatever had provoked such a reaction from Natakia and disheartened her so firmly, I wasn't sure. I simply hoped that if she was hungry, she would drink her milk without fuss when the time came.

As the wagon moved onward, I eventually placed the sleeping Natakia back into the wagon seat, my mind and eyes wandering to my goal in Jonsten.

There was a writ of lordship waiting for me.

"I am very sorry, sir, but the writ you are asking for has already been given. There are no extras."

I blinked, a little surprised. "The writ has already been given away? To whom?"

The man, a willowy fellow with the garb of a scholar, looked down at his large register. "One Rakta Velbrun, the newly adorned Lord of Gelvurt."

Strange and peculiar, I could feel the discomfort building in the pit of my stomach.

I pointed to myself. "I am Rakta Velbrun. I just got into town a few hours ago."

"Ah, I see. One moment." The clerk's smile was tight and did not reach his eyes.

The clerk stepped away from the desk, and I followed his form as he ventured into the back room through a door I had not paid particular attention to upon coming in.

I took the opportunity to look back at the wagon through the window of the office, keeping an ear out for any cries, before turning back as the clerk returned.

And with him, a short girl with doughy cheeks and bright-red hair, looking confused. She struck me as an apprentice, but she looked at me as if she'd seen me before.

The clerk pointed at me. "Clarissa, is this man the Rakta Velbrun you gave the writ of lordship to?"

Clarissa gave me a once over, recognition still in her eyes. "I . . . uh, sir, he was dressed differently, but . . . yes, sir. I believe so, in any case. Did I . . . ?"

The clerk waved her away. "No, nothing. Return to your work."

The girl nodded, tentatively, before heading off, stumbling over her own legs as she left. The clerk gave a sigh as he watched her leave, before turning to me, his expression conflicted.

I watched the girl leave myself, before saying, "I was not given the writ."

The clerk furrowed his brow, before looking through the register. "This fellow came in three days ago, the day we received the writ. I'm very sorry, but it's out of our hands from here. If you want, I can send word to House Velbrun . . ."

There was no telling the kind of punishment that this man might face if an issue was made of this writ going missing, no matter the duplicity involved.

I shook my head. "No, I'll handle this. Thank you."

The clerk looked thankful, before bidding me farewell and good luck in my search. He even suggested hiring a band of mercenaries that had come through Jonsten a week or so ago.

I wasn't interested in looking for help however.

Losing the writ of lordship to an impostor would just give House Velbrun more reason to reconsider my lordship. And, no matter how minimal the arrangements were, the title of lord would be important in raising the triplets.

I bid the clerk farewell and returned to the wagon, where my children, my vulnerable young, lay sleeping. What would Lydia do in this situation?

"Oh, give me some time, and I'll just divine where they are," Lydia had said, referring to the family of doppelgängers that had taken our forms to cause mayhem in a small farming hamlet and escaped into the forest.

I smiled at the memory, before shaking my head. Unfortunately, I could not scry upon the impostor using magic.

So instead, I pushed Fretz forward and began to stoke my Vitae. Though I may be rusty, I had my own ways of finding people.

3

The forest was alive around me as I stopped the wagon a few miles outside of Jonsten. The trail to Gelvurt was not well traveled, which would make any trace of travel more apparent to the naked eye.

Still, finding an impostor, a perfect impostor from the sounds of it, would not be easy. Unless the impostor was both perfect . . . and careless.

I focused my Vitae, going through the subtle, practiced motions of my body to direct the energy as I crouched down and focused my senses. My arms tensed, a pounding began to rise in my eardrums, and I felt my technique, rusty from lack of use, bloom to life.

The sights and sounds of the world around me faded as the **Scourger Bloodhound Technique** took hold. No longer anchored to my other senses, even the feeling of my palms against the grass fading, my sense of smell expanded.

The scents of the world shuffled around me like the common folk of a busy Certillian street, each of them brushing by me, but I quickly narrowed my focus. Soon, the smells left behind by the local wildlife faded away, followed by older scents of travelers, left behind like scars on the road.

Of the fresher scents, I quickly discounted the smells of my children and the wagon, picking apart the fresh, familiar scents of me and my clothes, before I narrowed in on the scents that were left.

Old, but not too old. Fresh, but not too fresh. Yet to be muddled by the weather.

Travelers, a group of them. Old by a day or two, but there was no doubt that there were at least four of them, possibly five. There was a slight distinction between two scents, which I'd found common among siblings that traveled together for a long time.

However, what drew my attention to this group was a very familiar smell among them. The smell that I had been looking for, an impossible smell that I should not have found if I were dealing with anything less than a perfect impostor.

Myself. Older, traveling with the group and certainly making no attempt to mask itself. With a distinct scent of perfume weaved into my own.

I did not wear perfume, and I certainly hadn't left my scent here days ago.

It seemed whoever was posing as Lord Rakta Velbrun was heading toward Gelvurt as well. And I had to beat them there.

Impostors within the Certillian Empire were not rare. According to Lydia, doppelgängers, humanoid creatures with appearance-changing magics, were native to the nearby mountains and had bred with early Certillians long ago.

No matter the creature at hand, whether a purebred or simply a Certillian with enough doppelgänger blood to awaken their abilities, the idea of a loved one being replaced by another individual was not unheard of within these lands.

Not that those with such duplicitous bloodlines were inherently villainous, of course, but I rarely had the pleasure of dealing with pleasant ones. I imagined that there were some who had found ways to use their abilities benevolently.

And yet, the difficulty of this pursuit was not leaving me with many favorable thoughts about the creatures. It had taken me a week of non-stop travel, burning through my Vitae to travel unabated throughout the night, to catch up to the scents that evaded me.

Were I on my own, I could have caught up with them within hours, but the idea of leaving my children for such a time was unthinkable. I was instead having to push myself alongside my younglings to make any progress in catching up to the thieves.

Channeling my Vitae through Fretz had been the only thing keeping the ox from crumbling from exhaustion. Similarly, my children were not fond of the constant travel, ruining their sleep and making them irritable.

Perhaps, that was why I had them now cradled to my chest tonight, with plans to confront the impostor tomorrow. We all needed sleep.

"Buh," my very awake son cried.

"Wah," my irritated Natakia noted in response.

I looked to Daka, to see if she had anything to add, but she was sleeping soundly against my chest, a dollop of drool spilling out of her lips onto my clothing. She was the heaviest sleeper when she was not gripped by fear.

"You should both get sleep like your sister," I gently chided the two other babes, both of their bright sets of eyes staring defiantly at me. "Are you not tired?"

They did not seem to care for the comparison, both of them refusing to go to sleep after a few more minutes of gentle rocking.

Perhaps if I were willing to light a campfire, I could let Dalton tire himself out counting coins and solve one of my problems. Natakia might have better luck at sleeping in the heat of the flame.

And yet, being as close as I was to the impostor's camp, doing such a thing would not be wise.

Instead, I gave a great sigh and felt the rolling, rumbling echo build up in my chest as I recalled the dark, cold nights of the Ruskan desert, the distant sounds of skittering sand vermin.

And the way my tribe's Storyteller began his nightly tales.

"There once was a man of great power," I began, feeling the story flow through my Vitae. "They called him many names throughout his life and after, but Brota was the name his mother gave him."

The two babes were enraptured, an easy crowd for even my amateurish Ruskan storytelling techniques, but I faltered slightly as I noticed the third pair of eyes now wide awake and listening deeply alongside her siblings.

I had not meant to wake Daka up, but I persisted for the sake of my young audience.

"Brota was a warrior in a time of great war among the Ruskan tribes, fierce and bloody, and lost his brothers and sisters to the blade of another, a Ruskan by the name of Garrok."

I could feel the names pulse as they were remembered, the souls of the ancient warriors preening as they were once again paid homage by those still weaving their own stories.

"Disheartened by the death and destruction, Brota stood atop the highest plateau he could find and sought answers from the world around him."

Even now, I could see the stoic figure standing overhead, his expression unreadable as he looked out across blood-stained sand.

"And the world answered with the desert sands, pushing and pulling at his body. And so, Brota allowed it to move him as it wished. The first Ruskan Dance began."

I continued on, telling them of Brota's journey. As much as my memory allowed, at the very least. I was no true Storyteller, but I had grown up hearing of Brota's story.

Soon, both Dalton and Natakia had been lulled to sleep by the tale, but one set of clear blue eyes had not waned during the story.

I gave Daka a kiss on the forehead. "Go to sleep, my little one."

And unlike her brother and sister, she did not resist, her head falling against my chest and quickly beginning to slumber once more.

The lights of my life cradled against me, I relaxed against the edge of the wagon and allowed myself to sleep for a few moments.

I stalked the forests, allowing the natural sounds to conceal my approach. I walked with the chirping of the birds and the rustle of the bushes.

Within my grip, the familiar weight of my throwing axe, one of my Vultures. It was larger than a normal throwing axe that could, and had, doubled as a regular war axe when the situation called for it.

"So, my lord, what'll be your first decree when we reach Gelvurt?" The voice, deep, had a teasing lilt to it.

"Ah, my faithful follower, I shall decree that a feast will be held in my name! The Velbrun name! And we will all eat . . . like pigs!" It was strange hearing my own voice with such an irreverent tone.

I was not an irreverent man.

The voice, my borrowed voice, was loud and free of concern. As I got closer, I could clearly smell the smoke of the campfire and hear the bustling of others.

Soon in sight as I peeked through the idle leaves of a bush, the camp, small as it was with only four tents, was alive and well, even this early in the morning.

Five figures, all of them laughing and jeering at one another, sat around the burning campfire, their weapons close by to each of them.

Two of them, a man and woman, looked almost identical, both of them covered in darker-brown clothing, large daggers on their belts.

Beside them, a larger-looking man, slapped his knee as he laughed with a booming pitch. "Aha! Yes, yes! I cannot wait until we are finally fit to eat like kings!"

Laid against his back was a large war hammer, the iron of its head gleaming in the early sun. It was a practical weapon, without any ornate additions beyond a stray feather tied to the oaken handle.

Both his blond hair and large build gave me an impression of the lands north of Certillia.

A reedy voice broke through, coming from a smaller, skinnier man at the larger man's side. "Lords, Kal, lords. I think it might be a while before Doh gets a chance at a king."

No weapons on him, but the necklace he wore stood out, bright and with an iron-chained amethyst at the tip. A focus for magic?

And then, almost the center of the conversation, was a familiar visage. My own. Laughing and smiling alongside the rest of these strangers.

He posed, something Lydia would have laughed at. "Yes, well, King Doh just doesn't have the same ring to it as Lord Doh. Besides, the king is old! I'll wait until a nice, pretty prince or princess gets their hand on the throne."

He, or perhaps they, didn't seem very serious about making a go at the throne. These five seemed close and much more experienced than simple bandits, certainly more professional in their equipment.

Mercenaries attempting to settle into an easy life? How did mercenaries learn about the writ of lordship? Many questions, not enough answers.

It wasn't of my highest concern. My children were waiting on the nearby trail, so I did not have much time to waste here. Every second that passed was another moment for danger to happen upon my children without me there to protect them.

Still, I would do this as Lydia would have done.

I stepped out of the bushes and into the camp in one clean motion, no longer making any attempt to hide myself. "Good morning, my name is Rakta Velbrun. I believe you have something of mine. Please return it."

The laughing and jeering stopped instantly, replaced with the stunned silence of the disbelieving mercenaries as they turned to me as one.

Doh blinked with my eyes. "Holy shit!"

They went for their weapons.

My Vulture cut through the air, hitting the center of their campfire; the magic laden within the enchanted weapon pulsed as it hit, a sudden great explosion of whirling air sending cinders and ash dancing, with the weapon at its epicenter.

The mercenaries stopped, staggering to their feet as they coughed and put out small flames that had caught on their clothing.

I held out my empty hand, the Vulture ripping itself out of the ground and twisting through the air back snuggly into my waiting palm.

I gazed at the mercenaries. "Please return it."

4

My Vulture Axes were magically crafted, enchanted in a collaboration between Lydia and a magically capable blacksmith we had saved years ago. Since they were gifted to me, I'd rarely used anything else, to the frustration of some.

They were doubled-headed throwing axes, with a glistening silver coating affixed to the blade. They were heavy, heavier and longer than a throwing axe should be, but that gave them more impact.

They were not large enough to be considered battle-axes, at least not the heavier Certillian-style battle-axes made for close quarters, but the dark metal of their shaft gave them the strength needed to parry blows from heavier blades if needed.

And, of course, I'd been made aware by others that they were quite intimidating.

The clearing was quiet, the mercenaries having regained their composure after the miniature campfire storm had died down. Each of them tense, but unwilling to go for their weapons and provoke my wrath again.

And then, the form of the leader, Doh, began to shift and grow smaller, my stolen appearance beginning to twist into something, or rather, someone else.

"Uh, um, there's been a bit of a misunderstanding . . . yeah?"

Their form deflated, their dark, tanned skin fading into a much paler hue, and their assumedly stolen fine clothing that had fit their previous, borrowed form so well now sat loosely against a petite, softer frame.

With a round face, her naturally wide eyes were as dark as her hair, and she held up her hands in surrender with a playfulness that did well, but not well enough, to hide the tension in her body.

I watched on, glancing at her companions. "Misunderstanding?"

"Y-yeah, uh, huge misunderstanding." She fiddled around, looking uncomfortable with how close I was. "We'll get you the writ, okay?"

"Wait a second." Kal, the large man, frowned. "What about our riches? Our feast?"

The woman shot him a look, her words a hissing whisper. "Shut the fuck up! Did you not notice this guy's out of our league?"

None of the other mercenaries looked happy at the concession, but neither did they seem willing to fight against my threat or Doh's lead. It seemed Lydia's polite approach and my display were going to do the trick here.

Good, Natakia had only drunk half of her breakfast, and I needed to get back soon to help the other half down. A growing child needed a proper diet.

I watched Doh slowly lower her hand down to one of the loose pockets of her ill-fitting garb and rummage through it, taking out a leather tube casing.

I nodded. "Throw it to the ground at my feet."

She did so, tossing the leather tube over to me. I kept my eyes trained on them all, not letting my gaze falter for even a moment as it thudded against my leather shoes. Appearing vulnerable would only incite a fight.

A fight I did not have the time for.

And yet, I still had to know one thing for certain.

"Why did you steal this? Were you tasked with this by someone? Did someone pay you to do this?"

She blinked, looking a little taken aback by the pointed questions. "Ah, no. We'd been hanging out in Jonsten for a while, uh, just doing stuff. You know, keeping the ole ears open for a job? Heard some new nobility was coming to collect their papers and . . ."

And had taken the opportunity for what it was. It seemed that if this was a part of some Velbrun plan, then these folk were not knowingly a part of it.

"How did you know what I looked like to take my form?" My appearance was certainly not bandied about in honor like the others that I had once traveled with.

"Ah, uh, yeah." She shrugged. "Some of the people in town knew what you looked like . . . ? I'm kind of talented in . . . memory magic."

Even though Doh kept her hands carefully in view when she said that, I still tensed. Magics of the mind, even something as innocuous as memories, were worrying. Lydia had been very stringent about keeping away from such insidious magic.

Someone with both the blood of a doppelgänger and a talent in memory magic . . . no, I could not get involved.

With a sigh, Doh shook her head. "Kinda wish I'd dug a little deeper now though. Surface stuff doesn't always quite tell the whole story, does it, Lord Velbrun? So, uh, you gonna let us go? We're very sorry."

All the mercenaries had become more and more tense, ready to go out with a fight. A part of me was irritated at the theft, but annoyance was no foundation for killing others. I had what I needed, and the more time I spent here was more time away from my children.

I nodded. "Take a walk. I'll be gone by the time you're all back."

"Oh." She smiled, relaxing. "Sounds good, my lord. Come on, guys, let's get out of his hair."

And yet, as the leader stepped away, looking happy to leave this whole situation behind her, the others weren't quite as cooperative.

Kal's fists were tight. "We are just going to run away? Again?"

The twins, both of them giving me dark looks, seemed to share a glance, the female stating coldly as the tension in her body began to go on the offensive. "A duster shouldn't be given the grace of nobility."

The thin man standing beside Kal looked the most nervous. His hands were fidgeting closer and closer to the jewel around his neck.

Doh looked resigned. "Kal, Erika, come on, I got a bad feeling, okay? Let's just all take a deep breath . . . and walk away."

"You promised us riches." The female twin, Erika, sneered at Doh. "You've run us ragged from one scheme to the next . . . We're done walking away, Doh."

The look she got back from Doh wasn't an impressed one. "Well, I'm gonna walk away. I've never made you follow me. I'll be back in a bit."

And without another word, Doh began to shuffle out of the camp, with the nervous man beginning to follow her . . .

"No, Victor, you stay." Kal's large hand landed on his shoulder, stopping him.

Victor gulped. "Okay . . ."

I bent down to pick up the leather tubing, clipping it onto my belt, before looking at the remaining mercenaries. "So you intend to fight?"

The idea of being away from my children was distasteful. I was going to need to finish this fight quickly.

Erika stepped forward, her daggers drawn and her stance low and ready to take advantage of any weakness she could find. "Let's see how far your fancy magical toys—"

Ge-guh! Her head recoiled from the force behind the Vulture as it sank an inch into her skull. As her body fell backward, thudding to the ground lifelessly, the camp burst into motion.

"You murderer!" The male twin ran toward me, heavy daggers drawn, and dove at me, his blades slashing visible arcs of energy in the air.

I stepped out of the way of the arcs, tasting the unrefined Vitae behind the attacks, before clenching my fist and sending a punch straight into his sternum, hearing bones break.

"Raaagh!" Kal, his large war hammer in hand, rushed at me with a wide downward swing. I rolled to the side, feeling only the wind disturbed by the force behind the blow.

I lashed out with my Vulture still in hand, tearing into the back of his leg and sending him to his knees as I rushed to my feet and dashed past him, toward one of the more dangerous mercenaries.

Victor, his hand on his necklace, continued to utter words under his breath. "Nimbus strength, inner energy, **Strike of Lightning!**"

From his other hand, a bolt of lightning lashed out in my direction, my Vitae thrumming as I flexed my hand and altered the flow of vital energy within it, activating my **Redirecting Hand Technique**.

I thrust my empty palm forward, meeting the magically fashioned electricity and letting it flow through my hand as I gathered up every last drop.

Victor blinked, horrified. "W-what!?"

I gave no response as I reached out and grabbed him by the face with my other hand, which now sparked with the gathered energy, before releasing some of the tension in my static-covered hand.

Victor screamed as the electricity from his own magic flowed into his form, frying and short-circuiting his entire body, starting with the head.

My hand, somewhat smoking, released the corpse and let it fall to the ground. I glanced back at Kal and the remaining twin, both of them regaining their composure.

Kal, standing again, growled at the sight of Victor's corpse, his skin beginning to glow red. "Holt, we need to flank him."

Holt nodded, breathing heavy from the punch. "On it. **Nightingale Shift Technique!**"

I took out another Vulture as Holt suddenly disappeared from sight. Not from speed, no, but some sort of stealth technique.

Kal roared, "**Colossal Might Technique!**"

His clothes ripped as his form almost doubled in size, his war hammer now held aloft in a single massive hand as he rushed at me, the flat metal weapon held high above me.

I breathed deeply, finally taking my **Dancing Star Stance**. "I hope that you are remembered by someone."

My Vitae shimmered within my form, and I did a sharp twist of my body, throwing one of my Vultures out straight at the rushing form of Kal, the behemoth moving to dodge.

"Shit throw!" Kal rushed at me, even more energy in his steps as my Vulture spun through the air past him.

And then I pulled, the spiraling thrown axe suddenly stopping still in midair before it changed trajectory, spiraling downward and sinking deep into his back, bisecting his spine.

The goliath crumbled midcharge, rolling to the ground as his face filled with pain and legs stopped listening to him. "Gah, I . . . I . . ."

I ignored him, lashing out with a Vulture into thin air behind me and feeling it sink into flesh. With a shimmer of Vitae, the dark-leather-clad form of Holt revealed itself once more, my weapon deep in his neck.

Gurgling on his own blood, Holt gritted his teeth as he managed his final word. "H-how?"

I removed the Vulture, letting him slink to the ground cradling his fatal wound. "No technique is perfect. I simply heard you coming."

Holt's eyes were filled with disbelief and anger until that fled his body, alongside his life.

I walked over to Kal, the large man's form unable to move with such a grievous injury, and ended his life with another quick, efficient chop. His form released the tension it carried in life, becoming meat on the ground for the buzzards.

While impressive in their own ways, these mercenaries never had a chance. Still having to speak the names of their techniques to focus themselves was telling, and Victor's incantation was far too long for having a focus at hand. They could have improved over time.

Now they never would.

I put my Vultures away, grabbing the one lodged in Erika's skull, before giving the corpses a look. "Your names will be remembered in the stories I weave."

It was the only rite I had the power to give them.

With that, I left with the writ, thinking of how Lydia would have handled that situation much better than I.

"Bluh." Daka was in my lap as I cleaned my weapons, the writ of lordship tucked away safely inside my packs on the wagon.

The child was staring at the bloodied Vulture, looking unhappy. Perhaps it was the smell? The coppery scent was certainly not the most pleasant on the nose.

I gave her a kiss on the head. "Do not worry, Daka, I simply had to defend myself."

She began to pull at my clothing, looking at my dark skin as if scanning for any injuries I'd picked up in the fight. My children were certainly strange for their age, being concerned for their father so early.

And yet, on this lonely road, it was more than appreciated.

"They were thieves." Daka's eyes looked up to me as I spoke once more. "Mercenaries who took the writ of lordship that rightly belonged to me. Their names were Doh, Kal, Victor, Erika, and Holt."

I began to weave a story about the encounter, trying to honor the lives of the criminals as best as I could with a proper narrative. From their conversation as I approached, to the skill they carried with them into battle against me.

A proper Storyteller I was not, but if my children were as intelligent and aware as they seemed, then perhaps it was good for them to learn early the proper ways to honor a life taken.

5

The day after I'd handled the mercenaries, their shape changing leader having walked off to avoid the same fate as her companions, I was admittedly tense. Not to the extent I wasn't sleeping, although my nightly vigils had continued making that a moot statement, but I was wary of those I passed.

A memory-manipulating identity thief was not something I had expected to meet on my way to a small village in the outskirts, but it was by no means the strangest or most dangerous thing I had ever come into contact with.

Other things held such high regard.

Still, my tension remained, and I watched for attacks coming from any direction. My biggest concern, of course, were attempts to trick me into helping a traveler on the side of the road and leaving myself vulnerable.

"By the gods, please save me! Goblins!"

The scream from deeper into the forest was littered with pain, filled with a genuine desperation and fear of death. My body tensed as I stopped Fretz, a clock ticking away in the back of my mind as I considered the situation.

Was this really happening?

On the side of the road, I could see the scraps of cloth and blood spilled on the ground, right where the supposed goblins would have snatched the lone traveler. Their ambush likely took less than a few seconds of their time.

"Anyone!"

It could be a trick. And yet, the scream was coming too far into the forest for me to be certain. I doubted that any common traveler would have heard their distant pleas from the road with the sound-dampening forest between them.

I took out one of my Vulture Axes, looking around and trying to spot any of the telltale small, leathery bodies waiting in the trees around me. I saw none in the area, but if I were to help, I would . . .

Glancing back at my sleeping children, all three of them at peace in this moment, I took a deep breath. Could I really leave them alone when I knew goblins were in the area? The idea of this being some kind of tra—

The screams suddenly ended in a sharp silence.

My body moved before I could truly comprehend it. The forest flew around me as I jumped from tree to tree, the wind gathering around my body as my **Great Wind Sprint Technique** seamlessly spurred to life.

A clearing, hundreds of feet away from the trail, was covered in the remnants of a struggle, five goblins standing around a downed form, crowding around their prey with a vicious energy around them, the largest of the group poking the body with a crude spear.

I felt the leader's skull shatter inward as my knee rocketed into it, my Vitae-enhanced interruption instantly killing the ringleader of this pack of cretins.

The other four goblins got a small chance to realize their leader was dead before my axe cut them down, their milky-white blood splattering against the ground around the tortured soul they'd picked off of the trail.

"Mrpgh." The gagged traveler on the ground continued to cry into his bindings, blood, mud, and tears covering his cheeks.

I felt my heart untighten slightly. I'd gotten here before they could kill him. For that, I was thankful.

I bent down, gently picking him up as best as I could. "You're safe now. Give me a moment to heal you, and we'll be returning to my wagon."

Laying a hand on his bare leg, where the most obvious wound was, I began to channel my Vitae, deciding to not ungag him for the process. Vitae healing could be unpleasant depending on the injuries and one's experience with the sensation.

The last thing I needed to do was help him regrow a tongue.

* * *

"Thank you." The man took a sip of water from his flask. "I don't know what would have happened to me . . . No, I know what would have happened. You saved me from torture."

I nodded, feeding Daka. I'd managed to get the traveler back to the wagon after dipping into my reserves to heal him. I was no expert healer, but I'd done enough to get him back on the road.

"I wish I'd come to your aid sooner." I would have had to heal him less, saving me precious Vitae, and there would have been less pain for all involved. All I'd done was be wasteful in my hesitance.

The man waved his hand, dismissively. "I'm plenty satisfied with still being alive. Uh . . . my name's Tenon. The Certillian Empire's a little more dangerous than I thought, ha ha!"

The name was distinctly foreign. Not unexpected after getting the chance to give the man a closer look while he was not covered in his own blood.

With long, dark hair that fell down his shoulders and an olive complexion, he struck me as a visitor from the Prell Islands, or somewhere in that region of Derra. It was certainly not a common sight to see a Prellian within the empire.

"Rakta." I offered my name, being polite. "What brings you to the empire, Tenon?"

He had not struck me as a merchant, with his lack of goods. And the way he dressed, simple britches and a worn tunic, did not lend to the idea that he was courier or nobleman.

Tenon smiled, looking off to the forest. "Well, you'll never believe this, but I'm actually writing a bestiary on the monsters of the world. I guess I got a little too close this time."

He certainly had. The idea of a bestiary was an interesting one, of course, having read a few during my time traveling the empire. They were invaluable to an adventurer.

"I've read bestiaries before," I said, laying Daka down in her hay bed. "You're going to write one for all the monsters in the world?"

Bestiaries were often regional texts, bound to only the monsters that tread upon the land that the authors of said encyclopedias frequented. Others had compiled them into larger editions, of course, but I'd never heard of a single author taking on the task of writing about all of them personally.

"It's a project of passion. You know, the more we learn about monsters, the less we have to be afraid of them." Tenon gave a wry smile.

I glanced at the forest I'd just rescued him from. "Have you never heard of goblins before?"

"Uh." His smile fell, seeing my point. "Yeah, I've heard about goblins. Read about them. I guess reading about them and seeing them were two different things."

I nodded, understanding where he was coming from, but knowing that true monsters would always be dangerous. No matter how much one knew about them.

In any case, Tenon certainly had a strong passion for his project if he was still willing to pursue it after the day's events.

"You're an adventurer, right?" Tenon blindsided me with the question, tilting his head at me. "I noticed how quickly you took out those goblins, well, kind of. Hard to see through all the pain."

I tensed, glancing at my children. "I'm a father, Tenon. I don't adventure anymore."

"Oh, anymore?" Tenon hummed, as if looking for a story or two.

Ha, the less I said the better for myself in the long run. I wasn't in the state of mind right now to be pestered about my past.

"I used to be a member of CAD," I said, finality lacing my words. "I'd rather not say much more on the subject."

He nodded, looking like he'd finally gotten the message. He took out an old, weathered-looking journal from his satchel, the first thing he'd recovered from the side of the road after being saved.

"Well, adventuring aside." He seemed to struggle with how to frame his question, especially as my eyebrow raised. "Um, sorry. I really want to ask about the monsters you've encountered, but uh . . ."

I gave the man this, he was persistent. If he wasn't still wearing his bloodstained jacket, I would be wondering if the peril I had saved him from hadn't been an illusion of some kind.

And yet, monsters. I did not want to speak about my encounters with monsters as an adventurer; they were, well, connected to a part of my life filled with too many regrets.

An idea struck me. "I'm from Rusk. Perhaps, I could tell you a few stories about the creatures that roam the sands?"

Tenon's face lit up.

"That's simply amazing." The scholarly journalist wrote words at a breakneck speed, in chicken scratch I could not understand. "So, if I understand correctly, a sandworm will lay its eggs in the undigested food within its own stomach?"

I nodded, having put my children away from this story after Natakia began to look sick and started crying. Some of the terrors we spoke of were not appropriate for children to hear about so viscerally.

Sandworms were only the tip of the iceberg when it came to Ruskan horrors. Vortexes, gargantlions, and mesa scorpions all plagued the sandy hills of my homeland.

Daka already had problems with nightmares.

"Yes." I took a sip from my canteen. "The larvae will drink the mother's stomach acid and spit it onto the food to soften it up. Eventually, the larvae grow so big, they . . ."

I stopped suddenly.

Tenon looked up from his writing, tilting his head. "They what?"

"They explode out of the mother, killing her," I finished, standing up from the campfire. I had been talking for too long, and I needed to continue my way to Gelvurt. "It's been nice speaking with you, Tenon, but I must go."

The traveler blinked, looking around the slowly darkening day. We'd been talking for hours now, but it truly had passed quickly. Tenon was an avid listener that always enjoyed the longer explanation for things rather than settle for less.

"I suppose you're right." He sounded glum, but he cheered up again. "Thank you so much, again, for saving me. The stories, the quotes I can add to my bestiary, I think this meeting will truly make for some of the best pages in my book."

I was happy for him, but my mind was steadfastly trying to detach from this as fast as possible. "Thank you, I appreciate the compliments. I'm sure you'll find plenty of Storytellers in Rusk that will give you far better renditions of the creatures I spoke of."

"I hope so," he smiled, continuing to sit by the fire as I packed up my things. Goblins often traveled in very small packs unless a clan had been established, but the signs of that were usually obvious and nowhere to be seen anywhere near here.

Tenon would be fine on his own.

"Safe travels, Tenon."

"And a fine trip for you, as well, Rakta. May Preia help keep your kids safe." With that he returned to his journal, continuing to scratch away at the parchment with his pen.

I was not sure if his island gods were present this far inland, but I appreciated the sentiment. I felt like I might need it.

Hours later, after calming down, my mind wandered as it often did when I had nothing to distract myself with. The children were asleep, and Fretz was keeping a good pace, having rested earlier while I spoke to Tenon.

I'd spoken so much to Tenon about the monsters that roamed my homeland that I thought it almost did a disservice to the beauty of my birthplace.

"For every monster Rusk has," I spoke to the ether of the night, "it has countless more beauties to be discovered."

Like the brilliant-white sands of Tratak's Rest or the clean, sweet waters of the oases that were lush with beautiful wildlife across the Ruskan desert. I'd made it sound like a wasteland filled with horror, I felt.

In actuality, I'd go so far as to say that the empire had it beat when it came to the dangers scouring the land.

Rusk certainly hadn't been visited by the same kind of tyrant that the Certillian Empire had been fraught with up until recently. No, there were tribes of Rusk that rarely humored the likes of Garrok in the present day, seeking to unite the land under one banner.

Even in the horrid beasts that roamed the lands, I felt like I had focused solely on their most dangerous and grotesque aspects.

The sandworm mother died as her children burst forth from her, but it was a natural part of life, a way to protect them until the sandworm younglings had grown their own armored hide.

Even if the mother died, it did not take away from the beauty of the children.

My heart ached, and I thought of Lydia as the night continued to pass around me.

6

I had stopped the wagon for the day, another week from Gelvurt by my rough estimate, and found a nice grove off the beaten trail for Fretz to graze. The ox had been grateful for the easier pace I'd adopted after dealing with the mercenaries.

Both Daka and Dalton had relaxed as I laid them out on the nice, warm grass, but Natakia was of a different mindset.

"Guh, gah," the small babe complained, attempting to wave her arms in the air in protest. She was trying to twist away from me as much as her infantile form allowed her, working up to a familiar crying tantrum.

I kept my smile warm and gentle, speaking as softly as I could to the upset youngling. "Natakia, you have to relax, my desert flower."

The parental ritual of cleaning my children was something that had grown easier and easier to do. Except for Natakia, the children had seemingly grown accustomed to it.

Nothing had managed to make them cry more than when I first changed their undergarments.

Still, Natakia never made it easy. Similar to the ritual of getting her to eat, I spoke to her and comforted her throughout the process, distracting her as I cleaned her. She would always cry, yes, but I would tell her stories of my homeland and soothe her spirit.

The Velbrun midwife had mentioned that speaking to young children was very important to their growth, which made sense. My own tribe had practiced something similar.

"Wah, waaah." Natakia tried to roll over, but I stopped her, quickly finishing up and reclothing her, before finally letting her roll to her belly.

She seemed to ball up, her small face molten red with emotion. Did she not want to look at me? Was my baby ashamed of being cleaned?

I was not sure if my child seemingly feeling shame so early was a reflection on my parental skills or not. Or, perhaps, I was just reading too much into the actions of an infant.

Shaking my head, I tenderly rubbed my daughter's back as she slowly calmed down and basked in the warmth of the sun like her siblings.

Lydia would probably have known.

The next day, I made my way to the last stop before Gelvurt, a small farming town called Niers.

Near the edge of where the Velbrun influence faded into the border of the Certillian Empire and Rusk, I knew that this was not the kindest place to strangers.

Nomadic bandits from my homeland, barbarians and trolls from the mountains, the area was rife with threats that kept the locals cautious and paranoid. I was prepared for a less-than-savory reception to my heritage.

Another part of me wondered, with the threats common to this area, if my appointment as a local lord was less of a reward and more of a new, strenuous job.

"Ah, Lord Velbrun of Gelvurt!"

I had just finished tying up my wagon when the call came from the open doors of the tavern, a large, jolly-looking man hoisting a mug in the air toward me. The liquid sloshed about in his cup, small splatters of drink hitting the ground.

With flowing robes, he shook the jug. "Come, have a pint on me, my lord!"

"Lord Velbrun of Niers?" Looking him over, I certainly got the impression of small-village royalty.

He smiled, revealing clean white teeth. "Yes, yes, my lord! Now come, I had a keg set aside for your visit!"

For a moment, I was stunned by how quickly I had been picked out as nobility, but I had informed the guard of who I was as I entered. News truly did travel quickly. Quite a few of the villagers of Niers watched on from the buildings and streets.

And yet, I felt a strange sense of being watched by something much more interested than just a casual villager. Glancing around, I saw no one of note, and the feeling did not feel malicious, so I set myself to ignore it.

Motioning to my wagon, I apologized. "I'm sorry, my lord, but I need to look after my children."

And, of course, I was wary of any accommodations by Velbrun nobility. Even this far out, their machinations were often lurking just under the surface of every coincidence.

The Lord of Niers quirked a brow, but the refusal didn't seem to quell his good spirits. He crept closer, looking into the wagon and seeing the sleeping forms of the triplets.

"I see, I see." He stepped back, nodding. "Well, bring them in, and I'll have my wife keep an eye on them, eh? Better than hay, and I'd like to have a word with you, if you can spare the time."

Wary as I was, I'd come into town only to make sure I had my directions to Gelvurt correct, something the local lord would certainly know better than most.

While I wasn't keen on allowing my children out of my sight for too long, I truly sensed no ill will from the noble, which was somewhat surprising given his Velbrun allegiance. Most with the Velbrun name had an undercurrent of conspiracy to them.

Lord Velbrun of Niers's wife was a stouter woman, much like her husband, who seemed to take great care as she started her vigil over my children as I entered the tavern.

"Welcome to the club, Lord Rakta Velbrun."

I had just sat down, when the jovial expression of Lord Velbrun of Niers had faded to being something on the cusp of serious, his words lined with lead.

I glanced around, the warm atmosphere of the tavern soaking into my bones. "I'm not sure I understand what you mean, Lord Velbrun."

He smirked. "Jorge, Rakta, you can call me Jorge. Been a Velbrun since my mother shacked up with one of their less-favored ilk and had me."

"So the same club we are in . . ."

". . . is a club of the disfavored, given consolation titles and sent to administer the lesser Velbrun settlements." Jorge took a swig from his mug.

It certainly wasn't a far-fetched idea. This close to the border, these settlements had a lot of trouble. Trouble that I, and Jorge, would be required to deal with.

Jorge continued, "Away from the house, away from the larger public where we might scrape up some influence, we're more likely to die early out here than make a name for ourselves."

I stayed quiet, feeling like the man had more to say. He certainly had more to say than I did on this subject.

"But you already have a name, don't you, Rakta the Scavenger?" The jovial tone sewn into Jorge's words had waned as he continued to speak, a rising undercurrent of conspiracy I'd grown wary of from Velbruns taking its place alongside a genuine edge of curiosity.

The food suddenly arrived, a steaming plate of steak that I had not ordered placed in front of me by a young woman. I wasted little time in digging in, not one to turn down a hot meal.

Instinctively, I circulated my Vitae to keep any poison from having any real effect, but I doubted Jorge's intentions were to harm me. And if I was mistaken, I doubted a lesser lord could get ahold of strong enough poison to actually dent my resistance.

I wiped my mouth. "That's not the usual name people know me by. You've done your research."

Jorge looked satisfied, but I counted with a quick pulse of my Vitae that there were about six individuals in the tavern, most of which I could see.

If this turned violent, I would have to retrieve my children from Jorge's wife before they were taken hostage. That was something that I could not allow under any circumstances.

"Well, it certainly piqued my interest. Your group actually did work around here quite a while ago, before the war, and, well, people have long memories in these parts." Jorge was happily digging into his own food, somehow managing to speak whole sentences between the large bites he took from his steak.

We had? I hadn't remembered doing such a thing. Perhaps we had inadvertently done some work here? Maybe a minor goblin extermination mission or two? At the very least, the larger threats to the Certillian Empire hadn't gotten this far south.

Still, I nodded. "Well, you're welcome."

There truly wasn't much more to say. I'm sure we'd been compensated for any work we'd done in the area, so further reward was far from my mind.

Jorge grinned. "I guess what I'm trying to say is, if you ever need help over in Gelvurt, let me know, okay? We gotta look out for each other down here at the bottom of the barrel."

Slowly, I realized with growing horror in the pit of my stomach that this was politics. Not from the perspective of an outsider, as I was accustomed, but from a player within it.

Setting my fork and knife down, I frowned. "That is the way of lords, I suppose."

I'd lost my appetite.

"Geh." Dalton made a show of tossing the small trinket away, the small little thing thumping onto the floor of the wagon. It was a small copper bear figurine, one that Jorge's wife had gifted him as we disembarked after getting directions.

I glanced over, picking the figurine up and placing it near him. "It was a gift, Dalton; you should appreciate gifts."

It had been a day since we had departed from Niers, Jorge being somewhat disheartened when I had declined to stay the night.

The man was kind, certainly, but I was not ready to . . . deal with the Velbruns. Not emotionally, much less politically. It was not like I intended to seek out any more influence than I needed to keep my children safe.

Dalton paid no more attention to it, ignoring it and turning away toward Daka and Natakia, both of whom were enjoying their own eagle and cat figurines, respectively.

Daka, in particular, held the eagle figurine close to her chest.

Humming in the back of my throat, I wondered aloud, "Younglings should have plenty of toys. Perhaps I can have some made in Gelvurt?"

Natakia was petting her figurine. Perhaps a nice pet would be good for the children to grow up alongside? Finding a hunter with a litter of pups wouldn't be the hardest thing to do.

The hounds of Certillia were certainly tamer than the coyotes of Rusk. Although, in my experience, a proper tumbletooth was far better at keeping a sleeping warrior safe than any bloodhound or retriever.

Suddenly, I heard a soft little smack of flesh on flesh moments before the sounds of Natakia's wails erupted.

Whipping my head toward my children, I saw Daka's guilty face welling up in tears, her hand moving away from Natakia's cheek. Their figurines lay on the wagon, forgotten.

"Oh no." I stopped the wagon, clambering into the back to pick Natakia up as she wailed. "There, there, my desert flower."

Daka started crying, too, her hands flailing, and the stress seemed to disturb Dalton enough to make his eyes well up in tears.

I made small shushing noises, holding Natakia close as I picked Daka up. Natakia seemed to shift away from her sister, and I felt a pang in my heart.

"No, no, accident, Natakia! Daka would never want to hurt you intentionally." The thought of Natakia fearing her sister ate at me in a way I wasn't prepared for.

Daka continued to cry, and I sat down, rocking in place with them cradled in my arms.

A half hour later, I had managed to calm them down, shifting their sleeping forms back into their wagon seat alongside Dalton who, mercifully, had calmed down himself.

I looked at the two sleeping girls, their limbs tangled together with each other, and felt an old wound stir. As numb as I'd felt since Lydia's death, the thought of my children being at odds with one another . . .

It was a familiar pain.

It was four days later that I finally arrived in Gelvurt with my triplets, happy to finally have some rest and give my younglings a chance to sleep on comfortable silks and bedding.

It was an hour after I had tied up my wagon that I was saddled with the news of a monster feasting on the local children.

7

In my short time in Gelvurt, I had noticed quickly that it was a small settlement. Made up of a village center, mostly consisting of a market square, and scattered homes of farmers and their fields that took up the majority of Gelvurt's lands, it was far different from the cobblestone streets of larger towns and cities.

The Velbrun Keep, my inherited home as the local lord, was located about a mile away from the center of town, surrounded by stone walls and modest defenses. Enough room for both a small militia and servants to live alongside my family.

A place for both my family and the people of Gelvurt to feel safe in times of trouble.

"Five children, mostly boys, have turned up dead, my lord."

Orion, the local general store owner, had filled me in on the situation. For the past few months, there had been rumors of something moving in the darkness around the homes of Gelvurt's people. For a while, it'd been assumed to be bandits or the like.

Then corpses of animals, mostly livestock, had been found eviscerated, an act above and beyond the simple act of theft one might expect from bandits. The villagers had sent word to the Velbruns, but my arrival was the closest thing they'd gotten to a response.

It was close to a month ago that children began to go missing, instead of simple cattle.

I placed Dalton down into the proper beds that the keep had been furnished with, wrapping him with one of the warmth-enchanted blankets I had purchased.

Turning around, I nodded to Orion. "What do we know about the creature? Has the local healer or any of the hunters examined the remains?"

The general store owner, the most overtly trusting of my arrival, nodded. "Marge, our local alchemist, examined . . . one of the children, and we have plenty of testimony from hunters who examined the livestock."

"And?" I made a motion for him to continue. I knew the findings could not have been pleasant, but they were important.

"The monster has claws, my lord, and they punctured cleanly through the skin and muscle of the cows. From tracks, we've gathered that it's bipedal and has mismatched feet, but . . . nothing beyond that."

Mismatched feet? I wasn't quite sure what to make of that, but I filed it away for the time being. I certainly didn't know of a monster like that off the top of my head, but trolls often underwent mutations that could be to blame for the oddity.

I nodded. "Whether by stealth or magic, it escaped the notice of the local guard. There's a lot of land to cover here in Gelvurt."

Orion nodded. He was Certillian, with a light tan darkening the paler skin of his heritage, and had long, dark hair that was tied off into a tight ponytail. He was tall, close to my height, but thin and lacking definition to his build.

I looked out the window of the room, down to the courtyard of the keep, where the people of Gelvurt had retired for the night. They had been here when I arrived, the women and children seeking shelter.

"What are our numbers? Local militia?" Even a small settlement would have some sort of manpower to protect itself.

"The captain is, unfortunately, not available, but he has trained eight capable swordsmen that patrol the village center and the fields on rotation."

I frowned. "What is keeping the captain?"

"Mourning, my lord. One of the children was his."

I closed my eyes, feeling for the man. Without Lydia, I was already at the edge of fading into a shadow myself, but if the lights of my children ever flickered . . .

"Guh." Natakia sniffed at a crawling beetle that she had moved her arm to squish. Daka giggled at the sight.

It would break me.

"Alright, I'll need two of the guards to accompany me; the more they are familiar with the area, the bett—"

Orion frowned. "My lord?"

Something was niggling at the back of my mind. Something that he had said about the examination of the bodies. Not so much the information regarding the creature, but the examiner.

I turned back to Orion. "Why did your alchemist examine only the first child?"

"Mourning, my lord." He sighed, truly exhausted by the topic. "The week after the captain's son died, both of her sons went missing and were found dead soon after."

That set off an alarm somewhere in the back of my head.

I frowned. "The parents of the other children, who were they?"

"The local postman and the tavern owner." Orion didn't seem to have caught on to my thoughts.

I considered the new information for a moment, before shaking my head. "This is no monster idly seeking easy prey."

The general store owner stumbled at the words. "M-my lord?"

I settled a fierce gaze at him. "This is an attempt to intentionally cripple Gelvurt by targeting the children. I want eyes on my children while I'm gone, understand?"

The man took a moment to gather himself before he nodded, and I was off.

Gelvurt was quiet at night, especially now, but that did not mean my hunt was free of distractions.

"So, you're the new lord, huh?"

Dresden and Kingsley walked alongside me, both of them equipped with the rudimentary arms and armor of the local guard, the metal implements clanking lightly against one another as they walked.

I turned to the more talkative member of my accompanying guards. "Yes, I am."

Dresden gave a nod, considering me. "Pretty active for a lord. I don't think I ever saw our last lord leave the keep before he got posted elsewhere, you know?"

I really didn't. I wasn't sure if I intended to be an active member of the community.

Kingsley pointed, distracting Dresden from any other questions at my silence. "There. That's the Conroy home, where the last attack happened."

He was an older man, most likely served in the war to some extent. From what I had been told, he was an old friend of the local captain.

He'd been very eager to join me in dealing with this monstrosity.

Dresden, however, was a younger man, only a few years beyond his boyhood. His lips flapped easier than Kingsley's, and it felt like he was testing me with his questions.

Coming up on the scene of the most recent attack was a bittersweet reprieve.

The Conroy abode was posted on a slight hill, with a small, fenced backyard with a few pigs roaming about. I approached it, noticing one of the windows was shattered.

Kingsley spoke up, noticing my focus. "Ole Conroy said he heard a loud shatter and screams before the thing dragged his boy out. Didn't get a good look at it though."

I nodded, examining bits and pieces of the glass scattered throughout the grass. "Why are these shattered outward?"

Dresden shrugged. "Thing crushed through the window to get out, yeah?"

I nodded. "That means it got inside somewhere else."

Perhaps through the door? The cellar? Was this creature able to dig? Fortunately, it mattered little how it entered.

It had, ultimately, left from this spot, the beginnings of a trail.

I crouched, flexing my body as my vital energy began to move and shift, the beginnings of my **Scourger Bloodhound Technique**.

With my last moments before the technique took hold, I said quietly, "Guard me, I'm catching the scent."

And then everything went dark, my sense of smell expanding as I took in the smells of the grass, the old smells of blood, and . . . something that was off.

It was barely there, a faint aroma of cleaner fluid, something I had encountered frequently in alchemist labs and other facilities that needed to be devoid of natural contaminants.

A curious smell I might have thought lingered from the local alchemist, but she'd been in no state to examine the area.

Still, it was certainly not the smell of a typical monster.

I got the direction of the stench, heading into the forest, and allowed the technique to fade, my sense of smell receding as my others returned.

"—uch do you wanna bet this guy is in over his head?"

I stood up, turning to both of them and ignoring the idle chatter from Dresden. "I've got the stench; let's go."

As we neared the forest line, I turned to my companions once more. "How often are these woods patrolled?"

Kingsley shook his head. "We don't. The hunters are out here most days and report any strange sightings back to us."

I frowned. It made sense, especially if they had only so many guards to spread out, but things could fester in places like this if not routinely checked.

"So, uh, you mentioned this thing might not be a monster?" Dresden's thin, light blade was out, held with a skillfulness that made up for his hint of attitude.

Honestly, it was refreshing to an extent. Most that turned their noses up at me had little competency to their name.

I shook my head. "It isn't a monster, at least, not a dumb one. This one went after the pillars of the community, wanting Gelvurt crippled, but not evacuated."

"Any idea of what it could be, my lord?" Kingsley's own blade, heavier than Dresden's, was held ready in a casual two-handed grip at his side.

"If not a human dabbling in darker arts, then possibly a peak troll. It might have come down from the mountains, possibly chased by a predator. They're smart, but if it was involved, it wouldn't have left corpses."

No, the corpses were around for a reason. It started with livestock, to stir rumors, and now children to strike while the iron was hot. What scheme was at play here? I couldn't even begin to connect the dots.

Lydia would have already figured it all out.

I had been following the stench for about an hour now, routinely using **Scourger Bloodhound Technique** to stay on track. A part of me worried that I was playing into the hands of this creature by leaving the company of my children, but I could not stand and idle by as families were torn apart.

I heard a branch snap in the distance, my eyes darting to a distant bush. In the blink of an eye, my Vulture Axes were ready, my form dropped into the familiar weight of the **Dancing Star Stance**.

"Something's coming."

The two guards readied their weapons, dropping into their own stances.

For a moment, the bush continued to shake and stir, before a small animal hopped out, a gray-furred rabbit that sniffed at the air, before looking at us.

Dresden's stance fell, his voice light. "Oh, come on, it's just a fucking bunn—"

And then a dozen more rabbits hopped from the same bush, the lead one opening its mouth with a dry, cracking scream, revealing a set of inch-long serrated teeth.

"Holy fucking shit!"

The monstrous rabbits charged, their dull eyes focused on us and us alone.

8

ir Slice Technique!" Kingsley's blade ripped through the air, sending a wide slice of physical force flying toward the enraged wildlife.

Three of the rabbits were torn into scraps by the wide strike, the horde of hopping horrors not abated at all by the loss to their numbers.

Tensing, I dashed forward, twisting as I closed in on the rushing horde and began tossing my axes. Sinking deep into two different rabbits, the Vultures pulsed with magic.

Dresden raised his foot. "**Stomping Leap Tech—**!'

The world exploded as my Vultures detonated the air around them, one sending an explosion of fire and cinder into the air as the other coursed the area around it with merciless electricity that flooded the forms of the small animals.

The young guard fell, knocked over mid-technique by the sudden force. "What the . . . !?"

The rabbits had been knocked around by the explosions, as well, with many torn to pieces. I held out my hands, both of the Vultures ripping themselves out of the ground and flying back into my waiting grip.

"These are not normal rabbits."

Dresden staggered to his feet. "H-hey, can you fucking warn us next time you decide to blow up the forest!?"

I ignored him for the moment, watching as the remaining rabbits got to their feet. They were eviscerated, parts of limbs broken and their fur burned, but . . . they continued to get up. Not even a hint of self-preservation in them.

I sniffed, smelling the air. Ozone, burned fur, smoke, but no blood. Not even the singed copper scent of cauterized wounds.

"Knock it off, Dresden. Get back into your stance." Kingsley was still defensive, holding his blade out toward the rabbits as they regrouped.

"Yeah, yeah."

We made quick work of the last of the rabbits, the weakened creatures being unable to move fast enough to escape our counterattack after our initial surprise faded.

"Last one's mine!" Dresden took one large step, bringing his sword down in a clean overhead swipe that bisected the last razor-toothed mammal.

Dresden, for a young man of his age, was an excellent swordsman.

His stance, a common **Iron Knight Stance** that was popular with simple militia, was strong, and he held the form well. Yet, he didn't seem to have Kingsley's skill at channeling Vitae through weaponry. Not yet, at least.

"You use a lighter blade than most I've seen with that stance," I said as the excitement of the battle began to fade, my head on a swivel to make sure all the pests had been dealt with.

Swirling his blade, Dresden shrugged. "I learned with a lighter blade; the training stuck."

Kingsley cracked a half smile at that, but said nothing, his own blade, better weighted for the **Iron Knight Stance** that he similarly employed, slowly lowering at his side.

After we were sure there were no reinforcements in the area, I bent down, examining one of the rabbits that Dresden had slain, picking up a nearby stick to poke at its wound.

"Is it necromancy?"

I looked up at Kingsley. "Possibly."

The older man shook his head. "Foul sorcery, that is. I thought all those fucking witches died out when the empire gutted the Warlock King."

That wasn't true, but I'd learned not to contest that rumor a long time ago. It had never led to enjoyable conversations.

Shrugging, I peeled back the muscle of the animal, strangely preserved, and furrowed my brows. "This . . . is unlike anything I've seen before."

"Well, undead come in all shapes and sizes, my lord." Kingsley chuckled.

"It's filled with cotton and cloth."

The guard was silent for a moment, before he muttered under his breath, "Never seen that before."

Necromancy, a magic of imbuing once-living things with Mana to bring them back from unliving states, was not inherently evil.

At its foundation, the magical art shared common ground with a number of other arts, especially those involved with the healing of the body.

At least, that was how Lydia had explained it.

However, the actions of the Warlock King had stained the art with a blackness that could not be washed easily. Not that I blamed people for their wariness.

"So, it's a necromancer?"

I shook my head at Dresden as we moved. "Maybe, maybe not. Whoever is doing this is taxidermying animals and animating them."

"Whether that's necromancy or something else isn't a discussion to have in the forest." Kingsley didn't look like he much cared about the distinction regardless.

I agreed. Each of the rabbits had been filled with stuffing, their insides and skins being soaked with alchemical solutions. Stitched and glued together, the magic weakening had simply left shredded taxidermy.

"So, uh, aren't we gonna go get some reinforcements? 'Cause, I'm pretty sure rabbits aren't the only thing this witch has going for them." Dresden spoke lightly, but I could hear the tremor in his voice.

I shook my head. "We need to take care of this now. They can't have expected my presence, giving us an edge we can't lose."

Especially since, giving whoever was behind this time to realize I had children, with their modus operandi, would mean I'd be unable to freely leave my younglings' sides to deal with them after tonight.

"Fuck, if I see an undead bear, I'm gonna be so pissed."

"You should have taken me up on the offer to go bear hunting, Dresden. That experience would have been invaluable now, yes?"

"Well, don't ask me to join after making a joke about me being bear food next time." Dresden's lips twitched into a hint of a smile, despite the annoyance in his voice.

The levity with which the two guards spoke was refreshing, but I made a quiet motion to shush them as I flexed my Vitae, activating my **Scourger Bloodhound Technique**.

The alchemically clean scent was getting stronger. Much stronger. I was sure that, any closer, and it would be noticeable by my more normal senses alone.

As the technique faded and my vision came back, I noted that the forest around us had become denser as we headed deeper and deeper in. In the dark shadows, every bush and tree grew larger and larger, as if to encompass the hidden dangers within them.

"The trail is getting stronger. There could be more of those creatures in every bush and behind every tree." I spoke quietly, but firmly.

Dresden's grip tightened around his sword hilt. "How many of those bastards are out here?"

The other guard's gaze was level as he made a slow swivel motion, keeping his eyes out. "A single witch could have upwards of thirty monstrosities bound to their will."

I nodded. "The higher echelons could bind upwards of a hundred."

There was silence in the forest.

"Damn."

Soon, tracking became easier as the signs of unnatural movement in the area became more pronounced. Large claw marks engraved into the bark and old flecks of blood, among other telltale signs.

"I don't hear any birds, my lord."

They'd begun to quiet as we moved farther along the path, no longer hearing their songs, but the fluttering of distant owls and other fowl was still noticeable.

I nodded. "I want both of you to return to the keep. If I don't return by the morning, prepare an evacuation to Niers."

"My lord, we can't leave you to fight alone." Kingsley sounded pained.

I looked down at my hand. "I'm ordering you. Dresden was right; I'm not communicating well tonight. If I'm not careful, I'm liable to hurt you if I use one of my techniques without warning."

Dresden scoffed. "I think we can get out of the way of a few explosions."

"Also, the villagers need to be alerted," I continued, ignoring Dresden. He didn't know what he was talking about. "We can't all go back without giving this individual more time to prepare. If only one of you leaves, you'll be vulnerable."

Kingsley was quiet for a moment, before he sighed. "You make some good points, my lord. Come, Dresden, we need to bring word back."

He began walking back, motioning for Dresden to follow him. And yet, Dresden lingered for a moment longer, his throat bobbing as he swallowed, staring at me.

"People saw you come in with kids. Don't die a hero; live as a father." There was a rawness to his demand.

My children flashed through my mind. I had no intention of ever leaving them for as long as they needed me.

"I will not die."

Dresden continued to stare for a moment, before he turned away, jogging to catch up with Kingsley. For a moment, his gaze had been looking through me, at someone else.

Everyone had lost someone.

Turning back to the trail, I brought out two of my Vulture Axes and began to circulate my Vitae, letting it simmer beneath my skin.

The Warlock King had been the most difficult fight of my entire life, physically and emotionally, but the witches at his beck and call had been vicious in their own rights.

If this truly was a remnant of his army, I could not hold back. For those who had lost their lives in the war, for those who were mourning their lost children, and for those fearfully cradling their children tonight.

Gelvurt's people, my people, would no longer suffer as they had.

Ten minutes later, twigs snapped under my footfalls as I came across the mouth of a tunnel entrenched in the side of a large hill. From the ancient wooden beams outlining the dark maw, it could have only been a mine in the past.

Abandoned by the nearby settlements and by time.

"Well, well, look who finally decided to show up."

The high-pitched, cracking voice echoed out of the mouth of the tunnel.

"The local lord decided to come have a tea party."

With a stilted gait, a long, furred leg came out of the darkness of the tunnel, the sounds of cracking bones accompanying the unnatural movement. As the bear paw planted itself firmly in the ground, I could hear the sounds of clicking as the bones moved like a loose jigsaw puzzle within the confines of the flesh.

Pulling herself, for it was certainly a woman, out of the tunnel, the lanky form of the sorcerer was certainly monstrous in its own right.

Leathery, stitched skin, one hand tipped in scalpel-like claws, the other completely replaced with the large, serrated paw of a bear, and the legs of a similarly large mammal, the woman smirked, tilting her head at me.

Her stomach was bloated, like an obscene perversion of pregnancy. Her dull, mismatched eyes were vibrant with magic in the moonlit clearing.

I kept my eyes on her, even knowing without pulsing my Vitae that this woman was no living creature. "Your true body is further in the tunnel?"

It was a fool's errand to believe a necromancer, or any conjurer of any magical art, would greet a foe personally if they had an alternative.

The womanlike thing chuckled, a dry, rattling noise. "All you'll find in this tunnel is death, my lord. And all my pets."

And then the tunnel behind her began to echo with a cacophony of what once were animals.

9

Stitched together by animal tendons and horsehair, the first creature that dashed out at me from the darkness was an elk, its impressive set of antlers carved into a set of serrated blades.

Its dull eyes focused on me as it charged, my body surging with Vitae as I dodged out of its way, letting the creature run past me.

"Get him, get him!" the ugly creature screamed, pointing at me. It was almost childish.

Wolves dashed forward, each of them with an extra set of limbs and an unhinged jaw full of teeth far too large for canines.

I quickly settled into my **Dancing Star Stance**, letting my Vitae rumble in the familiar tumble of the learned position, before watching the first wolf approach.

"Gragh!" it loosely snarled, a lifeless growl that spilled from its unhinged, splitting lips. The beauty of the wild beast dissected and perverted by the machinations of this witch.

I grabbed one of my Vultures tightly. "**Horizon Throw Technique.**"

Power surged through my arm as I threw the axe, letting its extended edge cleanly bisect the taxidermied beast straight down the middle, with the axe catching two more of its pack as it continued onward.

The wolves fell, unmoving, but I continued with my other blade, spinning as I began to cleanly carve through the other wolves as they moved to flank me. Axe after axe, each throw downing the creatures as they got close.

Fur and stuffing rained upon me, stained by the stench of alchemical solvents that the creatures had been soaked in. An absent thought occurred to me that alchemy components weren't expensive, but to have this much would have required some wealth.

At the sound of beating hooves, I leaped, letting the **Grasshopper Leap Technique** shoot me into the sky, twisting into a flip as the elk returned, its antlers finding little purchase in the air where I'd once stood.

The creature, the woman, snarled, looking far less composed than before. "You . . . Who are you!?"

I hit the ground, easily settling back into my stance as I faced the monster and her endless brood of beasts. "My name is Rakta Velbrun."

That's all I was these days, the only person I needed to be.

I breathed deeply, letting my Vitae vibrate and recover as I took in the sight around me. Over twenty caricatures of nature strewn around me, torn apart cleanly by my Vulture Axes.

The creature had thrown everything she had at me, a pitiful collection compared to what I had fought before, which meant going inside the mine would be easier now.

It was often thought a fool's errand to waste your time and energy on the hordes of a witch, a thought I'd often agree with. And yet, while I could have gone straight for the practitioner, I fought better out in the open when such numbers were against me.

Now, the only thing left to end was the main avatar of this foul magician.

I looked at said monster, her head on a swivel as she digested this alongside me. Emotions were not often carried well through the body language of these remotely controlled creatures, but I could sense her rising anger and fear.

I got down into my stance. "I will say this only once: give yourself up, and perhaps your punishment for your deeds will be lenient."

Although, truly, the most I could do was have her sent for execution at the capital. It would still be a mercy compared to what the people of Gelvurt would have in store for her.

For a moment, the woman was silent. She seemed to understand how little difference there would be to her end. Still, I did not care much.

This woman, the one behind all this village's tragedy, would die all the same.

"You . . . have children, don't you?"

I felt a small chill run down my spine, but ignored it.

She chuckled, dry and raspy, before she looked me in the eyes once more. "A new lord with children comes to find his lands beset by a child killer? I can taste the paternal need in you."

The woman was still for a moment, her body lax. As if lost in a moment of her own.

"Disgusting."

She blurred, her razor-sharp claws suddenly in front of me in an overhead swing, her heavy bear claw of an arm gleaming in the moonlight.

Dashing away from the strike, my instincts flaring, I threw a Vulture Axe at the spot I'd just dodged away from. The sooner this thing was dispatched, the better.

The thing growled, spinning away from the axe, and even managing to maneuver out of its way again as it flew back into my hands, neatly cutting her in half had she not moved with such knowing grace.

"Sneak attacks won't work. I have eyes all over this forest." Her croaking voice was filled with a smug glee.

I glanced around, now noticing the vigilant birds watching the battle. Their dull gaze kept eyes on every sliver of the battlefield that I danced upon.

Feeling the air move, I turned, and the sound of steel on steel echoed as I parried another swipe of claws with one of my axes, the strikes never letting up as I continued to dash backward, looking for an opening.

"Run, run, Lord Velbrun! As fast as you fucking can!" There was no mercy in her eyes, only a vicious insanity that gazed straight through me and sought my death.

The creature's blows came from odd angles, not limited by the strain on its body, puppeted by a will that wasn't its own as it continued to slash and claw at me.

And it was fast, faster than one would expect looking at the bloated stomach of the monster.

Knocking aside a random kick, heavy and strong for the frame of the creature, I saw an opening. I struck out with an axe, ready to end this and get to the real enem—

I heard leathery flesh rip apart, and a cold, metallic sensation pierced my stomach, my warmth spilling out of me.

The woman was still, her expression twisted into a raucous, mocking grin that stretched too far. "You're not the only parent, my lord."

I kicked out, knocking her away as I held a hand against my stomach, feeling my Vitae course through my system to begin to passively heal. It was a deep blow, something I couldn't ignore, but wouldn't put me out of the fight as long as I had Vitae to spare.

"Did I do good, Mama?"

The voice was cracked and feminine, dry and lifeless. Like a paltry attempt at ventriloquism, it distracted me from my wound as I refocused on the creature and . . . and . . .

The creature's obscenely bloated stomach had exploded outward, another smaller form, stitched into existence from scavenged flesh, hanging out of the newly opened window.

It was a child, a taxidermied child made up of mismatching parts. Its hands were gone, replaced with two large pieces of jagged metal that swung around in the air loosely.

The woman gave the creature a pat on the head with the palm of its clawed hands, a note of twisted love in her voice. "Yes, dearie. You did . . . wonderfully."

A deep part of me felt sick. Repulsed. I'd been concerned about what the one behind all of this would need with children, beyond scaring the villagers, but this? Salvaging parts from their remains?

And all for what? To puppet these creatures? Make them act out this perversion of familial love? To tear apart happy families just to create this insanity?

My **Healing Flesh Technique** pulsed, my skin restitching quickly at the cost of large portions of my Vitae. The most important thing right now was that I survived for my children; nothing was worth leaving them alone in this world.

And with the rest of my Vitae, I was going to completely destroy the abomination behind all of this.

"You once asked me who I was."

The creature stopped petting its abomination. "Aren't you too busy choking on your blood to talk? Wait . . . W-where did the wound go!?"

I grabbed two of my Vulture Axes. "I'm a father, a widower, a Ruskan trying to make a world better for his children, to protect them from the hardships that he faced."

I got down into a different stance, one that felt like an old friend.

"But before that? I was a dancer." My voice echoed as my Vitae changed.

The world blurred around me, spiraling for I was the tornado. The eye of the storm, the Vitae of the heavens. I moved with each subtle suggestion of the sky and forest. Beckoning heat and warmth as I took control of the duet.

For that was the way of the **First Dance Stance**.

The creature dashed at me, her claws outstretched alongside her child's. "S-stop this. I won't let you!"

The four-pronged attack surged at me with brilliant speeds, ready to skewer me.

"First Dance Technique: Sunrise over the Mesa."

And the night became daytime.

A minute later, I was sitting on the ground, putting out the last of the flames that had caught on the drier tinder of the nearby forest.

The smoldering remains of the creature and the other taxidermied beasts were unpleasant, the solvents applied to their bodies making for a pungent smoke that I dared not breathe in for too long. I couldn't recognize chemicals, but I knew enough to not inhale them carelessly.

I was tired. My Vitae had not been pushed so far in . . . since Lydia had gotten pregnant. Had peace truly rusted my skills this quickly? Vitae was a muscle; it weakened when one allowed oneself to lounge in the luxuries of nobility.

Perhaps the fault did not lie in peace, but rather, my own recent actions. Nights spent wide-awake watching over my little ones, while not straining on Vitae, left little time to recover.

And with that added on top of pushing myself with the bandits and . . . yes, possibly being rusty, I . . . perhaps I should not have been so confident as to go alone. Arrogance could have been the true killer here had my foe not been victim to it first.

I shook my head. "A single **First Dance Technique**, and I'm completely drained. Natakia would be laughing at me."

Natakia . . .

My thoughts of the past were set aside as I heard the sounds of footsteps coming from the mine entrance. I picked myself up, trying to scrape together the last bits of Vitae for more fighting.

Out of the darkness, came a woman, her blonde hair cut in uneven tangles, her pale skin splotchy with old, soured bruises and wounds, and deep bags under her glazed green eyes.

She wore a number of furs, each of them smelling the same as the creatures. In her weak grasp, she held a long cooking knife.

". . . Kill me."

The blade dropped from her grip.

I nodded gravely. What was the purpose of the beasts? Why make so many? Why create the facsimile of a mother and her child to hide behind? Why pursue necromancy and yet be so eager to die?

I'd often thought about similar questions while killing the witches of the Warlock King.

The only answer I had to any of my ponderings was from Lydia.

"Every one of them probably thought they'd regain something they had lost," Lydia had said on the cusp of our final fight with the Warlock King.

I stared at the woman, pondering once more, "Before I kill you, tell me your story."

The woman, who would later introduce herself as Vera before I slew her, hesitated for a moment, before beginning a tale of motherhood, empty promises, and madness.

"You're back, my lord!"

I nodded at Orion's astute insight, exhausted as I returned to the Velbrun Keep. "Yes, I've returned. Vera, the sorcerer behind the attacks, is dead."

The crowd that had gathered to greet me on my return erupted into cheers, all of them looking relieved and joyous at the news, none more so than the untouched families that could still take solace in the lives of their children.

"D-did she suffer?"

A woman stepped, almost stumbled, out of the crowd, her dark hair frazzled and deep bags under her brown eyes. Another woman tried to reach for her, to pull her back, but the woman ripped out of the grip, staggering toward me.

"My lord, d-did she suffer?" she asked again, struggling with a sob in the back of her throat. "Was she, was she torn apart? Did you hurt h-her? The same way . . . the same way my, same way my boys . . ."

I thought back to the story I was told and gazed at the woman who looked just a stone's toss from walking down Vera's dark path.

"Yes, she suffered. She suffered for a very long time."

The woman, smelling of alchemy, smiled, "G-good . . ."

10

G uh." Natakia handled my finger with care and curiosity, her eyes going to her own finger, as if comparing the two. I almost mistook her curiosity for frustration, but simple interest was more likely.

"I'm a fair bit bigger than you, desert flower." I was exhausted, more emotionally than physically after I'd had a chance to recover from my fight with Vera.

Which made the current conversation a little frustrating to be involved in.

"They're just . . . how old are they again?"

Marisha, Orion's wife, had watched over my children alongside a guard. Certillians were quite beholden to the idea of raising a child being a tender trade reserved for women, a departure from the share of child-care duties that Ruskans typically employed.

"They are about a month old."

"They are remarkably, uh, aware for their age. Active too." She sounded disbelieving, as if I might be pulling her leg.

I shrugged. "Children born with potential grow faster than others. Their mother and I were both considered strong in our own rights."

That was, of course, on top of the tendency for Ruskan infants to have to do their own small parts in moving away from threats that got too close. Guidance from the desert, my tribe's Storyteller had called it.

The redhead smiled, looking a little strained. "I see. We don't have children like them often."

For a moment, I considered whether she was speaking of their growth or of their heritage, their dark skin that was only a few shades lighter than mine.

"It's just . . . it feels like they're watching us, my lord." Her words were nervous, as if she were suddenly aware of whose children she was speaking about.

Ah, yes, the eyes. I'd grown fond of them over the month, in the same way I'd grown fond of everything about my children, no matter how odd others might have found them.

I smiled. "Daka has her mother's eyes. They are all intelligent though. Dalton, even more so. He began counting things when I wasn't looking one day."

Letting out a breath, Marisha seemed to gather herself. "Well, I hope they'll be nice playmates for my own children, if I can be so bold, my lord."

That sounded . . . pleasant. The idea of my children playing with other younglings, free from danger, was a nice salve on the wounds of the night's events.

I nodded. "I believe they would like that."

Dalton started crying, fat tears streaking down his cheeks onto his new, comfortable sheets.

Marisha giggled. "They must be hungry. Big as they may be, they haven't been weaned off of milk yet, have they?"

"No, I've been feeding them an alchemical milk substitute I purchased before I came here."

"Well, a substitute is no match for real milk, my lord. If I could . . . ?" She tugged at her clothing, giving me a meaningful look.

Her words, along with the implication, registered after a few moments. I nodded, having considered hiring a wet nurse of some variety for the next few months.

"I will, uh, leave you to that."

In the next room over, I breathed a heavy sigh of regret. I was no prudish whelp unable to watch a woman feed a child, but . . .

Appreciative of Orion's wife, I certainly was, but . . . in my heart of hearts, I knew it should be my wife feeding her children, not a kind stranger.

Lydia . . .

Was it the moment now? I was finally in Gelvurt, my children watched by another that I could trust nearby. Was this when I could rest for a moment? Allow myself to truly feel?

The decision was made the second I acknowledged what I'd been holding back.

My heart unclenched for the first time since life had left my wife's body, and the grief began to flow alongside the wetness pouring down my cheeks.

"Thank you, Lydia. Thank you for bringing these children to me. Thank you for giving me a chance to live for them as I lived for you."

I cried into my hand, feeling the calluses, the evidence upon my flesh of every fight and battle I dove headfirst into alongside my beautiful sweetheart. The plans I'd followed, the lives I'd saved, the lives I'd taken. So much hardship alongside her, and now she was gone.

"They have your eyes, your hair, even their skin is stained with you, Lydia. I love them so much, but I am scared . . . scared that I will falter, scared that one mistake will tarnish their beauty."

My body was wracked with the weight of loneliness, of no longer feeling her soft hands interlaced with mine. The stories we had woven together flashed before me.

The victories, the failures. The friends, the enemies.

The look in her eyes as she softly stepped in front of my path, nothing but vengeance in my heart. The feeling in my heart as she turned away, letting me deal the final blow to the downed Warlock King . . .

. . . We rarely spoke about those moments. The Warlock King's death should have been celebrated, but it was the moment Lydia had walked away from everything.

And I had walked away right alongside her. I'd walked alongside her hoping for a long future with her.

"What if the others come, Lydia? How will I face them? Our departure was so sudden, words were thrown so hastily . . ."

Breathing in and out, controlling myself, I tried to sit up straighter. I needed strength, strength I could not scrape together alone, not without my wife with me.

So I called out to her in the only way I knew how.

"There was once a child by the name of Lydia Velbrun, who saw the world through the window of her room, and dreamed every night of running away . . ."

I continued, feeling Lydia alongside me for the moment, thinking of the future.

A night of rest and mourning later, and I was in my new office, taking my first visitor.

"Here are official documents of Gelvurt's financial situation, Lord Velbrun. I was entrusted with them during the exchange of dominion."

I took the papers from Orion. "Thank you, Orion. I'm curious, however, of why you were trusted in lieu of the local guard."

Orion smiled, but it was somewhat tight. "The previous Lord Velbrun and I were friends, something he had very few of within Gelvurt."

I hadn't concerned myself with the previous Lord Velbrun of Gelvurt, but it seemed I would have to at least become familiar with his remnants. A part of me wished to paint him with the same brush most Velbruns used, but there was every chance he was like Jorge and me.

A lord at the bottom of the barrel.

I flipped through the documents, idly reading them. "Was the previous lord not liked by the people of Gelvurt? Why?"

"Disliked? Not exactly." The general store owner frowned. "He was private, my lord. Rarely left this keep except to buy some of the tonics he had shipped here."

"Tonics? Was he sick?" I'd imagined even a Lord Velbrun of ill-influence would be able to find a doctor willing to treat him.

"No, merely seeking to be healthier than he already was, my lord."

Interesting. Still, that was of less concern to me than another detail I had just happened upon.

"I'm not seeing the dominion testimony here, Orion."

Orion blinked. "I'm sorry, my lord?"

I laid the documents aside. "The dominion testimony; it's a writ from the previous lord that notes all the issues of the land the new lord must deal with."

It was not a missing document that would deprive me of my authority in any way, but knowing the people of Gelvurt and the issues was an advantage I'd thought would be helpful.

Lydia had always talked about how the most difficult part about managing new lands was the particularities of the land and its people.

Rivalries, grudges, and other small details about the people I managed were important if I were to do my job.

"My apologies, my lord. I can recheck the safe where I deposited them, but . . . I believe these are all the documents I was given. Lord Zactrik Velbrun was likely not aware of what ailed us."

That was certainly a possibility.

"And the previous Lord Velbrun is now . . . ?"

"He never said where the house was transferring him to, my lord." Orion shrugged, looking down and away.

House Velbrun was a secretive one, that was for sure. Limiting information among the public was . . . important to them. For things both big and small, in my experience.

I nodded. "I see, thank you for bringing these to me."

"Of course. If you need me to explain the empire's economic system to you, I can, my lord. I know there may be some differences from the Ruskan tribes . . ."

I stared at him, waiting for him to continue.

He wilted. "Not to imply that you grew up among them, my lord. I did not, uh, mean any . . . any offense . . ."

I looked at the top document, perusing the rate of taxes and the monthly quota of corn, a popular local crop, that House Velbrun expected.

"There is no offense in thinking I grew up among my people, Orion. My people's ways were different, not lesser." Although I was sure some Certillians would disagree. "I may need you on some accounts, but I was taught the basics of your system."

Lydia had been a gentle, but firm teacher. She had even formulated a spell of her own design to increase the learning rates of her students . . . It had given me a headache, but a new appreciation for budgets.

Orion's smile wasn't overflowing with belief. "Of course, my lord. As you need."

Marisha was once again looking after my children, an arrangement I was not entirely confident with yet, but one that allowed me to walk the streets of Gelvurt without worrying.

I could feel the eyes of the people on me, all of them staring. Some of them with a hint of fear or disgust, a holdover of raiders in the area, and others with no small amount of respect and gratitude.

The families of Gelvurt were, on average, quite neutral toward me.

The man I was set to greet this afternoon was decidedly less neutral.

"Good afternoon, my lord." The greeting was rough and laced with a dull venom that seemed more apt to stain the whole world rather than me in particular.

It was as warm a welcome as I'd expected.

The captain of the Gelvurt guard was a morose man, fresh out of the mourning of his child. My heart broke for the destroyed man.

I do not think I would have even a sliver of the duty he'd maintained in agreeing to meet with me.

I nodded. "Captain, I wanted to introduce myself."

"Lord Rakta Velbrun, newest lord to grace this little stain on the edge of House Velbrun's graces." He spit off to the side. "I apologize if it's a bit late for first impressions. I've already heard quite a bit about you."

I nodded. "May I come in?"

At my motion to the garrison, the captain nodded and welcomed me inside.

A small tour through the modest building later, and I was sitting on the other side of an oak desk, a large portrait frame lying on the ground with its face placed against the wall. There was no need to question the arrangement.

The man stared at me, silently.

Considering my words for a moment, I finally met the man's gaze with a firmness. "My condolences for your loss."

The exhausted man flinched, breathing deeply as he regained his center. "My lord, we didn't need to come to my office to speak about that."

"No, we didn't." I looked around, my voice treading carefully. "However, we did need to come here to speak about what I found in the lair of the sorcerer Vera."

The man's expression screwed up into anger at the name, and his tone was chilling. "Explain."

11

Vera's lair, where she had been living for quite some time in the forests of Gelvurt, had been dark and dirty, with the sickening, pungent odor of alchemy sticking to every inch.

There was something, I'd realized while in her den, very uneasy about a place that looked so filthy smelling so chemically clean. It was so obviously unnatural to the senses that it instinctively raised alarm.

Her bed, a ramshackle pile of dirty furs and hay, had many older letters and messages lining it for the extra layer of insulation. I doubted warmth was easy to come by in the cold, desolate mine shaft she'd called home for so long.

I handed over one of the old, tattered letters. "It was no coincidence that she was here."

Captain Roland Barker snatched the letter out of my hands, looking over it closely. His expression grew darker and darker as his eyes flitted across the page.

I glanced at the unhung portrait frame in the room. "Vera was contacted by someone, directed here with the promise of materials."

"Like my son." Barker's voice was scratchy.

After Vera's death, the alchemist, Marge Rogder, had gotten back to work examining the victims and had made a full report of the state of the bodies, specifically which pieces of the children were missing. With news of what the sorcerer had been up to, it hadn't been a large leap of logic for the villagers to make.

I had made it clear that the remains had been dealt with and there was no need for the families to traumatize themselves by looking for them.

I nodded. "Yes, but the reagents required for her magic were not cheap. Marge reported no thefts from her supply and examined the solvents I brought back. She made it clear that a number of the materials were difficult to acquire."

The captain laid down the letter, considering it for a moment, before sighing. "Is there anything to go on? Anything at all!?"

Barker's words were punctuated by his hands viciously slamming down onto his desk, cracking the polished wood.

"This is the only hint at the orchestrator's identity." I brought out another letter.

The stained, torn correspondence was addressed to Vera and spoke of a summit of sorts in the northern parts of the Certillian Empire. A gathering that promised a "great opportunity" for all with desire in their hearts.

When I spoke to Vera, she said it had come by raven in the dead of night. The identity of the sender was unknown to her, but they had contacted the sorcerer in the same way before.

The captain tensed as he read. "A letter addressing a necromancer about a summit in the north? Are the remnants of the Warlock King reorganizing?"

That was certainly what it looked like, but I was somewhat doubtful. Before Lydia had revealed she was pregnant, we had destroyed many of the remnants in House Velbrun's influence.

From what word I had listened to, the others of our old group had taken up a similar responsibility in the areas of other parts of the empire.

Grimly, I shrugged. "It does not look good, but we can't be sure. Still, this is something that can't be ignored. House Velbrun and the rest of the empire must be informed."

"I'll go." The captain's tone was curt, demanding.

I motioned behind me. "Will the village not feel your absence?"

"Not with you around, and I'll leave my men here as well." His lips were set in a firm frown. "Kingsley can take up my responsibilities while I'm gone."

For a moment, I considered telling him no, but with the postmaster of Gelvurt still barely keeping it together as well, perhaps it was for the best. A change of both posts might be beneficial for Gelvurt and the mourning families.

"Alright, you'll go. Should we expect you back?"

That was the true question. Distance from a loved one's death made it easier, but once you left, it was difficult to return without good reason. I would not be surprised if the captain's wife accompanied him.

The captain gripped the letter tightly. "I will return once I've put my boy's spirit to rest. The monster behind this will pay."

Ah, revenge. As potent of a motivator as it was misleading. Well, I would not be the one to correct him.

With that, I left the captain to prepare for his journey, and I went off to prepare myself for a few more introductions of my own.

"Sorry, sir. Mom ain't home right now; she's out checking the off fields now that things are looking safer around here."

The small boy was certainly a Varnedoe, one of the larger farming families belonging to Gelvurt. With his red hair and the beginnings of a stoutness, the child would grow to be big and strong if kept out in the fields.

I nodded, looking around the house. "Will she be long?"

The boy shrugged. "Sorry, sir. Mom takes as much time as she needs. She rode Till out there, so she might be back before dinner?"

The Varnedoe boy didn't look particularly enthused to be speaking with me, which I assumed was a trait he'd inherited from his mother. The Varnedoe family was the largest producer of corn in Gelvurt, but they weren't fond of the local lords from what I'd gathered from Orion.

Not wanting to intimidate a youngling, I nodded. "That's fine. Can you let her know that I dropped by when she returns? I'd like to speak with her."

"Sure, sir."

My polite departure was broken by the sudden building sound of rumbling hooves from behind me, a yell echoing at me.

"Hey! Get the fuck away from my boy, duster!" The vitriol in the words could not be understated.

I turned around to see the redheaded matriarch of the Varnedoe family leap off of her horse, landing with a stride as she never broke her momentum, heading straight for me with her fists balled up and her face an angry red.

Taking a step away from the child to hopefully calm the enraged mother, I nodded. "Ms. Varnedoe. I'm glad I caught you."

"Ya didn't catch me, dick. I came back on my ownsome. Now, who the fuck are ya, and what are ya doin' botherin' Samuel?"

Ms. Varnedoe was a broad lady, with a stout build that belied a life of hard work and discipline. Orion had said that after her husband passed away a few years ago, she became the head of the family.

It was under her control that the Varnedoe family had become so successful in these parts. Ms. Varnedoe's penchant for pressing merchants into promising deals for her family having made the farmers quite a bit wealthier.

I smiled, a practiced, polite thing that Lydia had said would help with introductions. "My name is Rakta Velbrun, Ms. Varnedoe. I'm the new local lord."

"Fuck." She spit on the ground.

Samuel spoke up. "He wanted to talk to ya, Mom."

The woman's face went red, but she eventually motioned me into her house. "Alright, come say your piece, my lord."

With a heavy thunk, my Vulture Axe sank into the heavy skull of Helen Varnedoe, right between the eyes. Or at least, that was what I imagined as the shot went straight into the center of my oak target board.

The woman was like every Certillian who had suffered in some way from the Ruskan tribes that had dipped their toes into banditry, but with none of the cleverness to merely insinuate the racial insults.

"Not that the woman's feelings are all that misplaced." I recovered my Vulture Axe normally, walking up and ripping it out of the wood.

Helen's husband had been killed by a Ruskan, so I understood, to an extent, that what she felt, while not true about myself, did not come from nowhere.

And yet, that did not give her the right to speak ill of my children.

"So, you got hellions, yeah? Well, keep your li'l dust balls away from my boy, got that?" Her tone was rough, and had gotten less and less respectful over the course of the conversation.

I had merely wanted to introduce myself and discuss recent issues regarding her conflict with another family's property line.

After she had brought up my children in such a tone, I made a hasty retreat. I did not want to hurt someone for simply speaking, no matter how venomous their tongue was.

Still, I had not left with a favorable impression of the woman.

"Dah," Daka called out, sounding excited. I looked behind me, to where my children watched me train and let off some steam.

Dalton and Natakia were both watching intently, but Daka seemed the most enthused about the show. It seemed she would be quite the warrior, if she chose to pursue it.

"Is my little warrior interested?" I walked over to her, smiling. It would be nice to be able to pass down my techniques one day, if her interest did not wane.

She giggled, most likely not understanding my words. And yet, she was watching with that familiar intelligence that made me hesitant to treat her as an uncomprehending infant.

I walked over to them, their small bodies secured in their seats. "One day I will teach you to harness your Vitae, Daka. If that is what you want, of course. I'm sure you all have potential for magic as well."

I would have to find a teacher for them if they pursued magic, which stung a little. The manipulation of spiritual energy, Mana, was outside of my expertise beyond the stray insights I had picked up from my travels alongside other magicians.

Still, either through some old favors or through my new title, I would make sure they were taught well.

Suddenly, without warning or care for my thoughts, Daka's eyes shined, and she gave a small pulse of her . . . Vitae? It swept over me, like a small breeze in the wind.

I was stunned for a moment, watching as the little infant's head drooped dangerously low, suddenly looking tired, far too tired.

The same kind of tiredness that preceded death.

Shooting forward, I pressed my hands into her chest, channeling my Vitae into her, feeling adrenaline rush through me. "Daka, no, Daka do not . . . You don't have enough vital energy to be doing that! Please don't go to sleep!"

The baby suddenly gurgled, looking more energized, less pale, after I circulated my Vitae through her . . . something I . . .

Where had Daka learned to do that? Pulsing out Vitae into the air was an advanced skill, something no infant could pick up in a few moments. Had she . . . learned from me? I often pulsed my Vitae to keep track of foes or possible ambushes, but for her to learn that . . .

How . . . had she learned that? What else had she learned? Concerning questions that paled in comparison to the relief that my child was still alive.

I picked her up, the baby girl giggling as I cradled her, and I bounced her up and down considering what had just happened and what I had just done.

She could have died, just now. Taught or not, a child could not pulse out their Vitae so recklessly, much less a newborn. And for me to have channeled my Vitae through her . . . I did not want to think about it.

I hoped she would still be able to use magic, to make that choice between the two energies, but if she was pulsing her Vitae already . . . perhaps she had already made it?

I looked down at Daka, her eyes shining with a little bit of fear now, as if sensing my own worries. I kissed her on the head. "It's okay, it's okay. Please, Daka, do not . . . do not do that until you are older. Please."

Glancing at my other children, I wondered if they would suddenly reveal themselves as prodigies by almost killing themselves as well. Perhaps I was lucky Dalton had not shown his skill with math by eating coins.

As both Natakia and Dalton gazed up at me and Daka, a distant memory rumbled in the back of my mind.

Three souls from beyond

Born to a hero and a pawn

The same ancient lisp from a month ago, stronger now. It sounded so familiar, and yet I could not place where I had heard the words before.

At the time, it had seemed unimportant, so why did I now feel such a great sense of foreboding?

12

I had forgotten something. Something very important.

A void in my memories that had carried with it a sense of foreboding for the last few weeks as I integrated into the village of Gelvurt.

As Lord Velbrun of Gelvurt, it was my responsibility to settle disputes and certify trade and taxes and other unenviable tasks that took up a large amount of my time.

Yet, this burden in the back of my mind made it even worse. Every new face, every bond formed, my mind always wandered to the absence within my memories.

"I'm, uh, having a little trouble with Natakia, my lord."

I turned away from my thoughts to look at Mary Ascott. Only just of age, Mary was an aid that the Ascott family, one of the larger families in Gelvurt, had offered for employment after I'd met with the patriarch of the family.

Taking care of my children while I was gone, she meant well, but she unfortunately possessed little in the way of maternal instinct. A genuine inability to calm them down, missing their feeding times, and other innocent habits that made her a poor fit for the job.

I took Natakia from her arms, readjusting my daughter into a more comfortable position. "You were holding her wrong. You have to support her neck, Mary."

She was sometimes not worth the sils that I paid for her services, but she meant well and had never spoken poorly of me when she thought I wasn't listening.

A decent soul, just very bad with children.

Mary frowned, ashamed. "Sorry, my lord, I forgot."

The babe in my arms calmed as I gently bounced her up and down, giving her a kiss on the head before laying her down beside her siblings.

The triplets had become more manageable after they'd settled into the new home. Natakia and Dalton had both cried far less in the past few weeks than they had on the open road. They'd taken to their soft bedding instantly, compared to their sister.

Unfortunately, Daka's midnight woes had increased, happening almost every night. I had taken to walking her around the outside of Velbrun Keep to calm her down, but while I enjoyed these walks, I felt powerless to truly help her.

"Bah." Daka looked up at me with a smile.

I lightly pinched her nose, wiggling it and making her giggle at the playful squeeze. Perhaps she was afflicted with some kind of curse of terror?

Dalton was sound asleep beside her, with a number of toys scattered around him. Plenty of mothers had doted over the youngling, always mentioning his hair, and I'd received a number of old toys for the three of them.

He had ignored most of them, but I had noticed that a few had gone missing. I wasn't concerned about it enough to accuse anyone, but it was annoying to know that I might have a thief among my staff.

Natakia had received the nicest gift, however. The local seamstress, the sister of Captain Barker's wife, had sewn together a beautiful scarlet, blue-trimmed dress for the infant.

My little desert flower cried whenever I tried to dress her in anything else.

The door to the nursery opened, Marisha stepping in. "It's feeding time."

Nodding, I gave her and Mary the privacy they needed and took a walk, heading toward Gelvurt.

"My wife says you take care of those kids real well, you know?" Orion had gotten quite familiar during my time in Gelvurt. At some point, formalities had fallen to the wayside.

I smiled, sipping at some of the water he'd offered when I entered his store. "I try my best. I can't help but think that I will make a mistake one day."

Orion nodded, cleaning a cup. With the tavern still closed, Orion had opened up a small watering hole of his own in the corner of his general store.

He didn't sell alcohol like Joseph, the tavern keep, but water and milk had kept most of the locals happy and socializing for the time being.

Laying the cup down, Orion shrugged. "I'm afraid I can't give much comfort to that. Unfortunately, fatherhood doesn't make us perfect."

"No, it does not."

He chuckled. "Now, if you ask my wife, she has a few opinions about motherhood. She always knows best when it comes to Al."

Alan, or Al, was their child, a small infant barely a month or two older than my own children. It had struck me how active, physically and mentally, my own children were when I compared them to Al's sedentary lifestyle.

I did not wish to speak about that comparison, at risk of offending the kind store owner and his family, but I think I'd grown to appreciate how my children had broken the mold.

Still, the topic of motherhood made my shoulders sag. "Their mother would know best, much better than I at least."

Orion faltered, as he often did when I brought up my late wife. "I, uh, see. I'm sorry. I . . . didn't mean to bring up bad memories, my lord."

I shook my head. "Only good memories, Orion. Lydia, my wife, I traveled with her for years before we married, but it was when she was pregnant that I believe I saw her truly happy."

The familiar feeling of forgetting something echoed in the back of my head for a moment.

"She would have made a great mother."

"Yes, yes," I chuckled. "She did not have a great childhood. I think the idea of giving to her own children something she did not have . . . made things bearable for her."

Looking across the general store, I noticed a few people wandering around the border of Orion's watering hole corner. Few people wanted to drink while I was here.

Continuing on, "I'll give them what she would have wanted. Thank you for the water, Orion."

"Of course, Rakta."

With that, I left to finish out the day.

A month had passed in Gelvurt, and the people had begun to finally put Vera's horrors behind them. Both the tavern keep and the postmaster had finally been encouraged by their friends to recover from their mourning, a slow, aching task that I did my best not to rush.

Their replacements had, well, done the best they could, but they lacked the experience of the true owners of the establishments.

I wasn't involved in their recovery personally, but I was grateful for the people of Gelvurt. Looking out for one another in ways that I, a fresh outsider, could not even begin to.

Unfortunately, one had not returned to the public eye in quite some time.

I knocked on the door. "Marge, are you there? Marge?"

The alchemist had been distant from the village even before her children had been murdered; the people of Gelvurt not keen on her expertise except when required.

Getting no answer, I tried the door handle and found it open, pushing inward into the home of the reclusive herbalist. A part of me feared what I would find.

Alchemy was a study of the mind, body, and the impact that different materials of the world had on both. Many advancements in medicine had come from alchemists, although the empire did not boast any prominent ones.

"What, um, what do you want . . . ?"

My gaze swept across the cluttered, dusty room toward Marge, her clothes tightly bound around her as she peeked at me from around the bend. The one eye, uncovered by a ruffled bang, was bloodshot and tired.

And yet, even with her ragged appearance, I could tell she was young, almost too young to be a mother. Certainly too young to have lost her children.

"I want to talk, Marge. About what happened. It isn't healthy to keep to yourself like this." I frowned as I stepped closer.

The alchemist snarled. "What do . . . what do you know!? I, um, I . . . I know what's healthy!"

"I know you do. Can I please sit?"

Caught between anger and pleasantries, Marge gave a sharp nod, but continued to stand and watch me from around the corner as I sat down in one of the chairs in the dusty living room.

"I'm sorry about Vierno and Benjamin." My voice was soft as I uttered their names, but Marge looked like she had been shot as they left my lips.

Tears welled up in her eyes as she finally stepped forward, like a frail doe, and crumbled into the chair in front of me, her hands coming to viciously wipe the tears away from the heavy bags under her gaze.

"I-I miss them . . . so much . . . I was a horrible mother . . . How could I have let them . . . ?"

I reached forward and gripped her hands. "You weren't a bad mother. You cared for your boys, Marge."

She snatched her hands away from my grip. "No! No, I . . . I shouldn't have stayed here . . . I should have left! Left as soon as I heard what happened to Roland's boy! As soon as I saw it!"

I did not disturb her crying, letting her vent for as long as I could, before I asked, "Marge, can you tell me about your boys?"

"W-what's the point?" Hiccuping, she gritted her teeth defensively at me, as if she thought I was mocking her.

"Because when we lose someone, the most potent remnants are the stories we tell about them. Vierno and Benjamin . . ."

Marge flinched when I said their names again, but I pushed onward.

". . . I'll help you remember them if you let me."

For a moment, the room was silent, before I watched Marge slowly close up. When no answer came, I thanked her for her time and let her know she was welcome at the keep when she was ready.

The next day, with my children sleeping in the next room over, I meditated as the sun slipped into dusk. While I would rather meditate outside, my bedroom had enough floor space for it.

I let my Vitae rumble and ripple as I swayed my body, moving my limbs and allowing the physical energy to slowly simmer down until it cleared my mind and allowed it to wander without distraction.

The words I had been hearing, remembering, were important. Of that, I was sure.

And yet, no matter how many weeks I spent trying to discover more of it, the further I felt from truly learning the details of what plagued me.

I froze in the middle of meditating as a familiar wail echoed through Velbrun Keep. A warbling infant scream of terror and nightmares.

Daka was having one of her nightly episodes.

I shook off the clarity of meditation and began to make my way to her, grabbing a blanket to wrap her up with for our nightly walks. It was beginning to get colder, and I did not want—

I froze as Dalton and Natakia began to wail alongside their sister. Not annoyed nor hungry, but with the same terrified tremor of Daka's nightly terrors.

The door exploded as I surged forward, opening up the door to the nursery within seconds, my Vitae pushing me into the room.

A tall, dark figure in a ragged cloak, standing above the beds of my children, had its finger outstretched to touch them.

It looked sharply at me, an echoey gasp leaving the darkness of its hood, as I stormed in. "You!"

Weaponless, I gripped the air and surged it with my Vitae, my **Wind Axe Technique** molding it into the transparent facsimile of one of my Vulture Axes, before throwing straight into the skull of the beast.

The thing's head knocked back as it took the blow directly, shrieking in pain and delight. "The Dancer! The Dancer!"

And then it leaped into the wall, evaporating into a fine black mist that escaped out of the keep before I could pull another weapon from the air and end it.

My children crying, my heart pounding, I immediately went to them, making sure that they were okay.

The younglings wailed, but I saw no scratches on them. No obvious enchantments, no weaved magical curses . . . I channeled Vitae to my eyes just to make sure.

Imprecise as it was, able to see only obvious magic really, the crude technique still managed to assuage my worry somewhat.

The only thing that made me pause was Dalton. In his weak grip, barely able to hold it, was a tiny, crude knife. More akin to a crude shiv than a true sidearm blade.

I stared at where the creature had left . . . Had it given Dalton this weapon? I picked it up from the child, examining it, and . . . no magic, certainly not high quality enough for any kind of enchantment.

I channeled a bit of my Vitae into it, and I could already begin to see cracks forming in the numerous flaws in the blade.

"What is going on?" I couldn't even begin to answer my own question.

The wails of my children continued, and I gathered them up into my arms. They would no longer sleep alone, away from my sight.

I had no idea what that thing was or what it had wanted, but it knew of me. Perhaps my first mistake as a father was believing my children would be safe from my past.

13

That does not bode well for Gelvurt." Kingsley's face was grave, mir-roring my own.

I'd spent the last hour discussing with him the mysterious stranger in the night. While my concern was mostly for my children, Kingsley had mentioned that this news would not go over well with Gelvurt.

I shook my head. "They've barely recovered from the last scare."

"It's my opinion that we keep this quiet, my lord."

I wasn't keen on secrets. It was far too similar to how House Velbrun operated, but it might be for the best. I was confident this entity was targeting me and my own.

And yet, the townspeople had a right to know. For all that right, how-ever, there was still the fact that it would only cause panic.

Lydia would have been fine with keeping things secret; she liked being mysterious, but I wasn't keen on it. Honesty, being open with things, was the essence of Ruskan storytelling.

And yet, I'd already betrayed that core value with some of the stories I kept to myself.

"Let's put off telling them, at least." I sighed and rubbed my eyes, feeling frustration build in the pit of my stomach. "I'll need Dresden to watch my younglings; I can't stay on the defensive during this."

Kingsley looked alarmed. "You're going after it?"

"I wanted a nice, simple life that was safe for my children. I can't wait to let this fester into something that actually has a chance of harming them." Lydia had wanted the children to possibly redeem our mistakes, not be consumed by them.

The guard, having taken up Captain Barker's responsibilities in his absence, nodded. "I see. I'll station Dresden and a few more rotating guards. Gelvurt will notice your absence, so make it quick before I have to start answering questions."

I smiled as much as the situation allowed. "Thank you, Kingsley. I won't be long."

With everything said, I left and made my way to Velbrun Keep to prepare.

"Dah." Daka giggled up at me as I held her close in my arms, before putting her down to give both Natakia and Dalton some quick hugs as well. Natakia was cranky after last night, but made a noise of contentment in my arms.

I gave them all a fond smile as I laid them back down. "Try to treat each other well, alright? I'll be gone for a day or two, but I'll be back. Marisha and Mary will look after you. Dresden will keep you safe."

"Yeah, that fucker won't know what hit 'em if he comes to mess with us."

I slowly looked over at Dresden. "Yes, thank you."

I wasn't keen on swearing around my children, somewhat wary of what they might pick up with their odd awareness, but I would not go so far as to correct Dresden for it.

The young but capable guard was polishing his blade, keeping it ready for any dangers. Only he and Kingsley knew of the exact reasons for my absence, but Marisha and Mary were told to stay wary.

They were curious, of course, but I'd asked them not to question it too much. Thankfully, it seemed the Velbrun influence in these parts had successfully rooted out any instinctive nosiness from those within their borders.

Suddenly Natakia started to cry, and the swelling of stink in the air implied all it needed to.

I smiled. "Well, one last change for the road."

As I got to work cleaning and changing my little desert flower, Dresden suddenly spoke up, marking the first time I'd ever had a conversation during this particular fatherly task.

"So, my lord, I gotta ask. Any reason for the names?"

I glanced over. "Natakia is one of the names for a rare and beautiful white flower that grows around oases in Rusk. Daka is a Ruskan name that means 'great one.'"

"And Dalton?"

"It was the name of my wife's brother. I don't know what it means." I slightly shrugged.

Although, I did know what the name meant to the select few who had been informed about Dalton's role in the war. I was still not entirely comfortable with my wife's decision to give our child such a burdensome name.

"Huh, I'll have to look it up. My mom has this old book of Certillian names she got from a passing trader. She loves that thing. Dalton's Certillian, right?"

I glanced over. "I assume so. I appreciate the interest."

"Names are important." Dresden went back to polishing his blade, his tone wistful.

On that, I agreed.

With Natakia cleaned and dressed in her pretty dress, calming down from her dirtied tantrum, I gave them all one last look before nodding to Dresden. I would trust the swordsman with my children, no matter how hesitant I was to do so.

It was time to head out.

The figure from the night before had a scent. It smelled like a cooling corpse, the first vestiges of rot percolating in the recesses of draining life.

It had stuck to every tree branch and bush with a strong odor, leaving little black stains of rot behind as it escaped through Gelvurt's forests. By simple examination, I'd found that the trees and plants the rot stuck to quickly shriveled up and decayed.

It was unfortunate that I had nothing on me to take samples with.

With my **Great Wind Sprint Technique**, I had been running and jumping over trees for the last few hours, but still the scent persisted.

This thing had been fast, very fast, and I was beginning to worry about my destination if my course didn't correct itself soon.

Unfortunately, another hour of rocketing across the landscape of the Certillian Empire, and I was greeted by a familiar and unwelcome scent and sight.

The blackened smell of the intruder leading straight into the heart of the village of Niers.

The large, well-dressed figure of Jorge Velbrun sat comfortably in his office, the walls adorned with trophies of past hunts and old books that had no names.

Quite the collection for the lord of a minor village.

Jorge was not quite as jolly as when last I'd spoken to him, his face screwed up with thought as he considered the news I'd come with.

"A rotting corpse of the night, come to Niers? What am I supposed to make of this, Rakta?" He tapped his stomach with his fingers, humming to himself.

I frowned. "The scent never wavered. I expect the creature escaped to here, yes, but I also believe it came from here. The thing's scent is too strong to not leave a trail, if it had come from somewhere else."

"Undead, eh?" Lord Velbrun of Niers gritted his shiny white teeth. "A wolf among the sheep. I'll raise the alarm with the guards, but . . . I assume you didn't come here to just warn me?"

I shook my head, "I'll be taking this into my own hands, if you would allow me. This creature threatened my children."

Jorge clapped his hands, looking relieved. "Well, usually I'd trust my guards—we certainly pay them the sils for threats such as this—but your reputation precedes you, Dancer! Please, investigate where you wish!"

Getting him to agree was the easiest part, unfortunately. I had yet to bring up my most major concern.

"Thank you, Lord Velbrun of Niers. Unfortunately, my investigation must begin here in your keep."

Even saying that as softly as I did, Jorge still started, his eyes widening in alarm as he stood up. "What, uh, Lord Velbrun? You . . . want to investigate me?"

"Not you, specifically." I motioned to the keep around me. "The scent grew weaker once in Niers, as if hiding, but I followed it here."

"But I . . . never." Jorge looked flabbergasted. "Yes, uh, yes, Rakta . . .

Lord Velbrun of Gelvurt. I can allow you to investigate my premises, posthaste!"

Was his distress because of a creature hiding within his walls and threatening the lives of his family and staff? Or because he was in league with the monster?

I hated the doubt I held for the man, but it was hard to truly shelve such idle considerations. Especially when such machinations had been leveled against me before within this empire.

Relieved at the permission, I smiled. "Thank you. Can you bring your staff to the main hall? It'll be easier to examine them for any markings I may have left on the beast."

"Yes, yes, absolutely," Jorge stood up, before his eyes flashed with sudden insight. "Lord Velbrun, while I gather them, perhaps you should look into my most recent hire."

I knocked on the servant's door, "Excuse me, Dorothy?"

A small voice came from the closed door. "Yes? Who is it?"

A moment later, before I could answer, the door opened up a crack, revealing a pair of green eyes that widened as she opened the door.

"Oh fuck," the servant squeaked.

The familiarity in her eyes, the way she tensed like I was going to attack her, made me move before my mind completely registered the connection I made. Any words she tried to mutter were gagged by my hand around her throat.

I slammed her backward, planting her against the wall of her room a foot off the ground, her legs kicking in panic. The blonde servant clutched at her throat as she tried to pry off my fierce grip.

"Wh, guh . . . meh . . ." Dorothy struggled, trying to utter some sort of curse. "Fuh . . . !"

I was about to begin questioning her, when her form suddenly shifted. I almost beheaded her before I realized that this was by no means the same inky-black shape-shifting that I had witnessed the night before.

It was a different, familiar variety of shape-shifting.

The blonde hair quickly darkened into a deep black, the subtle tan of the servant fled, replaced by a recognizable paleness, and her panicked green eyes darkened into charcoal.

Dropping her, I took a step back. "You aren't the creature I'm looking for."

Doh, the doppelgänger, fell to her knees coughing. "Ha, fuck, ha, thank the Great Beyond for that . . . What the fuck is your problem!?"

A few minutes later, Doh was sitting on the edge of her bed, having regained her breath, but still looking very unhappy for obvious reasons. She stared at me, almost unblinkingly with annoyance in her eyes.

The silence in the room was somewhat difficult to pierce.

With a slight cough, I tried my hand at it. "I'm . . . sorry for my rash actions. I'm looking for a shape-shifter of some sort that attacked me, and . . ."

"Yeah, I've heard we all look the same." Doh's tone was dry. "How the fuck did I manage to run into you a second time?"

I looked around. "Niers is the closest village to Gelvurt. I'm surprised you came here knowing I'd be a lord there."

"Yeah, well, after you slaughtered my little circle, I kind of had to find a place to work. And honestly, servant for a lord seemed like ironic employment after my last little stunt."

Her words were flat at the mention of her companions, little, if any, emotion leaking into the mention of her old traveling group. Perhaps she wasn't very close with them? The mercenary lifestyle must require more detachment than I had previously understood.

I looked around the room, unsure of what to make of the words. "I . . . see."

Doh smirked, looking much more interested. "So, you're looking for a shape-shifter, eh?"

A part of me was wary of the doppelgänger for obvious reasons, but the aid of a shape-shifter would be helpful in finding my true prey.

Putting aside my concerns, I told the truth. "Yes, one that I believe is undead. It's hiding somehow, possibly as someone within the keep."

Doh hummed, her smirk smoothly shifting into a smile. "I see . . ."

"Do you know something?" I was almost hesitant to ask, but any lead that got me closer to my quarry was one I must pursue.

"I might. What's in it for me?"

The doppelgänger leaned forward, her eyes glittering with a secret.

14

I don't have any money."

Doh's eyes widened. "But you're a lord! Don't you Velbruns have a huge vault with a bunch of money!?"

"If they do, they would rather melt it down than give me access. I'm not beloved by the other Lords Velbrun." As Jorge might put it, they'd rather throw the money down a ravine then let it slip down into the bottom of the barrel.

The doppelgänger flopped backward onto the bed. "Damn it, of course I go after the only poor lord in Certillia. I bet the Iriends don't have poor lords . . ."

The Iriends were another royal house of the empire. I'd met only a few of them, but they were assuredly the wealthiest of the empire's nobility. The one I knew best would not have taken Doh's attempt at theft quiet as lightly as I did.

"So, what do you know?" Money or not, I was going to get this information out of her.

Shaking her head, Doh sat back up. "No, no, no, this ain't free information. You've got to have something for me! What about one of those magic ax—"

"No."

The doppelgänger sniffed, tears suddenly springing from her eyes like they'd been readied in advance. "You're an ass! I just wanted to live life in luxury, and you keep making it difficult!"

It was subtle, but I was pretty sure she'd made herself slightly younger looking, more vulnerable. Was this manipulation? Was I supposed to feel bad?

I shifted, feeling a little awkward at Doh's childish tantrum. It was one thing for my children to throw such things, but an, assumedly, grown woman? "You already have a job with a richer lord. What could I possibly give you?"

Doh's tears dried up, a little too quickly, as she checked her nails for dirt. "Yeah, ole Jorge is richer, but he's kind of a pervert. Let's just say my earlier outfit was a little more his speed."

Jorge had not struck me as that sort of noble, but it was not like I knew the man on a very personal level. I was not fond of the idea of the man not being faithful to his wife, who'd proven to be a sweet woman.

"So, what is it that you want? I'm not going to force the information out of you, but this creature I'm hunting threatened my children." There had to be something I could offer her.

Doh's eyes sparkled once more, making me somewhat concerned.

". . . Children, eh? I'm pretty good with children."

I was suddenly very concerned.

Five of the servants had been stained by the scent of the creature I was following, but Jorge seemed to be accosting one in particular.

"What did you do, Quentin? Is this one of your foul little games again!? We've talked about this time and time again!"

I had never seen the rotund man look quite so angry before, but the Certillian giant of a man that he spoke to was looking paler and paler with each question.

He was tall, even taller than me, with long arms and legs that made him seem gangly. His servant attire was ill-suited to his frame, squeezing in the worst of places.

There was a strength to his build, but not one that looked especially trained.

"No, uh, my lord. None of my games, dah, I promise, mah, my lord." Quentin spoke with a scared, soft voice that belied his towering frame. He stumbled over his words often.

"Lord Velbrun of Niers, may I take it from here?" I stepped forward.

Both Jorge and Quentin glanced at me, with the former nodding his assent and stepping back, letting me take his place.

I craned my neck back a bit to meet the eyes of the slouching man, wondering just how much giant blood must run through his veins, before addressing him.

"Where are the books you took, Quentin?"

The servant frowned, shifting uneasily, "I, uh—"

"He took books!?"

I gave Jorge a look, quieting the irate lord for the moment, before returning to Quentin. "You were seen leaving your lord's room with a book a week ago . . . Where is it?"

"The, uh, the . . . I put it in the attic . . ."

There was a different fear in the servant's eyes. One that was more primal, as if simply uttering the words was the equivalent of signing his own death writ. Was Quentin truly under threat of death by Jorge or was he intimidated by the promise of another?

Nodding, I looked over to my fellow lord. "I'm going to investigate."

"Please . . . Please do." He looked faint as he nodded, the realization of what may have been festering above his head suddenly gripping him.

Each wooden step creaking, I slowly creeped my way up to the attic of the keep, one of my axes held firmly at my side. Whatever was up here, alive or undead, could be waiting to ambush me.

I was thankful I was not using my **Scourger Bloodhound Technique**, for even without it I could smell the rotten stench clinging to more and more of the keep around me as I reached the door at the top of the stairs.

Gently, I pulled the handle, listening for any disturbance behind it. I couldn't even hear traces of rats skittering, but a soft metal thud interrupted my focus as the locked latch hit the doorframe when I pulled against it.

"Hmm, so much for quiet," I whispered to the door, as much of an apology as it would get from me.

And then I slammed through, kicking up foul-smelling dust as the attic door crumbled against my force, the scatterings of wooden debris barely fazing me as I jumped inside, my Vitae ready for battle.

"Come out, creature!" My voice kicked up dust around me, but my eyes were on a swivel, taking in all the corners this creature could be hiding in.

My grip around my Vulture Axe was tight, but it loosened as I truly digested my surroundings.

Dark and musty, with cobwebs covering the various pieces of time-worn furniture, an old, forgotten mirror on the wall, reflecting my own careful gaze.

Ritualistic symbols were scrawled across the floors and walls in circular patterns seeming to emanate from the epicenter of the setup.

And at the center of the ritualistic symbols was an open book, the scrawls of a madman upon the pages of the manuscript.

The place smelled of magic. A very sickening magic. Something that went beyond the simple magics and spells of necromancy and pursued something older, forbidden, and entirely unknown to me.

I vibrated my Vitae, readying myself to dispel any attempts to lay a curse upon my person, and approached the center of the ritual. I felt dirty as I got closer, as if there was a physical illness in the air that tried to tug at my bones, but found no purchase.

Whatever had happened here felt old, something that had already occurred. Was this what I had smelled? Had the creature truly fled to this keep?

Or had it spawned from here?

"Lord Velbrun, d-did you find an—!?"

I frowned at Jorge. "What were you doing with that book, Jorge?"

The noble flinched, patting himself nervously. "Well, uh, I'm not quite sure of the one you speak of . . . ?"

I held out the book, rescued from the center of the ritual. It was the product of a madman, written in languages I did not speak, and made my Vitae shrink back in disgust.

"This one, Lord Velbrun of Niers. What have you done? And why do you try to hide it?"

"Wait, wait, really, I, uh, promise . . . !" The large noble raved his hands in fierce surrender. "I have no idea what's in that book! I, well, I knew it was filled with craziness, but . . . I just acquired it for my collection! For parties!"

Ah, yes. The shelves of books in his office.

"Who did you buy this from?"

Jorge wiped his brow. "When the last Lord Velbrun of Gelvurt left, he came by and sold it to me for a pittance! I, uh . . . I'd always heard he was a learned man . . ."

The last lord of Gelvurt? I was less and less enthused about the mysteries surrounding the man. Perhaps I should take a greater interest in his identity?

I shook my head. "Whatever was here is gone now, but may return. You'll want to burn everything in the attic, in case it's left behind something foul."

"But . . . some of those items are surely artifacts . . ."

He weakly trailed off at my disdainful gaze. The day's frustrations had made the large man seem much smaller, all in all.

"Additionally, whoever was involved in this had been in there for quite some time." I took out an old tunic with blood on it, stained too deeply in black ichor to be of any help. "I found a side room, small and cramped, but far less dusty than the attic proper and filled with crumbs."

"We will"—he paused, thinking for a moment—"I'll put out some feelers. Perhaps one of the townspeople has seen something suspicious."

It was as much as I could ask for.

"I'll be requesting the service of your servant Dorothy. She aided me in return for employment in Gelvurt." And I could not argue with how much help she had been.

The noble said nothing, but nodded, looking eager to make amends in any way he knew how. He was no sorcerer or ill-minded tyrant, but a part of me did worry about what else might fall into his collection and pose a threat.

Spending the day examining each of the servants, and interrogating Quentin, the identity of whatever or whoever the creature was still eluded me.

Quentin had said he'd simply helped a sickly voice in the attic that he had befriended months ago, a friend that had always spoken kindly to him.

Getting them the book, the giant had said, was just one of the many things he'd done for her, for he assumed it was a her by the softness of the voice.

Food, material, many things that Jorge had been inflamed about hearing becoming victims of Quentin's theft, but one day the voice had threatened him before disappearing.

That had been a week ago. With nothing to continue my investigation on, I aimed to return to Gelvurt.

And yet, not alone.

"Okay, so, what . . . You're gonna give me a piggyback ride?"

I was similarly unamused by the idea. "I aim to return to Gelvurt quickly. I said I'd be gone only for a day or two."

Doh was dressed in some of the same garb I'd first met her in, although properly tightened to fit her frame compared to my own, but looked primed for the road rather than the halls of a lord. Thankfully, she did not own much, or I would have been hampered even further.

"You know, I'm gonna be really pissed if you drop me."

"If I drop you then there will not be much of you left to be pissed." I bent my knees, dropping into a crouch.

"You really know how to comfort a lady."

Usually, I tried to be more polite to those around me, but it was very difficult to do so with someone who had tried to steal my identity.

Feeling her wrap her legs and arms around me, holding on tight, I straightened up. "Do not open your mouth."

"Why—gah!"

The world blurred around me as my Vitae rumbled to life and my **Great Wind Sprint Technique** surged me forward, my limbs emanating with power, sending me toward Gelvurt.

As Doh screamed very loudly straight into my ear, I considered a number of things. This would not be as cut-and-dried as dealing with Vera. I couldn't leave Gelvurt and my children alone to investigate things properly.

I had to deal with this like a true noble. It was time to send some letters to the capital.

15

The capital city of the Certillian Empire was Cerula, where the highest of lords from each house beseeched the high royals, those of the king's blood, for more power and land and other things that they busied themselves with.

While perhaps I was disrespecting tradition by not sending my letter to Velbrun, the epicenter of House Velbrun's influence, I had asked the postmaster to send a letter to the capital itself.

Specifically, to the capital headquarters of the Continental Adventurers of Derra.

The adventuring guild, known as CAD, while oddly named, was perhaps the only thing bearing resemblance to legal power behind the benevolent explorers that bore no other national jurisdiction.

Membership was easily granted and, in my own experience, made it easy to find work across borders for travelers seeking to help for coin in return.

Travelers, or rather, adventurers that I required the aid of.

"You think they'll truly send help, my lord?" Orion's tone was hesitant.

I nodded, watching the bird fly to the north with purpose. "I was an adventurer once, so it should be handled carefully. CAD organizes its members efficiently and will send individuals with the skills I need."

In fact, although perhaps due to my bias, I trusted CAD and their members to handle a problem more so than any local collection of guards. The lifestyle simply attracted the experienced and competent.

"I hope so, my lord. The people are . . . nervous."

Nodding, I considered that. Upon my return, I had informed the village of the circumstances, now that I had a better grasp. I'd used the small bit of the sils I had left to pay for this commission for help, but other villagers had pitched in as well.

The farming families were of great help, but I'd found aid from the local tavern keep and postmaster as well. Of course, I found no help from the Varnedoes.

I'd even received a small bit of coin from Marge, although I'd received it by the hands of another. The alchemist had kept to her home, but it was good to know she was not completely shut off from the rest of the village.

Gathering my things, not wanting to give myself time to doubt my actions, I agreed. "They have reason to be. We'll persevere."

And yet, as open as I had been with the townspeople, there was one topic I had not yet broached since my return.

"Orion, tell me about the last Lord Velbrun of Gelvurt."

"He was a cold man with a dry sense of humor." Orion sipped at his drink. "Zactrik gazed through people, I think, more than he ever truly saw them."

I took a sip of water. "And these tonics he purchased, did he ever say what they were for? Besides health?"

The general store owner shook his head. "Never—he would outright ignore any questions about them. Frankly, I never trusted the claim that they came from the capital . . . Something never smelled right about them."

"You didn't mention this before."

"He was a friend." Orion's words seemed aimed to convince himself more than they were meant for me. "A friend even, uh, even if he was dabbling with drugs as I thought. I'm not one to question the habits of a Velbrun."

I couldn't fault him for that. Some of the nobles I had met would certainly go to great lengths to hide their various vices.

The store was empty, most back at the regular tavern enjoying themselves, and allowed for a great privacy that was beneficial for this conversation.

"Did he ever say anything about his studies? Did he ever order any books?" Building such a large collection of them, as Jorge had attested to him having, could not have been a simple task.

Orion shook his head. "Never, my lord. I knew he had a great collection, but he purchased that from a traveling trader after the war."

A number of the Warlock King's forts and holds had been plundered by scavengers after the tyrant had drawn his last breath. I wouldn't doubt some forbidden knowledge had been sold to the highest bidder.

The idea that my predecessor had been dabbling with darker studies was a chilling one.

Only one of my curiosities lingered. "Did the prior Lord Velbrun of Gelvurt ever mention his reason for being stationed here?"

At that, Orion frowned. He took a long drink of his ale. He didn't speak, but I could tell he was struggling with my question. Moments before I gave up and asked him a different one, he gave a rough nod.

"One night," the general store owner rasped, glancing around. "A few nights before Zactrik left Gelvurt, he came to me and said a great many things. I didn't ask, specifically, but he said . . . he said he'd been stationed here because he'd killed someone, that he was a murderer."

I watched the general store owner wrestle with himself for a moment. "That . . ."

He looked haggard. "If I'd known, I'd never have let him into this place, noble or not. He met my eyes that night, and I saw something in that man's gaze that I've rightly never wanted to think about again."

"Alright, you little stinker, come here. Yeah, yeah, I know it sucks to smell, but I've got some nice flowery perfume with your name on it that'll make you smell as pretty as you look. All you gotta do is quiet down, alright?"

I watched as Doh handled Natakia, currently in the form of Marisha, moving about in the mature woman's form. The shape changer had claimed it helped to get into character, especially after Orion's wife had to attend to her own child elsewhere.

Daka had started crying when Doh first shifted into a new form, but Dalton and Natakia had taken it much better. In fact, Natakia had grown quite attached to the new maid. She seemed to enjoy the attention Doh lavished on her, soaking it up like a sponge.

Mary, well, I had put her on duties elsewhere in the keep. She seemed to be having a much better time keeping Fretz and some of the keep's horses tended to.

How horses were easier to handle than children, I would never understand. I disliked the animals, and they seemingly held no love for me either. Mary seemed to corral them with but a single tap of her foot, a born caretaker and rider.

"You do have a way with children, Doh." Daka was much more comfortable in my arms than Doh's embrace. No matter what form she took, Daka always seemed able to sniff her out.

Another exciting oddity of my beloved children for me to take pride in.

Doh smirked with Marisha's face. "Marisha, my lord, while I'm in character."

An interesting notion considering her ineptitude at impersonating my own character, but I could not fault her ability. She had been studying Marisha over the past few days, watching her take care of the children as well as talk with me and her husband.

Now, if I had not seen her transform or had not known Marisha was assuredly elsewhere . . . well, I had been considering informing Orion of Doh's true nature, if only to quell future mischief.

I laid Daka back down, my little warrior sleeping, before glancing over as Doh settled Natakia down for sleep as well. Dresden would be here soon for his shift.

There had been something I was considering recently.

Something that Doh could help me with if I trusted her.

"Where are you from, Doh?"

Back in her usual form, Doh swirled around the last dredges of wine I'd poured in her glass, "Eh, here and there. Pretty sure I'm Certillian at the end of the day."

"When did you begin traveling?" I'd never gotten the chance to sit down and speak with an individual of so many faces before.

Setting her glass down, Doh sighed. "Young, real young. And no, I don't really wanna talk about it. Not everyone has a story they wanna share, yeah?"

Well, it was the response I expected. Doppelgängers, or those with the blood of the creatures in them, were never known for their openness.

"I just wish to know more about the woman who puts my children to bed at night."

Doh raised an eye. "Who says I'm a woman?"

I waited, not responding.

She eventually shrugged. "Okay, yeah, I'm a woman. Right now, at least. That kind of stuff gets hazy when you can shape-shift, but I like my current equipment."

It was good that we were alone for this conversation. Such admissions would have been slightly more bizarre than I think Orion or the staff could have taken.

"If you don't want to tell me, I understand." I certainly wouldn't force her. A story forced was no true telling at all. "I'm simply trying to make it clear that my interest has no ulterior motives. I simply want to build trust by sharing stories."

"Well, I already said my piece on that."

Very true. Perhaps more time spent together would lower her walls. I was not without my own barricades, of course.

Still, I moved on. "So, you practice memory magic, correct?"

"Yeah, but don't worry, it's not as subtle as the blowhards at the capital academy would like you to believe." She waved her hands dismissively.

The way she said that raised some questions, but none I'd approach tonight. Had she gotten close to the capital academy in her past? Was that where she'd learned her magic?

"I've heard that practitioners can warp a man into a stranger given enough time and finesse." Simple rumors, but concerning ones.

Doh looked a little more guarded. "Hey, I just got comfortable in my room here. You better not be getting cold feet, Rakta."

I shook my head, not concerned for myself. I knew how to fight off the influence of magic, although I may have been more wary of the village and my children if Doh actually seemed malicious.

"I've also heard that they can aid in the recovery of lost memories."

A month later, I watched as emerald-green horses thundered up the trail from Gelvurt's main street, the spirited steeds of any CAD member that had proven themself worthy, each of their riders cloaked in the familiar silver garb of official CAD members.

Watching them from the steps of my keep, they quickly came to a halt in front of me, each of the members dropping off of their horses.

"Thank you for coming so soon." I stepped forward to greet them.

The lead member chuckled mirthlessly. "Well, what are old friends for?"

They threw back their cloak, the familiar dark eyes meeting mine as the cold, feminine voice registered.

She was short, but she still managed to look down on everyone around her as if they had not proven themselves.

With her utility belt loaded down with various tools and magical gadgets, Penelope Iriend crossed her arms, her head tilted upward in a fashion that made my stomach rumble with displeasure.

The only silver lining to this was the other cloaked members revealing themselves to be strangers.

DAWN INTERLUDE: DAKA VELBRUN

Hey, BTO, you playing later? Not writing a report for ole Mama Derby tonight?" Johnson was an asshole, but his annoying jabber was the only thing keeping the men sane.

I didn't sign up for this. Well, I had, but I was looking for something easier. I hadn't made the cut as an officer, hadn't made the cut as a medic. Honestly, maybe that was for the best.

I wasn't sure if I had it in me to watch someone die while I tried to fix 'em up.

No, whatever it was that I wanted, well, there was a word for it. What was the word being passed around? Cushy?

I wanted cushy.

When I was seven, I read *The Wonderful Wizard of Oz* for the first time. It was a foggy memory now, more of a vague recollection of the idea, but ever since my rebirth, I'd been thinking about it more often.

A colorful little novel about a dame that had found herself in a mysterious new land of fantasy. She'd met a lion, a scarecrow, and a man made out of metal.

She eventually got home if I was remembering right.

I was basically that girl now, uh, Dorothy? Dorothy was her name. Gone from a basket case to being loaded around a strange world by my new dad.

I'd heard his name thrown around, Rakta, but I preferred calling him Dad.

And, uh, he called me Daka. It was terribly different from George, but as the months passed and I'd had nothing to do but listen and enjoy the heartbeat of my father, that name felt more distant. I enjoyed that distance.

I was Daka Valbrun now, uh, a girl. That had been, well, I was still finagling with that last part, but I tried not to give it too much thought. Guess there was a sacrifice in this new world business?

Ha, my dear old mom would cuff me on the ear if she heard me talking about the fairer sex being a burden . . . although, I can't imagine she ever thought about me becoming one. She'd probably have thought me strange, probably wouldn't recognize me.

I wouldn't have.

Sometimes, I wondered when the devil would let the other boot drop.

"Daka, are you hungry, my little warrior?"

The deep, accented voice broke up my dark thoughts.

The large frame of my father moved into sight, my little neck not great at the whole business of turning quite yet. The way he glowed at my strange, fanciful sight was comforting though. Like a tree of fire that didn't burn me when he hugged me.

My stomach rumbled, and I tried to explain that, yes, sir, I was really hungry, and I'd like to eat something soon, please.

"Bluh," I managed to get out.

I'd rather take a white feather than have anyone from before see me like this. Johnson would have pulled my cheeks hard like some of the other old women in the town had, probably would have called me a daddy's girl.

I wondered, for a brief moment, if Johnson had gotten the same chance as me. A life away from . . . from the trenches.

Taking out a familiar bottle, Dad picked me up into his warm arms, and my body did most of the work for me, instinctively taking the suckling nub and having at it with gusto.

Any shame I felt was calmed by the gentle beat of my father's heart.

"Brooks brought in a reporter, can you believe it? Taking photos of this hellhole?" I checked my hand again, my same bad cards having stayed as shit as ever.

I spit out some tobacco. "Thought they didn't let them out in the trenches?"

There wasn't anything to see here. Unless the folks at home wanted to spend their teatime with scones and death.

"Nah, not anymore. I saw him taking photos of Curt's trench foot earlier. Sick bastard." If there was one thing I could appreciate about Johnson, it was that he didn't hold his tongue.

He was even funny sometimes.

I wish babies could be court-martialed. I knew they couldn't help themselves, but I wish I could really dekko Dalton in the eyes and really tell him, show him, how I felt right about now.

"Guh," said the little shit.

'Cause he had to be doing this on purpose, right?

He'd been handling my fucking toy, a little wooden man Dad had carved for me, for the past hour, and I was about ready to scream and cry to get it back. 'Cause damn it, that shit was mine, and I loved it, alright?

The roads had been rough with Dad's pace and the rough, dirt trails, but now that we were in a nice stone castle, or, uh, keep, my siblings had been getting to be right bastards.

Natakia, who'd cry if her fanciful little dress got dirtied, even by accident. I could barely control my bowels, and the dame thought I could go about aiming my upchuck?

And Dalton still hadn't given me my toy back!

I let my displeasure gurgle in the back of my throat, feeling my tubby little cheeks begin to bunch up. A wetness began to grow in my vision and . . . and . . . !

"Waaah!" I knocked my head back, letting my personal air sirens go off.

I didn't want to, it was so embarrassing, but I was a baby and babies got to cry, right?

The dame that'd been taking care of us while Dad was away came over, gently pulling my toy from Dalton's greedy mitts. Her own gentle glow was nice, but barely a whisper compared to Dad's brightness.

And where Dad's glow was an intricate spiderweb, like some

of the maps I'd got shown in school once, her glow was just some bloody rivers! Nothing very beautiful about it, but at least it was nice to look at.

Still, I slowly let my crying die off as I began to play with my little wooden boy again, Dalton sulking. He'd get over it; he had plenty of toys.

This life was a lot simpler than my old one. It was nice.

"They say the Germans are gonna make a run today."

Johnson had refused to run yesterday, said he'd rather face his dues than go out there to his certain doom. They'd taken him home, but I'd heard what happened to cowards.

At least he had more time to say his prayers.

"Well, I best put on my shooting glasses, then." The joke was as funny as the last time it was said. I couldn't really remember who'd been saying it all this time.

I polished my rifle, not really sure where the bloodstained metal ended and my body began.

After a night of having a nasty blighter almost assault me in my own crib, I hadn't realized that something much worse was about to happen.

"Try to treat each other well, alright? I'll be gone for a day or two, but I'll be back. Marisha and Mary will look after you. Dresden will keep you safe."

My dad was leaving me. He'd be back, maybe, but he was leaving me, and I hated it. The world was just a bit dimmer without him to hold me. What would I do if . . . if . . .

And who the bloody hell was Dresden?

The little boy waving around a sword!? Right shit, I thought this all was. Least his Vitae was okay, and the way it moved was nice and rhythmic, like a well-played drum.

It still had nothing on Dad's Vitae though.

After watching Dad train and explain Vitae, it'd become a lot easier to understand the glow most seemed to have in this world.

Vitae and Mana, he'd explained. Vitae was life; everything living had it from what I'd seen. Magic was beyond me, not sure what it looked like, but Vitae lit up easily!

And even easier was doing what Dad did with my own Vitae! Even if pulsing my Vitae, like my dad did, almost killed me. That'd been one hell of a way to remember I was a baby.

It felt amazing though! Not just using this new fancy energy I had, but just getting to do something! And getting focused on by Dad! He'd even mentioned training me!

When I was bigger, able to move and such, I knew he'd work with me! We'd spend all day running around and getting stronger. And I'd move like he did when he trained! Like a big, muscular circus . . .

Muscular . . . circus . . . ?

I think I felt another bloody nap coming on.

"Hey, Derby, you okay? Haven't heard your whistles in a while! I liked your tunes!" I just ignored the voice, not really sure if they were talking to me or not anyway.

I shot a man today. I had blasted plenty of Germans, truly, but this man was different. I'd had a flight of fancy that he'd be the last man I ever put down.

And then another man's head popped up, and I'd broken that promise without even thinking about it. I was having trouble sleeping, but killing? It was easy.

"Hey, come flap your gums with us for a bit, yeah?"

I missed Johnson.

I missed Mary.

Well, maybe *missed* was a strong word. She held me wrong most of the time and was always just a tad bit too forcible when she was feeding me, but . . .

At least she was normal.

"Alright, kiddos! Daddy is doing some very important work right now, so we're gonna have a great time together, okay?"

Doh was an abomination. I hadn't realized it at first, but when she kept showing up as different people, but with the same messed-up-looking Vitae, I'd caught on quick.

And damn, it was messed up. It looked different, bizarre. I didn't like it. I hated it. It was like someone had shit on a piece of art.

I'd rather eat a serving of iron rations than spend more than a couple of minutes with the monster! The worst was when she looked like Marisha . . .

Marisha was a good sort of woman who didn't deserve such a thing wearing her face and making a mockery of her!

"Buh." I cursed the woman, hoping to drive her back as I started wailing.

She frowned. "Why can't you be more like Natakia?"

The traitor was cradled in her arms, looking as pleased as a plum about her state of affairs. That girl was gonna grow up to be horrible, I could tell.

"Beh," Natakia sputtered at me smugly.

Yeah, well, Dad likes me more.

Still, it was strange how Dalton and Natakia would focus and look at things sometimes. Not like a baby would though.

Well, at least they'd grow up quickly if that was the case. While we'd been born at the same time, I felt like a big sister to them on account of my added years.

And with age comes wisdom. Wisdom I'd use to keep them safe.

The sharp, steel-coated whistle reverberated through the trench.

I started running, as fast as I could, trying to get my legs and eyes to work in the dust and gloom of no-man's-land.

I hated this. I hated everything.

And then something hit me, a loud concussive explosion that sent fire and brimstone through every inch of my body.

And I died.

And then I heard the voice of God.

I woke up in the middle of the night with a wail, the memories flashing through my mind with such vibrancy, the smell and taste of the trenches a permanent stain on my tongue . . .

I felt like George more than ever, and I hated it; I hated George. What had George ended up doing besides killing? Fearing his own country as much as he did his enemies?

And yet, his life gripped me, my life, my horrible life.

And suddenly, warm, strong arms picked me up, and I was gently cradled to a familiar warmth, the rhythmic beating of my dad, not George's, suddenly there with me. A rock to lean on.

"It's okay, my little warrior, it's okay."

I was his little warrior. Yes, his little warrior. I didn't fight for any country right now because I was Daka. I wasn't George.

I was Dad's little warrior.

A man who knew blood and conflict like me and yet held himself with a strength I didn't have. The strength I wanted to have.

"Calm, Daka, calm. Let me tell you a story, Daka. A story of an ocean as blue as your eyes."

And he painted a story for me, a story of great waters, of vicious pirates, and of adventure. There was so much of this world that I hadn't seen, but every tale Dad whispered to me made me yearn to see it for myself and brought me back to reality, Daka's reality.

My wailing quieted as George's scars slowly retreated back into a dark place somewhere in my mind, some hole I wish it'd die in, replaced by a heartbeat overflowing with love.

I would be a warrior that made him proud, a hero that accomplished what George had failed to do.

Protect what he loved.

16

Well, Lord Velbrun, you certainly have a lot of nerve asking CAD for help."

This was going about as well I thought it might.

I muttered my gratitude to Mary as she set out some tea for me and my guests, feeling like I would need something a little stronger for this conversation. Honestly, I was still a little unsteady from the shock of seeing my old friend so suddenly after so long.

Trying to keep stalwart, I frowned. "Penelope, I paid all my dues before I left. CAD does not require lifelong membership."

Taking out one of her marvelous inventions, Penelope set her own teacup down on her personal self-heating coaster.

Her lips tightened as she watched her tea begin to simmer. "My first name, Lord Velbrun? That is a very personal way to refer to a stranger."

I closed my eyes, feeling a headache coming on. And, I'd admit, a little pang in my heart at the idea of being strangers now.

"Miss Iriend, thank you for—"

"Never mind, I hate that." She closed her eyes, taking a sip of her tea. "Go back to first names, Lord Velbrun."

Opening my eyes, it was easy to notice her discomfort. She'd always hated her last name, always enjoying any distance she could keep between her reputation as one of the empire's brightest minds and her noble lines.

Still, I felt the small hint of a familiar smile tug at my lips. "Only if you refer to me in the same way, Penelope."

I realized I might have overstepped as the cold look in her eyes became absolutely frosty, her gaze narrowing at me like icicles about to drop. "Rakta."

If her weapons had been drawn with that tone in her voice, I may have felt more than just a chill run down my spine. Even weaponless, Penelope had a knack for making anything within reach deadly.

Attempting warmth, my response reeked more of guilt than familiarity. "Penelope."

I glanced at her aides, the other adventurers that had arrived in response to my letter to the Continental Adventurers of Derra.

There were three of them, two of them men and the last a woman. They looked foreign, none of them from Certillia. The men resembled each other and the fierce blond tint to their hair spoke of northern Fjordic heritage.

The woman was a more alien sort, her eyes large and wide and her fingers long and willowy. The touch of the Mana Wastes upon her was as subtle as the bright-pink hair that seemed to glow.

Still, they enjoyed my tea silently, seeming enraptured by Penelope's discourse with me. Certainly, I enjoyed having a captive audience at this warm reunion I was having.

"So, Rakta, what finally dragged you away from Lydia's side long enough for you to send a letter? You mentioned a threat against your children?" Penelope looked around the room, as if grading the decor. "Congratulations by the way, on the children. Would've been nice to hear about it before now."

Her words were lined with a venomous edge. I felt a sting somewhere deep within me as I realized a crucial flaw in this reunion. Penelope was not . . . aware of Lydia's passing.

"Are the Velbruns really so unhelpful for their runaway hero daughter that they couldn't give her a village with more guards? Send some of their elites?" Her words were prodding me for an answer, taunting me.

I frowned, not sure how to bring it up. I cursed my heavy tongue, unable to blunt the tip of my words when they mattered most. And yet, it was not like I could simply keep Lydia's fate to myself.

No matter how things had ended, Lydia and Penelope had been friends.

"I'm afraid that House Velbrun wanted little to do with me after Lydia passed."

There was silence. I kept my gaze low, down at the table watching my tea cool. Penelope's cup remained hot, warmed by her own magical coaster.

". . . Damn it."

I slowly looked up, unable to meet Penelope's gaze, but watching as her fists paled from the tightness in which she balled them up.

"This . . . This isn't fair . . . I was going to be mad at you, insult you for abandoning us . . . but how . . . ?"

I glanced up to see the first and only tear slip through the cracks of Penelope's control, rolling down her cheek. She looked uncomfortable, gritting her teeth.

"How can I do that now?" Her words were bitter, lost. Like she'd been beaten in a duel I wasn't aware I was a part of. I didn't feel like I'd won anything though.

Grief could be a difficult, selfish thing. I hadn't even thought about informing the rest of my old adventuring group about Lydia's death. I'd assumed they would hear about it eventually, but . . .

Well, House Velbrun had not allowed the world to know of Dalton's death, had they? I couldn't imagine they'd be public about Lydia's demise.

Sighing, I tried to keep my demeanor. "You've been riding for some time. Mary will show you to your rooms."

"So, these are the Velbrun spawn."

I smiled, letting Natakia play with my fingers as Dalton focused on Penelope with his keen gaze. "They are my precious younglings. Smart, something they get from their mother."

"Yes, Lydia was certainly bright." There was much left unsaid by the words, but I didn't care enough to pick it apart. I knew that Penelope and Lydia's relationship was complicated, especially when it came to their magical work.

I motioned to each of my children. "This is Daka, my little warrior; Natakia, my desert flower; and Dalton, who was very brave in the face of the dark thing that threatened him and his sisters."

Penelope hummed, her eyes flitting from each of my children before they wandered off to look at the walls and the ceiling, examining the room. "Garrick and Varn are taking care of the perimeter, seeing if there was anything you missed, and Zerota is looking for any remnants of energy in the keep."

She walked around the room, zeroing in on the wall into which the creature had fled through after I had attacked it.

"This wall . . . you haven't cleaned it? Since the thing came through?"

I shook my head. After giving her a day to rest from the trip and the news of Lydia's passing, I had informed her of everything that had happened.

Cold and superior, she often was, but Penelope was efficient. She did not have to be told the same thing twice, and there were many times that her skill with magical apparatuses had saved lives.

"Alright, give me a moment."

She pulled out a metal device, adorned with runic designs and components that were well out of my understanding. Her grip around a long handle, the flat, boxlike extension from the handle was waved over the wall.

After a moment, some of the runes began to glow, emanating a small whining noise that quickly faded.

"Something was here alright. It isn't undead as far as I can tell." That came as a surprise to me. She continued. "It's still cranking out a lot of energy. Where's the book with the details of the ritual?"

Moments later, I had fetched it and offered it to the most scholarly of my old adventuring group. "I didn't know what to make of it. It's madness."

Penelope looked over a few passages, her eyes growing wider and wider. "No, this is . . . this is in code. I can see a few repeating phrases, but gah, it definitely hurts to read this."

"Anything you can make out?"

"Not really, but whatever came out of this ritual probably isn't done growing. I'm seeing at least one design here that mentions a larval state." She shuddered at the idea, before closing and pocketing it. "I'll have to do some research about what this is, but . . . I don't know if I can do that here."

I frowned. "I sent for adventurers to hunt this thing down, not study it."

"Getting into your role quite well, Lord Velbrun. I know you weren't always a part of this step of the process, but before we kill, we often like to know what we're trying to kill."

The way she said that did not sit well with me. Still, perhaps she had a point. I was no longer an adventurer, just a concerned father and noble. And even when I was, it was not like I was the brain of the group.

"Hey." Penelope's voice was a touch softer, perhaps seeing something on my face. "I'm . . . not trying to downplay your part in what we did, okay? This is an unknown, and unknowns have the highest fatality rate among CAD."

Put like that, it felt better. I didn't want people to recklessly sacrifice themselves just so my children would be a little safer. And yet, a part of me simply wished to gather up the strongest of the lands and hunt down the creature.

I wasn't even sure why it was here . . . except for the accursed thoughts of the Warlock King's death at my hands. The idea of my past coming to haunt my family terrified me.

Shaking my head, I grunted, "My children are in danger for as long as that creature persists. They are vulnerable, and I . . . I am not perfect. I will make a mistake eventually."

And if my children got hurt, never forgiving myself would be the least of my punishments.

A gentle hand on my shoulder brought me out of my thoughts, my gaze locking with Penelope's dark eyes, her look revealing little to those who did not know her well.

And yet, for me, the softness tucked away deep within them touched my aching heart and soothed it.

"We won't leave you with nothing, Rakta." She turned away from me to scribble a few notes down in her own journal. "I'm going to set up some protections, and we'll go investigate Niers as well. If we find it, research or not, we won't leave it alive if we can help it."

I nodded; that was all I could ask for. At a certain point, this was out of my hands unless I wished to leave my children again. One comfort, I supposed, was that the creature was out of the keep for the time being.

There was a soft knock on the door, both Penelope and I glancing at it, our moment broken.

"Yes? Come in." Penelope's command came as easy to her as breathing.

The door creaked open, revealing the wide-eyed Zerota, her willowy fingers threading between one another as she made an expression that somewhat resembled that of a surprised fish.

She looked around the room, as if trying to find us, before her gaze eventually settled on Penelope. "I found something."

My cellar had a basement.

Hidden underneath a smattering of empty boxes and barrels, covered in dust and cobwebs that I had yet to tend to, was a trapdoor that opened up to reveal a ladder that went straight down.

It was a rough job, more likely dug with a shovel than magic. It led all the way to an underground room that could barely be anything more than a closet space, and yet every inch was covered in reasons to be concerned.

Blood, runic symbols, elixirs of horrid concoctions, and magic that spoke of the work of a madman. Something, the universe seemed to be trying to tell me, was wrong here.

"I'm going to presume this was the work of the previous Lord Velbrun of Gelvurt." Penelope's tone was clipped, similarly horrified by the same sight as I was.

The withered remains of an adult, their naked body decomposed to the bone and a serrated dagger lodged into the remnants of their rib cage.

17

"Thank you for letting us stay the night, Orion."

The man dotted his head with a rag, still looking disturbed by the tale I had woven for him just a few hours ago. Finding a ritualistic sacrifice below Velbrun Keep had, well, understandably put both of us on edge.

While Penelope had not found any remnants of magic on me, my children, or the staff, there was no telling what machinations had been performed there. It could, truly, be waiting for the right time to affect us, infect us . . .

I was not comfortable with the idea of my children sleeping there until Penelope and her company of CADs cleared it of all remaining filth and got up some proper protections. A few nights away from the keep, while it raised Natakia's ire, were worth the precaution.

"It's quite alright, my lord, I just . . . to hear about what you found, it truly brings every disappearance and missing traveler into a new disturbing light."

I frowned, taking a drink of ale-tinged water. "Was that a problem in this area?"

Thankfully, the man shook his head. "Not particularly; nothing beyond what we expect here at the border. We had a performer come through here a few months before Zactrik departed, a minstrel."

He had a strange expression on his face. As if the words he considered were heavy in his throat.

"He seemed . . . taken with Lord Velbrun, as if he enjoyed the challenge of speaking with him as an equal. One morning came after a raucous night, and he had departed without a word . . ."

Not abnormal for some performers, but with this new revelation . . . perhaps a clue to the identity of the corpse? If his corpse was cleansed of the remnants of Zactrik's ritual, then perhaps it could be returned to a relative.

"What was his name?"

"Circei Wale."

It was an unfamiliar name, but perhaps enough knew of his exploits to fashion a narrative for his life. A life gone untold was surely a punishment he did not deserve.

"So, this is your spawns' maid?"

Doh held Natakia with a comfortable ease, tilting her head at Penelope. "So, this was the best CAD could send, huh?"

"I am one of the best in these lands; don't test me." Penelope's gaze was frosty, eyeing up Doh like she was a machine she was planning to take apart.

"Shouldn't one of the best in these lands not have to go around calling themselves that? Doesn't sound as genuine when it rolls off your tongue so easily."

I stepped in before Penelope could pull out one of her contraptions. "Doh, please stop questioning my friend. Penelope, please stop responding to Doh so easily. It's what she wants."

Doh pouted at my words, but thankfully Penelope disengaged, turning her attention to me. I was glad my old friend had finally managed to pull away from the jabs of others. "Where did you even find this woman? Were you so bored you decided to hire a jester?"

Ah, so perhaps she had not fully disengaged.

"I met her on my travels." I motioned to the shape changer. "It's a longer story than I believe is appropriate for right now, but she aided me in my cursory investigation in Niers. In return, I hired her."

"You? Afraid of a long story?"

I frowned at Penelope's version of a teasing smile, which looked more like a shark ready to take a bite. "I'm not afraid. We just have other things to tend to, and the story can come later."

Doh was suddenly a few inches closer to Penelope, whispering to her in mock conspiracy. "Rakta? Afraid of stories? That's like saying a pig is afraid of mud!"

I let them rattle on for a while longer, tuning out as I was obviously being ganged up on by the two women. A dangerous scenario, one I had learned to simply endure so as not to escalate.

Even though a part of me wished to defend my people's way, the two had no true ill intent in their words. I had heard enough truly malicious perspectives on the matter to know the difference.

Eventually, I interrupted their back-and-forth discussion about my storytelling. "So, the news you had for us, Penelope?"

Penelope's smile, which had grown while speaking with Doh, dampened down into a more professional one as she returned to the matter at hand.

"We've examined the site of the ritual in Niers," she said. "It uses familiar runes from the journal, but looks more incomplete. If I had to guess, I think the ritual performed here was a more complete one."

I frowned, stroking my chin. "So, Zactrik used the ritual with a sacrifice, but the one I saw in Niers had no such sacrifice."

Penelope nodded. "Either a different or incomplete version of what we saw here. No one noticed anything odd about Zactrik after the time we presume the ritual happened, so . . ."

"He may be another problem, independent of this other creature," I finished.

Doh laid down Natakia. "So, why'd the messed-up one come here, then?"

"Perhaps it knew that Zactrik's estate might have something that could help it, some sort of tonic, but didn't find the underground ritual site."

Neither had I. Had I not called for CAD's help, how long would it have taken for me to find it? How long would my children have been influenced by the lingering magics?

I had wanted this keep to be a haven for my children so badly that I allowed that hope to blind me to this harsh reality living right underneath them.

"Rakta, you had no reason to believe that kind of thing was here," Penelope lightly snapped at me. "You thought that the creature was here because of who you were, not where you were living. That's a reasonable assumption."

I tried to relax, letting go of the tension in my bones. "It's a bittersweet relief. I thought I was dealing with remnants of the Warlock King, and I let that blind me to other possibilities."

"Wait, you fought the Warlock King!?" Doh blinked.

Penelope smirked. "We did, yes. Together."

"Fuck, I really shouldn't have tried to steal from you!"

"You what!?"

And suddenly it became the time for a long story.

"Well, it's time."

Penelope and her companions had been in Gelvurt for a few weeks now, putting into place special protections and cleaning out any stains from the creature or Zactrik's actions. I didn't think I would ever walk the halls of the keep with the same comfort again, but I was appreciative of the work she'd done.

Watching her get ready to leave now, heading back to the capital to do some proper research and launch a full-scale investigation was . . . strange.

Perhaps I had gotten used to having her here? After the sting from Lydia's and my departure had faded between us somewhat, it had been nice to speak of things like before.

"Be safe, Penelope." I pulled back from the goodbye hug. "Trust your companions as much as you trust your devices."

Penelope sniffed primly. "I've learned my lessons, Rakta. The true question is if you will ever learn yours."

Downcast, I shifted slightly. "I am truly sorry, Penelope. When Lydia made to leave, I knew I had to go with her. I wanted to wait until morning, to make it proper, but . . ."

"Rakta, I don't think Lydia ever really enjoyed being around us." My friend's smile was brittle.

I flinched. "That . . . isn't true. She had many fond memories of you, and spoke of you often . . ."

"Memories, yeah. When she was actually talking to us? Walking with us?" Penelope shook her head. "She never connected with us like she did you, you know? She trusted us, was loyal, but I think she was more Velbrun toward us than she was toward you."

I wasn't sure how to respond, but my heart hurt in a strange new way. A mixture of grief and defense, as if I should be defending Lydia's legacy. I was probably one of the few willing and able to do so.

And yet, Penelope was not simply speaking to hurt me. There was a truth to her words, genuine facts that I wasn't sure if I was ready to fully accept.

Looking back up to Velbrun Keep behind me, I tried to keep my voice steady. "Lydia was a peculiar soul, a beautiful one. After the Warlock King's death . . ."

"She took it hard, I know. Was there a funeral?"

I shrugged. "Perhaps a small ceremony. The Velbruns don't like to hold funerals . . ."

". . . It helps them hide how many of their agents are alive or dead." Penelope finished for me.

With them being one of the most secretive royal houses of the empire, I wondered how many of the Velbruns had known about Zactrik's actions, his interests, without raising a hand to stop it.

"I'm still angry at you, Rakta, the others too. We thought you'd been kidnapped or ambushed . . . The letter Lydia sent us a week later to tell us what happened . . . Rakta, it was almost insulting."

She shook her head, as if clearing her thoughts of the detached, clinical phrases and explanations Lydia had offered to them. She'd wanted to write the letter, but I knew I should have done so, no matter how bad my handwriting was back then.

"I'm glad you're okay," Penelope eventually managed. "I'm glad your kids are okay, but it really hurt us. And I know you feel horrible about it. I just think that Lydia probably didn't."

I knew for certain that she hadn't.

With that, Penelope departed. She promised she'd be back, but warned that having found me, she wouldn't be keeping my location a secret from the others.

It sent a chill down my spine, but made my heart yearn for the reunion. I could only hope it went as well as it had with Penelope.

* * *

"So, you really want to do this?"

I sat down in my office, taking deep breaths and letting my Vitae vibrate. "Yes, I believe it is necessary. I've forgotten something, something I think is very important."

Doh sat cross-legged in the chair across from me, the shape changer watching me as I began to force my body to relax.

"Cool because this kind of magic ain't supposed to be for remembering birthdays." She smiled, standing up out of the seat and walking around to stand behind me. "Now, the spell I'm going to use is going to be kind of touch and go. It'll be up to you to remember things, alright?"

I nodded. "Okay?"

That seemed like how memories usually worked, so I believed I had some experience to lean on.

Doh blew a bit of hair out of her face. "I mean, fuck, this is hard. I'm heightening the memories, but you gotta point them in the right direction, yeah? If you aren't focused, you'll get lost and we'll be here for a while, possibly a really long while."

That made sense. It had taken me some time to trust Doh to perform this kind of magic on me, but any concern I had about her intentions paled in comparison to the concern I felt about these foggy memories.

Finally managing to relax into the chair, I began to focus my mind, sharpening it like a knife. Meditation would help here, keeping my mind focused on what I needed to learn and nothing more.

Behind me, Doh began to chant, "Mother of Memories, I beseech thy grasp to pull from the waters a golden fleece of the past."

Her words had a somewhat religious tone to them, as most magical chants did, but I could tell that this was nothing like the zealot chants of some disciples of various divinities.

"From a foggy torrent, from a cracked mirror, ordain this one with insight of yesteryear, of that which has passed and become dormant."

I thought of the ancient tones of the voice, the undercurrent of tension within the words, like that of a warning, a message. For myself and . . . Lydia?

Wait, Lydia had heard this as well?

My eyes widened at the revelation.

"Brush away the dust, **Clear River of Memories!**"

The sudden insight had come at the worst of times, the magic surging through my mind as I tried to refocus it . . .

And then all went dark.

18

H i," the stranger said, the polite, almost shy voice coming from the small figure inching their way through my door.

Everything hurt, my bruises and my pride. I had not asked for a fight and yet the belligerent folk of this town seemed starved for something, someone, to take their anger out on.

I should never have left Rusk. There was nothing for me there, but there was less than nothing for me here.

I turned away from the voice, bandaging the cut on my arm. "My name is Rakta. If you've come to poison me, know that I grew up drinking sunset cactus juice."

The figure crept forward, a small little giggle filling the empty, dark tavern room. I almost mistook it for bells, an undercurrent of innocence dancing under the amusement.

"I thought that was simply a myth passed around by merchants and minstrels." The voice was teasing me, waiting for me to drop my guard. And yet, there was something enticing about it.

Frowning, I tied off the bandage, the pressure from the bindings a familiar feeling. "It isn't. We boil the pulp in water collected from the sand, and it cleans the water, giving it a sweet taste."

Not that a Certillian would understand the delicacies of a good drink with their hard liquors and spiceless food.

The figure approached my bedside. "Then it is good that I have only come to poison you with kindness. I heard that you were hurt."

I ignored the ways my bruises pulsed from being acknowledged. "I think sleep is the only solace I need right now. I do not need a mob seeking revenge on me for speaking with one of their women alone."

"I'm not one of their women."

She stepped into the shine of the cloudy moonlight, her bright-blue eyes shining like jewels and her unmarred pale skin glistening, as if it were the surface of a celestial body.

Playfully winding her long, silvery hair between her fingers, the woman smiled. "My name is Lydia Velbrun."

I wanted to ask her to dance.

This wasn't right . . . This was too early. I knew this moment, the moment I met Lydia. She'd invited me to travel with her, and I, there was no resisting her.

But I had to resist now. No matter how much I wished to linger, I could not.

I had to . . . focus . . .

"Are you sure about this, Lydia?" It wasn't often I worried over my beloved's plans, but this one seemed stranger and riskier than most.

And I had never enjoyed underground passages. Movement was so limited and constrained in these tight tunnels.

With a familiar confidence, Lydia smiled. "My magic doesn't often lead me astray, dear. While the others distract the trolls, we're going to cut the head off the lion."

I smiled fondly. Still, I held on to my worry, if only to keep my senses sharp. Lydia never had doubts about her plans, but that never kept them from encountering unforeseen obstacles.

She sulked quite a bit after getting blindsided by something her magic had not divined from her silver mirror, so I needed to work extra hard to make sure everything went according to the plan.

"Will the others be okay?" Penelope had crafted some interesting weapons for the local militia, calling it a field test for new designs, and Shawn and Ulric were both strong in their own ways.

And yet, I worried.

"Hmm, I'm not sure. I didn't check."

I frowned at the slight dismissiveness in her tone. "You told them they would be fine, Lydia."

"Of course I did." She turned back at me and smiled. "I have faith in our friends, Rakta. They wouldn't let a band of trolls be the end of them."

She said it with such confidence, but calling the force they faced a simple band of trolls underplayed their true force of numbers. They were up against the largest facet of the Warlock King's fighting force, but perhaps I was simply splitting hairs.

"We're here." That was a persuasive end to the conversation.

The tunnel we had been walking through opened up to a large room decorated with similar tunnel openings. Ours had opened up into a smaller hole on the ceiling, hidden by a stone overhang.

Something only Lydia's magic could have found without any investigation.

And yet, I could already see Lydia sulking after we were through as we both peered down at where the leader rested with a skeleton crew of trolls around him.

"He . . . looked smaller in my mirror." I would have sacrificed much to see her face, her whispers nearing the edge of what a braver man might call whining.

Fourteen feet tall and with a frame of corded muscle, a troll of impressive size drank deeply from a barrel . . . and with his additional head, chewed on a cow leg.

Brushing my beloved's hair aside, I smiled. "Do not worry; this hurdle will not keep us from the future you saw."

She smiled, a precious thing, and we got to work.

I wrenched my thoughts away from the memory, not wanting to get swept up in the pain and action of that fight. Dargon, the two-headed troll leader, had been one of my closest experiences to death.

Was I getting closer to my answers? How did Lydia play into this?

"I can't believe her!" Lydia was pacing as I came in, which was never a good sign. Our group had decided to take a break for a week, but sudden issues had prompted Penelope to extend our downtime.

Closing the door behind me, I wrapped my arms around her, letting her fall back into my chest. She sighed, the stress flowing out of her as we simply stood together.

I sat her down on the bed. "She cannot help her heart; you know this. She owes the local church a new roof after her last field test."

My love's expression soured in a way I disliked. "If we aren't at the King's Summit soon, we're not going to have any time to prepare."

"Prepare for what, Lydia?" I brushed her hair gently, to remind her I was here and to see more of her beautiful eyes.

I asked out of interest, but with no real intent to get any answers out of her. The others had yet to learn that Lydia shared her insights only when she wished, but I had made peace with it quickly.

She was like the wind. She was not required to respond to every call.

Sighing, she held me close. "The Warlock King."

I breathed deeply of her scent, the familiar vanilla perfume she personally enjoyed. "What about him, Lydia?"

"Do you promise not to tell the others?"

"Yes."

The Warlock King was a rising threat and, after joining the Continental Adventurers of Derra alongside Lydia and meeting the others, we had heard more and more about him.

Lydia's voice was trembling. "It's going to get very bad, Rakta. I know how I can make it better though, how to have everything end the way I want it to."

She said the words like they were a sin to be hidden from the gods, as if she was scared that I would balk at her words. And yet, I loved her.

"How do you want things to end, Lydia?"

. . . I stopped the memory there. It hurt to remember the promises I made, my inability to bring the future she wished to see into fruition.

She was never the same after my failure.

I had to continue. I could not let this stop me.

And yet, I could not stop myself from thinking of what relit her flame after my actions snuffed it.

"Rakta, I'm pregnant."

Lydia said it to me with a fond smile, her eyes glistening. She had lost so much these past few months, but now, right here, I saw the woman I loved alive again.

And then the words registered.

I fell to my knees, feeling the world tremble below me at the revelation. Looking up at her, I saw her amusement clear as day. It was a balm for my embarrassed soul.

I weakly picked myself up, taking her hands in mine. "Truly? Is it, uh . . ."

She leaned forward and gave me a kiss, silencing my foolishness. I simply basked in her presence, in the news, in the absolute truth of Lydia's pregnancy.

My wife broke off the kiss. "Yes, they're yours. Of course they're yours."

I nodded, before I choked. "T-they?"

She nodded, a bittersweetness flashing across her visage.

"I told Mom, and she . . . looked ahead for me." Lydia rested her head against my chest to hide her expression. "I didn't ask her to. I wanted it to be a surprise."

My joy lessened for a moment at the Velbruns ruining this joyous occasion for us, before I kissed her on the forehead tenderly. "Be happy, Lydia. Our lives will be blessed with two darling younglings."

She ducked her head into my chest and made a noise that vaguely sounded like a word.

I brushed some of her silvery hair back. "Lydia, darling, what did you say?"

Looking up, meeting my gaze, Lydia smiled. "Three."

And then she screamed as I took her into my arms, swinging her around as I began the happiest dance of my life, its only contest being the dance I shared with Lydia on our wedding day.

Too far, the answers here . . . why had I not noticed how sad her smile was? Was I so happy I could not see that something was bothering her? What had her mother told her?

No, no. I had to take control of the spell, control my mind. My thoughts, my wishes.

I focused on the words, the ancient words that had fallen from my mind.

I needed to hear them again, know where they had come from.

* * *

This was supposed to be a simple mission, something that Lydia and I could do on our own with the others invested in their own works.

Penelope had become infatuated with one of the great minds of the capital's Grand Library, working with them on some sort of project together. Lydia had mentioned to me on the way here that it wouldn't work out, but I was hopeful for my inventive friend's chances.

Shawn had been snatched up by some representative from CAD to go speak with interested heads of state that wanted an update on the War-lock King. He was heads and shoulders above the best to represent our group's findings.

And finally, Ulric was barred from leaving the CAD HQ until the local authorities were more confident in his ability to walk the streets without causing collateral damage. Too many destroyed bars had damaged the trust he'd been tenuously given.

Leaving Lydia and me to find a local bandit crew that had escaped from guards the prior week and moved house to the nearby hills.

So how did it come to this?

"I've . . . never missed something this big before, Rakta." Lydia's voice was worried, scared.

We had found the hideout, built out of one of the natural ravines of the Certillian Empire's countryside, and with it, we had found the bloody corpses of the criminals. Their bodies torn limb from limb, at least, that was what the scene would have us believe.

I examined the wounds. "These wounds are too perfect, efficient."

"Magic?" Lydia's voice was soft, but there was a tinge of something else in her voice that I could not put a name to.

"Magic or Vitae." I flipped one of the torsos over with my Vulture Axe, looking at the wounds. "A normal swordsman couldn't cut this cleanly through bone."

Lydia stepped around me to the opening of the ravine, a ladder descending downward. "I want to go down there, Rakta."

I dragged my gaze from the bodies to her. "This is dangerous."

"I have to know. There's something different here."

There was a resoluteness to her voice that I was weak to. There was no chance of stopping or abandoning her to this new quest.

I would walk alongside her anywhere.

Standing up, I nodded. "Can I convince you to wait until we have the others with us?"

The sly look she sent me over her shoulder was more than enough as an answer.

We descended into the ravine, Lydia acquiescing to my request to go down first. I helped her down the rest of the ladder after I reached the bottom, gently setting her onto the ravine floor.

"It's cold down here." My beloved's insight was boundless today.

As if sensing my dry thoughts, she gave me a look, but I could not argue with her about the temperature. It was cold down here, a chilly draft that was different from the warm summer day of the surface.

This deep into a ravine, I was somewhat worried about rocks falling from above, but did not voice my concerns. I would save myself from Lydia's comments about seeing such things coming.

Stepping off of the ladder down onto the rocky ground, Lydia took a few steps away from me, her gaze slowly swiveling from left to right. I waited patiently, ready to slay anything that attacked us.

After a few moments, Lydia looked at me, taking out her silver mirror. "I'm going . . . to try something, okay?"

She sounded unsure, a rarity from my wife. A nervous energy around her form as she began to circle her fingers around the frame of her mirror, I had never seen her look so hesitant before.

"What are you—?"

"Let the chambers of fate greet this Lady Velbrun, let the world shrink before my omniscient gaze."

The reflective surface of Lydia's mirror flashed.

*"Bring forth my **Boundless Prognostication**."*

And then the world went white.

An ancient voice that hurt my ears to listen to flooded my very being.

Three souls from beyond

Born to a hero and a pawn

Death and destruction

Peace and function

Lies within the strength of a bond

I heard a scream that sounded like Lydia, but nothing could keep my world of white from fading into the darkness of unconsciousness.

I awoke with a start, once again firmly in my keep's office.

"Oh thank goodness, you're alive." Doh started removing valuables from a rucksack, placing them back around the office.

I blinked away tears, dealing with fresh memories and new insights.

19

A prophecy, a prophecy I had forgotten somehow. One that Lydia had called forth from the cosmos? How had she done such a thing? Why had she?

"Hello? Anybody home? Rakta?"

I breathed deeply, finally looking up to meet the gaze of Doh, who had been needlessly trying to get my attention after returning her stolen goods. Subtle about it, she was not.

Perhaps if they had been my own possessions, rather than historical pieces belonging more so to the Velbruns, I would have been keener about the attempted theft.

As it was, I had other matters to concern myself with right now.

"Thank you, Doh." Without her, I would still be racking my brain for the lost prophecy. I doubted that would have yielded any results quickly.

She blinked, tilting her head. "Oh, uh, you're welcome? So, did you find what you were looking for?"

I nodded, standing up. My body felt stiff, a hint at how long I had been submerged within my own mind, but I pushed through it. There was no time to allow for simple aches of the body to keep me from moving.

And yet, while I had my answers, it had awoken so many new questions. Why had I forgotten this prophecy? What did it mean? I had an inkling, but it would be rash to act upon mere ideas.

All these questions had left me tired, not helped by my troubled heart and aching head at the memories of Lydia becoming so fresh.

"I need time to think, Doh. Go put the children to sleep. I will be in soon to kiss them good night."

Doh snorted, muttering to herself as she left, "I wish someone would kiss me good night."

Ignoring her, I let my strained body begin to settle into familiar stances, one after another, letting my Vitae thrum as I meditated on my new insights.

There was so much to consider.

Finishing up my meditations after a moment, I quickly went to kiss my younglings good night and wish them fond dreams. Hopefully Daka would have a peaceful slumber.

The three sets of intelligent eyes slowly succumbed to sleep, and I wondered if perhaps I had already experienced the first part of the prophecy.

For perhaps my children were bound with souls not of this world? Ancient intelligences of old? Was it possible? Were there any true impossibilities in this world?

I had never heard of such a thing before, not sure what world such souls would even come from if not this one.

"Hey, what do you feed these kids? Natakia's getting heavy." Doh seemed intent on breaking up my thoughts, putting away the little toys the kids, mostly Daka, had been fumbling with before bedtime had rolled around.

And then, as if understanding her words, my little desert flower startled from her waning consciousness and started crying.

I shot Doh a look, something she flinched at. Perhaps the night was weighing on my patience? It was not like Doh's words had caused Natakia to cry.

Or had they?

Cradling my upset daughter, I gently swayed her back to sleep. "Calm, Natakia, calm. You are a growing child, Natakia. Growing to be as beautiful as your mother."

They were familiar comforts, sweet truths that were a balm to the infant's hurt feelings, and Natakia's tantrum quickly calmed, my desert flower gently falling asleep completely as I laid her back down alongside her siblings.

"Man, she is gonna be a handful when she gets older. Why'd she start crying?" My shape-shifting maid seemed ignorant of her words' impact on Natakia.

Perhaps, I would have been as well before I truly realized the intent of the prophecy. Just how much did my children truly understand from the speech of those around them?

In my tired mind, a thought occurred that I would need to keep Dresden from swearing so much around them.

"Good night, Doh."

"Good night, Lord Velbrun," She teased, closing her door.

I gave her a nod, leading her to her room by the light of a candle, before returning to my own chambers for the night.

The magical protections that Penelope had installed within the keep would ward my children from harm, allowing me to give my mind the rest it needed after tonight.

A door opened behind me. "Rakta?"

Doh's voice stopped me, sounding a bit different than usual.

"Yes, Doh?" I turned back, somewhat wary of whatever comment or witty remark I'd be getting on the way to my room.

It was hard to see her expression in the candlelight of her own room, but I could see the nervousness in her body language as she half stood outside of her bedroom door.

"My magic is very involved, Rakta," she offered hesitantly. "I don't see everything, but I see enough."

For a moment, I tensed. I was not entirely sure of what to make of the prophecy, of the events, and thought I had at least a night to consider it before I shared what I had learned.

"Your wife, uh, I saw her."

Oh. Now tense for an entirely different reason, I tried to keep myself calm. I knew that allowing Doh into my mind, allowing her to affect my mind, would require trust. That she saw Lydia . . .

"You saw her." I repeated her words, mulling them over. The implications were obvious, Doh's bloodline abilities coming to the forethought of my mind.

Doh's words came a bit faster. "She was beautiful, um, and I know that there probably isn't a chance in Derra that you wanted me to see her, but I, well, it just kind of happened . . . ?"

Was she scared? Alone in this empty hallway with me, no room for trickery? Had she faced reprisal for her actions in the past? I did not have the energy for these questions.

Still, Doh had not been required to be so open about this.

"Doh." She tensed as I said her name.

Exhausted as I was, I could never have hurt her for doing exactly as I asked her to. And yet, one concern had nestled itself into my heart that I could not keep myself from voicing.

"I'm not going to blame you for what you saw, but . . . if you ever take the form of my wife, I hope you understand that I will not appreciate it."

I wasn't even sure what I would do if she did so, but my memories of Lydia were too fresh, far too fresh to see Lydia in the flesh once more and be okay with it.

I wasn't sure I would ever be okay with that.

"Hey, that's . . . reasonable, yeah? Don't worry, Rakta. I'm really not a pillar of honor and morals and shit, but I won't pull something like that." She shuddered. "I let the dead stay dead."

Her voice was thick with an unheard story. Something I suspected neither of us had the energy to delve into tonight.

I nodded. "Good night, Doh."

"Good night, Rakta."

"Bah." Dalton was counting again, clumsily spreading out golden sils onto the ground and muttering to himself as he laid his tubby, fat hand on each one.

I watched him, Natakia and Daka out of the room for once. Doh had wanted to show them the stables, but Dalton had cried at the idea.

With my new insights, I simply watched him play with the coins.

"You and your sisters are remarkably intelligent, Dalton. Sometimes I wonder how smart you are, how far your intelligence will take you."

I watched as Dalton stopped counting, looking at me with his intelligent eyes and waiting for me to continue. Over the past month, his silvery hair had begun to grow thicker and push down toward his neck.

His first haircut might be quickly approaching.

One thing that I hadn't thought about in a long time, perhaps criminally long, was the blade that Dalton had brandished against the shadowy creature.

Crude, yes, but for a child to pull it out of nowhere, with no inkling of where it had come from, it was still strange.

Taking him into my arms, bringing a few coins with me so as not to upset him, I gently cradled him in my arms as I rocked back and forth. "Fatherhood has been strange, Dalton. I had seen this as a chapter in my life that I would enter alongside your mother."

I'd been prepared for a partnership, a team effort from the both of us to face down the obstacles of parenthood.

"And yet, recently, I've been cursed with nothing but questions."

Questions Lydia would not have had difficulty with.

Dalton brushed up against my beard, making a little noise at how rough it must have felt. I had not shaved recently, leaving my facial hair unmanaged.

Still, he did not cry, in fact, he did not cry often, not like Daka and Natakia.

"And yet, perhaps there are questions that do not need answers. The love I have for you and your sisters is not one based on answers or fate."

If my children were truly from another world, did that change anything? Were they not still of my own flesh and blood?

"I hope that whatever the future holds, Dalton, that I am strong enough to prepare you for it, teach you how this world works . . ."

As I tried to think of how to finish my thought, deciphering my own feelings as I poured them out to my son, I felt a little pulse of something indiscernible.

I looked down to Dalton in my arms, his hands coinless. Had they fallen? What was that unfamiliar feeling?

And then I felt it again, and suddenly Dalton was holding something else. A short, collapsible edged blade that he was waving slightly too close to my face for comfort.

Was that a straight razor?

"Duh." Dalton was giving my unshaven cheeks the dirtiest look I had ever seen from a baby.

* * *

My son knew some sort of instinctual magic that I had never felt before, nor did it seem to use Mana at all. On the other hand, my ever-cheerful daughter already knew how to manipulate her Vitae in ways some adults had trouble with.

I was not sure whether I was more concerned about whether Natakia would have some peculiarity of her own or if she ended up without one. Perhaps she would simply be unceasingly cute and disarming.

A father could hope.

And yet, while my thoughts lingered on the subject of tutors and lesson plans, neither of which were my forte, I had my hands full with a different matter.

"There's a prophecy!?"

I had really thought Doh would take this better.

"Fuck, this isn't a prophecy where the maid dies, is it!? Shit, I can't outpace fate!" Doh was pacing around the room, her form flickering through hundreds of faces I didn't recognize.

I placed my hand on her shoulder. "Doh, calm down. I didn't tell you this to make you panic."

Doh frowned as she got her form under control, shifting her weight from foot to foot. "Then, fuck, why tell me at all!? How am I gonna help at all with a prophecy!?"

"I don't need your help with the prophecy; all I need for you to do is help me figure out one more thing." I'd asked a lot from Doh, but this could be the most important part yet.

The memory manipulator looked reluctant. "Yeah?"

"The reason I forgot about it."

20

oh had sat me down in my office, looking about as serious as she could manage for an extended period of time. Maybe it was the stress from the revelation of a prophecy, but she wasn't making jokes right now.

In all honesty, I might've appreciated some humor in this moment. The idea of someone having messed with my mind was an unnerving one.

"Okay, so, forgetting things is natural, alright?" Doh began, scratching the back of her head. "There isn't always a memory-eating aardvark sipping on your brain stuff through your ears at night."

I supposed that was a slightly humorous image, if nothing else. "I'm sure I would have noticed if one tried."

"Not if it ate those memories." Doh's smile was teasing, but her tone was anything but flippant. She didn't seem like she wanted to joke about losing memories.

I was not an expert on the monstrosities of the world, although I knew that they were wide and varied, but I'd put this new addition closer to the top of my list of creatures to be cautious of.

Still, I shook my head. "I had remnants, flashes of this memory before you helped me remember. It was not eaten, I feel."

Doh dragged over her own chair, getting comfortable across from me and crossing her legs. "*Suppressed*, *bound*, and *locked* are all good words for what you're talking about."

They certainly were. I wasn't sure if having a proper term for it would help me though.

"The problem," Doh continued, "is that doing that kind of thing, locking a memory, requires a lot of power; it's really only beneficial if you have a bunch to spare or a catalyst to hold the memory back."

"And you are certain there was no catalyst?"

Something tangible holding my memories at bay was more comforting than a being of great power being involved.

"If there was, it broke. Something like a diamond or rare crystal, probably. Otherwise, I'd have had to push through a lot more barriers for you to remember this prophecy of yours." The doppelgänger made a face at the idea of having to push herself.

So, someone or something with a lot of power had suppressed my memories? I can't imagine forgetting such a prophetic moment otherwise.

My expression must have given away my thoughts because Doh was nodding along.

"Yeah, yeah, can't imagine a guy like you forgetting a prophecy, and, well, if you're powerful enough to go up against the Warlock King, then a lot of power would have been necessary to suppress your memories long enough."

I shook my head. "Why suppress them at all? Why not just take them? Eat them like that, uh, aardvark you mentioned?"

Doh shrugged. "More humane? Iunno, Rakta. If they had this amount of power, to suppress something that happened more than a year ago, then splicing or modification would have been easy."

The idea of someone modifying my memories was a terrifying one, but here I sat with a practitioner of such arts. My Vitae thrummed in instinctive protectiveness.

Still, I trusted Doh once. I could do so again.

"So, you'll be examining me?"

Doh began to weave streams of purple energy into the air, letting her Mana drain from her fingertips into the space between us, where it solidified for her purposes. "Yeah, well, every magic leaves a mark, even memory magic. Just sit back and think about when you learned about the prophecy the first time."

That was reasonable. Relaxing, I tried to empty my thoughts, although it was somewhat more difficult to do so without the more physical, rhythmic meditation dances I was familiar with.

Still, I focused my thoughts on the cave, the prophecy, Lydia, and all the events that had led up to that strange, forgotten encounter. The questions I had, the concerns that felt like rocks in my stomach. I just wanted answers.

"Memories of memories, mind eye awakening, **Map of Consciousness!**"

I felt a prickle in my head, as if something under my scalp was wiggling, but I tried not to let it disturb my focus.

"Hmm, hmm. Alright, I think I got something, but it's not . . . hmm . . ." Her voice trailed off, with a slight worried edge to it.

I opened my eyes as the prickling feeling faded. "It's not . . . what?"

Doh looked up from her findings, her magic in front of her contorting in a way that only she and other magicians would be able to decipher.

The look in her eyes was almost too flippant, like she didn't trust herself to handle this if she took it seriously.

"Yeah, I think a god did it."

The gods of Derra were not strangers to meddling in the affairs of mortals, although very few had proper evidence for such meddling.

Gods were, at least how I had been taught, great spirits of power that moved the world and nudged events as wind might scatter sand into the air. Invisible, but felt.

Ancient histories and stories told of times when these gods, divided among countless pantheons and domains, spoke to mortals more directly. Avatars of these great spirits walked upon the ground of Derra, leaving footprints that could still be felt today in the right spots.

And yet, that was a thing of the past, surely?

"This seems oddly direct for a god." I had spent the last hour considering Doh's findings.

Doh started, having kept herself busy by mindlessly shifting her hands into various different skin tones and sizes. "Huh?"

"My memories—why would a god go so far as to alter my memories? Lydia's memories?" I could not see the reasoning behind such contradictory action.

Doh hummed in thought, before she smiled uneasily. "Well, uh, not sure about the why, but I have a hunch that Lydia didn't forget."

"Of course she forgot; she would have told me something this important." The idea that she'd keep something like this from me was ridiculous.

"Really? No secrets between you?"

"Lydia kept secrets, had me keep secrets." Many, many secrets. "The one person she trusted everything with is . . . was me."

The shape-shifter shrugged. "A prophecy has to be known to someone. It's kind of like a tree falling in the woods; someone has to be around to hear it."

"I was around to hear it."

"You were around to forget it."

A bit of old, familiar anger crept into the back of my mind, an acrid frustration that I knew was not healthy. I needed to meditate on this, clear my thoughts, before I fell prey to it and paid back Doh's kindness with words that could not be taken back.

I returned to a simpler concern. "Why would a god do this?"

"Iunno, why did the Depth of Death help the Warlock King?"

"They did not."

Doh blinked. "Really? Fuck, someone should have told the Church of Radiance that."

Someone had wanted to; we all had. And yet, that was out of my hands now. I wasn't proud of not speaking up at the end of the war, but when the Velbruns needed to muddy the water . . .

"Perhaps someone will." The words were weak and promiseless, even to my own ears. Regardless, it was not like there were many followers of the Depth of Death to redeem in the eyes of the public any longer.

My companions had stayed quiet at the behest of Lydia, but perhaps that promise would fray now that she had passed.

If I was being honest, my concern for broken promises paled in comparison to a god playing with my mind.

Perhaps it was time to send another letter.

Deep in thought on the steps of my abode, I felt my heart beat with a sense of hope and dread, even hours after I had met with the postmaster.

And then, thankfully, a call distracted me.

"Rakta!" Orion's form came over the hill to the keep. He looked bedraggled, and his clothes looked slightly torn.

I took swift steps to meet him halfway, feeling the urgency in his steps. "What is it, what's happened?"

"There's a fight in the village center! Joseph tried to calm it down before it got out of hand, but there's no stopping it now!"

I idly registered the name of the tavern keep, my mind going to all the brawls that I had been swept up in due to the words of a drunkard or my more excitable companions. Now, I had to be the one to break it up.

This, I thought, was the duty of a lord, I supposed.

"Lead me." I began walking, my pace as fast as I could go without leaving Orion behind. "What is this fight about?"

Property conflicts and ancient grudges could be the motivator for a murder or some other darker offense, but bar fights rarely began due to rational reasons.

Orion flinched. "I, uh, well, I couldn't say exactly, but I know a lot of the Varnedoe and Ascott families are both involved."

The Ascott family? I thought back to Mary and her skill with the keep's horses. I certainly couldn't let any of her brothers or uncles be hurt in this madness.

My mind flashed to Helen Varnedoe. I didn't like the woman at all, nor did she have any love lost for me, but I still wouldn't allow her relatives to be maimed.

"I'll rush ahead and handle this." Every second I took was another moment for the fight to escalate to the point that someone got truly hurt.

With a burst of Vitae, I left Orion's side and made my way to the village center.

"You son of a whore!" The sounds of fists meeting flesh greeted me as I rushed onto the scene, the crowd of Gelvurt's people quickly moving away from my arrival.

The two present guards, both of whom had been keeping on the edge of the fray and trying to curtail the brawlers, helped herd the audience to a safer distance.

As Orion had warned me, the Ascotts, a family of shorter, black-haired Certillians, were currently battling with the redheads of the Varnedoes.

I had not, however, expected the matriarch of the Varnedoes to be in fray.

She rammed into the side of an unsuspecting Ascott, grabbing the man by his clothes before flinging him over her shoulders and into the dirt. "Stay down! Before I put you down for good!"

The Ascott man glared up at her, groaning in pain from the ground.

"Enough!"

My Vitae filled the clearing as my roar echoed off the nearby buildings, the combatants flinching and stumbling as the command reached their ears.

I watched as every man and woman involved, even Helen, turned to look at me as I stood, the dust having yet to even settle around my feet from my arrival. Some smiled, as if they thought themselves in the clear, some flinched, as if my wrath were certain.

My head on a swivel, I took in the crowd. Bloodied lips, bruises, and assuredly some aches that'd make themselves apparent in the coming days. These were farmers; they gained nothing from taking themselves out of commission.

"Who wants to explain," I began, "what happened here?"

Gazes shied away from me, even some grown men who seemed finally possessed with enough rationality to be ashamed of their actions.

"Just a fight, my lord," one of the young Ascott boys said, spitting some blood onto the ground along with one of his teeth.

I nodded, expecting an answer like that. "Just a fight. Does a fight often go out of its way to involve the majority of two of the most prosperous, competitive families in my lands?"

There was silence. I hadn't been aware of any deep grudges between the two bloodlines, but I had no doubts they could be lying just under the surface after so many years.

Helen stepped up, her expression set in a stern frown. "Just send the boys off; we can handle this between the heads of the family, elsewhere."

A cursory glance revealed no fatalities from the fight. Taking a peek inside the tavern revealed no different, other than Joseph looking frustrated over the remains of a few broken chairs.

"Next time"—I looked back at Helen and the few Ascott and Varnedoe men loitering around—"do not allow this to escalate. We'll meet to discuss this tomorrow."

I had to review what I knew about the property lines of the two families and any documents pertaining to past difficulties, but I doubted I'd find anything of worth. Something else I could blame on the previous Lord Velbrun.

All I knew for certain, in this whole debacle, was someone was paying for those chairs.

21

There was a room within the heart of my keep that I suspected saw very little use until today, an assumption I gathered from the many revelations of Zactrik's true nature.

In it, a long table rested with a silken covering of the green-and-gold colors of House Velbrun spread across it, a set of candelabras arranged up and down the meeting table.

I sat in a chair at the end of the table, the largest, most ornate chair in the room. The light from the midday sun fell on my shoulders from the single small window behind me.

Before me, on either side of the long table, sat Helen Varnedoe and Robert Ascott, the heads of the brawling families. Both had come alone; neither looked happy to be here. Although, I had yet to see Helen happy to be anywhere.

"We're here today," I began, "to speak of the fight that occurred yesterday. You've both had time to speak to your kinfolk. Who wishes to have the floor first?"

Robert looked over at the Varnedoe matriarch across from him. "If I may, Helen?"

"Go ahead." She seemed distinctly unconcerned about all this pomp and circumstance. It was not my preference, either, but with so many injuries, something had to be done.

Not to mention, I did not wish to risk the chance of the elders of House Velbrun claiming I was not performing my due diligence as the local lord in keeping the peace between the families of my land.

Turning to me, Robert's lips thinned. He was well-dressed, as much as the local trade would allow. Unlike Helen, he had actually made an effort to clean himself up for the meeting.

"Yesterday"—he coughed, a touch of embarrassment to his cheeks—"members of the Ascott family were the instigators of a fight that got out of hand."

I blinked. "Are you sure of this?"

Truly, I had not been expecting one of the families to readily admit their own fault. I was much more used to the back-and-forth of leadership that readily contested any hint that blame fell anywhere near them or their people.

"A member of my family, David Ascott, made a rude remark regarding Ms. Varnedoe here and her brother, Ben, responded in kind." He shook his head, as if he was there watching all of it go down before him.

Helen spoke up. "He called 'em a dustkisser. Everyone knows he slept with one of 'em that tumbled their way across the border for ah week before heading back. Good riddance, I say."

Robert let out a slow breath of air that wheezed its way out of his pursed lips. I, myself, was simply stunned at the absolute gall of the woman.

She turned to me, as if waiting for me to let the offense rest where she had placed it.

I looked over to Robert, my stomach turning. "And this started the fight?"

"Yes, my lord." The Ascott patriarch firmly agreed. "David threw the first punch. I won't try to deny that."

Considering that for a moment, I nodded. For her comment, I wanted to simply hand off any and all punishment to the Varnedoes and their continued distaste for all things noble and Ruskan.

"Robert, the Ascott family will be paying for the repairs to the tavern." I gave a firm nod to the patriarch, getting one back in return. "Please speak with Joseph about the exact costs."

To do that, however, I thought went beyond the realms of what I was here to do. I was not here to reward the family that was less subtle about their lack of respect.

No, that was an issue to be handled separately.

"I'll do it on my way back to the farm." The man seemed content with the punishment. It was really the least he could do.

"Then you are dismissed."

Robert stood up and made to leave, Helen following suit as she pushed her chair back to stand up.

I held up a hand. "Helen, sit down. We need to talk."

"I'm not getting any younger, my lord," Helen said, my title a mocking little addition she gave to the end of her words. "Did what my brother say get under your skin? I thought you Ruskies had thicker skin."

A part of me wondered if she knew that I was, at my core, a reasonable person who would not slay another simply because of some offensive language. Otherwise, I could not imagine what she hoped to accomplish with this.

I shook my head. "I hope to take as little time as possible, Helen. The last time we spoke, we shared some words."

Most of them consisted of her bad-mouthing me and saying outright that she wanted nothing to do with my children. At the time, I wasn't familiar with the Varnedoe family, nor were they familiar with me.

"Out with it." She leaned back into her seat.

I looked her square in the eyes. "Very well then. I can understand where your dislike comes from for the Ruskan people. I've heard that bandits from across the border were involved in the death of your husband."

Helen tensed, crossing her arms, but said nothing as I let the words linger in the air.

"And yet," I continued, "my understanding of your reasons and my experience with such sentiments before have prepared me for such a thing. Your family obviously does not appreciate my authority."

If she agreed with that, she made no obvious sign.

"My children, however, are innocent. They have not been ridiculed yet for their heritage." It was a fine blessing that I wished to retain as they grew up. "So let me put this very plainly."

The thrum of my Vitae picked up, filling the room with my presence, Helen growing pale as her body began to naturally shake and shiver from the pressure filling the room. It was an expected reaction to suddenly feeling like a large predator was staring you down.

"Insult me all you like, but never forget that I am Lord Velbrun of Gelvurt." I began easily, my true concern having little to do with my lordly title. "And if I ever hear a single word of derision against my children from the Varnedoe family, Helen, that will be when you need to worry. You will not be dealing with the lord of these lands, if that happens. You'll be dealing with me, their father."

And I would be unkind to those who thought to treat my children the way that I had been for my entire life within the empire.

Helen held her locked gaze for a moment longer before she peeled it off, looking away with a disgruntled look on her face.

"Do we have an understanding?" I leaned in, making sure that I spoke clearly for the Certillian widow.

She nodded her head, one jerky, rough motion. "I understand."

"Good, you are dismissed."

As she left, I sighed, letting my Vitae recede from the entirety of the meeting room. I was sure the situation was not over, but a lord's job was never truly done.

I had other things to attend to.

I was hot and sweaty, having been dancing in the sun for over an hour now. And yet, the movement was nice and gave my mind a chance to clear from the weeks of disturbed thoughts.

My mind had been endlessly cluttered with Doh's revelations and the messy politics of Gelvurt for far too long.

And nothing cleared the mind like a good spar.

"**Swordspear Technique!**" Dresden thrust forward, his Vitae-infused body shifting toward me across the dirt as he extended his blade toward me.

I deftly dodged, grabbing the blade with the crook of my Vulture Axe and tossing the blow to the side, moving in closer.

"Fuck!" Dresden tried to move, but stilled as I gently placed the cold steel of my weapon an inch away from his neck.

"Call the time." I wasn't even winded.

Kingsley checked the hourglass where he sat outside the fenced training arena. "About three minutes, my lord."

I backed off of the boy, his cheeks reddened from frustration. "You're getting better, but you need to polish your basics."

"I'm falling behind, so I need to start at the very beginning," Dresden huffed. "Great advice, my lord."

I ignored the snark, noticing he'd certainly been listening to my advice. It had been a few weeks since Dresden had come to me asking for lessons. As he was one of the few guards stationed here in Gelvurt, I thought it important to aid where I could.

I was not entirely selfless, of course. Dresden was often the guard of my children while I was away. The stronger he became, the safer my children were.

And yet, while he had come far, Dresden seemed very upset by his own perceived lack of progress.

"Come on, Dresden, who are you so concerned about outpacing you? Charles?" Kingsley called out from the sidelines.

The young guard spit on the ground. "Charles couldn't outpace molasses."

He didn't truly answer the question, instead getting back into a stance, but I made no similar motion.

Instead, I sheathed my axes. "It's getting late. I need to return to the keep and check on my children."

Dresden gritted his teeth, and for a moment I thought he was going to argue, but he eventually nodded. "Yeah, of course. Thanks for the spar."

He sheathed his blade and left the training field, looking exhausted and unsatisfied.

"That kid, he's got too much of his father in him." Kingsley came up and handed me a towel for my sweat.

I dried off, looking off to where Dresden had walked off to. "His father?"

"Yeah, he was a guard once, when Dresden was just a child, my lord. Good with a blade, had a bit of a temper. It, uh, didn't end well for him, I'm afraid."

My thoughts went back to Dresden's warning on the night of Vera's death.

I was going to ask more, but the sound of a loud, achingly familiar trumpet blew through the air. Another Velbrun had come to Gelvurt.

"I wasn't expecting you to come."

"I wasn't expecting you to write me a letter. You shaved?"

I reached up to feel my smoother cheeks, tamer than before. "It was heavily suggested that I keep my beard trimmer."

Daka and Natakia seemed to like the change as well.

Markus, Lydia's brother, gazed at me with a familiar anger, but it was older now, time and distance having perhaps quelled his intense dislike of me. And yet, the gaze bore into me with many questions, some that I may not be ready or able to answer.

"I have questions"—I looked to the side, shifting uncomfortably—"that no one else can answer."

"It's about our family then." He had never included me like this before. It was almost suspicious, but a spark of hope lit in my chest.

I had certainly never been against getting closer with my brother-in-law.

I nodded. "Yes, but first, would you like to see your nieces and nephew?"

22

R uh." Natakia was glaring at Markus. I had just introduced the younglings to him, seeing as their uncle had been unwilling to spend any time in the same room as them when they'd been born.

"So, these are Lydia's kids."

Markus's gaze was warm, warmer than I had expected, as he carefully let the children, mostly Daka, curiously play with his fingers. My little warrior seemed delighted to have new fingers to play with, gripping onto them with not a worry in the world.

Whereas Dalton was cautious of the stranger, Natakia seemed to be instantly discomforted by his presence, twisting in her bed and trying to shy away from his hands. I'd never seen her react to somebody so negatively before.

To be honest, it put me on edge. I trusted my children's instincts. It was said a Ruskan child could almost sense danger whipping about on the desert wind.

"Yes, they resemble her, don't they?" It was the most charming thing about them, truly, the gifts their mother had given them before she passed.

He nodded, admiring Daka's sparkling blue eyes, Dalton's silvery tufts of hair, and Natakia's paler skin. While I loved my children for many reasons, these inherited traits of their mother's were certainly one of my most treasured.

Markus turned away from them, looking at me. "I'm glad to see them in good health. I wasn't sure if you'd manage."

Perhaps a friendly jab from another's lips, but the words came with audible barbs. Perhaps I had gotten ahead of myself regarding the age of his distaste.

It seemed as young and fresh as ever.

"I had help," I admitted. Although certainly none had come from the Velbruns. "It takes an entire tribe to raise children right."

And even then, mistakes were always around the corner.

Markus was quiet for a moment, his eyes watching the children. "So, you had questions?"

"Let's speak in my office." Motioning him out of the room, I signaled Doh to continue with her duties with a nod as I headed for the door.

Markus passed a glance to my shape-shifting maid, before nodding. "As you wish."

He was quiet as he mulled over what I had revealed to him. I had not trusted him with the details of the prophecy, only the existence of said prophecy, still unsure of what to make of Lydia's brother at this moment.

Truly, I was not inclined to reveal the whole prophecy to anyone, with it undoubtedly having to do with my children in some regard. The closest to learning the contents, Doh, had wanted nothing to do with it.

I did not blame her. I barely wanted anything to do with it, and yet, it must be handled by someone.

"A prophecy." Markus's first words since I had laid out the strange circumstances surrounding the strange, god-given insight that Lydia had procured.

I was hesitant to reveal the mere existence of a prophecy to another Velbrun, the whole lot of them having a fascination with the future, but only they would have an inkling about what had happened.

"After Lydia used the spell, one I'd never heard before," I added, "a bright light flashed, and, well, I've only just now remembered the experience, the prophecy."

Lydia's brother leaned forward in his chair. "**Boundless Prognostication** is a Velbrun secret, an ancient spell that is known by only the elder Velbruns and their most trusted."

The elder Velbruns' most trusted? "I was under the impression Lydia was the farthest one could get from trusted by the Velbruns."

"After she left and came back, yes, few Velbruns would have trusted her with the local gossip, much less an ancient spell." Markus lightly rolled his head. "Before she left . . ."

The man took a sip of his wine, seeming to be considering his words. Lydia had mentioned that her initial departure from the family had not been a pleasant one.

"She was a prodigy, heralded as the next Velbrun Oracle, a title we have not had granted for decades, possibly a century."

I frowned. "I knew she was talented, but she never mentioned she had such acclaim with her family. How did I not hear of this before?"

"Once you're a black sheep of the Velbruns, no one knows about you anymore. I'm sure there are some out there who aren't even aware I had siblings." The nonchalance in his words sent a chill up my spine.

Lydia had received the same treatment as Dalton? How had I not noticed?

I grimaced. "This family is cruel."

"Be careful, Rakta. Our family has given you a title and land. I doubt that House Kire would have been as compassionate to your plight in a similar situation." The glint in Markus's gaze was near malicious.

The words did nothing to help my souring mood. The Kires were known for their harsh stance against those from Rusk.

I kept my breathing careful. It would not do me well to rise to Markus's taunts or threats.

"Be that as it may," I pushed onward, "my memories were suppressed. Does this spell involve the gods to a great degree?"

His tone taking on a more scholarly tone, Markus coughed. "Yes, well, from what I know, yes. The spell is a remnant from a time when gods moved through mortals more directly."

Markus's eyes twinkled as the symbol of the Velbruns suddenly appeared in a subdued magical light arrangement.

"Some Velbruns," Markus mused, "have even reported the spell to be less of something a mere mortal casts and instead a god's spell that simply requires a mortal vessel primed for the ritual."

"And my memories?" I felt resignation building up in the back of my throat. A god was involved, after all? Truly, my children were burdened in this life.

"Prophecies are sacred, private things, held only by the one that is used by the spell. While we certainly don't have documented evidence of its casting, stories go that observers are exempt from remembering the process." Markus took another sip of his wine.

Leaning back in my seat, I considered the main implication of all of this: Lydia had known, well and truly, that this prophecy existed and had never told me of it.

Feeling old, older than my bones and flesh truly were, I gazed at a nearby wall. "Why didn't she tell me?"

"Should she have?" Markus's voice was a light whisper, sounding like the rattling of a snake.

My gaze snapped to him. "It would have been appreciated. This . . . prophecy is difficult, something I do not fully understand."

Markus smiled; at some point the aged anger in his eyes had become renewed. "Perhaps she knew you wouldn't. Perhaps she couldn't trust you with something this important after you killed our brother."

I flinched. "That was—"

"We had a plan, Rakta. A great plan, one that would have worked. A plan that Lydia and I poured our blood, sweat, and tears into, and it took you but a moment to make it crumble." Markus looked ready to murder me.

The sounds of Lydia's anguished screams echoed in the back of my mind.

And yet, I remained stalwart and looked him squarely in the eyes. "Then why didn't she tell you?"

Markus looked struck for a moment, blinking. "I . . ."

He fell quiet, following me in a long, drawn-out moment of silence. Did either of us deserve to be told of this prophecy? Had Lydia even told anyone? Did she have others she trusted more than us?

Would we even know if she did?

The only thing I was sure of was that I loved my wife. I was confident in her decisions, even if I did not truly understand them or know of all of them.

My sigh broke the silence. "Thank you, for answering my questions."

"You're welcome. Perhaps you could return the favor by revealing the prophecy to me?" Markus's gaze had a glint of steel in it, as if daring me to deny him.

I dared.

"No, I don't believe I will."

He bristled. Would this make it harder for me? Most likely. And yet, the idea of the Velbruns wanting a prophecy that only I knew . . . It may be the only thing I'd have as a defense if they got personally involved.

Another moment of silence passed.

"I'd like to talk about something else, then, Rakta." Markus had an air about him now, as if he was suddenly towering over me in his superiority.

I motioned for him to go on. Perhaps he was going to move to the discussion of the monthly taxes? Gelvurt had been managing to meet quotas, from what I had seen from the reports.

He smiled. I did not like it.

"The elders of House Velbrun have made a decision regarding your children."

The carriage rode off, surrounded by the personal guard that had escorted it to Gelvurt in the first place. The glimpse of Markus smiling at me was the last I saw of my brother-in-law.

He'd left me answers and some disturbing questions, but most of all, he'd left me with a choice.

The heads of House Velbrun had asked for one of my children.

To preserve the heritage of their bloodline, of Lydia's exceptional potential, they wanted to educate and raise one of them in Velbrun. Provide for one of them, according to the elders, an opportunity to excel where their mother had failed.

Somehow more insulting than the slight against my wife, Markus had the audacity to ask me to choose immediately, and had even intended to leave with one of them today.

I had made it extremely clear how unlikely that was.

And so, he had left. No matter how protected he thought himself to be, he would not dare try to take one of them by force while I was around.

"House Velbrun wants to take my children." I spoke to Doh standing at my side. "They sent me away and wanted to reel my children back in, leaving me with nothing."

"Fucking dicks." Doh's eyes burned with emotion as she watched them go. She'd had to clean up the slight display of force I'd needed to show to get Markus to realize the gravity of my displeasure with the Velbruns.

"If I don't comply, I know they'll get more forceful, draw on other legal means." Anger simmered in my voice. "Perhaps even resort to off-the-books kidnapping attempts."

"They'd really get away with doing that to a hero who fought the Warlock King?"

"I'm not one for the public eye. I don't have the presence that my companions do, and . . . my skin would put me at a disadvantage."

"Damn."

I nodded. "Damn, indeed."

We watched the sunset as the carriages disappeared into the distance. Eventually, they were gone, and the moon had risen to take the sun's place.

How long had we been standing here? I needed to go check on my children. I needed to see them after today, after the revelations and the threats.

As I turned to head inside, Doh surprised me with a comforting hand on my shoulder. "Don't worry, Rakta. They're not taking these kids without a fight."

Surprised at the determination, I glanced at her. "You would fight for my kids?"

"Eh, probably. They're just too cute, what can I say?" She shrugged, smiling.

Feeling light at her familiar irreverence, I managed to chuckle. It was nice to know that my relationship with the once identity thief had come far. "Well, I appreciate— Get down!"

I pushed Doh out of the way, sending her flying toward a nearby pile of hay, as the night sky suddenly cracked and shattered into pieces, sending an unbearable wave of magical pressure headed straight for me.

I moved to dodge, but the ground underneath me suddenly shattered into pieces, leaving me vulnerable for just a moment.

Long enough for Ulric's signature magic to slam into me with the force of a bull.

23

Ulric was from Fjord, a coastal nation embedded in the cold northern lands across the Crest Sea that invested itself into the art of war and battle.

A land composed of clans and families that held a deep appreciation for pushing the boundaries of warfare, not purely for the act of waging war, but simply the performance of battle. A battlefield or arena to them was as a painter might see an empty canvas.

To that end, there was a notion that a Fjordic warrior could make any spell or technique into a weapon given enough time.

As I caught my breath, my entire body shaking from the impact of Ulric's magic, I certainly felt the truth of such a statement. I could feel the light fractures in my bones healing, my torn muscles screaming at me as my Vitae pumped through me quickly.

"Ah, Rakta, I didn't see you there, my friend." Ulric's form crept from the forest line, his muscular body an indistinct shadow in the moonlit night.

My Vitae thrummed, and I began to channel the beginnings of the **Great Wind Sprint Technique** into my recovering muscles, a necessary act they certainly did not appreciate.

Additionally, I gathered up the rest of my Vitae and circulated it through my body in other areas for my **Instinctive Reflex Technique** and **Skip Dash Technique**.

Outrunning and dodging Ulric was the only way to truly last in a fight with him. Taking even a single hit wasn't good for one's health, my body reminded me.

"Ulric, I heard Penelope was going to . . . inform you. I'd ask you not to hurt my maid, if you could." My voice was strained, still lacking a bit of breath to it.

Doh groaned from where I had thrown her, her form swallowed up by the hay pile she'd landed in. It was far better than being paste splattered against the side of my keep.

It struck me that, had I been just a few seconds slower, Ulric would have very likely killed Doh.

"Don't you trust me, Rakta." Ulric's voice was decidedly untrustworthy at this moment. "I can rein myself in quite fine."

The air in front of me shattered, releasing a deadly burst of air pressure that fractured the ground I had just been standing on before I blurred away.

"I see you're as fast as ever, my friend." He sounded amused, but the undercurrent of anger was familiar. Ulric would joke with even his most hated of enemies, but I had never personally been on the receiving end of his jovial edge.

I'd never thought I'd be deserving of it, frankly. And yet, here I was, dodging one of my oldest friend's sincere attempts at hurting me, having to listen to him joke around like old times.

It felt wrong.

I took a deep breath, feeling my air come back to me as my body finally recovered. Dodging Ulric's attacks was difficult, his wordless shatter magic able to come from anywhere at any angle.

I relaxed my arms and legs and settled into a different stance, a simple but effective **Grace Stance**, and observed Ulric as he came into the moonlight.

"You look quite serious, my friend. Something wrong?" He chuckled, talking with me as easily as if we were sharing a meal.

With long, braided blond hair that came down to his hip and a simple cloth-tunic-and-pants outfit, Ulric was a large man. Standing a few inches taller than I, he had not taken being gifted in magic as reason to forgo physical fitness.

I frowned. "Can we take this elsewhe—" I blurred out of the way of another attack, sending up dust and dirt a second before only a crater remained where I'd been standing.

"—re? I have—" Another shattering, another blurred dash moments before it hit me.

"—sleeping younglings." At this, I watched the man, tense for the beginnings of new shatterings. Truly, Ulric was a terrifying magician, able to use his magic without any sound or movement.

He had stopped, however, the night obscuring his expression. "Younglings? Penelope mentioned you had a family now."

The keep, I noticed, he was looking over at the keep. Where my children were trying to sleep after meeting their snake of an uncle.

I nodded. "I do. It has been a stressful day. I'd like to give them peace tonight."

"Peace?" Ulric moved closer, smiling as if I was joking. "Hmm, sure. Come, friend, let's find somewhere else to settle this."

I nodded and made to move toward the forest, feeling confident that Ulric would not attack for the moment, as another voice broke through.

"Uh, Rakta, are you going to be okay?" Doh had finally managed to climb out of the hay pile with her wits about her, calling out to me with a hint of concern in her voice.

I called back, "Make sure the children are sleeping well. I'll be fine."

Even a struggle such as this would be easier to deal with knowing that my children were being kept safe in my absence. I did not put it past the Velbruns to somehow use this to their advantage with their insights into the future.

"Widower for only half a year, and you've already got women after you again, eh?" Ulric's jest wasn't appreciated, but I channeled my frustration at the joke into my Vitae, letting it thrum.

Looking back at him, I frowned. "Come with me."

"Not going to use your axes?" Ulric stood thirty paces away from me, his voice raised for me to hear it.

I kept my Vitae thrumming, my techniques still flowing through me. "I will not need them for this, Ulric."

"You think you can beat me without weapons?" His voice was colder now, like Fjordic winds. Ulric was not fond of the idea of holding back, for better or worse.

"This isn't about beating you." I certainly felt no desire to hurt him. "I don't want to hurt a friend."

"Ah, I see. So, you're just going to be running away again, Rakta?" There was a violent edge to his jovial tone. I could see his smile from this distance, and it was not kind.

Out of a fight, I may have flinched, but my body remained lax, my mind ready. "I ran away for a reason then, Ulric, as I am running away right now. I don't want to hurt you."

"Then maybe I'll hurt your kids." He said it casually, like a cloud in the sky had caught his interest.

I stilled, unprepared for the idea. I knew, rationally, that Ulric would never hurt a child. He was speaking from anger and hurt, and yet . . .

And yet, I pulled a pair of my Vulture Axes off of my belt. I was tired of people bringing my children into the business they had with me. Mere infants did not need the weight of my mistakes, my past, pressing upon them.

"Ah, the Dancer has finally shown his teeth!" Ulric's satisfied tone only irritated me further. As if this were a game he had mocked me into playing with him.

My Vitae thrummed as I drew from it more, replacing the relaxed gait of the **Grace Stance** with the familiar **Dancing Star Stance**.

". . . Ah, still taking it easy on me, eh?"

Ulric rumbled, or rather, the world around Ulric rumbled. Cracks in reality began to creep across the sky and the ground, fissures that the shatter magician guided into existence.

"I will not be doing the same, my friend." His tone was grim, that of Ulric the World Breaker.

I was glad I had taken my enraged companion far away from Gelvurt, for this battle would leave the land scarred for years.

As I took my first high-speed step in this torrid dance of arms, the entire world crashed against me.

Shatter magic, from what I understood, was rooted in the same schools of magic that mending magic was. An inversion, really, of putting things back together, shatter magic took them apart.

Perhaps, in a less determined man's hands, it would have been limited to breaking apart simple structures or solid objects that the magician's magic pulled apart.

As I flipped and dashed through the air, using my **Air Dance Technique**, I was reminded that Ulric was not lacking in determination.

"Run, dusty feet, run!" Ulric shattered the space in front of me, sending me flipping through the air to dodge the barely aimed rush of pressure.

I reared back midflip, throwing out a Vulture Axe into a quick spiral that headed straight for Ulric's center mass.

Ulric grinned, not even deigning to move from his spot. "Ha ha!"

The air shattered right in front of him, breaking the Vulture Axe's momentum and sending it flying into the distance before it began to naturally come back to my hand as I landed on the air.

Ulric didn't move when he fought, not really. He shattered anything that got close, and that was, more often than not, enough. Still, he wasn't used to dodging.

So if he took a hit, he usually took it head-on. A practice that the average magician would balk at.

I sighed. "I don't like fighting you, Ulric."

"You didn't like leaving, either, I bet, but you still did it, yeah?" The Fjordic man's words were merciless.

Letting my Vitae surge, I let my **Swift Throw Technique** coalesce within my arms, and suddenly all six of my Vulture Axes were flying through the air.

Ulric watched them with interest, his fingers twitching, before I pulled on my **Dancing Star**–influenced Vitae.

And the axes began to dance as they fell from the sky like shooting stars.

Self-driven spirals that dodged the very air they flew through as Ulric shattered the sky, trying to throw off their trajectory. I had to keep moving, shatterings thrown my way, as well, but he couldn't ignore my axes.

Each of my axes moved with my own finesse, possessed by my will, and I danced with them, dodging just as they did, getting closer and closer to Ulric. A whirlwind of movement and metal that would eventually overwhelm the sedentary shatterer.

As one axe neared, Ulric's eyes flashed, the air around the axe shattering and throwing it to the side, before he gasped in pain.

Another Vulture Axe, having danced into a blind spot, ripped into his shoulder before it glowed a deep, deep blue.

And erupted into ice.

"Gaah!" Ulric quickly ripped the heavy-layered ice off his shoulder, taking skin and muscle with it and letting the blood run free.

As the rest of my axes fell toward him in similar not-fatal spots, I realized, far too slowly, that the air of the battle had suddenly changed.

"Derra, I demolish, **Shatter Thy World**." Ulric's form glowed, and my axes stilled as the world shuddered in a new, foreboding way.

It was only instinct that sent me sprinting into the distance, as far as my few seconds allowed me. The world around Ulric broke into one large crack, shearing through air.

And my Vulture Axes.

The sound of air imploding filled the empty space, my eardrums crying out at the sheer noise of the attack. The sound of rending metal could barely be heard over the crack.

Relatively unharmed by the attack, managing to make it away from the epicenter, I still felt the tingling of my skin from the sheer destructive force of the spell.

And yet, that was not what stilled my heart.

I dropped to the ground, stepping solemnly through the air, as I came close to examine the remnants of my weapons, their scattered remains dug deep into the cracked earth and surroundings. They were ripped apart, rent completely asunder by the destructive spell.

Even Ulric quieted, blood dripping from his wound, as we both ignored the earthen crater he now stood in and looked at the scrap that remained of my axes.

The ones Lydia had made for me, had poured parts of her magic into. A magic that she had burned in order to have precious moments with our children.

"Rakta . . . I'm sorry; we can get, uh, get Penelope to fix them."

A magic that no longer walked upon Derra.

I met Ulric's gaze, feeling something large uncoil inside of my core. "Penelope cannot bring my wife back."

My Vitae hummed as I moved with the wind and the gaze of the moon, the heat of the sun, the rising tide, and the beginnings of a maelstrom.

For that was the way of the **First Dance Stance**.

24

As Ulric's eyes widened, as he got back into his own readied stance, the anger in my bones cried for war and bloodshed. Everything was tinted in red, in Lydia.

I was tired of Markus and the Velbrun family, tired of their chains around me growing tighter and tighter. I was tired of how they saw my children as assets of their arrogant family, stepping stones to further their beloved greatness.

I was frustrated by my allies, my former traveling companions. This guilt I felt for abandoning them when they perhaps needed me most, for chaining them down with promises, had eaten at me for years, and yet they still sought to attack me further?

And perhaps, most distant of all, I was confused and lost in grief. Had Lydia seen this coming? Had she known what tribulations I would face without her? Why had she not trusted me with the truth? Why did I have to face this alone?

"First Dance Technique." I funneled all my heartbreak, all my anger into the roaring maelstrom of my Vitae. **"Twister Through the Valley."**

"Wait, Rak—"

I was gone to the wind, a thick wave of air crashing around me as I moved forward with the speed and ferocity of a twister, destroying everything in my path. The crater I dashed across was scarred, dirt and stone flying around me as I lifted my fist up into the air, coming down on him.

Ulric threw up his arms, attempting to shatter the air I had brought forth upon him, but it was suffused with my Vitae and would not bend to his attempts to break it, break me.

He flew back as the air hit him, cuts and tears beginning to tatter his tunic and skin, small, shallow wounds that let the blood flow.

His arm in tatters, soaking in blood, Ulric looked for me in the storm. "Rakta, fuck . . . !"

I felt free, riding the air and the storm I had brought it to, a massive cyclone that was just as much a part of me as I was a part of it. I was unrestrained in this moment, released from my mortal doubts, allowing me to, perhaps, find the calm within the storm.

And yet, it only allowed my rage to flourish more so.

"Derra, I demolish," Ulric began uttering the magical incantation, focusing his Mana. "**Shatt**— Urk!"

As if I would let him even attempt to shatter the vengeance I had wrought.

My fist was suddenly embedded into his stomach, blood splattering from his lips as he registered the cracking sounds coming from his ribs.

I growled into his ear, barely audible over the rushing cyclone around us, "You come here, threaten my children—"

Another punch to the chest sent his large frame flying. I had the momentum of a storm behind me; physical strength and speed meant nothing right now to me. Trees bent to my presence, and even the strongest castle would crumble to my rage.

I was there in a moment's gasp, catching his flying form in a headlock and pushing his face into the dirt. "—mock my faith and loyalty to Lydia—"

Picking him up, I threw him into the wall of wind that had formed around us, the cyclone whipping him around until it sent my old friend straight back into my waiting fist.

Knocking him to the ground with a solid fist to the chin, I stared down at him, speaking with the tempest. "—and destroy some of my last vestiges of her! And you think I'll just turn the other cheek!?"

Ulric's eyes flashed with anger, his voice tired but strong with determination. "Ya abandoned us, leaving us to clean up a mess that Lydia made. Good people died, Rakta!"

Lydia had died. The most wondrous person in all my life, the light guiding my path, had died.

I felt my anger skyrocket, my foot raised above his chest. "Then I guess neither of us have been good friends." It was time to end this for good.

He looked up at me, his eyes shining with acceptance. There was no fear in the Fjordic man's gaze. "Are ya going to kill me, Rakta?"

I was. I was going to kill him. I was going to kill him and take my children somewhere they would never be bothered by anyone ever again. The mountains, Rusk, wherever.

I had to break these chains that the world had wrapped around me, these terrible bonds that kept me from my children's future. The chains that threatened to strangle them in their infancy.

My Vitae, tinged by the ferocity of the storm, begged me to do it.

"Then do it quick." Ulric closed his eyes. "I've tired of living these past few months."

He had spells that could stop me, terribly fast, land-crushing spells that would equal my storm. I had seen them in action, had seen them tear fissures into Derra's horizons.

I had not beaten him into submission; he had simply given up.

"I have faces I want to see."

Ulric was not afraid to die. He welcomed it.

My Vitae sensed the decision in my heart before I had even truly recognized it. The cyclone around me began to fade, the roaring thrum of the storm fading into the gentle whistle of nighttime.

Exhaustion hit me as my Vitae relaxed from the **First Dance Stance**, my techniques fading alongside my will to finish this fight. "I don't want to kill you, Ulric."

Ulric continued to simply lie on the dirt, his eyes still closed. There was no relief in his form as the storm halted, his life rescued by my sudden mercy. "Aye, neither do I want to kill you."

"You destroyed my axes." It was the most treacherous crime he had committed, but even now I felt too tired to truly express the anger I felt. It had been a long night.

"Aye, I did. I've broken lots of things, Rakta." Ulric's voice was soft, filled with memories of the things he'd ruined. "I'm sorry I can't put them back together, friend."

It was almost humorous, calling me a friend after all of this.

"Are we still friends? The things you said, the things you did." I did not feel like a friend. "I almost tried to kill you. How are we friends?"

"I don't know." Ulric shrugged. "I came here to see you again, like a big surprise, but when you got hit, when I actually hit ya, I don't know, it felt right. Maybe I came here just to hurt ya, to make you feel like we did."

I sat on the ground, my Vitae slowly thrumming as I digested his words and recuperated from the fight. "We?"

Ulric still hadn't moved from his spot on the ground. Did he plan to stay there all night?

"The war didn't end when the Warlock King died, Rakta." His lips tightened. "People he trusted, corrupted, still rampaged across parts of the empire, just not the Velbrun part of it."

I frowned, having heard little of any continued war efforts. Living in the heart of Velbrun, I had been informed of very little that the heads of the family did not wish for me to hear. Perhaps to be expected from a house known for controlling what their people did and didn't know.

"Who did we lose?"

"Piper, Gregory, Froschia, Wilfred . . . Birdy." The familiar names of past allies filtered through my mind, each of their stories having gathered dust. I had not thought of them for so long.

And yet, "Birdy?"

It was not a name I remembered, and yet Ulric spoke the name with more sentiment than I had ever truly heard from him. He was companionable to most, but he'd never gotten truly close to one person during our travels.

Ulric grumbled, "A magician, fresh recruit from one of House Saren's settlements. Young thing and didn't have much training at all. She has . . . had potential."

I looked down at my wedding band soaked in Ulric's blood. "I'm sorry. How?"

"Was struck by a boulder. I didn't shatter it in time. She couldn't . . . shatter something that big yet." The grief was palpable in his voice.

He was teaching her shatter magic? From what I knew, those from Fjord taught only those of their families. I . . . wasn't sure how to respond. If there was even, truly, a response to give.

And so, we sat in silence for a while, living in our own minds for the time being. So much had been said; so much had been done. Wounds that would not simply close overnight now littered my heart.

And yet, even at the heart of this tragic moment, I thought I felt somewhat at peace.

After Ulric had fallen asleep on the dirt, his wounds beginning to close after I applied some Vitae to them, I picked my way through the scrap that remained of my Vulture Axes.

They were scattered around, each enchanted piece of metal flickering in the darkness of the night. Even destroyed, their metal ruined, the remnants of their craftsmanship were obvious, and yet my eyes caught on one piece in particular.

One piece that flickered just a tiny bit brighter than the others.

I gathered up the scrap, placing it into a small leather bag, before approaching the brighter piece, and gasped as I knelt down to inspect it.

It was damaged, torn and shredded by Ulric's magic, but before me lay a mostly intact head of one of my Vulture Axes. It shimmered, the handle having been broken off and torn, but . . .

I picked it up gently, admiring it.

"Normal weapons aren't going to be enough, Rakta." Lydia had smiled. "We need you equipped with weapons that befit a man of your stature."

I could remember her looking adorably smug, tossing her hair back.

"Of course, I'll be personally making sure that their magic is a masterwork."

I stared at the shimmering Vulture head and placed it against my cheek, feeling the remnants of Lydia's magic within it. A hot wetness began to spill down my cheeks, and I let it flow.

The Velbruns had sent me on my way long before they held a funeral for Lydia, a private affair that only her closest relatives would attend. Not something they thought her husband deserving of.

And yet, with the remnants of Lydia's magic, her essence, within these broken pieces, perhaps I finally had something to bury myself.

"It's probably best that you left." Time and rest had given me enough energy to once more be angry at Ulric, my gaze filled with heat as I trained it on him.

It was the morning after, both of us having returned to the outskirts of town and nearing the edge of the comfortable distance I was okay with Ulric being near my children. The threat he'd paid them was still fresh in my mind.

He turned and watched the morning birds chirp. "Yeah, probably best . . . You know I wouldn't have hurt your kids, right? I . . . shouldn't have said that."

"I'd prefer if you didn't come back." I glared to emphasize my point, but softened it a moment after. "Not until I . . . I have time to think. I think we're both different people now, and I . . . I need to work out if those people can be friends again one day."

Ulric nodded, looking sad but understanding. "Friends or not, let me know if you ever need help from an idiot."

I hesitated for a moment, before I nodded.

With that, he began to walk away from Gelvurt, heading east, but stopped a few paces away. For a moment, I thought he'd changed his mind, was readying his magic to have one more round with me before he left.

And then he spoke, sounding old and bittersweet.

"I miss the good days."

I let silence reign, and, after a moment, Ulric continued on, disappearing into the forest.

I was nearing Velbrun Keep when I heard the distant crack of noise, almost like thunder, as Ulric began to throw himself across the empire with his magic.

Some things never changed.

25

Rakta,

I'm sending this letter by way of Ulric, so forgive me if you have to put the pieces back together because the hardheaded fool couldn't keep his magic under control.

I told him what you told me, so maybe he'll offer to help. I don't expect it though. He took it the worst when you left in the middle of the night.

Regardless, on to more important matters. We've had some more sightings of the creature you encountered up north, close to the mountains.

More concerning, we've also had some sightings of a wandering lord that resembles Zactrik in those parts.

We're getting together a team to investigate and deal with them, but I just wanted to let you know that the dangers seemed to have moved on from Gelvurt.

Between you and me, Rakta, I think this has something to do with that taxidermic necromancer you dealt with as well.

Let me know if you encounter anything else,

Penelope Iriend

P.S. Apparently, Doh didn't learn her lesson when she posed as you. I had to explain to one of my companions that it wasn't me flirting with him while we stayed at your keep.

Make sure that doesn't happen again.

I closed my eyes, feeling a bit of a headache coming on. And yet, it did not ruin the relief that I was feeling in my chest at the news my friend's letter had brought.

After Ulric had left, I had the pleasure of fighting back a number of surprisingly concerned questions from Doh. I would have been a bit suspicious of her protectiveness had she not been doing so while returning valuables to the halls of my inherited home.

Now, though, I was alone with my thoughts and Ulric's bloodstained letter from Penelope.

The soft breath of my sleeping children filled the quiet air of the nursery. With my troubled thoughts, it was easier to think clearly here with them. Physical proof that they were safe, that the Velbruns had not sneaked off with them during my fight with UIric.

I laid the letter down, leaning back in my chair. "Oh, Lydia, what do I do? Did you have any plans for this? You wanted to travel and teach our children about the world, but your family . . ."

Politically, I was inept. I knew only the bare minimum of the law within the empire, mostly for civilians and things related to taxes. Ruskan politics were more about the spirit than the letter, with some of the well-worded trickery ample in Certillian law edging toward dishonorable.

In the empire, however, the complicated twists and turns of a law were far more complex. Lydia had explained that very few laws had ever been decommissioned, so the whole system was a labyrinthian hallway of conflicting and overriding laws.

Perhaps, I could write a letter to Penelope? She was from House Iriend, yes? She would know the laws. And yet, she was quite busy herself. A part of me was somewhat hesitant to continue leaning on those I had abandoned, my own desires for aid poisoning any sense of the honest reconciliation I hoped for.

So no, I needed to do this myself, at least try.

Breaking my thoughts was the sudden, familiar start of Daka's breath, the only warning I got before she began to cry and wail into the night.

I was by her side in an instant, cradling her gently in my arms as the other two sets of bleary stares gazed up at me and their sister.

Daka's bright-blue eyes were so scared, almost glazed over with fear. What did she see? What horrors had her soul brought with it? I wondered, for a moment, if the terrors of Derra could even compare to what my daughter had experienced.

And yet, she soon relaxed in my grip, her wails dying out slowly as I whispered calming words to her and gently took her away from the terror that had taken her for a moment.

The tired smile she gave me, as bright as a smile could be in the middle of the night, made my heart lurch. I gave her a kiss on the forehead and gently placed her back down alongside her siblings, both of them looking relieved to have peace and quiet once more.

I stared down at all of them in their beds, feeling Lydia in the room with me. "The world is a hard place, little ones. Scary monsters and dangers abound."

Dalton sniffed, not looking very impressed by my warning, but Daka's eyes seemed to grow even brighter in the dark room. Of all my young listeners, it always felt like she hung on to my words the most.

Smiling, I gave Natakia and Dalton kisses on the forehead. "Stay strong together; love each other. No matter where you are, your bonds are always with you."

I pointed to my heart. These were words I needed as much as they did, even if they did not know it.

"Dah dah." Said heart almost stopped as Natakia spoke up, her words sounding somewhat frustrated with me. Out of all of them, she looked the most irritated at still being awake.

And yet, I couldn't help the rush of emotions that leaped at me at the almost words. It hadn't quite been there yet, but . . .

I was their father, and I wasn't going to give them up without a fight.

It was a warm day, the sun only barely hidden by clouds as Doh and I relaxed in the backyard of my keep, the grounds large and impressive and suitable for my needs.

"Is this really okay, Rakta?" When had Doh given up the pretense of calling me Lord Velbrun? I wasn't sure, but I hadn't heard her refer to me as such in weeks.

I certainly didn't mind having a friend during all of this.

Still, I nodded. "The Velbruns leave their graves unmarked as tradition, but nothing prohibits me from doing as I like."

House Velbrun could, of course, complain, but as they were already bordering on what my temper found acceptable by demanding one of my children, I doubted they would push me too much.

"Hey, you know this law stuff better than I do." Doh bounced Natakia in her grip, the baby looking pleased to be in her arms.

I almost chuckled. I had spent the last week reading the empire law books my office had come with, trying to find an answer to my problems. A pleasant side effect was learning about my rights of property.

And so, sitting down with Daka and Dalton resting in my lap, I smiled at the crude headstone I had carved from some nearby rock.

Lydia Gelna Velbrun

Above all else, a Dreamer.

It had taken only a day to get everything handled. Finding the perfect spot had been more a matter of my own pickiness, somewhere elevated so it did not wash away during the rainy season.

After finding the right spot, the scrap of my Vultures had been buried in the ground after only a few hours of digging.

I, myself, had kept the largest intact piece of Vulture that I had found after fighting with Ulric. I planned to get it refurbished, if possible. Not to fight with, but . . .

Something to help preserve my memories of Lydia. There was no getting her back, but to have a reminder of our time together, the greatest gift she had ever given me.

"Guh." Daka smiled up at me.

I corrected myself. The second-greatest gift she had ever given me.

All the while, Dalton silently stared at his mother's headstone.

"Thank you for helping me, Orion."

The general store owner shook his head. "This is the least I can do. Some in Gelvurt may not have the warmest reception toward you, but there's plenty of gratitude to go around."

His words make me think of a certain alchemist. I hadn't heard a word from her in some time. I hoped she was doing well.

Regardless, after stepping my foot into the bear trap that was Certillian law, I'd eventually had to call in some help with dealing with the complexities of the system.

Numbers were universal in Derra, making tax work and quotas easier, but the language? While neighbors, the empire had adopted Nevian from the Donns of Neve centuries ago, although plenty of their ancient laws were still written in their original Certillian.

The Rusks, however, had never abandoned our original tongue, Shahis, or the language of the winds. It was an oral language, the only writing involved mostly revolving around the complex musical notes that the musicians of our country had developed.

It was a beautiful language, truly. Nevian was a pragmatic, rigid language, but Shahis? It was evocative, almost like a song with every conversation a harmony.

Regardless, my inexperience meant that I did not have the most solid foundations of the written languages, Lydia's teachings aside. With Orion here, I hoped he might have better luck finding a loophole or answer to my problem.

"What about this lex that royal children cannot be unwillingly taken from their homes until the age of ten?"

I shook my head, dragging another book over. "A ruling made years later made it so that the royal cities of each house were included in the definition of home provided by the original lex."

"Doesn't seem quite fair." Orion sniffed, pulling the book close to him and taking a look for himself.

"Unfortunately, fairness has very little to do with this legal system, I've found."

If it had, then I doubted I would be trawling through this legal maze just to try and keep my children from being taken from me without any just cause.

"I'm curious, my lord, are you aware of which lex they are using to do this in the first place?" Orion was rifling through one of the law books on education.

I thought back to what Markus had explained to me. "Something about rightful upbringing . . . Give me a moment, I'll get it for you."

I had found the lex before, stared at it for hours. It really wasn't a fun lex to look at. Still, it was easy to find again.

"The Rightful Upbringing Lex. It states that all royal children have a right to an upbringing that involves a proper academic education, attendants, prosperous culture . . ."

I read on and on. At the end of the day, it allowed the higher lords of a house to request children from lower lords and hold them hostage. It was just about more control, although from what I'd seen, most of these laws were.

"Can I see it?" I handed the book over to the man.

Hopefully he could do more with it than I could.

I busied myself with other laws for the next few hours, such as the Right of Duels Lex, which would have been perfect had it not been complicated with obstructive rulings.

It allowed royalty to duel for the right of a favorable exemption to a lex, however said royalty could not be of foreign blood, possess years of military service, have a membership with certain extraterritorial organizations . . .

Effectively, not usable by anyone other than higher lords that could keep themselves from the battlefield, as they most certainly intended. Again, more control, more power.

"Rakta . . . I think I have something."

I slowly looked up at him from my book, curious and hopeful.

He was biting his lips, looking at the words. "If I'm right, out of all these requirements set by the Rightful Upbringing Lex, by legal definition, the only one that we couldn't arguably have here in Gelvurt . . ."

"The proper education, yes," I finished for him, knowing where he was going.

Gelvurt's teaching was more of a family affair and the only proper education that existed within the Velbruns' lands was in their royal city of Velbrun. Unfortunately, even though my children weren't of schooling age yet, the lex could be enforced regardless of the age of the child in question.

"So, we'd need a school here in Gelvurt."

"Yes?" That was what I'd gathered myself. I didn't think it was that simple of an answer, however. "I don't think I have the power to create one out of thin air, unfortunately."

Orion was quiet for a moment, rereading a few passages from one of the education-law books I'd seen him with earlier.

"I, uh, I actually think you can, my lord."

26

Upon further reading, Orion was proven correct. The creation of a school required only the sponsorship of the local lord, as all construction in the local area did. There was no special lex disallowing the approval or any lengthy process to go through for it.

Now, while this was certainly the best answer we had found yet, it came with a few struggles, such as resources and man power.

Still, the most pressing was that the more influential Velbruns could move to block it if I did not have the support of other Lords Velbrun. And they certainly would if, or more appropriately, when they got wind of my plan.

"And he will support you, my lord?" Orion was rereading other empire law books to make sure we hadn't missed some crucial detail that could undermine our plan.

I nodded. "Lord Velbrun of Niers seems inclined to go against the higher lords."

My last visit might have strained that relationship slightly, but Jorge was genuine when he had wished to be political allies of sorts. I'm sure he would like the expanded freedoms of having a school as well.

"Also, feel free to drop the formality, Orion." I glanced at my companion, in a much better mood than I had been just hours ago. The general store owner had a tendency to slip back into a more formal tone when we were in my office. "I don't like titles between those I fight alongside."

And this would certainly be a fight. One stained with ink rather than blood, but a gruesome, merciless fight nonetheless.

Orion nodded, looking faintly honored. "Uh, Rakta, then. Are there any other Lords Velbrun for you to draw support from? A qualifying local school for the surrounding villages would be easier than one specifically for Gelvurt."

After I finished penning my letter to Jorge, I took out a map of the surrounding land, spreading it out across my office table.

"I haven't been very active politically"—which certainly didn't make this situation any easier—"but there are some smaller villages I could speak to the lords of."

Orion came over to look at the map, as well, pointing to one of the small inked names to the east of my village. "Might I suggest Alwur? The village has always been on good terms with Gelvurt, and we share some lineage."

I looked at Alwur on the map, estimating that it'd take me only a few hours of sprinting if I went alone. "And the local lord is amiable?"

"The Lordess Velbrun of the area is fair, from what her people say. Unfortunately, she is, uh, very distant." The last few words rolled hesitantly off his lips, as if he was unsure how to feel about them.

I imagined he was thinking of the similarities between this noble lady and the distant calm that preceded the storm that was Zactrik Velbrun.

Still, if I could get the Lordess Velbrun of Alwur to lend her support, I would have the influence I'd need to protect my school from the machinations of House Velbrun. Not to mention, their support would benefit the actual construction.

Niers would be a great help. While it was still primarily an agricultural village, it had a better reputation as a trading hub for merchants coming through from Rusk.

Close enough to be a nice resting place, far enough away that bandits and criminals from the desert nation wouldn't get very close before getting stopped by a patrol.

"Alright, I'll head to Alwur soon. I'll need to send a letter to introduce myself and my intentions, so I can't just run there as I please." If I wanted the aid of nobility, I had to play by the rules of nobility.

And nobility did not just drop in unannounced.

Orion pulled out a few more documents. "With that settled, the influence is only part of the problem. I made a quick estimate of the personnel and resources we're going to need for our school to be seen as proper education."

I heard the faint echoes of the death knell for my plan as I saw the numbers. I'd never seen that much sil in my life, much less had it in my coffers.

"Damn."

My companion nodded, not looking enthused either. "Damn."

I would need a benefactor, a non-Velbrun patron that could front the costs of construction and hiring the proper personnel.

Technically, as the local lord and an honored veteran of war, I could act as the personnel required for the physical arts a proper education was required to provide.

Unfortunately, I lacked any proficiency in teaching etiquette, higher mathematics, history, and the assortment of other subjects that were required. Such experts were not common in this part of the empire either.

And while I could twist the arms of the locals in Gelvurt to find that money, it wouldn't help my chances of getting them invested in the idea of sending their children to school. Not to mention, of course, that requesting aid from the royal funds of House Velbrun was out of the question.

"Finding that support won't be possible here in Gelvurt." I didn't need to look to know that Orion had jumped a bit as I finally spoke after a long moment of silence.

"It . . . would be easier to do so at the capital, yes."

I shook my head. "If I go, I'll be away for too long. I can't leave my children unattended. House Velbrun, they'll notice, catch wind of where I am and use the opportunity."

Even a week away would be a risky amount of time; the Velbruns most likely already had a plan in place for when such an absence arose. How many mercenaries were lurking in the countryside waiting for me to leave?

The idea made my blood boil.

The destruction I would unleash if they hurt my children would make them wish for the Warlock King, but that wouldn't win me any favors. It would just alienate the few in my corner, make me an enemy of the empire.

"Sounds like you need someone to go for you, Rakta." A new voice piped up from the doorframe.

Doh twirled her bangs, smirking at me as she sauntered into the room, giving Orion a coy look. The poor man looked confused, having not had much of a chance to speak to my maid.

At least, while she looked like herself.

I stroked my chin, realizing the implication. "That . . . is an interesting idea. What keeps you from using this as an opportunity to help yourself?"

"Rakta, you wound me!" Doh dramatically placed a hand on her chest. "After all we've been through together?"

The various thefts? I wanted to question her, but I had other things on my mind as I mulled over her offer, something at the tip of my tongue.

Orion piped up, "Sending a lone woman traveling all the way to the capital . . . That feels risky, Rakta. No offense, uh, miss."

"No offense taken. I don't usually travel as a woman anyway." Doh was far too casual about the comments she made sometimes.

I let the poor general store owner deal with that confusing comment for the moment as I considered Doh.

Sending her to the capital wasn't a horrible idea, but my influence was already minor. Trying to leverage it through a dignitary would be even more difficult, and, well, some of my best chances of finding support wouldn't appreciate me sending a messenger after so long.

The idea of Doh possibly going as me, however, was ridiculous. I couldn't even begin to imagine the social disaster that would lead to.

And yet, Doh's comment stirred something in the back of my mind. The Velbruns were waiting for me to be absent from the keep.

What if I never was?

"Orion, this is my maid, Doh." Proper introductions were important as I slowly put together my plan. "Doh, I'd like you to introduce yourself properly."

"Oh, uh, are you sure?" Her features were already beginning to shift, Orion's confusion fading into recognition at what Doh really was.

Nodding, I felt a very Lydia-like smile pull at my lips. "I have a plan."

I sat down with my children in my lap, corralling them gently with my arms as they watched the world with their intelligent eyes. I whispered to them comforting words as I tried to settle the difference between my heart and my mind.

"I'm going away for some time, my younglings." They stared up at me, their attention gained. "Longer than I ever have before. There are . . . There are people who wish to take you away."

"Fuh." Daka's eyes were bright, with the kind of anger I'd once seen when Dalton had stolen one of her toys. The other two tensed at my words.

It was almost a relief to have children capable of understanding how dangerous the world was, yet disheartening to have them confronted with it so soon.

I kissed the little warrior on the forehead. "I'm not going to let that happen. I have a plan, one that requires me to speak with people far away."

Even with my techniques, the travel would take a few days, there and back, which didn't even include the time I would need to convince others to aid me. That could take much, much longer, even with the favors I'd already considered calling in.

I had never been away from them for so long. I was going to have to trust the people of Gelvurt, Orion, and, most importantly, Doh. The same criminal who had tried to steal from me a time ago.

And yet, she had helped me recover my memories. If I could allow her into the sanctity of my mind, could I not trust my children's lives to her?

The logic was sound, perhaps, but my heart was not in it. The sanctity of mind meant nothing compared to the young sparks before me.

"Guh." Dalton had relaxed slightly, his hand awkwardly coming up to give me a pat on the arm. Was he trying to comfort me?

Truly, I was a lucky father to have a son willing to comfort me so soon. "Thank you, son. Now comes the hard part. Doh? It's time."

The figure that came into the nursery was tall, darkly skinned, and broadly built. Muscular, but with the lithe grace of an acrobat in his gait.

Doh smiled with my face and threw out her, well, his arms for a big, exaggerated hug. "Come to dear ole daddy, kids!"

They all started crying.

"Ha ha, oops."

I gave him a look. Doubts about my plan were building.

INTERLUDE:
DOH

My breakfast wasn't half as tasty coming up as it had been going down this morning. Acidic, horrible, I wiped my mouth as I stared down at the gray, mottled mess on the ground. Was I dying? Why did dying taste so bad?

"Oh my god, Delilah, honey!" Mom dragged me away from the mess I'd made, her hands pulling at my cheeks and hair. "Are you okay!? How are you feeling?"

She was pretty worried. I guess I should be pretty worried, too, but everything felt a little sluggish and placid all of a sudden.

My stomach rumbled, like it hadn't just thrown out all the precious food I'd given it this morning. "Iunno, I guess I'm fine."

I might've been ill? I wasn't sure really. All I knew was that looking down at my fingers, the back of my hands, the little flowery dress I wore, I felt . . . wrong.

"Oh yeah, this is the good life." I cracked my strong, muscular back as I propped myself up on what would be my bed for at least the next week. It wasn't actually any softer than my own bed, but the room wasn't the only benefit to this arrangement.

Having Rakta's deep, throaty voice at my beck and call, by permission of the man himself, I couldn't help but feel a bit of excitement run through my body. Of course, I wasn't quite the man down to the last detail. I didn't have his strength or prowess, but his physique? His chiseled abs? His privilege?

All mine for me to do with as I wished! In a weird little happenstance, my original plan that I'd had upon hearing about Lord Velbrun coming through town had actually worked!

Suck it, Kal! It would've felt better throwing it in the big guy's face if he were still around to laugh about it with me.

"And now," I practically sang as I stood up from my lord-sized bed, ignoring that emotional nonsense, "it's time to check on my lovable, adorable younglings!"

Dancing out of my borrowed room and to the nursery next door, I had to remind myself that, as a father, I couldn't play favorites. Still, I smirked, for I was not a father. Only a pretend father!

So while I only pretended not to play favorites as the little gremlins looked up at me, I gently picked up the palest of the bunch, Natakia, the best Velbrun child, and held her in my arms. "Ah, my little desert flower, did you sleep well?"

The most beautiful of the three children looked up at me with that strange intelligence that Rakta seemed to adore. I wasn't going to dip my toe in it, mostly because I was pretty sure it had to do with that prophecy bullshit, but I saw the appeal.

After a moment of considering me, my borrowed form, the baby made an attempt at nodding its head like someone far older. "Guh."

Yeah, just ignore the weirdness. I wasn't sure what these kids were gonna say for their first words, but I'd heard stories of prodigies and legendary warriors doing shit like this as toddlers.

Now, did I have proof that Harruk the Red killed his nursing aid a day after he was born by slicing her neck? No. Did I need proof to be worried? Never.

"That's great, honey." I bounced her in my grip, wandering over to where Rakta kept his magically preserved milk for the kiddies. "Time for breakfast milk!"

Marisha wasn't here today, so the babies would have to deal with the preserved stuff. I certainly didn't want to go to the trouble of breastfeeding.

The look on Natakia's adorable face wasn't pleased as I brought out the bottle, but I knew how to get her to not make a fuss.

"You're looking so nice today, 'Kia." I softly rubbed her angry little cheeks. "You're practically glowing, you know? You're gonna be beautiful with all this healthy milk you're getting to drink, aren't you?"

Could a baby be vain? In general, maybe not? Natakia? Oh boy, the way she lit up at my compliments could have put the sun to shame. Her future suitors, of which I foresaw many, were going to have to get really good at paying lip service.

Also dodging axes, probably.

"Duh." The little girl eyed me with a little suspicion, but that didn't stop her from accepting the milk bottle as I got her to drink from it.

And the other kids got some milk too. Look, I tried to assuage my little speck of guilt; it wasn't like I didn't take care of the other little spawn, but they didn't exactly go out of their way to be cute!

Dalton hated it when I held him, although that wasn't specific to me, and Daka tried to bite me! And those little baby teeth hurt! Honestly, I was a little unnerved by how capable the babies were at sniffing out who I was. Daka and Natakia seemed to dislike and enjoy my presence respectively, regardless of whom I looked like.

That's why, as young as she was, I never kept my eye off of Daka for long. She definitely didn't like me for some reason, no matter what I looked like. If any of them were going to pull a Harruk the Red . . .

I laid Natakia down and leaned up against the post. "Ha, you're gonna have to teach your siblings how to be cute one of these days, 'Kia."

Daka growled at me. Growled!

As her pretend father, I should be proud. As the maid with a distinct lack of enjoyment of harm, I was a little concerned.

"Please, Geoffrey, I'm worried about Delilah. She hasn't . . . she's ill and hasn't been the same recently. Is there anything you can do?"

The old burly man that had taken up residence in the village as a healer grumbled. "Macy, I'm not a miracle worker. I can cast a quick spell to boost her health, help her fight off the ick, but I mostly work with animals, okay?"

I swung my legs back and forth on the big chair I'd been placed on.

Wasn't really sure what I'd done wrong or how I was hurting. I felt fine, right now.

"Please, she's been throwing up this horrid mess every time she tries to eat, and she's obviously in pain! She hasn't smiled or laughed in a week!" She was real upset.

I wasn't really in pain; everything just felt numb. I wasn't sure what was going on, really. Sometimes Macy, uh, Mom would call for me, and I'd forget that Delilah was my name. I was kind of worried about that, or at least, I wanted to be.

Regardless, it wasn't hard to notice the way the doctor stilled. "Vomiting? What . . . color is it?"

Sometimes, it was hard even remembering the village's name. Something . . . Dunstock? It felt like a Dunstock, but maybe that was just a fun rhyme.

"Ah, my lord! Good morning!" One of the rare smiles of Gelvurt graced me as I walked through the village. A young lady with her children, all of them looking healthy thanks to Rakta.

Well, me.

"Ah, Gina, good morning to you as well," I waved, smiling like Rakta always did. "I hope the recent weather made its way toward your fields."

Gina McDay blushed. "Yes, my lord. It's been a blessing."

Humming, I grinned. "I'm sure it has."

Gina's son dragged her away to where her husband, Peter McDay, was a few paces away talking to some of the other men of Gelvurt, and I couldn't help but watch her go. I didn't miss, of course, Gina glancing back at me before turning away with red cheeks.

It took every speck of willpower I had not to wink. Rakta did not wink at deliciously cute women walking back to their husbands.

Did Rakta realize how attractive a strong, tall man with a gentle smile was to some ladies? No, but I certainly did. And, of course, while I'd never besmirch his identity with any kind of tryst . . . a shape-shifter could fantasize, couldn't she?

I certainly thought so. Maybe, for my birthday, whenever that was, Rakta would let me have a night on the town in his form.

Ha, yeah right.

Still, Rakta Velbrun, the honorable, honest widower of Lydia Velbrun, would never even consider such a thing so soon after his wife's passing . . . if ever.

It was a little disappointing, but disappointment was an old friend, almost like family, really. Still, for now, Lord Rakta Velbrun had a few meetings and property issues that he needed to sort out, so I was off to go fetch Orion, the general store owner and apparently trusted Doh minder.

As if I needed a minder, ha. I could do this in my sleep.

"Bloodlines!? What are you talking about, you mad coot!?" Macy was really getting into with the healer now. She hadn't gotten this angry since . . . since something had made her really angry before.

The healer was pale. "When, uh, monsters, supernatural creatures, intermingle with families, they, well, they have sometimes . . . someone, an ancestor, must have mingled with some kind of creature! And these changes, they . . . can come with problems, okay!? Our bodies weren't meant to harness the power of monsters!"

Oh, so Macy had fun with some sort of monster? Was that where my other person went? My, uh, my dad. Wow, things were getting kind of foggy. I noticed it was pretty bright outside.

I wanted to go outside.

"Well don't just talk about it. Fix her!" That woman needed to . . .

"What do you mean fix her!? I can't do anything for that thing!"

"That thing is my daughter!"

"Not anymore, Macy!"

I went outside.

I picked my teeth as I left the Varnedoe family household. "Wow, that woman is a bitch."

"Yes, well, she did have understandable issues." Orion shuffled the documents he'd brought. "But the personal comments weren't needed."

I glanced back. "Didn't Rakta save Gelvurt? Why's that bitch acting like Rakta was the monster going around eating kids?"

"Bad blood between her and those from Rusk, I'm afraid . . . my lord." Orion had that look on his face that meant he didn't want to discuss the matter in detail. I didn't really either.

I understood the concept of racism and hating the people of other countries, but, well, I was just too flexible to ever really get it. I certainly didn't change much, no matter what I had my skin look like.

"Yeah, well, she better keep to her side of the cornfield and not make trouble." I glanced back at her abode. "I can't imagine Rakta would be all that pleased if she went around spouting shit about his kids."

Surprisingly, I wasn't very fond of that idea either. Natakia certainly didn't deserve that kind of vitriol pointed her way.

Orion smiled. "I'm sure she's smart enough to not start anything. I actually knew her when we were younger before, well . . . never mind. Regardless, she isn't a bad person."

"Yeah, well, take it from a bad person—she isn't great."

He gave me a reproachful look, but I just focused on his lips. It was too bad I couldn't shift into Marisha right now or I could let off a little stress. Orion was quite the looker, too, in his own scholarly way.

I stared at the road ahead of me, my favorite dress torn at the bottom and my bare feet dirty. It'd been a few months since the fog had rolled in, and I wasn't sure what to do now.

The lady was gone, driven mad by her monster daughter, according to some of the louder people at the tavern. I don't think they noticed me.

I was her daughter, wasn't I? What did I do? Why was I alone?

Nothing made sense, but a deep grief kept gnawing at me. Who was I mourning? What was I mourning?

Who am I? Was I tall or short? Blond or brunette? Female? Male?

I began to walk down the open road, out of the nameless village. Even if I couldn't find answers, at least there'd be fewer questions.

I relaxed on my bed after a long, hard day of being a father and lord of an entire village. It was satisfying, but not as satisfying as a feast in my name would have been. I'd talked to Orion about having one, as a little treat for myself, but apparently that would have been "out of character" for Rakta.

One of these days, I'd have a feast. I swore to whatever god of feast there was out in the world.

I could feel my body flexing, spurred by a flux of energy that felt like magic, but always came from somewhere more instinctive. I'd certainly never run out of it like I'd come dangerously close to doing with Mana.

As the reflex tugged at my form, Rakta's muscles deflated, slothing off of me, and I was left with the lithe frame of my most common form, something I'd picked up on my travels.

I think I got the hair from a nice little waitress in Cerula, and I'd come to love the petiteness after some fun I'd had with a professional lover somewhere over in House Kire's lands.

And yet, my mind went back to how everything had eventually worked out for me. A nice room, sweet kids, wanting for practically nothing except a feast.

"I wish my plan had worked out sooner," I sighed, relaxing into my borrowed bed. I'd run with a lot of crowds, hatched a lot of schemes, but honestly, I didn't blame those fools for turning on me. I'd been running them around raw, promising them too much and coming up empty half of the time.

Of course, they were still idiots to go against a guy who said hello by throwing a magical exploding axe in the center of our fucking camp. Like, come on, how had I been the only one to get the danger vibes from Rakta's toned ass?

And yet, if my plan had been better, they'd be here too. Now, they only existed in my mind, and Rakta's quaint little stories, which was a very precarious place to be.

So precarious, that I needed to make sure I kept up the nightly ritual.

Sitting up in my bed, I felt my magic stir as I let my hands begin to dance in the air around me, Mana dripping from my fingers and lingering in the air as I began my chant. "My House of Yesterday, Open To Me, **Palace of Memories.**"

As the familiar spell took hold of me, shoring up my memory, I wondered if everyone with doppelgänger blood dealt with the same issues that I did. I'd never met another like me to know for sure, but I hoped and prayed it was just a me thing.

I didn't have much attachment to the person I was before I'd managed to learn enough memory magic to keep my thoughts from deteriorating, but . . . sometimes, I remembered a woman and a smile.

And I just felt sad.

27

I traveled to Alwur first for a few reasons. For one, it was closer, and secondly, any financial support I could garner while in Cerula would mean nothing if the Lordess Velbrun of Alwur didn't weigh in with her influence on the creation of the school.

Money would mean nothing if I didn't have the power to defend the school from the Velbruns' interference. They could end the school in its infancy if I did not do this right.

So, having given my letter to the local lordess time to arrive, I descended upon the stalwart village after a night of sprinting across forests and the deep ravines of the empire.

Surrounded by large wooden palisades, Alwur was considered one of the safest villages sitting on the border of Rusk and the leading supplier of lumber to the rest of House Velbrun's land. While I had noticed some housing and farms outside of the walls, most of the Alwur community seemed nestled inside the walls, the taller buildings built close together.

And the only proper way in was through one of the two gatehouses that were built into the palisades on the northern and southern sections of the walls. It was manned by a few armored men, even this early in the morning.

"Halt." One of the guards stopped me as I walked up. "What's your business, traveler?"

I eyed the two men standing a distance away from me, both of them holding their halberds with caution, but not hostility. "I am Lord Rakta

Velbrun of Gelvurt. I've come to speak with Lordess Caitlyn Velbrun of Alwur about political matters."

A more cynical part of me wondered if I was going to have problems proving that I, with my heritage, was actually a Lord Velbrun. Perhaps I should have brought my writ.

The guards stood a little straighter. "Ah, Lord Velbrun of Gelvurt, we were told to expect you. Where is your company?"

They seemed a little suspicious, but I wouldn't allow myself to fault them for doing their jobs. "I came alone. I'm traveling and, while comfortable, carriages and company merely slow me down."

A small lie, really. Carriages were a little too cramped for my tastes. Running with the wind and through the air was much more calming and relaxing than the pace of a horse.

Finding my answer satisfactory, the guards allowed my passage through the gate, sending a runner to alert Lordess Velbrun of my arrival. I was curious if she would be up at this time in the morning.

Nobles often kept a more comfortable sleeping schedule, but perhaps she rose with the sun? Of course, when the runner came back, I was slightly surprised by the news he brought.

"The lordess is willing to meet you at noon, my lord." The young man seemed less surprised at the news he brought.

"Is the lordess busy with another arrangement?" Jorge's insight on the matter confirmed through letters that Lordess Velbrun of Alwur was very private and isolated. I'd expected her to have a free schedule.

"No, my lord." The runner shook his head, smiling wryly. "The lady only meets people at noon."

Strange tradition, but I would not question it for the time being. "Then I shall wait."

A few hours of waiting would be the least of my problems if I ruined this chance by forcing the issue. Problem was, I had very little idea of what to busy myself with while I waited. It was still quite early in the morning.

"Might I offer the honored Lord Velbrun a tour around Alwur?" The runner's smile had yet to fall, his arm offered for me to take.

I considered the young man for a moment, before nodding. I had no reason to decline.

Compared to the spaced-out placement of Gelvurt's homes, even the closest storefronts within the village center, the compacted arrangement of Alwur was novel.

It reminded me of Cerula or Velbrun, cities that made use of all the space they had, but even they allowed for cobblestone alleyways and spacious alcoves.

Alwur, however, was a single, tall building that simply had been fashioned out of different buildings stacked on top of one another, but the people seemed content. No matter how high they walked above the ground.

"Lordess Velbrun's grandfather was the first to begin Alwur's ascension after we had a surge of refugees from a troll attack." The runner, who had introduced himself as Julian Carnline, said. "The walls you see were originally a lot tighter, so the honored Lord Velbrun built up."

He waved and chatted with civilians passing above us. Julian struck me as a popular man here in the village, and he seemed knowledgeable about the history of his home.

I watched a father carefully tend to his young son playing near one of the guardrails for the upper platform built between the homes. It was a heartwarming sight, but a question nagged at me. "Why the wooden pathways?"

"Yeah." Julian shrugged, looking up at them alongside me. "Not really necessary, but enough people were living in the second story of another home or store that the idea came up, and we had the carpenters and wood for it. The current lordess's parents supported it when they were in charge, so it happened."

"And what of a dry season? An errant spark and the village center goes up in flames." The engineering of some of what I was seeing was beyond intriguing, but I wasn't sure if it was worth it. I'd seen wildfires consume a home in minutes.

Julian kept walking, the question barely breaking his stride. "We asked that question a long time ago, well, ha, not me, but Alwur actually found an answer to that back when we built the wooden walls."

He pointed to the sky, and I turned to look, my eyes widening.

"Is that what I think it is?" I almost couldn't believe it.

An amorphous blob of water floated in the air, a blue light at the center of the aerial puddle. It danced around the wooden structure of

Alwur, lazily dodging the citizens that walked past, small kids running their fingers through it when it got close.

"Yep." Julian smirked. "A water blorp, born and raised here by the Auqkers. They're a water-magic family, willing to help out and teach anyone with talent a spell or two to keep our home from burning down."

Blorps were effectively magical energy that had mixed together with an element. Harmless and easily controllable by elementalists, but I'd never seen water blorps used as fire retardants. I'd certainly dealt with fire blorps causing them though.

I stroked my chin. "Very interesting. They teach?"

"Yeah, teach and more. We get dry spells pretty commonly here this close to Rusk. The Auqkers help the farmers keep their crops irrigated."

I hadn't considered it, but dealing with the aridness of Rusk's lands would be a problem the closer a village got to the border. Alwur's lumber had to come from north of here, where the forest thrived.

Maybe if the relationship between Alwur and Gelvurt grew with this deal, a conversation could be had regarding this irrigation prac-tice. I was sure the families of my village would appreciate the help with their fields.

"Well, thank you for the lesson, Julian." We hadn't been walking for long, and yet I already felt this tour was worth it. Truly, the Velbruns must pay little attention to their lesser nobility if this had happened under their purview.

"Don't mention it." He smiled. "Besides, I haven't shown you the best parts, my lord!"

"Welcome to the Oak Eatery." Julian gestured out all around us to the quaint restaurant that he had led me to.

Although, while I called it a restaurant, it was much more akin to a street diner or café, with rustic wooden architecture, from the chairs to the tables. Strange, as well, was the awareness that I was currently stand-ing on the second floor of Alwur.

Below us, below the Oak Eatery, was in fact the general store of the entire village. Julian had introduced me to the man behind the counter, Hector Pint, as we used his stairway to reach this part of the village.

I looked around, relatively enjoying the smell of bark that was heavy in the air. "It certainly is as nice as you'd mentioned."

Sitting down at one of the tables and motioning for me to follow, Julian nodded, looking pleased to rest his feet. He struck me as a young man who was on the move more than most, even for a runner.

"Oh, just wait until you fall in love with the food." He tapped his fingers on the table, meeting eyes with the lady at the counter of the establishment.

Soon, we'd been served, and I found myself enjoying a delectable meal of chicken soup served in an oddly fashioned wooden bowl with a bark outer shell, as if they'd bent the part of a tree into the shape of the container.

Silently enjoying my meal, I broke the companionable quiet between us. "This is quite good, certainly. Are you a regular here?"

"Yeah." He shrugged. "I'm a horrible cook, so I tend to come here for a bite to eat when I get tired of bread and water, you know?"

I certainly did know. Rations prepared for the trail were hardy and kept your energy up, but nothing encouraged finding a good meal more than having to eat them for a long time.

Although, bread and water did not sound like it'd be horrible, as long as the bread had been spiced. Not that Certillian cooks really knew how to use spices correctly from what I'd found. They much preferred their food to be almost flavorless compared to Ruskan delights.

"So, forgive me for asking, my lord." Julian winked. "But what brings Lord Velbrun of Gelvurt all the way over to Alwur? I've made the trek before; it's not a short one."

Even with how friendly the young runner was, I wasn't sure if I should be open about my planned arrangements with the lordess.

"I've an offer to the lordess," I said, speaking as openly as I felt comfortable on the matter. "A, well, business arrangement that could benefit our neck of the woods, so to speak. I'd just need her support."

Julian took a sip of his drink, nodding along. "Mm, very vague. Still, I guess this really isn't a conversation meant for me, after all. I hope everything works out. Caitlyn has done a lot of good for the village."

"Caitlyn?" I hadn't expected a villager to address her so casually, but I supposed there were plenty of people in Gelvurt that did so in regard to me. "Are you a friend of the lordess?"

"Oh yeah, we grew up together." He swirled his drink. "Of course, she's not as out and about as she used to be. It's a real shame, honestly. It feels like it's been years since we went out and saw the fireflies."

Beneath his bright visage, I could recognize the face of a man who was missing a friend. I understood the sentiment completely.

After a few hours of being shown around the best parts of Alwur, I was taken to the Velbrun Keep on the outskirts of the village as it neared noon.

"How long has it been since Lordess Velbrun of Alwur took to having her meetings at noon?" It was a strange habit, but not as concerning compared to only meeting someone during the night. That would have been a grave sign I could not ignore.

Julian waved to some of the guards as we passed, the guards waving back. "Since the passing of her mother and father, my lord. Lordess Velbrun doesn't go out for more than an hour every day."

Only having meetings at noon was one thing, but to only leave at a specific time? What, I wanted to ask, did she do for the remainder of the day? Simply read and drink?

Julian's concern about his friend not being out and about as much as she used to be struck a darker chord all of a sudden.

I kept my guard up. If I was dealing with another Zactrik, I could not let myself be taken off guard by a pleasant tour. Not when I had three younglings depending on my good health.

So I stayed quiet, watching my surroundings as I was welcomed into the keep. It was familiar, the gold-and-green colors of House Velbrun on every tapestry in the main hall, with even the smell resembling that of my own keep.

"Alright, well, I hope you and Lordess Velbrun get on well." Julian gave me a small, informal salute and whistled his way out of the noble household. The guards let him pass without pause.

I wasn't sure of what to make of the runner. He was confident and seemed like the kind of fellow to be in good spirits regardless of what they day brought. No one seemed to pay him much attention and let him go as he pleased.

And he was quick to fashion himself as a friend, even to a stranger like me. It was appreciated, if not slightly concerning how easily he had done so.

"I'm sorry if Julian's company wasn't exactly up to par with the taste of a Lord Velbrun." A melodic voice came calling from behind me, the hair on the back of my neck rising.

Turning to the voice, coming from the top of the stairs, I frowned at one of the most beautiful women I had ever seen. With caramel skin and silken brown hair, the woman's curves were accentuated by the gold-and-green dress she wore.

She walked down the steps with confidence, as if she were a great spirit venturing from the heavens to greet a mortal that had called for her. The acidic glint in her eyes, however, made me desire little to do with her beyond what I had come to speak with her about.

And, of course, I knew a Vitae-enhanced personality when I felt one.

I thrummed my own Vitae and felt the air around me vibrate for a moment, dispelling that sense of awe that had filtered into the room as she made her presence known, overwhelming the attempt at grandstanding.

Lordess Caitlyn Velbrun's eyes widened, her bravado broken for a moment. "You . . ."

She would have needed a stronger Vitae than my own to affect me, an uncommon occurrence among the nobility. Perhaps I should have simply endured the aura instead of dispelling it? It wouldn't have influenced me, not to any true extent.

I certainly didn't want her to think of me as an enemy simply due to her snubbed pride.

"Lordess Velbrun of Alwur, this lord thanks you for welcoming him into your home." I bowed to the noblewoman; the formalities I'd managed to skip with Jorge, unfortunately, held a tight grip on me here.

"You, uh, yes, welcome." The Lordess Velbrun seemed to fall back into the formal script without much trouble. "Lord Velbrun of Gelvurt. Please, join me in my study."

She made a motion of her hands, her gaze now cautious but her movement not quite as inherently seductive or distracting without the

Vitae empowering it. I was relieved she had not made any additional attempts to grandstand before me.

The last thing I needed was for Lordess Velbrun to call for a duel of honor or some other time-wasting endeavor.

Putting such thoughts aside, I followed her up the stairs, mentally trying to recount the fine details of the plan that Orion and I had crafted over the last few long nights leading up to this meeting.

28

A school?" Lordess Caitlyn Velbrun did not look amused at my idea. We had gone through the usual small talk for a few minutes, discussing the local crops and making polite complaints about taxes, before I had brought up my reason for visiting. Even without her pleasing Vitae aura, I would admit that the lordess was pleasant to speak with and had a cautious, but straightforward attitude.

I nodded, not buckling under the look, pushing over the document that Orion and I had penned. All the resources required for such a task, as well as some of the benefits, were included in a nice, succinct handwriting that was not my own.

Unfortunately, I had a heavy hand, and, while it was legible, my writing was certainly not pleasant on the eyes, as opposed to Orion's practiced script.

"Gelvurt, Niers, and Alwur are the farthest villages from Velbrun. For any proper education," I said the words with a little distaste, annoyed by them after many long nights, "our villages' children have to attend a school that is both a month away and difficult to attend without the right connections."

"You seek to give commoners a proper education?" Her eyebrow was quirked, her eyes glancing to the documents. "Any particular reason as to why?"

Orion had given me a number of reasons to justify the school. Distance, uplifting the local community, creating and enhancing relations with the lower lords, and an assortment of other practical arguments that backed up the proposal.

And while those were all well and good, those were reasons we had come up with after the fact. I already had my answers for why I was pursuing this school.

"I have two reasons, Lordess Velbrun of Alwur. One is that I have children of my own." I took a sip of the wine that an attendant had poured for me before departing.

She seemed to relax, a glint of uncertainty fading at my admittance, and nodded. Her smile had become a little more rigid, and I couldn't help but feel more distance between us.

"The Velbruns have requested that they are raised in Velbrun, but if I am able to provide proper education, they won't be able to make such claims." I stared down into my drink. "They want to hurt me."

Lordess Velbrun of Alwur took a sip of her own wine with a controlled delicacy, as if she were mulling over the weather rather than the forceful taking of my children.

"So, you've vexed the higher lords of Velbrun, and now you wish to escape their wrath." Her voice held little sympathy. "How quaint."

Her summary felt unfair. I had done little to vex the Velbruns beyond existing and having the gall to fall in love with Lydia. Still, she did not know my story, nor did I know hers.

"Are you displeased with my first reason?" I'd never know for sure if I didn't ask.

She sniffed. "Hardly. I simply find it unsurprising that it takes self-interest for a Velbrun to begin improving anything. I can see why you married into the family."

At the very least, I supposed, she wasn't lashing me with comments about my heritage. Still, being likened to a Velbrun was a novel strike against me, certainly one I had never felt before.

I did not like how it felt.

"You think I'm at fault for wanting to keep my children away from the higher lords?" I frowned.

The lordess hesitated, considering her words. "You . . . would not have come to me about this school had you not required it for your children. And yet, I see many of the benefits it has could aid the local region."

"Do you fight fires when they do not exist?" The question was defensive coming from my lips, trying to protect myself from the accusation.

"No." She squinted. "But I am always looking to improve my village's preparation for such disasters, not just when those disasters threaten me."

I considered her words, mulling them over. I was struck with frustration that another Velbrun was impeding my plan, but such thoughts would serve only to hurt this conversation. From her words, she was treating me like any other Velbrun. I gained nothing from doing the same to her.

"So you consider me selfish." I kept my words calm. "Only working to improve our lands when I have something personally to gain from it."

"As nobles, our responsibility is improving the lives of those who have placed us on this royal pedestal. And for all they'd like to believe otherwise"—her gaze was heated—"that does not only include the higher lords or our families."

She had my respect, if that was worth anything. I had met only a few nobles with such a mentality but had certainly never met one with ties to House Velbrun. I supposed those of the house with such feelings were put out here in the outskirts for a reason.

And in a way, she was right. I would never have considered a school if it weren't for my situation. Improving Gelvurt was not really one of my major concerns.

Still, I persevered in the face of her scorn. "My first reason may be self-interested, I won't argue that point, but my second reason still stands."

"You have the floor, Lord Velbrun." She seemed almost amused by my resolve.

"House Velbrun"—I gave my voice weight—"wants control over their region. The use of the laws they have in place to take my children is not unique. We suffer under their control because we, the lower lords, fight alone against their influence."

I remembered Jorge's words, how he had said that he had been ousted to the border of the Velbrun influence due to his lack of favor. Not because of some grand sin that he had committed, like Zactrik, but rather simply having no one willing to stand with him.

We, the lower lords of House Velbrun, would have no voice if we did not speak together as one.

"This school can be the first step to having some agency to truly do something for the region," I said, motioning to the documents I'd given her. "Do you think this responsibility you speak of is limited to the borders of our villages?"

She looked hesitant to agree with me, obviously seeing the implication of my question. "No. As nobles of the empire, we should seek the betterment of all citizens, within my village and without."

For a moment, there was silence. I stared into her eyes, and she stared back unflinchingly. No deceit hid within her eyes, only a true devotion to her people.

"When I fought against the Warlock King"—her eyes widened at my admission—"I saw many things, Lordess Velbrun of Alwur, things that never reached this region."

I stared up at the map of the Certillian Empire hung on her walls, the lands that I had fought and killed countless souls to keep safe. "Before I was a lord, a father, I was an adventurer risking my life for this empire alongside my future wife, Lydia Velbrun."

If she recognized my wife's name, she didn't make it obvious. If the Velbruns truly had wiped her name from their records, I doubted many within their influence would.

"She died in childbirth after the war, leaving me with three beautiful younglings, and I would rather feel the pain of dying a thousand times than see harm come to them." I broke my gaze on the map, looking down to the floor.

"I'm sorry for your loss." Her voice was soft, her eyes glancing away.

I nodded, saving my tears back for a more private time, before looking up and meeting her gaze once more. "So yes, my reasons are self-interested, but I know what it means to help others. I want to keep my children safe, my part of this world safe, so will you help me take that first step?"

"This will be your room for the night, my lord." The attending maid smiled at me. "I hope it's satisfactory."

Wanda Bellshep was much more put together than Doh usually was during her professional hours. A nice clean outfit, her long brown hair tied back into a ponytail, she walked with a dutiful hurry in her steps that never ruined her demure presence.

I glanced around the spacious room, the comfortable bed and the large windows helping give the room a welcoming energy. "It's fine, thank you."

"The pleasure is mine, Lord Velbrun of Gelvurt. The lady of the house will meet you tomorrow at noon to give you her answer." With that, the maid departed for the rest of her daily chores.

Once again, I would be waiting until noon to meet the lordess. Truly a curiosity that I still had little answer for.

From what I had gathered, Wanda was one of the most trusted maids in the keep, Lordess Velbrun's only personal attendant. My respect for the noble's privacy kept me from asking the maid any questions, but that left me with many unaddressed concerns.

Still, I was a guest, and I had felt no threats to my person beyond the attempt at grandstanding upon introductions. I wondered how many other Velbruns had been swept off their feet by such a display.

Removing my cloak, I sat down on the edge of my bed, and carefully looked around the borrowed room. It was nice and felt like a good place to get some rest after the night spent traveling here.

Technically, I could roam about as I pleased if I wished, only restricted from entering Lordess Velbrun's personal wing that her room was located in. Only Wanda was allowed entrance, if I'd understood correctly.

Still, an entire wing of the keep closed off to the entire staff except for one maid. It made one wonder what activities happened behind those closed doors.

"Ha." I kicked off my leather shoes, letting my toes breathe after being cramped for so long. "I've been on my feet for too long."

It was time for a nap. I'd need my energy for the trip to Cerula once the lordess gave me her decision. While not one for prayer, I sent a small plea to the ether that the odds were in my favor before laying down.

The bed was comfortable, so I was sure I'd have no problem closing my eyes for a bit. Perhaps an answer to problems would come to me within a dream?

Lydia often liked to think so.

An hour later, I continued to stare up at the ceiling. It was difficult, I'd quickly realized, to fall asleep so far away from my children. Not having them close to me, close enough to protect, it stoked a worry in my stomach. What if the Velbruns had already kidnapped them?

There was no certainty that Doh's ruse would work. No certainty that an attempt would not still be made, mercenaries attacking the keep under the cover of night to take the children by force.

And yet, a part of me was still tangled in the words of the lordess. Was it wrong of me, I wondered, that I cared more for my children than the greater whole of the empire? That I only cared for the betterment of their lives rather than the greater whole of my lands?

Perhaps it was not wrong of me as a father, but as a noble? The figurehead and ruler of a land, vested with great privilege and even greater responsibility? I had turned a blind eye to the struggles of the empire in my marital bliss alongside Lydia, and now it seemed as if I inched toward the same slope with my children.

"I killed the Warlock King," I muttered, sighing. "When do I get to rest, if not after that?"

Unfortunately, while the decorations on the wall were nice, swirling gold designs on a green background, they offered no nugget of wisdom.

Having eventually managed to nap for a small time, I was jostled from my rest at the sound of a knock on my door. A light, gentle knock that seemed to be scared of being heard.

I glanced over to the windows, noticing the light had dimmed from noon. Not quite dusk, but certainly heading there within the next few hours. Perhaps this was an invitation for some food?

"Excuse my interruption." The familiar voice of Wanda spoke through the door. "Lord Velbrun, but may we speak for a moment?"

I instinctively felt for my Vultures and grunted at the empty air my hands met, before pulling myself out of the bed and onto my feet. I felt naked without my weapons on hand.

"Good afternoon, Wanda." I opened the door, comfortably barefoot. "What can I help you with?"

The maid looked scared, her eyes darting to either side of the hallway, as if worried someone would notice her. "My lord, would, um, would you . . ."

She stopped, trying to gather herself.

I waited patiently for the young woman to collect her thoughts. I knew how difficult it was to speak sometimes, especially in Certillian.

She took a deep breath before letting it out. "It's about the lordess."

"Is she in danger?" My fists tightened reflexively. Or perhaps, my mind wondered, was she the danger I was about to be warned against?

"Uh, yes, well, no." She fretted with her fingers. "How . . . experienced are you with curses?"

Suddenly, I wished Lydia were here.

29

Curses, one of the many dangers that terrorized the people of Derra. Only the individuals most studied on the matter understood the limitations of curses, which I personally thought were few in number.

Horrid enchantment laid upon the mind, body, and soul of an individual, the difference between a curse and a spell with lasting effects was simple.

Magic was born from Mana, an energy that was within the mortal realm, but curses were born from the same primal energy that fueled the esoteric abilities of the monstrous creatures of Derra.

Where a spell-breaker magician might be able to dispel an enchantment laid upon a poor soul by another mortal spell, such a task was much more difficult when it involved a curse.

And so, sipping on some tea that Wanda had fetched me, I considered the woman sitting across from me. "Lordess Velbrun is cursed?"

The suddenness of the revelation had taken me off guard. It was not often you accidentally happened upon someone with a curse.

"You can't tell her I told you." Wanda shifted nervously, glancing around as if scared someone was listening in. "She'll be . . . oh, she'll be very cross with me, but . . . yes."

It was somewhat frustrating. Primal energy, or Primus among the more scholarly sort, was strange, unpredictable, and much harder to deal with than Mana or Vitae. Any sort of manipulation of the energy was considered the magnum opus of any academic.

And so, getting rid of it was no easy task outside of the means provided by the curse itself, which were unfortunately often complex or immoral in my experience. A man kept from drinking water until he had given up all his secrets to his enemies, a woman beset by ravenous wolves at the stroke of midnight no matter where she was until she accepted the engagement of her ex-lover.

They were never pretty.

"Can you tell me about this curse?" I asked gently. "I can't say if there is anything to be done until I know . . . the circumstances."

There were curses that could put one into an eternal sleep, render a merchant unable to bear the sight of gold, and many more horrific things, but depending on the context, there could be an answer to the lordess's issue within the problem itself.

"Well, it was a few years back," Wanda began. "The lordess's parents had just passed away from a horrible illness when an old woman walked into the village with a proposition for the new Lordess Velbrun."

She leaned back into her seat, her face scrunching up with distaste and anger at the thought of the woman.

"The woman was a hag." I tensed at the naming of the monster. "A vile crone from the darkest parts of the forests that promised freedom from illness and death for the people of Alwur. All she asked for in return . . . was for Lordess Velbrun to provide her annual tribute."

I frowned. It was the kind of deal a hag would offer. I'd met only a few, but they were all the same, opportunistic creatures with ambitions that they kept close to their chests. Although, if the hag was behind the curse, then . . .

Wanda continued. "She wanted flesh and blood, a pure woman and man every summer solstice. I have no idea why she needed them, but Lordess Velbrun, well, strongly refused . . . and that made the hag angry."

My respect for the lordess grew upon hearing her refusal. While she seemed capable, curses were not the only weapon of the hags. Their skin was as hard as iron, and their talons were swift. To deny one would take tremendous bravery or, perhaps, ignorance of the danger they entailed.

"And that was when the hag cursed her?" This made it both difficult and less complicated. A hag could end any curse they gave, but the curse's effect would strengthen if the hag was killed while it was still in effect.

"Yes." The maid nodded. "I was there with the lordess when it happened. A flash of blackness, a horrible rumble, and then the hag was gone . . . and the lordess was on the floor . . ."

Her fists were tight, balled up and white from their tightness.

". . . She looked older, drained and tired. I went to fetch someone, anyone, but she woke up and stopped me. She . . . was scared . . ."

I nodded. "Hags are terrifying monsters and their curses . . . You had every reason to be frightened. Did anything else happen?"

Wanda nodded. "I . . . Lordess Velbrun is prideful, hates the idea of looking weak. I and the head of the Auqkers family are the only ones who know. If word got out to the other Velbruns about her state, she'd . . ."

I squinted. "And what does this have to do with her specific schedule? She seems skilled with Vitae. Does she simply forcibly rejuvenate herself to fight off the curse for a short period of time?"

There were tales of monks that wandered the land south of Rusk that did such a thing. It was said that even their elders enjoyed youthful bodies up until they perished in battle. I'd never been interested in such techniques myself.

"Well." She glanced around the room. "The, um, curse . . . wasn't just making her old."

After hearing about the curse, I made it clear to Wanda that I needed to speak with Lordess Velbrun about it personally. Even if, as Wanda said, she'd be crossed that I knew.

She'd asked me to wait until early the next morning, saying that the lordess would be in a better mood then, but even now, as the time came, she looked quite worried.

"I just, well, what if . . ." Wanda fiddled with her fingers as we walked to the lordess's private wing. "Oh, this is going to be terrible when she gets ahold of herself."

Ahold of herself? I'd thought this was simply a curse of the body.

I quirked a brow. "The curse changes her behavior?"

"Well . . ." Her voice trailed off. I waited for her to finish, but after so many years of keeping this secret, it seemed she had said all she could.

That did beg the question, perhaps one easier to answer for the poor maid. "How did you hide this from the other servants? You may be her only personal maid, but I can't imagine that the others haven't been curious."

"Well, they know a little." She perked up a little, that being an easier topic for her thankfully. "I act as a go-between for the lordess and the others, but they think that she's ill, conserving and building her strength through Vitae meditations."

"Is she?" Vitae meditations were the foundation of stances, the act of slowly working your Vitae into new states of being. Not every cultivator bothered with them, but I could attest that they were worth the time and effort.

"She is!" The maid looked happy to talk about that. "Her Vitae is affected by the curse, like the rest of her body, but she's been meditating on the changes, and . . . and . . . that's sort of all I understand."

Wanda blushed at her own ignorance, but I didn't think less of her for it. Vitae was complex, and even my own teachings were more practical than academic. There were plenty of scholars half my age that knew more about the theoretical side of life energy than I.

Eventually, we came upon a door, one that Wanda looked at with no small amount of trepidation before approaching it and looking over her shoulder at me. "One moment."

I nodded, stepping to the side out of the way of the door as she opened it and went inside. I heard conversation inside, but I kept myself from eavesdropping. I'd learn everything I needed to eventually.

And then the shouting started, followed by furious yells and a very frustrated scream, which sounded strange through the walls. The door suddenly catapulted open, Wanda running out with tears streaming down her cheeks.

I watched her leave, feeling very uncomfortable.

"You . . . You . . ." I turned toward the door, blinking at the higher-pitched voice.

Lordess Velbrun of Alwur was glowering at me with a Vitae-enhanced heat, her eyes almost glowing with distaste and hurt and betrayal. I might have been more alarmed at the look . . .

. . . had it not been coming from a child.

With the youthfulness of somewhere around eight or nine, the lordess could have passed for her younger sister if she had one; her angrily puffed-up cheeks did little to intimidate me.

". . . big meanie! Come back at noon, you idiot!" She stomped her foot, the ground cracking a bit under the force.

I nodded, feeling a slight headache coming on. "Of course, Lordess Velbrun of Alwur. I'm sorry for—"

"Just leave!"

I darted after Wanda's retreating form. Currently a child or not, Lordess Caitlyn Velbrun was still an angry woman.

Hours later, after I'd been welcomed back into her private office at noon, she continued to stare at me with the entire force of her Vitae. This time, I decided to endure the enhanced intimidation attempt and not press my luck.

She was right to be angry. I could not fault her for it. Nor would I take away the comfort she found from bearing down on me with her Vitae.

"Do you think that holding this over my head is going to make me agree?" Her glare was impressive, but I wasn't sure what she was talking about.

"I'm sorry." I cleared my throat, a little confused. "Could you clarify?"

Her glare somehow became even more fierce. "Don't play dumb, Lord Velbrun, you weaseled my secrets out of Wanda, that traitor, and now you think that gives you power over me?"

Oh, the meaning behind her words finally struck me.

"I believe there has been a misunderstanding."

"Oh really." Her smile was cruel and amused. "Enlighten me about this misunderstanding, oh great Lord Velbrun of Gelvurt. How am I misunderstanding your actions?"

Could I fault her paranoia? Had I been any other Velbrun, perhaps even Jorge, I could imagine the possibility of taking advantage of . . . her state. And yet, I could not even bring my heart to consider such blatant blackmail.

"Wanda asked me to help you, Lordess Velbrun," I said plainly. "She wanted my help in breaking the curse. I don't have, and never will have, intentions to use your curse, one you gained in the defense of your people, as a weapon against you."

I'd done many things in my life, things that I struggled with in my sleep, but I would never callously use someone's vulnerable state, their shame, against them just to further my own ambitions. Say what she might, I was not entirely a Velbrun.

Although I wore their colors, I was not their breed of viper.

For a moment, the noble stilled, like her body was trying to relax at my words, but the mind wouldn't let it. And yet, the anger drained from her gaze as it fell to the table between us.

"Can you?" It sounded shaky, a tiny chink in the armor that she put on at noon. The only indication she gave of the burden that she'd been dealing with for so long.

I considered her for a moment. "Finding the hag that cursed you would be difficult, unless you already knew where she was. Curse breakers could . . ."

". . . I've asked for them, subtly. Private messengers, but their price is too much. I would have to drain Alwur for years just to afford it." Her tone of voice made it clear that that would never happen.

Curse breakers, effectively master spell breakers, could untangle a curse from a soul, but they were few and far between, and most were already in the employ of the rich and powerful. Not to mention, their work was far from perfect.

Most often, they would simply be able to change the curse or lessen the severity of it. A man cursed to eternally sleep may be brought back to the waking world with an extreme case of narcolepsy, as an example.

"Can you tell me more about the curse, Lordess Velbrun? The more I know, the better I'm able to help." As Penelope had said, it was better to know thine enemy before confronting them. And this curse was certainly an enemy.

"You truly wish to help? Why?" She squinted at me.

I looked down at my hands, not sure how to be both upfront and convincing. "Don't think me a saint. I want us to work together to build a place for our people; that can only happen if we trust one another to lend aid. This is my best foot forward."

Additionally, although I wouldn't admit it at the moment, it pained me to see someone punished for standing up for their people. A lesser noble, one like Zactrik, wouldn't have batted an eye at the hag's request.

I suspected he would probably welcome such an opportunity from what I'd discovered about the man.

"Please." I met her gaze. "Tell me about the curse."

After examining me for any deception, she sighed. "Well, you already know most of it, so why not? It's called the Curse of the Waxing Maiden, from what I've read. In many ways, not the worst the hag could have used against me, but . . ."

She paused, hesitating. I'd never heard of this curse, but my study of hags was exceptionally lacking. It was interesting to know that specific curses had been identified and studied. Perhaps there was a scholar with more answers on the subject?

"My age is decided by the hour," she eventually managed to continue. "At noon, I'm in the prime of my life, but as the sun sets, I grow older, meaner, and filled with bitterness. And then I wake up a child, with an innocence and maturity unbefitting of a noble."

I nodded. "Your mind is affected, too, then?"

"Yes." She nodded. "It's torture. It's not even how I was as a child, and I certainly have no intentions of being as . . . grouchy as I get when I'm older. It's like the curse idealizes the purest archetypes of age, the most childish of children, the cronest of crone, and burdens me with them. I have to second-guess every decision I make, every action, because Alwur suffers if I slip."

The idea of being young again, a boy years away from adulthood, and the dangerous innocence that came with it certainly was not enticing. Especially with those counting on me, such a state would be horrible.

"And you have to keep this secret from the village because of spies?" She didn't strike me as someone who would have hidden this long from her own people out of simple pride.

Lordess Velbrun nodded. "Exactly. I trust my people, but House Velbrun? If they learn my timetables, when I'm most gullible or physically weak . . ."

It'd be easy to dismantle everything she'd worked for if one of the higher lords turned their gaze upon her. A few honeyed words in the morning or an assassin at night, and she would be nowhere capable of putting up a fight.

"And this prime state at noon"—I motioned to her form—"it's your original age?"

She smiled a little at that. "Was, to begin with. I've had this curse for years and a lot of time to examine how my Vitae changes throughout the day. I guess you could say I've tamed this hour, enhanced it. I'm stronger, smarter, and . . . I feel like myself."

"That's . . . quite impressive." Turning an aspect of a curse into any kind of positive was extremely difficult. I'd certainly never done it myself.

"And this hag," I started. "She never came back? What reason did she have to give you this particular curse?"

She shrugged, looking sour at the mention of the hag. "Her name was Zunia, and no, she never came back. As for why she gave this particular curse . . . I have no idea. I got reports from other villages that she had visited them, as well, but no reports of any curses, not that I reported my own either."

Reports of any kind within House Velbrun's influence were quite bare-bones. Evil truly festered within the cracks of their little information games.

"I see. Well, I have good news and bad news." It was difficult to know how she'd react to either.

"Bad news first. I don't like wasting my time enjoying the good news before I know how shitty the rest of it is."

Certainly a way of looking at it. Lydia had always liked to relax and enjoy the good news for a little bit before the bad news ruined her mood.

"I don't have the funds right now to hire a curse breaker for you, nor do I have the time to hunt for Zunia." A part of me had hoped she had simply kept in the area. "But if you've already made strides in conquering your curse, then perhaps I can offer my aid."

"Your aid?" She seemed interested, but unsure how much I could truly help. I was somewhat unsure myself, but confidence was my greatest ally right now.

"Yes, my aid." I stood up, straightening to my full height. "Lordess Caitlyn Velbrun of Alwur, I, Lord Rakta Velbrun of Gelvurt, the Dancer, the Slayer of the Warlock King, will help you with your curse."

The woman blinked, her eyes going wide at my titles and my offer to help. It was grandiose of me, I thought, to lay them out on the table so openly, but she needed to know who she was dealing with, who was willing to lend a hand to her in this time of need.

And perhaps, I needed the reminder of who I was for the people of this empire.

After a moment, she let a deep breath of air leave her lips. "I see . . . Well, Lord Velbrun of Gelvurt, I think if you're going to teach me anything, we're going to need a school."

I smiled.

30

Leaving Alwur was a must, now that I had enough support for my plans. Caitlyn, as she'd asked me to drop formalities with our alliance, had been understanding, but made me promise not to reveal what I'd learned to anyone.

I certainly didn't intend to share it with anyone. Doh would probably get a kick out of it, but I doubted she had the kind of respect in her to treat the cursed noble with the delicacy it required.

As the forests of the empire blurred past me, the **Great Wind Sprint Technique** boosting my travel time beyond the mundane, I considered my options in Cerula.

I had already pulled on my connections with CAD to get an investigation going into Zactrik Velbrun's mysterious ritual and whatever nefarious means he was up to, so I was hesitant to do so again so soon.

Additionally, getting funding from CAD for the school would most likely require it to become an extension of their facilities, perhaps a part of the land allotted for the school to be a training area for provisional CAD members.

An interesting idea, but I wasn't sure how I felt about my children growing up so close to the adventuring lifestyle. It was seductive, and, well, I didn't want to encourage my younglings to lead the life I had lived so readily.

There were some higher lords of other noble families that I could call upon, but getting more nobles involved would have to be a last resort, seeing as that would encourage House Velbrun to dig their feet in faster and deeper. No house wanted to lose face when one of the other noble families was involved.

Of course, I could also drudge up support from the local merchants. Since I was primarily looking for funding, I had a few wealthy patrons in mind that could possibly be persuaded to fund the school, but I was worried what they might want in recompense.

Gelvurt was not in an extremely profitable location, so the compensation they'd seek might involve deals that sought more control over the village or trade agreements.

I didn't have much confidence in my ability to decipher the hidden meanings of contracts or complex negotiations, so I was hesitant to make them my first option.

No, I needed someone I trusted, someone whom I had fought alongside and had developed a rapport with. Even if the negotiations weren't any easier, I would be more comfortable with any long-standing deals.

Slowing to a stop at sunset, I began setting up camp for the first and last time on my trip to the capital. Letting my Vitae replenish with rest and food, I considered my options, and one man kept rising to the top despite the reluctance building in my stomach.

Shawn Hanchett, the only adventuring companion I had not seen since Lydia and I left the group.

Cerula, the capital of the Certillian Empire, was a large city surrounded by massive stone walls that hadn't been breached in over a century. The Warlock King had once planned to siege the capital of the empire, but the magical defenses and royal guard were not to be trifled with.

Waiting among the long line of commoners and traveling merchants waiting patiently as the guards at the massive gate saw to everyone, I idly wondered how quickly the war would have ended if the king had decided to send his royal legions to aid in the war rather than allowing them to hold their place here.

Would Lydia and I have had the time to get married? How would Lydia's plan have changed if she had been put on such a tight schedule? Many questions that made me tense, but it was just an idle fantasy. Simple thoughts of things that I could have been.

Nothing to worry about any longer.

"Hello." The guard greeted me as I came up, his eyes giving me a suspicious look. "Welcome to Cerula. We'll need your name and your intended business."

There were five guards stationed here, all of them looking a little more on edge as I stepped up to be let into the city. Their Vitae was just on the edge of what I would consider a threat.

"My name is Lord Rakta Velbrun. I am here on royal business concerning Gelvurt." I flashed the signet ring I'd received upon arriving in Gelvurt, the symbol of House Velbrun on it.

Some of the guards glanced at one another, some muttering under their breath about never having heard about Gelvurt.

The guard, however, blinked. "Ah, uh, I see. Well, we'll send word to the Velbrun delegation and have someone meet you."

"No, that won't be necessary." I shook my head. "My business is not with the Velbrun delegation."

And the fewer Velbruns that knew I was away from Gelvurt the better.

"Even so, we'd appreciate it if you'd stay here while we get confirmation." I felt his suspicion growing, although I had no idea of what confirmation he spoke of . . . unless . . .

I frowned. "Do you think I'm a thief?"

"What, uh, n-no, sir." The guard shook his head, suddenly defensive. "We just . . . we haven't received word of any new Lords Velbrun."

I tilted my head, looking down at him. "Do guards at the gate often receive such news? Regardless, my business is pressing. Will there be a problem in letting this Lord Velbrun inside?"

I let an inkling of my Vitae echo into my words, letting them know that I was no simple thief that they could simply deny.

It was a threat, something Lydia wouldn't have enjoyed, but it was somewhat of a subtle one, something she loved. I only wished she were here so I would not have had to make it.

For a moment, I thought I would have to defend myself from city guards, but after a tense moment, the guard acquiesced, and I was let in.

The line into the city continued behind me without pause.

I'd dealt with prejudice barring me from entering the city easily numerous times, but I'd thought nobility would have alleviated it.

Unfortunately, it seemed a duster trying to pass as a noble was too far-fetched for the common folk of the empire.

Would my children have to deal with this? The very idea made me want to go back to those guards and teach them a lesson they would never forget.

I needed something to eat.

Cerula was the heart and soul of the empire, where the noble houses came to seek power from the king and his blood.

King Arwin Certimov, the most politically powerful man in the empire, had inherited his father's skill in weaving laws and policy that, while benign, cemented the power of the nobility.

"And now, you're one of them, ha ha!" The old man guffawed behind the counter, slapping the old, tired wood of his cane. "Now that's a good joke!"

I rubbed the back of my neck. "Yes, well, it wasn't intentional, but . . . I cannot say that I haven't enjoyed some of the benefits, 'Abi."

Adoabi nodded, still reeling in his chuckles. "Yes, yes, Rakta, I bet your kids will grow up nice and spoiled with all your servants running around to please them."

"No, no." I waved my hand. "That . . . my children will be taught respect and humility."

I was certain I could instill the right values in them as they grew up, as long as I learned from the stories of my ancestors.

"Hmm, hmm." The old man smiled, obviously unconvinced. "Well, what can this humble chef get for ya? The old regular?"

I nodded and smiled, watching the man quickly get to work. Adoabi's Corner was a small, secluded eatery in one of the less refined districts of Cerula. It was also one of the only places in the empire that served Ruskan cuisine, a fact owed to Adoabi's own Ruskan heritage.

Lydia had found this place for me after I'd had an episode of homesickness, and it was nice to return here after so long. And yet, the empty seat next to me . . .

"Get that sad look off your face." Adoabi came back with a steaming bowl of poda soup and cray rice. "And another thing, why didn't ya bring your kids!? I want to see 'em! And you know you can't cook a Ruskan meal that's worth a damn."

A cook, I assuredly was not.

I chuckled, before swallowing some of the soup while it was still piping hot, the best time to eat it. "They're young, 'Abi. I can't travel with them so soon."

"Ha, your tribe would shed a tear at such words." Adoabi shook his head with no small amount of good humor. "How's the grub?"

I let a spoonful of the rice sit in my mouth, letting the hardiness of the spicy, steamed cray rice melt into my mouth. The stalwart cray rice was a mainstay crop of Rusk, a hardy rice that grew in the harshest of environments.

"It's perfect, 'Abi." The man nodded at my honest compliment. "And I'm sure my tribe's tears for me dried up long ago."

It was better that way. I was sure of it.

His genial smile became somber, laying a hand on my shoulder. "Hey now, Rakta, I ain't exactly been back in a long time, either, but that don't mean they're not still family."

I shrugged, saying nothing. Continuing to enjoy my soup and rice, I could almost hear the distant words of my sister echoing in the back of my head, but I tried not to dwell on them.

That was not a story I was ready to share; I wasn't sure if I ever would be. Letting the silence settle between us, Adoabi returned to preparing for the next customer.

He'd certainly had a boom of popularity once it'd been leaked that the empire's heroes regularly ate here. I couldn't say if the others had continued coming after Lydia and I had left, but I was glad the Certillian clientele had realized how good the food was.

All in all, I was glad I came here. I made a promise as I left that my children would eat here one day as well.

"I'll be waiting." Adoabi tipped his hat at me.

The streets of the capital seemed longer than I remembered as I walked the cobblestone steps. Building after building, I passed with less and less enthusiasm as I realized that I truly needed to begin figuring out whom to ask first.

Going to Shawn, I was still doubtful of such a plan. The very idea of even possibly taking advantage of him after what I'd done . . .

"Is that . . . ? It is! Rakta!" I started at the unfamiliar voice, my eyes glancing around before they locked onto an approaching man waving his arm through the air.

With an olive complexion and a rough set of britches and tunic, for a moment, I wondered what this perfect stranger wanted with me.

He came up to me. "It's me, Tenon. Remember? You, uh, saved my life."

Recognition hit me like a wagon. I could just about faintly remember this man. I'd met him on my travels to reach Gelvurt so many months ago. "Tenon, I remember. How have you been?"

"Oh, me? I've been great!" He rifled through his satchel, the same that he'd had so long ago. "This big merchant, he got wind of my little project. He decided to fund the whole thing!"

I blinked. That certainly was quite the fortunate turn of fate.

"Congratulations." I gave him a nod. "You were writing a book, correct?"

Smiling, he brought out his journal. "Yep, a bestiary for the entire world, every monster above and below the surface of Derra, for all to learn from."

Ah yes, I'd spoken to him about the creatures that wandered the sands of my homeland. I hoped I'd been of some help to him.

"You're as passionate as I remember." I certainly couldn't fault the man for such a project. As long as such a task were feasible for one man alone, then plenty of CADs would be interested in his book.

The man was barely paying attention to me, though, continuing to rifle through the pages of his journal, before he stopped and turned it around to show me. Beautiful sketches, illustrations, of sandworms and gargantlions.

Depicted alongside chicken scratch, of course, that I assumed were quotes of some kind. Possibly even mine. "These pictures are very detailed. Did you draw these?"

"Oh, uh, no." Tenon laughed. "I mean, man, can you imagine? No, uh, a guy found by the merchant sponsoring me did. He'll be my illustrator! He's a pretty great guy, honestly."

I was glad he would not be on his lonesome on his journeys.

"Well, I hope you weave long and fruitful stories, Tenon." I gave him a nod. "Perhaps you should hire some protection for them."

"Oh, wow, are, uh, you offering?" He was already going for his coin purse.

I shook my head, slightly amused at his excitement. "No, no. I'm afraid I have my responsibilities here. Perhaps, though, we'll be seeing each other around. I'll keep an eye out for your name."

"You better." Tenon grinned. "It's gonna be everywhere one day."

With a stomach full of food and, after meeting Tenon, slightly more confident, I tried to bring myself to knock on the door in front of me. I was not a coward, but it felt wrong to crawl back in these circumstances.

I was no liar. I knew that even after abandoning them, I had better chances striking a fair deal with my past companions than any other patron in the city. At least, I hoped so.

And yet, to abuse these bridges that I'd already tarnished . . . perhaps this was a mistake. No, it finally occurred to me, this was most definitely a mistake. To come here like this was a disservice to trust and loyalty we'd once shared.

I straightened up, finding my resolve, and made my way to go back onto the streets, toward the home of a different possible patron. One that I would not be abusing the trust of for coin.

And then the door opened behind me.

". . . Rakta? Buddy, is that you?"

I turned around, seeing the freckled face and ginger hair of my most savvy traveling companion, and gave an uneasy smile. "Ah, Shawn. Hello."

Shawn's face lit up, his dimples beaming.

31

So, how've you been, man?" Shawn's earnest stare didn't waver for a second as he sat in the chair opposite of me, my friend having led me into his warm abode.

It was a street-side manor, humble for what it was, but still indicative of a rich lifestyle. I saw a few servants attending to their duties, but not many. I wouldn't be surprised if Shawn did a lot of the cooking himself; he'd always had interesting tastes.

"I've been well," I said, glancing around his nice home. "As well as I could be, at least."

Shawn frowned. "Yeah, I heard about Lydia . . . and, uh, what Ulric did. I would have gone after him, you know, if I'd known. I learned, uh, a little bit too late though."

I nodded, feeling my chest pang at the memories of that night. "I don't have anything more to say on what happened between me and Ulric."

"I get that, man, I really do." He gave a nod, his smile full of genuine understanding.

If there was truly someone worthy of the title of hero among those I traveled with, it was Shawn. A mysterious stranger, really, that had taken up the banner of the empire and spearheaded the defense against the Warlock King.

I'd doubted he was even a native to the empire when we first met, something that had made it more comfortable to connect with him.

I coughed. "And how have you been, Shawn?"

"It's been nice, honestly." He leaned back, looking comfortable. "Not easy though. Even with most of the Warlock King's remnants accounted for, we've got something big going on in the north."

My thoughts went to Gelvurt's captain of the guard. "Big? Should I be worried?"

"Well." He shrugged. "I don't know yet. We think the smarter followers went to ground, and now we're thinking they've got this small Illuminati thing going on among some of the houses."

I blinked. "Illuminati?"

Shawn blushed. "Uh, sorry, saying from my hometown. It's basically, uh . . . a secret group? We think a few nobles that secretly supported the Warlock King are trying to finish the job he started."

That was concerning. Were the Velbruns involved? They hadn't exactly provided much aid to the war, but Lydia had never spoken of any major support for the Warlock King among the higher lords. Although, perhaps she would not deign to tell me such things.

"So yeah, Penelope and I are getting a force together to clear the air and get some names. Arwin needs evidence before he can be convinced to do any kind of deeper investigation on the houses."

"Speaking of King Certimov, are you still courting—"

"He is."

With a little yawn and a delightful stretch of her arms, a young woman walked in from one of the back rooms, her curly blonde hair falling a few inches below her shoulders and her sparkling red eyes gleaming.

I watched as all of Shawn's blood went to his cheeks as he stood up. "Tracy, you're up! Uh, I was just . . . talking to Rakta . . ."

Princess Tracy Certimov gave me a polite smile before moving over to give my friend a chaste kiss on the lips, rendering him speechless. No matter how long they'd known each other, I doubted Shawn would ever get used to the princess's affection.

As she sat down, Shawn following her example, I looked at her tousled clothing. "Congratulations."

I was both relieved to see my friend had found love and . . . a mix of jealousy and grief that I tried not to think about. It was unfair to let my thoughts linger on what I'd once had when I should be happy for the couple in front of me.

"No, uh, no." Shawn tried to find his words, his blush getting brighter. "I, well, unfortunately King Certimov still doesn't entirely approve, but, well—"

"He's coming around," Tracy finished, leaning her head on Shawn's shoulder. "At least, he must be to turn a blind eye to some of the activities we've gotten up to."

From what I understood, Shawn had met Tracy after a gala thrown in celebration of the successes amid the war against the Warlock King. He was never quite open about it, but Shawn always found new ways to meet up with her, one way or another.

Lydia had kept me from the party, not that I had wanted to go. I believe only Penelope was in attendance with my heroic friend at the time.

"Ha ha." Shawn was steadfastly looking at the ground. "Yeah, uh, activities."

I was struck with the strong notion that I was intruding. I'd already felt somewhat villainous for coming here for funding to begin with, so I stood up. "Perhaps I should give you two some privacy."

"No!" Shawn looked alarmed. "You can't leave just yet, uh, we haven't really talked that long. You have kids, right?"

Tracy's eyes glimmered with interest. "You're a father, Rakta?"

"Well, yes." I slowly sat back down, lured in with the promise of speaking praises about my children. "I have three beautiful younglings, each of them intelligent for their age and growing more amazing every day."

The thought of them brought a smile to my lips, only tempered by the distance between us.

"Man, Rakta, I never thought I'd see the day that you were a father." Shawn shook his head. "It sounds like you're going to be fine."

I couldn't help but frown. "If the Velbruns allow me to."

I realized my mistake when both of their gazes became concerned, having said far too much. Both of them were aware of the treacheries common among the Velbruns.

"It's nothing, just politics." I waved my hand dismissively.

Shawn reached out and took my hand. "Rakta, what's going on? You're a horrible liar, and I can tell something is bothering you."

I could feel the Vitae humming with his hand, easily harmonizing with my own after years of battling side by side. It was comforting, far too comforting for a man like myself.

I breathed in and out. "I don't deserve the aid you would offer after I abandoned you all—"

"Stop." Shawn's voice was strong.

His gaze was warm, but commanded attention. Suitable for someone that had spent years leading militias and keeping our group together.

"What you did was wrong," Shawn said, speaking plainly but kindly. "We worried, we thought you'd been kidnapped or worse, we made mistakes that cost us. Lydia's letter, when we finally got it, was dismissive of the years we fought together."

Cold knives pierced my heart, even as a part of me leaped to defend my wife from . . . the truth. I'd read the letter. I'd been convinced that it was fine. And yet, she was so distraught after what had happened, I knew I should have written the letter. She'd thought I'd done enough.

My friend continued, "We didn't deserve that, Rakta. And you don't deserve going through whatever is happening to you alone either."

"I should have come back sooner," I said, the words falling uselessly out of my lips. "It's wrong of me to knock on your door when I am in trouble. It isn't right."

"Yeah, it is a little scummy." Shawn chuckled. "But we've almost died for each other, Rakta, countless times. Remember the scylla?"

A horrid beast of the depths that had been fished from the ocean by some of the Warlock King's enslaved sirens. One the most dangerous fights we'd been involved in.

"That made for a good story." I nodded. Ulric and I had to keep the creature contained while Penelope and Lydia worked together to aim and fire one of the former's larger pieces of weaponry. Shawn had been the one to finally strike its heart.

"It was a great story," he agreed. "So, what's going on?"

I gave him a long look, glancing over to see Tracy having moved to his side and wrapped an arm around his, a show of solidarity. While not as warm, her gaze was full of compassion for a friend of the man she loved.

Lydia's gaze had never been so warm toward those I had called friends.

"I need help." And I told them everything.

"So, uh, wow." Shawn slowly digested all that I'd told him. I had left out only the particulars of the prophecy, my friend having understood my reservations to reveal it to anyone so soon. I still wasn't sure what it meant, so how could I speak about it to others?

I nodded. "It's more complicated than I would have liked my young-lings' life to be before they even begin learning to walk."

Although, with how active they were already, I wouldn't be surprised if they started walking early. Or their first words. If I missed either, I would be devastated.

"Okay, well, don't worry." Shawn crossed his arms. "Uncle Shawn will take care of everything."

I blinked. "Uncle?"

My friend blushed, rubbing the back of his neck. "Oh, uh, that was just . . . you know, I know we aren't brothers, really, but I'd like to be there for your kids . . . I know you'd be there for mine. Like family."

I closed my eyes and felt my heart almost give out at the sheer kind-ness of the man before me. I'd witnessed it firsthand many times, but now, to feel it myself after so long, I was left awestruck.

"You—" I shook my head, amazed. "Shawn, I would be honored to have you as part of the lives of my children."

Shawn smiled. "The others would love to, as well, you know?"

I wasn't quite as confident. Penelope's coldness and Ulric's actions were not as encouraging as Shawn's forgiveness.

"They are not as forgiving as you are, Shawn." And I was still wonder-ing if that was a mistake on his part. "Perhaps, in time, we can all make amends."

Try as I might, it was difficult to think fondly of Ulric. Perhaps, with Shawn to mediate, I could begin to rebuild these bridges that I'd thought irreparably burned.

"So, you need money," Shawn continued on. "I can handle that. How much?"

Hesitantly, I brought out the documents with the tallied costs of everything, from personnel to construction, with a healthy margin for additional costs that Orion and Jorge had predicted.

Shawn's eyes widened at the final number. "Wow, that's a pretty penny."

Shawn had never explained what a penny was in all our time travel-ing, but I nodded. "Any funding would help. I can always have more than one patron—"

"So, do I give you all this money now, or do I hand it over later?" Shawn handed the document back.

I checked the document, making sure I had marked the right amount. There was no mistake. To be so casual about this sum of sil, it was almost breathtaking.

"Since we are in the capital, we can make the largest purchases here . . . Are you truly willing to pay for everything? You have that much money?"

"Even if he doesn't"—Tracy came back into the room, having left for a shower during my explanation—"my father doesn't mind how I use my own personal funds."

A weight on my shoulders suddenly lifted as I realized, with a cer-tainty, that my children would be safe, one way or another.

An hour later, Shawn and I walked from building to building, discussing the best prices for all the material and manual labor the school would require.

It felt like old times, really. Shawn was much more talkative than I, but he was insightful. He knew much more about economy and numbers than I did, something even Penelope had noted on our travels.

Most of his wealth, from what I understood, was investing in local businesses that he had helped get off the ground. And he'd even given our group's artificer some new ideas for magical inventions, his imagi-nation supplying her with inspiration throughout the time we'd adven-tured together.

Truly, he was an enigma. One that we, or at least, I had never truly understood. Perhaps that was alright.

As we stepped out of the Adamant, a construction business, Shawn grabbed my arm, stopping me.

"Yes, Shawn?" I looked down at him with some concern.

He smiled up at me. "Rakta, your kids are a part of the prophecy, aren't they?"

After a moment of hesitation, I nodded. I'd alluded to that point somewhat, but I'd kept myself from outright admitting it. If there was one man I trusted with that much, it was Shawn.

"Well," he said, his smile tightening. "Be careful. Prophecies are . . . don't let it rule their lives, okay? There's a lot more to life than fate."

I nodded, considering the gravity behind his words. "I will remember that, Shawn. Is . . . is there something you want to talk about?"

The very least I could do was listen to the hidden struggles of my friend, who had provided more help than I truly felt I deserved after all I had done.

"Nah, buddy, it's fine. This isn't about me anymore." Shawn smiled, but the sadness in his gaze did little to calm my worried heart. He continued on, as if nothing had been said, leaving me to recover alone from the finality in his words.

32

Alright, that's the last of it." Shawn scratched off the last item from the list he'd made before we had set out on our shopping trip.

We'd been at this for most of the day, going from merchant to merchant. Where I thought I'd have favors to pull to aid in the purchasing of the materials, Shawn had truly outmatched me. Discounts for the hero of the empire were freely given.

I checked my own papers. "Personnel will have to come later. Teachers are not so easily purchased as wood and stone."

To convince the great minds of the empire to live in the small village of Gelvurt, I would have to market the opportunity in very specific ways. Jorge would help. He was far better at sounding enticing than I, but my name would help.

My friend shrugged. "Yeah, but we can trust the Dover Trading Company to get the word out about that, and the Adamant will get the construction started as soon as the supplies reach the area."

"I'll have to let Jorge know; these workers will need a place to sleep and eat." Although, from what I'd understood, the lord had been eagerly preparing Niers for the surge of men and women coming. He was very excited for all the new business.

Shawn nodded, beginning the trek back to his abode. It had been amazing, honestly, to see how expertly my friend had swayed the merchants and business owners to our side. Shawn was good with a blade, but his true skill was always with people.

The way he demanded attention with a smile outmatched the Vitae-enhanced charisma of most nobles. In the eyes of the empire and its people, he was truly a beloved hero.

I was happy for him, finally having what he deserved. The spotlight had never suited me, for reasons beyond my heritage, but Shawn relished in it. And yet, he had come a long way from being the glory hound that I had first met all those years ago.

"So, are you staying the night? It's a long walk back to Gelvurt." Shawn nudged me as we walked, getting my attention.

I nodded. "I'd already planned to stay two days to get everything sorted. I think resting here for the night would be fine."

"Great! Tracy has this new recipe she's been trying out; she really got into cooking after we went to this new place near Ori Park. The chefs cooked the food right in front of us!"

I listened to him chatter on, enjoying the conversation, and asked questions here and there to keep it going. It was relaxing.

After a delicious meal of only slightly burned chicken breast and fine wine, I had retired for the night, leaving Shawn and Tracy to enjoy the rest of their night alone and in the privacy of their shared room.

Or at least, that had been the plan before I heard a knock at my door a few hours later, stirring me from my light sleep.

I crept over, opening the door gently. ". . . Tracy?"

Princess Tracy Certimov, dressed in her fine nightwear, looked apologetic for a moment, before her expression melted into the more severe bearing of royalty. "Rakta, we need to talk."

In my heart of hearts, I truly hoped she did not need help with curses as well. I doubted that was the intent, but I was still trying to figure out how to aid Caitlyn with her own.

"Of course, Tracy." I nodded, opening the door and letting her inside. "Does Shawn know you're here?"

"No," she said, stepping inside as I closed the door behind her. "He sleeps deep when he's had a few glasses to drink. I wanted to take this time to make a few things clear."

I nodded, feeling a little bit of worry build in my chest. Clarifications had very rarely ended up going well for me in my experience.

"First, Shawn is kind, too kind. You know this, I know you know this, and I don't appreciate that you've come to him for help without . . . without making proper amends." She looked cross. "There was never a chance he wouldn't have helped."

I had no defense against the accusation. I shifted, unable to meet her gaze. "It isn't right of me, I agree. I'm almost overwhelmed by his forgiveness, one that I truly don't feel deserving of."

It was hard to say what I could do to feel deserving of it. Nothing but time and years of being there for him could ever repay him for this forgiveness.

"But you can be."

I looked at her. "What do you mean?"

"Shawn is kind," Tracy repeated. "So kind that when he heard you had kids, he stopped himself from asking you to help with the situation up north."

I blinked at the mention of the north. "The situation? He didn't tell me much about it."

"That's because we know basically nothing," she said. "But there have been sightings, Rakta, sightings of monsters moving around a small village called Crest."

"And Shawn is heading there soon?"

"There's a Taine there," she continued. "Shawn, Penelope, and Ulric are going to investigate him alongside a small contingent of guards in the next few weeks."

House Taine, another of the noble families. They were one of the coastal houses, with a strong grip on the fisheries and production of boats. I'd not interacted with members of their house much, but the Warlock King had certainly had a few outposts within their influence.

Still, I saw where Tracy was going with this. "And you want me to go with him."

It was a reasonable request.

"No." She shook her head. "This isn't about me. You should want to go with him, Rakta. If you truly feel bad, undeserving, then you should be right where you should have been in the weeks after the Warlock King died."

She pointed toward the door, out to where Shawn slept.

"With them."

My heart lurched in my chest. The idea of going into battle once more, alongside my . . . friends. Even if I couldn't truly call Ulric that with the same confidence, could I truly pass on the chance to aid them once more?

And yet, what of my children? What if I was slain? Their lives would be forfeited to the heartless Velbruns that would see their intelligence, their prophesied existence, and use them as pawns.

I took a deep breath. "Thank you, Tracy. I have much to think about."

"Yes, you do." She nodded, looking less severe now, before turning toward the door. "Good night, Rakta. I'm . . . sorry about how the chicken turned out."

"It was delicious." I chuckled, giving her a genial smile. "By the way, does your father know you're here this late?"

The look the blushing maiden shot me was filled with horrible promises. I decided that teasing the princess was an exercise in courting death that I'd distance myself from in the future.

"I know about Crest."

Shawn and I had walked to the gatehouse of Cerula the next morning, my friend wanting to see me off on my way back to Gelvurt.

He blinked. "Oh, uh . . . Tracy told you, didn't she?"

"Yes." I nodded. "She said you kept it from me intentionally."

"You have kids, Rakta. The only world you should feel responsible for right now are in their cribs, probably crying for you to get back soon." Shawn stared off into the distance, not meeting my gaze.

I looked off into the distance as well. "And yet, I also have friends. Friends that I abandoned when they needed me."

My night after Tracy left had been one filled with hard thoughts. I tried to find wisdom from the stories of my people, sought inspiration from the trials and tribulations of past heroes.

And yet, nothing had helped. There were not many tales of cowards among my people or, at least, none that had survived in my tribe's telling of history.

"You could get hurt. You could die. What's going to happen to your kids without you?" Shawn's voice was rising in heat.

"That's why," I continued gently, lightly placing a hand on his shoulder, "I'd like to be unreasonably selfish of your kindness."

I turned toward him, and he finally met my gaze. His eyes were moist, seconds from shedding tears. Shawn had always been one to cry when he got emotional, from anger to laughter.

"There is a chance I will die, Shawn." There was no sense in hiding the risk. "Yet, there is a smaller chance that we both die. If something happens to me, in Crest or in the future, can I die knowing that you will take care of my children?"

Shawn let out a choked gasp. "Shit, Rakta, that's . . . how can I say no? Of course, man. Buh, but please . . . don't die. Don't throw your life away just to feel better."

I nodded. "I won't."

"Well then . . . we, everyone, would be happy to have you along." He said it with a teary smile, his dimples positively shining.

I had almost run away from the responsibility I had to the group. Returned to my children as a man who left his friends to risk their lives without him.

And yet, I remembered my friends. I knew them. While I only had Shawn's word, I knew that neither Penelope nor Ulric would simply leave my children to the wolves.

And that had made my decision much easier to make.

Would Lydia have agreed with it?

"Thank you, Shawn. I'll be back in time for the expedition."

With a surge of Vitae to my legs, I leaped into the air and began the long journey home.

Returning to Gelvurt days later, I was surprised at the relief I felt as I walked into the center of the village. I was comfortable here, I realized with a bit of a start.

When had Gelvurt become a home? It wasn't perfect, there were still villagers that looked at me with distaste, but most saw me as a hero for dealing with Vera. It was more acceptance than I'd really thought possible within the borders of the empire.

And it was where my children would grow up. The children I saw running around would one day be the peers of my younglings.

It was no Ruskan tribe, but the closeness of the small village community felt familiar, familiar enough that I realized that Caitlyn was right. Doing the best for this village, for my people, it truly was one of my responsibilities now.

Still, I rushed to the keep, wanting to see my children and relieve Doh of her duties. I hadn't worried much about her on my travels, but now I felt a small bubble of anxiety begin to build in my chest.

"Doh? Doh!" I entered the keep, heading up to my room, where we'd planned for her to sleep in my absence.

The door to my room slammed open as I approached, Doh stumbling out barely clothed. "Oh! Hey, uh, Rakta! You're back, uh, early!"

I stilled. ". . . Doh? What did you do?"

"Uh." Doh blushed. "No one."

And then Dresden's voice, sounding barely awake, called from the open door. "Mm, Doh come back to bed."

Doh's blush brightened, small blotches of her skin shifting hues as she glanced back into the room. Wisely, I decided to go check on my children before dealing with this, walking past the maid.

33

D ah!" Daka waved her arms up at me as I peered over into her crib, her siblings staring at me. Natakia giggled at my return, but Dalton met my gaze with a cool scan of his own.

I smiled, picking them up and sitting down with my precious younglings. "It's good to be back. I hope you were on your best behavior for Doh."

Although she certainly hadn't been on her best behavior, from the looks of things. I wasn't sure if I wanted to congratulate the shape changer on her deception or her audacity to spend time with Dresden in my bed.

Daka's face screwed up like she'd bitten something rotten, but Natakia nodded her head. Dalton didn't respond, still watching me intently as his sisters engaged. It was adorable.

I was so glad to be home.

"Yes, yes, I know it must have been strange." I could only begin to imagine if one of my loved ones had begun acting as strange as Doh did on the regular. "But it has paid off. You will all have the finest education possible in the empire."

For once, it was Daka and Natakia that were slow to react, but Dalton . . . actually smiled. I'd gotten the impression that he would be fond of going to school.

"Guh." Dalton closed his eyes, like he was content and ready for a nap. I had gotten here close to nap time, after all. Natakia quickly followed him, her eyes closing as she started to snore. Daka's eyes were brilliant with excitement.

I gave her a kiss on the forehead as I placed the other two back into the crib. "Well, my little warrior, perhaps it is a good time for a walk."

She let out a little giggle, and I felt a comfortable warmth fill my chest. The last few days had been difficult, racked by worry for my children and guilt for my actions.

But now? I knew it had been worth it. My children would be safe and happy here. I'd have gone through countless sleepless nights for that.

"Hey, uh." Doh crept in slowly. "Are the kids asleep?"

I glanced over, thankful that she'd gotten properly clothed. "I'm going to take Daka on a walk. I think I could use some relaxation. Is Dresden . . . ?"

The maid's cheeks reddened, her fingers weaving together nervously. "He had some . . . training to go do."

I'd have to talk to him about his intentions with Doh. A relationship was fine, of course, but, really, I doubted my chambers were the proper place for it.

Ignoring my infant daughter's narrowed gaze at the maid, I stood up and walked out. "Join me, Doh. I want to be caught up on recent events."

Hearing about everything that Doh had taken care of in my absence, with the help of Orion, I was pleasantly surprised that no real issues had come up.

Much like me, Doh had kept to herself when not doing her duties, but had continued to walk through the village regularly and made herself available for discussions.

"Uh, the only thing that kinda surprised me," Doh said as she walked alongside me, "was this alchemist woman, uh . . ."

She trailed off, so I spoke up. "Marge?"

"Yeah! Her." Doh snapped her fingers. "She came by. It was, uh, a really heavy conversation, but it sounded like you said some things to her? She said she was getting better, dealing with her loss."

That was a relief to hear, albeit bittersweet with the duplicity involved. "That's . . . good to hear. I wish I'd have been here to truly hear her out."

"And, uh, if we're being really honest, I kind of cheated while you were gone." She seemed hesitant to say the words out loud.

I blinked, lightly bouncing Daka in my arms. "Cheated?"

"Well." She coughed. "There was a slipup here and there . . . you know, villagers realizing I was, well, you were acting strange . . ."

Unease built in my chest at the scenario she was painting for me. "And you . . . cheated?"

"Well, if they don't remember I messed up, did I ever really mess up?" Doh batted her eyelashes at me, trying to look innocent. I was absolutely sure, this time, that she was subtly shifting herself to look slightly younger as she did so.

Daka hissed at her. My daughter truly did not like her for some reason. It'd put me on edge, the first few days, but she'd proven herself trustworthy despite my infant's dislike of her. I imagined her penchant for changing her shape disturbed the youngling.

Still, Doh's admittance was a tad disturbing and certainly not something I wanted to encourage. It bordered too closely to how the Velbruns operated in their darker corners.

I took a deep breath, before I looked around and tried to enjoy the surrounding forest. "Please don't say things like that. Don't mess with the memories of my villagers, Doh. Not without their permission."

Having a memory-altering shape-shifter in the village was one thing—it had proven to be a boon more than once—but I couldn't let myself get comfortable with the idea of her altering memories as she liked. That could become a serious problem.

Doh nodded, looking surprisingly guilty. "Hey, it didn't feel good, you know? I'm not sure how to feel about getting this . . . familiar with everything, everyone."

My tension was mollified by the genuine discomfort she was feeling. I wasn't sure if that was something I would have seen from her months ago.

"I understand." I smiled softly. "Settling down is hard. Thank you for trying . . . But how did Dresden get involved?"

"Oh, uh, well that is a great story that involves him walking in on me as I was transforming into you one morning and, uh . . . Did you know Dresden can draw his blade faster than I can cast a spell?"

"Yes." Dresden was always quick on the draw. We'd been working on his reaction time for months.

Doh giggled. "Yeah, well, I explained it all, and Orion was brought in . . . One thing led to another, and I, uh, invited Dresden for a little bit of fun."

"In my room?"

"Well, I was in your form when I asked." She had the audacity to giggle at the memory.

I frowned. That really didn't make me feel any better. I doubted that would have made anyone feel better.

Her eyes widened, her words suddenly in a rush. "Buh, but, I was, uh, me the whole time after we . . . got into the room. Well, uh, at least, I wasn't you."

"Well." I sighed after some time. "At least this means you'll stop pining after Orion?"

Doh nodded slowly, but a part of me wasn't really convinced. Regardless, I let silence reign and enjoyed the rest of my walk with my daughter and maid.

"So, you'll be leaving again in two weeks?" Orion's face scrunched up like he'd swallowed a lemon. "Please don't have Doh stand in for you again."

"Was it that bad?" I was double-checking the documents needed for the academy, getting letters ready to send off to Caitlyn and Jorge to update them on the process.

"She was, uh, excitable as you," he said. "Smiling far too much."

"I smile plenty." I raised an eyebrow at him.

"Around your children, yes, but your smiles while out on the streets are rare." Orion shook his head, organizing some of the paperwork. "Doh smiled a lot."

Despite wanting to contest it, I doubted I'd have any luck. My first few months within the empire, I had wondered why Certillians smiled so much on the streets for strangers, so perhaps I was the odd one out.

I shrugged, returning to the original topic. "So, yes, I will be gone. I don't know how long, but there is something going on in House Taine's land."

"Up north? That's where the captain headed, right?" Orion's attention was undivided now.

"Yes." I nodded. "He'll either be a part of the expedition or already be up there. Hopefully he's in good health."

There had been little to no word from him since he'd left.

Orion agreed, nodding as he went back to the paperwork. We'd been hammering out the last few details, such as the different positions and number of students we'd be allowing for the first year.

Suddenly a knock came at the door, Doh quietly stepping in with a letter. With the way she moved, I almost thought she was about to admit to further crimes.

"Rakta." Her voice was worried. "It's from the Velbruns."

Not even a day back and I was already accosted by the family once more.

Hours later, I dropped the letter onto the sheets of my bed as I stepped outside onto the balcony that overlooked the forested hills of my domain, my land.

Only mine by the power of the Velbruns. Nothing I had, it seemed, came without strings that led back to them.

"I don't care about land or power," I muttered to the wind. "Only the safety and comfort it allows my children."

I would not allow the Velbruns to attach their strings to them.

They had learned of my movement, my plans. It was inevitable, really; nothing could escape the web of information that the Velbruns had built throughout the empire and beyond. The alliance I had with Niers and Alwur was now common knowledge among the Velbruns, it seemed.

Markus had penned the letter, but I could taste the poisoned honey of the other higher lords on it. He had complimented my plan, had even said that, with the backing of the princess, it would be difficult to contest within the royal courts of the empire.

"And if the Velbruns are threatening the one reason I accepted their land and power," I pondered, "why would I even continue as a noble? Why would I not run off elsewhere?"

They would contest it, according to Markus. The higher lords were already prepared to pull on every string, every favor, to gain custody of my children. They didn't want to go to such lengths though.

House Velbrun finally wanted to sit down and compromise, find a middle ground that we could both agree on. Because, while they could pull on everything they had, they wouldn't have anything left afterward. Not to mention, they seemed hesitant to truly rile me.

At the end of the day, they were cowards. Had they not foreseen that I wouldn't want to give up my children? It was laughable that they thought I was detached from the affairs of my children, but the alternative scared me.

That this, the demanding of my children, the forming of the academy, this offered compromise, was all a part of their plans. Lydia had been intelligent, and her divination magic had snatched victory from the jaws of defeat.

But now, it had been turned against me, and Lydia, the only Velbrun I trusted, was gone. The pawn was left on the board, just waiting for its string to be pulled by the next one to come along and grab them up.

"If I tell them the prophecy, they'll never let up." I frowned. "They would like nothing more than to have the prophesied children in their clutches."

Sighing, I let my Vitae thrum and felt the world around me still. I sought answers from the stories of my ancestors. Muttering their stories under my breath, I felt their names pulse upon my tongue.

Could a story truly help me here? A story of the past? What story held the wisdom that I needed in this time of struggle?

"You named for the future, Rakta, but I must respect our past. Perhaps our mistakes can be cleansed through them." Lydia's words suddenly echoed through my mind.

I felt a strange certainty grip me. What if the story I sought, with the wisdom I needed, was a story that had not been told yet? One that was kept close in the hearts of those Lydia had bound by promise?

A story the Velbruns would do anything, agree to anything, to keep from the light of day.

The story of the Warlock King.

34

I wasn't expecting you so soon," Markus said, opening the door of his home. It was a luxurious home, one of the many estates in Velbrun that had been offered to those with influence. Lydia and I had lived in one during our time staying here.

I gently took off my traveling cloak and set it aside on a nearby coatrack as I came in. "I want to take care of this before I get wrapped up in later business."

Not to mention, if I did not do this now, and died during the mission, I would be hard-pressed to make the same point as I'd come to impress upon House Velbrun.

"We didn't expect you to be so calm about this." Something about how relaxed I was must have made him tense. "I take it the academy is being funded?"

"Yes," I said. "Shawn is providing funding. Of course, Princess Certimov has also offered her resources if his treasury comes up short."

My brother-in-law flinched. "We had . . . heard rumors that might be the case. However, even with the princess's backing giving you confidence, I'm glad you came to compromise."

The words stank of Velbrun manipulation. They certainly had not wished to compromise when I was but a simple lesser lord to put pressure on as they might. I was happy to remind them of who I was before I had left my adventuring days behind me.

"I came to hear you out, at the very least." I wasn't fond of having to burn precious days I would rather spend with my children before I would have to leave for the north to meet Shawn and the others.

However, the situation required it. I would still be able to return to my children for a few days before I was called once more by my responsibilities and duties.

He nodded, giving me a brief scan. "I see. Well, make yourself at home. I'll be acting as the representative of the higher lords of Velbrun for this conversation."

Gesturing out to a few leather chairs in his sitting room, he left me to sit and ponder until he returned with a stack of documents. This one was thicker than others I'd seen, neatly compiled in a leather folder to keep them all together.

Passing them to me, Markus smiled, an expression filled with a sheathed edge. "The higher lords were interested in the prophecy, Rakta, very interested. It was unfortunate, they thought, that you would not share the details."

"Was it?" I looked at the documents. Mostly signatures of the various members of House Velbrun, a symbol of collective support for the conversation. Nothing of worth here, other than names to pursue if something were to happen to my children.

For all of them were in support of taking one of my children, one of my triplets, into their greedy hands and raising them to be the perfect Velbrun.

"Yes, it was." Markus's tone was colder at my nonchalance. "I had to listen to it for quite some time until this arrangement was figured out."

I paused. "Figured out?"

"Honesty works best, in my opinion." He waved a hand dismissively, lying as easily as he breathed. "Some of our specialists were to scry upon the various possibilities regarding you and your children."

Now that was an expected, yet still disturbing, truth if I had ever heard one.

"I don't appreciate the higher lords scrutinizing my children and me, Markus." He already knew that, of course, but it had to be said.

"No one does." Markus shrugged. "But it keeps the empire safe from unexpected attacks, within and without."

The usual response, with none of the usual variation to keep it from sounding trite. Markus wasn't even trying. Was he truly invested in all of this?

Getting comfortable, Markus smiled. "Well then, let me say right now that a single child is all that the higher lords are requesting. We believe that at least one heir or heiress of Lydia's blood should grow up . . . closer to Velbrun."

I watched him, feeling my body instinctively tense at the sheer gall to ask me to acquiesce to such demands. Still, this was not the time to lash out unnecessarily.

"Of course," he continued, "visitation will be well within your rights, and we will schedule monthly visits between you and the child in our care."

"Do you think the higher lords are right to ask this of me?" I kept my voice neutral, but nothing could hide the tenseness in my voice.

"My opinion is meaningless," he said. "Although, I have been tasked with taking care of the child in question, seeing as I am their uncle."

Hiding behind his responsibilities, his duties to his family. What about his duty to his nieces and nephew? What about his duty to keep them where they would be loved without conditions?

I frowned. "Your opinion is not meaningless to me, Markus. You are my brother-in-law. That means something."

A part of me wanted Markus on my side. Not even on my side, per se, but at least some show that he didn't agree with what the higher lords were doing to Lydia's children.

That he was not as purely Velbrun as I had been led to believe by all other traces of evidence.

"It means I'm the one who will have to take care of them." Markus said with finality, a familiar undercurrent of anger in the chill of his voice.

A silence followed, my hands steepled together as I considered that. If that was all he made of our familial connection, then so be it.

"Once a year." I slowly raised a finger. "My children and I will visit Velbrun for a week until they are of age to decide where they go. You will not raise any of my children."

Markus raised an eyebrow. "So you want to do this the hard way, Rakta?"

That was where I knew Markus completely misunderstood me. There would have been nothing harder than simply giving Markus one of my children.

I would have rather ripped out my own heart and given that to them instead.

"No, I wanted to do this the right way," I admitted. "The way a family should. Without deceit or coercion, I sought support from a family that had no warmth for me and my children. All the Velbruns know is greed for a tomorrow that they wish to own."

"Careful." Markus frowned. "Rakta, the elders don't take kindly to slander. We've given you more than most would; don't you think it's time to give back? Perhaps you'll understand the depths of our kindness if it's taken away for a time?"

"Perhaps you and House Velbrun will understand the depths of my patience once it breaks?" My fists were clenched. Threatening Lydia's brother felt like an affront to her memory. Is that why the Velbruns made him act as a middleman? To limit me?

He tensed, his eyes subtly glancing around the room. There were guards posted outside, of course, but if anything happened, they would not reach us in time to truly stop anything if I acted with haste. The idea they thought me on the edge of murder was ridiculous.

Although, I was certainly close to breaking something.

I shook my head, clearing any thoughts of violence. "You and the higher lords will accept my offer. We will visit, continue acting in the circles of House Velbrun as I have done so far, and in return . . . you will not bother my children until they have the responsibility of making their own decisions."

While it would hurt, I would not stop my children from seeking the Velbruns out if they grew up wishing to align themselves with the rest of the family more closely.

"And why would we ever consider that deal?" Markus was glaring at me now, a shock mixed in with the anger that swam in his gaze.

"Because," I began, "if you do not, I will tell everyone that Dalton Velbrun, the former treasured son of House Velbrun, was the Warlock King."

There was silence in the room. If there were any listeners to this conversation, I wondered if this revelation would be their doom.

Markus suddenly paled, his hands beginning to shake as my threat, no, my promise truly registered. I sat in silence, letting him digest my words in peace, if he was able to find any in the face of my proposal.

His first words were but a whisper, but the sheer vitriol in his voice was palpable. Like a glacier slowly appearing over the horizon.

"You . . . you would break your promise to my sister?"

"You think she would oppose me?" I let my Vitae begin to vibrate. Markus was not a combatant, not really, but most skilled in manipulating Mana could form simple blasts. I'd much rather be ready for them than not.

My brother-in-law seethed at my words.

"Lydia and I spent months crafting our plan to get him back alive, to talk him down from his madness, and you . . . you want to destroy his reputation now too?" He looked at me like I was mad, his voice becoming a fierce, desperate whisper. "After killing him and ruining everything?"

Either no one was listening in or Markus simply did not care about who heard us.

"What reputation, Markus?" I gestured to all around us. "You said it yourself: the higher lords put a black mark upon him. Few even know he existed."

"Shut up!" Markus's grip on his chair was tight, Mana pouring off of him. "Murderer! Brother killer! Lydia is rolling in the grave! She hated you!"

At his fierce words, I nodded. "Perhaps . . . perhaps she did. I did everything she asked me to, Markus. Every mission taken in the dead of night, every enemy killed before his identity could be revealed, I did it."

"And now," he muttered, "you want to destroy whatever remains of him."

"I could not stand by, however," I continued, "when after Lydia made her final stand, offered him open arms, he tried to kill her."

"She could have taken it."

"She was exhausted by that point, Markus. Lydia had seen that we needed to fight him to his final breath before giving him a chance to surrender . . . and he didn't." I remembered Lydia's screams as my axes tore her brother apart. I wasn't proud of it.

"So, that's it then? You wish to blackmail your family with our hidden sins? I see you are a pinnacle of Ruskan ideals. Lydia would spit where you stand." Markus growled at me, resorting to pulling my heritage into this.

I thought about that, about Lydia. I'd taken her into my arms and promised her anything and everything. All she had wanted, she had cried, was her brother back. Her loving older brother that had made the world shine.

I thought of the manipulations, the friendships she threw away when everything was over, the bloodshed that I had wrought at her persuasion, and the sheer uncertainty of whether she truly loved me or not.

But there was one thing I was certain about.

"Recently, I've heard many things about Lydia." I trained my gaze on Markus. "Some true, some not. Sometimes I felt the furthest from ever understanding the mysteries within her mind; sometimes I felt moments of knowing more than ever before."

I closed my eyes and breathed deeply, before opening them again with new resolve.

"But as my wife died in my arms, she wanted nothing more than to be there for the children she loved with all her heart. No prophecies, no plans," I said. "And that is a love that I will move mountains and break promises for."

Standing up, I let my gaze linger on Markus's shocked face before moving to the door and grabbing my cloak. I looked over my shoulder. "If the higher lords take this as a reason to go beyond the law, to take my children when I'm not around, remind them that I've killed a Velbrun once. It won't be difficult to do so again."

He didn't stop me. Nothing could have.

I was going home to spend quality time with my kids.

35

I felt lighter: a part of me that I hadn't realized was dragging me down was now gone, or at least, no longer quite as heavy as it'd once been. After my talk with Markus, coming back to Gelvurt felt like the calm before the storm that was the trip to the north.

A calm that I enjoyed as much as possible while I had the chance.

Daka clumsily clapped her hands, giggling as I juggled a few of the toys in the room. I'd no talent as a juggler, not really, but my coordination and speed were enough to make up for my lack of skill.

Natakia smiled, not looking as amused as her sister was, but enjoying the show I was putting on as much as I expected her to. "Roh."

"Where did I go? Where did I go? I'm right here, ha ha!" Doh was having her own kind of fun, trying to get Dalton to play along with her little game of hide-and-seek with her hands.

My son stared up at her, glaring as much as an infant could.

After a moment of getting nothing out of him, Doh leaned back and watched me add another toy to my dazzling display. "This isn't fair. Why am I entertaining the boring kid?"

"None of my children are boring, Doh," I reminded her, my eyes on the toys flying through the air above me, ready to come down to my waiting palms. "All my children are unique and beautiful."

Doh snorted, and I gave her a look. She smiled cheekily before bending back over Dalton and cleaning his mouth of a little drool that'd collected.

"Look," she said after straightening back up. "All I'm saying is that counting is not the most exciting thing a baby could be doing."

I wondered what she'd rather have Dalton be doing. Shape-shifting? I wasn't sure if bloodlines presented themselves that quickly. A part of me was curious about when Doh's own abilities had awoken, but she'd made it clear how she felt about sharing.

"Counting is an invaluable skill that is a testament to how intelligent Dalton is." I had no doubt that he would be a merchant or scholar of repute. Honestly, I doubted that any of my children would have problems pursuing whatever they set their hearts on.

My thoughts lingered on the words of the prophecy. As long as fate did not sabotage their lives, they would be happy and successful. What else could I, as a father, wish for them?

Doh lightly pinched Dalton's cheeks. "He's going to be just like one of those little academy scholars, aren't you? Aren't you?"

I stopped my juggling as Dalton made a noise of distaste, before Daka spoke up. "Rah! Rah!"

She was shaking her arms at Doh, as if to fight off the maid for the sake of her brother. I picked her up, carrying closer to where Doh was playing with my son.

"It's fine, Daka, it's fine." I showed her that Dalton was okay, just annoyed. "Doh wouldn't hurt your brother, although she certainly has no qualms about annoying him, it seems."

Doh giggled, sticking out a finger to tease Daka, which the baby slapped away. I would never understand why my sweet daughter disliked Doh so much.

I hoped she grew out of it. I certainly thought Doh was doing, well, as much of a satisfactory job as I'd expected of her.

"What?" Doh looked up at me.

Had my thoughts peeked through? I shook my head, returning to playing with my children and showing off a few party tricks I'd learned from my time with Shawn.

The teleporting coin was an amazing feat of sleight of hand.

"Ha ha! Oh, it truly is a time to celebrate!" Jorge drank deeply of his wine, only being careful enough to have it not drip onto his shirt or the floor.

I raised my own glass. "It certainly is a fine arrangement."

The collection of wines in my keep, although slightly less expensive since Doh had sniffed them out, were quite good at loosening up an evening. Jorge had come from Niers once he'd received word of Caitlyn's support and had wanted to celebrate.

I certainly wasn't planning on denying him.

Jorge swallowed his drink down slowly, taking great care into tasting it. "Oh, this is definitely some finely aged drink. It is a shame that Caitlyn couldn't join us."

Lordess Velbrun of Alwur had been invited to celebrate, as well, but unfortunately had to decline due to personal conflicts. It'd made Jorge concerned; a noble often made time for those they had agreements with. I'd waylaid it.

"Yes, I'm sure she'll one day join us for drinks, perhaps once the school is up and running." We might have had a chance to solve her problematic curse by then.

For a few hours, we discussed some of the business involved of the project, which of the workers would find rooms and places to stay in Niers, and what kind of business would float my way. Jorge seemed convinced that the school would be drawing a lot of attention to the area.

Especially, he'd said, with one of the empire's heroes personally teaching at it!

"Well, I'm not sure what I would be able to teach." I'd considered the idea, but wasn't sure about what I could actually pass on beyond my skill with Vitae. "I'm not a great teacher."

"Oh, physical education is very integral to the curriculum," Jorge assured me. "There'll be plenty of demand just to hear your stories, I bet! You could be your own personal history teacher!"

My own stories, hmm? That was quite the idea. I didn't think there was anything interesting about the tales I'd woven, but perhaps I was being needlessly down on myself. Those who saw the most value in stories, I'd found, were those not a part of them.

A thought occurred to me, and I silently cursed myself for not having thought about it sooner. If I did not come back from the north . . .

"Jorge," I said. "I need to talk to you about something important."

Jorge's grin faded as he realized I was serious, his jolly demeanor shrinking as he put down his glass and gave me a nod. "I'm a little too far gone for serious, but I'll listen."

Keeping as many of the details as I could, such as the reason behind the trip or the realities behind the lord that had sold him that journal, I told Jorge about my planned excursion to the north.

And the chance that I would not come back.

"That would be bad." Jorge had certainly sobered up as he considered the concept. A lot of the dealings we'd discussed had me as a cornerstone.

I, in a way I was almost uncomfortable with, provided legitimacy to the school. Not helped, of course, by the fact that the support from Shawn and Tracy had come through me.

And yet, it was not as grave a concept as I made it out to be. "The funding won't be frozen if I die, I promise. The school can still be built; the agreements are still set."

"Do you think you will die, Rakta?" Jorge's eyes were big and blubbery. I didn't know when we had become friends, exactly, but I certainly saw it in his gaze now.

"Well." I considered the question. "I can't be certain, really. I will be standing alongside my old companions, my friends. We survived against the Warlock King; we can survive against this."

Jorge leaned over and gripped my shoulder tightly. "See that you do, Rakta. I'll do what I can to keep your kids safe if I don't hear back from you. The Velbruns won't lay a hand on them!"

The offer of protection warmed my heart.

"Thank you, friend." I nodded. "I can fight easier knowing that my children will be safe if the worst happens to me."

With that, we got back to drinking and enjoying the fine wine the previous Lords Velbrun had stored in the keep.

A few nights before I left for the north, after putting my younglings to bed, I was surprised to find Doh waiting at my bedroom door.

"Doh? Are you alright?" She'd been out with Dresden, the two of them having been getting along very well since they'd spent time together in my absence.

I'd long since forgiven them for the dalliance, but I was not above teasing the two of them at times.

Doh scratched the back of her head. "Hey, Rakta. Sorry, I . . . I just wanted to talk."

Perhaps, I should have been wary. Even with all my trust, I knew that Doh was uniquely capable of a great many insidious things, and yet, it was uncommon to hear Doh so vulnerable.

"Of course." My door was certainly always open for a friend. "What did you want to talk about?"

"Do you think we could share stories?" Doh smiled crookedly, as if trying to play off how important this felt to her.

I blinked, before smiling. "I would be honored."

<h1 style="text-align:center">36</h1>

You threatened them? Just like that?" Shawn sprinted through the wind by my side, both of us dashing through the forests of the empire to meet up at the rendezvous site where the others were waiting.

He was armed with his longsword, Road Less Traveled, and had donned his usual attire for conflicts, a set of enchanted, flexible full plate that was polished with a red sheen and protected him from most forms of harm, even environmental hazards.

Conceptually, I understood the use for armor, but I'd not found any set of armor that did not hamper me more than it would ever do me good.

I nodded, somewhat uncomfortable remembering how the conversation had gone. "I was frustrated. Lydia wouldn't have wanted me to threaten them though."

"Well, buddy." He shrugged, "She probably wouldn't have appreciated them trying to take the kids away either."

She wouldn't have, and yet . . .

"If she were still alive"—I pushed off from one tree branch to another—"House Velbrun would not have gone to such lengths to take them from me."

Many things would be better if she were alive. So much more would make sense; the children would be so much safer.

We traveled in silence for a moment, Shawn glancing around as I did the same. While we currently outpaced most possible threats, there was no reason to not be cautious.

"It's good that you're still alive, too, you know?" My friend finally spoke up.

I absently nodded, my doubts distracting me. In Lydia's passing, I believed that I sufficed as a father. And yet, compared to the life and love she could have given the triplets, I was not sure if my own parenting, the things I could give them, matched up.

Loving my children with all my heart was easy, but I could not see into the future and deal with threats before they arose, as Lydia could. I was too reactive, dealing with issues only once they became problems. One day, I feared I would not react swiftly enough.

The last thing I wanted was to one day have to avenge the death of one of my children.

"Alright, well." Shawn smiled, getting my attention. "Let's speed it up and get to Penelope. She's got a surprise for you."

A surprise from Penelope? Such things were always pleasant.

Nodding back, I pumped more Vitae into my leaps, sending me soaring higher and faster through the forest. The sooner the mission was underway, the sooner my heart could finally rest a little easier.

And perhaps, with this mission, I could solve a problem before it ended up affecting my children.

A few minutes later, we came upon a large campsite, with at least forty empire guards encamped in a large, man-made clearing. The sight of recently cut trees and multiple campfires scattered around was a familiar one. We'd often traveled alongside larger forces during the war.

"Humph, you actually showed," Penelope greeted us upon arrival, walking out from one of the larger tents. "I wasn't certain you'd grace us with your presence, Lord Velbrun."

Her tone was frosty, but far less cold than it had been in our original reunion. Shawn took a step forward, smiling brightly. "Come on, Penelope, give Rakta here a break. We both know you were excited to show him what you made."

The artificer blushed lightly, shooting Shawn a glare, before sniffing haughtily, and turned back to me. "Well, regardless, I'll need to go fetch it. Wouldn't want you being useless out there, Rakta."

I was relieved that she called me by name. We'd left off somewhat cordially after she departed from my keep, but I knew that our friendship was still healing.

Glancing around, I turned to a pleased Shawn. There was one concern I had that was still walking around here somewhere. "Is . . . Ulric here?"

Shawn's expression dimmed. "Uh, yeah. He is. Do you want to talk to him?"

I rubbed my neck lightly, looking around. "I'm not sure. We didn't, well, he said things that I would kill others for even implying."

The old anger of his threat to my children, empty as I knew it to be, still rankled at my heart. And the destruction of my axes was still a vivid memory. I wasn't sure if I knew how to forgive him for the things he had done and said.

"Yeah." Shawn nodded. "He fucked up. Don't feel like you have to make amends right now, okay? I made sure he knew it'd be best if you came to him when you're ready, so he won't bother you."

"That's kind of you." It was uncomfortable to have Shawn suddenly be between Ulric and me, but it was a welcome discomfort. A mediator was what I needed, and he was the face of our group for a reason.

It was hard to be diplomatic when I was emotional. And unfortunately, the Ruskan stories I knew did not have much wisdom regarding how to forgive, and I certainly hadn't grown up learning how to forget.

Except when it came to prophecies, of course. Even if the source was from some god, I couldn't begin to forgive myself for allowing such a thing to happen.

I had been weak, and Lydia had had to carry fate on her shoulders alone.

"I'd appreciate it if you looked more excited." Penelope broke my thoughts as she came back up, a large carrying case in her arms.

I made an attempt at a smile. "Sorry, Penelope. I am eager to see what you've made for me. I was just thinking about other things."

Honestly, I was more than touched that she had gone out of her way to do such a thing. It gave me hope for rebuilding the friendship that we'd once had.

"Yes, well." She shrugged, tapping her fingers on the case. "Shawn thought it wouldn't be right to have you go in half-cocked or whatever, so I designed and built a new axe for you."

"I . . ." I didn't even know what to say to that. A new axe? Losing my old axes still felt so fresh. To get a new one so soon . . . I wasn't sure if I was ready for such a thing.

"Rakta, I swear if that face means you're going to say n—" Shawn stepped in front of Penelope before she could break into a rant.

He smiled. "This could be dangerous, buddy. We're glad you're here to help and all, but I think everyone back in Gelvurt would be even happier if you came back in one piece."

Including my children.

"You're right." I sighed, moving to meet eyes with Penelope. I hadn't meant to insult all her effort. "My apologies again, Penelope. I don't want it to seem like I don't appreciate your hard work. I was just . . . attached to my old axes."

The artificer's cross expression faded into a sympathetic one. "They were some fine work, Rakta."

Her words were surprisingly touching. It felt like Lydia was receiving the kind words. I wish she were here to finally hear Penelope complement her work.

For a moment, we let silence honor my fallen weapons, before Penelope began opening the case. "I didn't have time to make a full set like the Vultures, but I thought this was a good opportunity for an upgrade."

Inside the carrying case was a single axe of a similar size to my old Vulture Axes. With an ebony blade and a solid metal handle, the axe looked deadlier. Said dangerous appearance was aided by the flickering red spiderwebs of energy that seemed to course through the handle and into the base of metal of the throwing axe.

It looked like a solid weapon that, designed and built by Penelope, I had no doubt would work perfectly out in the field.

"It will be strange to only have one, but thank you." I reached in gently and took the axe, feeling its energy coursing through my hand and meeting with my Vitae.

And yet, as I focused on the axe in my hand, I looked down back to the case and noticed something. A duplicate of the axe in my hands was still displayed in the opened carrying case.

Penelope's smirk at my confusion was filled with a smug pride. Like

I'd answered a question incorrectly, so she now had a chance to explain everything to me.

"Oh, did I say I didn't have time to make a full set?" Penelope's batted her eyes innocently. "Let me rephrase that. I had time to make a single axe that could be duplicated into a full set."

The Mana Wastes was a region stained by the leftovers of a long-forgotten empire that had flooded the area with Mana after its collapse. People born there often grew up with strange traits, not helped by the odd cultures that had developed there.

However, while no kingdom or empire held claim over the Mana Wastes, none wishing to take responsibility for the bizarre and rebellious denizens, many delved into its depths for raw material that had changed and mutated due to the high intensity of spiritual energy.

"I'd already pulled some strings for duplinium a few months ago for a personal project." Penelope shrugged. "The project fell through due to . . . reasons, but I had some duplinium left over."

I stared at the axe in my hand, having carefully picked up the real version by the part of the handle that wouldn't trigger the duplication effect.

"This is," I began. "So, the metal is what duplicates itself? And it does this forever? How long do the copies last?"

She pointed over to the copy I had made, and I watched as it slowly began to break apart into dust. "Not long; no more than a minute. See, duplinium splits a copy off when it comes into contact with Vitae or Mana, anything that disturbs its equilibrium."

She took the axe from my hand and pointed to the larger part of the metal handle that had grooves in it. "This part of the handle is null, enchanted to not connect with outside energy. That stops the duplication from happening."

"Interesting." It certainly wasn't a simple weapon. My old axes had been simply made from magically enchanted metal, nothing inherently strange about the metal itself. I felt like I was going to hurt myself with something this complicated, but it was still an axe.

I knew how to throw an axe.

Shawn was listening intently, as well, most likely in the dark about all the details himself. "So, when Rakta channels his Vitae through it, holding on to this part of the axe"—he pointed to the smaller part of the handle, where I would usually rest my thumb—"it'll throw out a duplicate instead of itself?"

"Exactly." She smirked, obviously happy to hear she'd explained it well enough. "Should keep the channeled Vitae and the techniques used intact as well. And, of course, I haven't even gotten to the more exciting enchantments yet."

My head began to pang slightly as Penelope rattled off more and more about the axe, but while I continued to listen, I spoke up with one question.

"Does it have a name?"

Penelope blinked, taken off guard. "Oh, uh, not really. During the enchantment process, I just referred to it as the Many-Axe." She shot Shawn a pointed look as he chuckled at her naming scheme.

"I see." That was good. I was glad I got to name it.

As she continued to rattle off the various enchantments, from increased durability to corrective aim, I pondered what would be a suitable name for the new weapon. While my Vultures did not have individual names, a singular weapon deserved one.

Also, I wondered how long Penelope had been working on this. It felt like it would take much longer than the few weeks it'd been since I'd agreed to be a part of this.

Of course, I dared not doubt her claim openly. I wanted to get back to my children in one piece.

<h1 style="text-align:center">37</h1>

House Taine, from what I understood, was a pillar for the empire's naval presence on the Crest Sea. The Certillian Empire had not fought a war across the seas in quite some time, but they still maintained an impressive fleet that was hosted in the house's largest city, Taine.

Crest, the small coastal village we were headed to, was named after the body of water it sat on the edge of. Nothing, from what we had been told, was very peculiar or special about the village of fishermen, beyond the lord that governed it.

"This Lord Taine of Crest," I asked Penelope as we walked down the trail, "has there been any word from him? Does he know we're coming?"

Penelope looked up from her map, a frustrated grimace decorating her expression. "Unfortunately, yes, he knows that we're coming. Allowing a force of this size to move into a noble's lands without proper introductions would be unthinkable unless we had evidence of treason."

"And do we?" The forces we'd brought could move at a good pace, all the soldiers being adept cultivators of Vitae, but we'd still been traveling for close to a week now.

I was getting anxious for my children, but I took solace in that I could smell the sea in the air. The scene rankled at my senses, but it told me we were getting very close to Crest.

"Well, yes and no." Penelope went back to her map. "Recently, Crest's quota for fish has dipped, but that's been made up by an uptick in corn. However, the sightings of monsters by the locals are enough just cause for us to come and investigate."

I nodded. "So, while he might be involved, it isn't an absolute fact."

"Yeah, no real evidence." Shawn came up, having been speaking with Ulric at the rear for the last hour. "Still, he didn't reach out to us, and these sightings are too frequent for him to be so unconcerned. So, officially, we're here to take out monsters; unofficially, we're here to ask a few questions."

I nodded. Even with my experience at killing trolls and goblins, I wouldn't be shy about requesting aid in the face of large numbers. No one could fight forever.

"Any descriptions of these monsters?" It'd be better to know the enemy going in.

Penelope and Shawn read off a few testimonies from the runner from Crest, the man who had brought word of the sightings. Large, hulking beasts, leathery skin. Sounded like trolls, but one thing felt off.

"No disappearances?" I rubbed my chin. Trolls were eternally hungry monsters, for both food and conflict. With their regeneration, trolls were unafraid of solo raids against larger threats, much less farmers.

A lack of missing people was suspicious.

"None," Penelope answered. "Someone or something is keeping these monsters in line and is doing a good job at it."

My mind went to Captain Barker, who had ventured north to find vengeance for his son. I hoped he had found it rather than one of these monsters finding him. He wasn't among the guards I traveled with.

I shook my head, clearing it of worries. "When do we reach Crest?"

"Tonight." Penelope put away the map, and we resumed our faster pace.

It was the quiet that first piqued my concern as we approached Crest on the main road. I held up a hand, Penelope and Shawn stopping at my signal, the rest of the guards pausing as well.

Penelope opened her mouth to question me, but a finger to my lips stopped her. Something was off about the area. There were no bird chirps, no crickets.

All the natural noises of life had ceased a minute ago.

I bent down and let my Vitae rumble into my senses, letting the **Scourger Bloodhound Technique** take hold. My senses faded, and in return, I got my answers.

Blood and monsters. A deep stain on the area around us, as if it had been drowned in the scents of a horrid battle of trolls, goblins, and something else.

Something that smelled distinctly inhuman. A familiar scent of death and foulness that chilled me to my core and made me want to gag.

Letting the technique fade, I opened my eyes and stood up to my full height. "Blood, an ocean of it. Trolls and goblins. And the scent of the creature that invaded my home."

Knowing that horrid, malformed creature was here, or had been here, put me on edge. Why come here? How was it involved?

And yet, this was my best chance to finish what I had begun during my introductions to the pest. Perhaps, my presence on this mission truly was a chance for me to proactively protect my children.

Some of the nearby guards paled, but Shawn simply frowned. "We haven't seen any traces of a conflict, no blood, stray weapons."

"It must have been quick," Penelope said, looking around the clearing. "Crest may have never seen it coming."

One of the guards stepped forward from the contingent accompanying us. "Should we leave and return with a larger force?"

Going into a possible ambush with only the moonlight to aid us didn't sound appealing. While our senses could be enhanced with Vitae, rendering the darkness somewhat meaningless, it still put us at a disadvantage.

"If we leave now," Shawn said, "we might find nothing but ruins on our return, with any trace of the enemy gone. Not to mention the survivors we may abandon."

"Understood. At your orders, sir." The guard resumed his place, his halberd firmly gripped.

While anxious at the risk, I agreed with Shawn. It was better to do this now with the force we had rather than let the chance for answers disappear. I saw no better moment to take care of this thing that had terrified my children.

I readied my new axe, which I had taken to calling Crow. I still wasn't entirely familiar with the new weight, nor the slightly strange way I had to throw the axe to instead throw a duplicate. I would learn better out in the field.

Or at least, I would have to.

Penelope took her own weapon out of the holster on her belt, a small, *L*-shaped magical weapon she called Blaster 7 that I had seen blast holes through tree trunks. A product of her discussions with Shawn.

With that, along with her magical bracers, the slight shimmering of a magical shield of force around her, and the various other unseen threats she had stowed on her person, she seemed ready. A part of me wished we had one of her larger vehicles of war.

Those had always inspired confidence in me when we went to battle alongside one of them.

Shawn, like me, merely had his weapon drawn and activated the magic of his armor, an extra lump of polished red metal around his neck moving upward into a flexible helmet around his head that left his mouth unarmored.

More heroic that way, he'd once told me.

The literal tension in the air, like the sky itself was glass about to break, was the only sign I needed to know that Ulric, at our rear, was ready as well.

"Then let's move," I said, heading down the road toward Crest.

Constantly pinging the area around me with Vitae to keep an accurate count of living creatures around me, I also had to regulate my breathing to keep my **Guard Periculum Technique** up.

I was willing to walk into a trap, but I was not willing to let myself actually be surprised by it. I was sure my companions were of similar minds, their bodies tense and ready for any kind of ambush.

Still, the closer we approached Crest, the more we began to see hints of the conflict that had happened here. Wooden rubble of a stray carriage wheel, the torn rags of a common dress, the stuffed toy of a child.

And yet, no signs of blood except the fading hint of copper in the air. Had the monsters cleaned up behind themselves? Or had they simply wasted nothing?

Trolls and goblins were not often this meticulous in salvaging meat from their kills, but I chalked it up to whoever was leading them. Lord Taine of Crest had plenty of questions to answer, if he was even still alive.

"Whatever happened here," I muttered, "is fairly fresh. No more than a few days old."

The others nodded as we rounded a heavy collection of trees and brush, the trail opening up into the larger village of Crest, the sounds of waves in the distance.

The salty air intertwined with the bloody scent, my nose cringing at the horrid mix of smells. I was never fond of the salty air to begin with.

And yet, while the air was thick with blood, the village was quiet. The chilling quiet that comes from an empty tomb. The kind of quiet that comes with an implied question.

Where were the bodies? I could almost taste the blood around me and yet not a single body. This went above and beyond simple human intelligence and leadership.

This implied something other than trolls and goblins in the area.

Shawn held up a hand, pausing the company of guards. He kept his head on a swivel. "We're going to continue down the main street. The Taine Keep is our goal; any survivors would head there."

I nodded in agreement. Doubling as a staging ground for naval defense on the coast, the coastal keeps were known for being far larger and more defensible than those found inland. Even with unmanned walls, trolls and goblins would have had difficulty getting over the walls.

As our group began to march through the buildings of the village center, keeping a close eye on the various buildings around us, I continued to pulse out my Vitae.

First pulse, there were fifty-three amongst us. Myself not included, that encompassed the entire contingent of guards, Shawn, Penelope, and Ulric in the back.

Second pulse, there were still fifty-three. A relieving consistency.

A chill ocean wind blew through the streets, whistling through the cracks of our formation. My hand tightened around the handle on Crow.

The third pulse of my Vitae went out.

We were down to forty-nine. My **Guard Periculum Technique** suddenly screamed at me, my body moving before my mind caught up.

I whipped around to look at the company of guards, Shawn in sync with my concerns, as Penelope raised Blaster 7 toward something I couldn't see in front of us.

A scream went out among the company as something beyond my

common sight began to tear the guards apart, blood spurting into the air from the rear.

"Battle formations!" Shawn's sword glowed, and he leaped into battle.

The world shattered, a blast of focused Mana shot through the air, and I gripped my new axe and settled into a stance. Among the chaos, I was comforted by the fact that I was fighting with my friends once more.

38

The difficulties in fighting an unseen monster could not be understated. Beyond the simple obstacle of actually hitting an invisible assailant, the chaos and panic that quickly filtered through the ranks could be as much of a death sentence as a transparent blade.

Rushing into the fray, I kept my Vitae thrumming as I watched other guards around take more defensive postures.

As some of their numbers scattered to be picked off, a majority of the company stuck together and kept their heads straight, their halberds braced as they made a perimeter, shoulder to shoulder, and settled into their **Iron Knight Stance**.

As one, the skins of the guards darkened into a deep gray and shined with the metallic glint of the **Iron Skin Technique**, a common technique among the empire's forces that would supplement their protective suits of armor.

My thoughts did not linger on defense however. Settled into my **Dancing Star Stance**, I readied my axe and aligned the Vitae within my body and allowed it to flow to my sight.

"**Deep Blue Technique**," I muttered, feeling my eyes burn as the world suddenly became tinted in a deep, deep cerulean blue, every individual, object, and obstacle outlined in a bright, vicious red.

Including the long-bodied monsters that skittered swiftly from guard to guard, cleanly swiping off arms and heads with praying mantis–like scythed appendages that extended from their upper bodies.

With large, bulbous eyes; reflective, scentless chitin that rendered them indistinguishable from their surroundings; and thousands of centipede-like needle-thin legs silently carrying them across the battle-field, I recognized the fearsome creatures. "Calkers! Keep an eye on the ground!"

A nearby calker turned its head at me, rushing forward with its mir-rored skin, before its body was eviscerated by a Crow, my arm having thrown on instinct with a quick **Horizon Throw Technique**.

"Shawn." Penelope's goggles shimmered as she blasted a calker. "Cover me while I work; we need to give the guards their targets."

As Shawn and Penelope moved closer to the rough perimeter of guards fighting fiercely to keep the unseen calkers at bay, their wide swipes doing little more than nicking the armored plates of the crea-tures, I continued filling the air with Crows.

It was only the days I had to practice that kept me from throwing my actual weapon at the monstrous insects rather than the duplicates. And yet, my Crows flew and danced around the battlefield as my Vitae directed them, filling the air with a murder of axes.

Calker after calker fell to the simulacrums of my weapon, and I felt and watched the world shatter as some of them were turned to viscera by Ulric's wide-area spells.

"How many more!?" Ulric's booming voice resounded across the battlefield. From anyone else, I'd assume they were desperate to be done.

From Ulric, I knew he was simply hoping there'd be plenty more to kill.

It was hard to keep count though. Calkers kept coming from every-where, moving fast and relentlessly toward us. They came from the doorframes and windows of nearby houses, the alleyways; some were even digging up from the ground.

"Just keep killing them!" Two more fell at my feet after trying to stab me in the throat and legs, getting far too close. I diverted some of my Vitae into my **Instinctive Reflex Technique** and **Skip Dash Technique**.

My eyes were beginning to burn more and more, the side effects of my **Deep Blue Technique** becoming more and more pronounced the longer the time ticked by. If I couldn't see them, then I'd have to rely on simply reacting to the blows.

"Wide Cleave Technique!" An empire guard managed to cut one in half with a lucky blow to the chest.

As one of the guards was slashed in the arm, nearly taking the appendage off, he bellowed, **"Counterstrike Technique!"**

His form surged with strength, and immediately the calker was beheaded by a swift blow powered by vengeful Vitae.

And yet, for every calker that a guard was able to fell, one more guard had to fall back with a grievous injury or was simply killed on the spot.

"Let the calcified eye rain dust upon th— Urk!" One of the few royal magicians in the company coughed blood as a bloodstained scythe-like hand penetrated their sternum.

We were dealing with the invisible beasts as best we could, but there were simply more calkers than guards. Unless something changed soon, we could lose our entire contingent.

Shawn was batting aside blows as they came, his armor taking slashes from the calkers around him, his sword cleaving through the mindless assassin brutes.

"Activate!" Penelope's outcry preceded a burst of blue energy that engulfed the bloody streets of Crest, soaking it in a blue tint even as my **Deep Blue Technique** faded, my eyes feeling worn out. A few more minutes and I would most certainly have been blind.

And as the calkers were coated in the blue energy, the guards cheered with vengeful glee.

"I can see 'em!" The defensive perimeter suddenly broke as the company of guards went on the offensive.

The world rumbled as Ulric's booming laugh echoed, "There you are, you fucking pests!"

Slicing one in half with a thrown Crow, I realized with relief that calkers were a lot easier to kill en masse when they couldn't hide.

I breathed deeply, trying to build my Vitae back up to a comfortable level as I pulled Crow, the real one, out of the corpse of one of the calkers. It was somewhat embarrassing, really, how many times I'd thrown the whole weapon.

"What are the numbers?" I stood up, looking over my shoulder as Shawn came from where the remnants of the guard were resting.

"Twenty-two dead, twelve too injured to continue on without

healing." He shook his head, "We'll need to devote about ten to keep them safe if we move on, leaving us with only five guards to accompany us . . . if we want them."

I looked over at him. "You think we should leave them all behind? Go forward with only us four?"

Shawn nodded. "Honestly, yeah. The keep is the most defensible, but that's probably where we'll face the most resistance. Penelope's teaching the remaining magician among the guards to use her device in case more calkers show up."

I nodded. We'd killed a large horde of them, but there were surely more underground. Calkers released a concoction of pheromones upon death to inform the rest of the hive in the area about hazards, so they wouldn't be attacking again until they'd rebuilt their numbers.

Penelope had already sent a self-delivering letter back to the capital on the subject, so hopefully it would get to the right hands. Alchemists could hopefully prepare something that could handle the nest before the hive recouped the losses.

"Alright." I cleaned Crow off with a bit of cloth. "Then let's continue on."

A hand on my shoulder made me pause, Shawn speaking more quietly. "I have a feeling. Keep your eyes open and don't act hastily."

Shawn's feelings were always strange, but usually insightful. Lydia had always made it clear that he wasn't truly divining anything through magic or the like, at least from her expert opinion, but I'd long stopped doubting his feelings.

One time, Ulric almost got him to tell us more about these feelings after a night of drinking, but he eventually said it was just a remnant from his distant village. Ulric stopped badgering him after that.

"I'll keep that in mind, Shawn. Thank you." His feelings could be the difference between life and death in times like these.

He smiled. "No problem, buddy."

As Shawn reunited with Penelope to organize and prepare the guards for our absence, Ulric finally made his way over to me. I tensed, but he kept his distance, simply giving me a solemn nod as he collected some of the things that had been tossed about in the battle.

So, he was truly dedicated to letting me come to him? I found myself appreciating that more than I had thought I would. And yet, if this was as dangerous as we rightfully suspected, could I simply say nothing to him on the eve of battle? Death came for us when we least expected it.

When we were least prepared for it.

I considered that for a moment.

"I like fighting alongside each other," I muttered, catching his attention, "rather than fighting against each other."

His eyes widened, his lip twitching into a smile, before he nodded. He did not say anything in response. Perhaps a time for that would come, but I felt a familiar peace between us.

Perhaps the new people we were could one day be friends again.

We approached the Taine Keep cautiously, under the stealthy guise of some protective coverings that Penelope had fashioned from the calkers' chitin while the rest of us recovered from the fight and organized the remainder of the guards.

While not perfect or permanent, powered by only the rapidly draining primal energy within them, I didn't mind placing the chitinous cloak around me for the added stealth.

It was a shame they'd be useless within an hour.

"I don't see anybody." Ulric looked at the walls of the keep, his magic keeping the air around him tense and ready to shatter. Once upon a time, I'd been uncomfortable standing so close to the man when he got this worked up, his magic even more uncontrollable then.

Now I was glad to be this close.

And I agreed with his words. "Perhaps they're waiting inside?"

"Or there's no one there." Penelope frowned. "Nothing's stopping them from waiting until we go inside and coming at us from behind."

"No," Shawn muttered, looking at the keep. "I'm pretty sure they're already inside. If they were gonna ambush us, they would've done it alongside the calkers. They're waiting for us."

I didn't like that. It was either supreme confidence or deep insanity that provoked someone to simply wait for their enemies to reach them. Neither boded well for a fight, in my experience.

"I could just take the keep down," Ulric suggested. I didn't doubt that if we stepped back, Ulric could do just that and take everyone inside out.

"No," I said. "I checked for scents. Villagers were taken inside, not all of them dead."

Shawn nodded, unsheathing his blade. "We're going in."

That was the end of the discussion.

Penelope and Ulric looked disgruntled, but neither made to argue. We gained nothing from arguing; that was a lesson we'd learned a long time ago when decisions need to be made swiftly.

The artificer primed her magical shooter, checking over her various gadgets stowed away on her person, before looking over Ulric and me.

"If we're going to do this," she said, "then we need to stay sharp and delicate. Ulric, look out for load-bearing beams, and Rakta, don't throw that weapon like it's a common axe, got it?"

I nodded, Ulric shrugging at the advice. It wouldn't do to lose my new weapon so soon in a fight I was confident I'd need it in.

Still momentarily hidden by our cloaks, we made our way inside.

Whoever had gone to such lengths as to clean and tidy up the forests and trails around Crest had done no such thing for the interior of the keep.

The blue-and-white tapestries of House Taine were soaked in the deep red of its people, the bloody gore that we'd expected to see littered outside gathered here into a single horrid display.

From stripped bones to bloody clothes, the mess of the sight paled in comparison to the corpses, both young and old, that were stacked on top of one another. I had to turn my head away from the slack form of an infant, my heart having softened to the horrors I'd become familiar with when fighting the Warlock King.

"Monsters." Shawn's eyes were hard. He'd never had much mercy for those behind these grisly scenes. I never held it against him.

Firmly inside the large welcoming room of Taine Keep, the oaken doors slammed shut behind us suddenly, all of us tense. It seemed Shawn had been correct—nothing intended to flank us once we'd arrived.

It was here waiting for us.

"Well, well, well." A familiar dry, whispery voice echoed through the room. "The heroes of the empire have finally seen fit to arrive at my little gala. You're quite late! Did my invitations get lost in the mail?"

I glanced over at my allies, Shawn and Penelope looking at me expectantly, and nodded. "The creature from my estate."

"Oh, he remembers me!" The voice seemed positively exuberant. "That sends a rush of pleasure through my collection of hearts, Rakta, dear."

I felt a sudden lump of anxiety form in my stomach. At the core of the insane affection, I felt an itch of familiarity. Something that tickled at the back of my mind.

Shawn stepped forward, his sword unsheathed. "Stop with the mind games, creature. Where are the villagers? Why attack Crest?"

"Well now, brown cow." The voice sounded distinctly feminine now. "I can't give up the little game so early! We've barely started, barely even begun!"

I frowned at the voice, recognition clicking. "Stop that!"

"Rakta, what's going on?" Shawn was worried, his eyes darting around and looking for movement to get too close.

"Oh, Rakta, dear, you've seen me at my worst. My most pitiful self, the ugliest stage of my brilliant new life." Flutters of movement happened around us, dark shadowy whispers that seemed to be pulling together before scattering. "When I heard you were coming, I had to . . . pretty myself up."

"Oh shit." Penelope's eyes widened, finally recognizing what I had moments before.

I tensed as the shadows coalesced into a solid form at the top of the stairs, the creature looking down at us from above, as if she were the lady of the house.

Shawn gulped, glancing at me. "Oh."

A parody of Lydia stood opposing us, her pale-white skin a deep obsidian, her silvery hair a long, slobbish mess of tangles and blood, her bright-blue eyes tinged with amused insanity.

"Rakta," the fake Lydia cooed at me, streaks of blood across her cheeks like the flustered blush of a maiden, "would you join me for a dance?"

And the blood and viscera around us stirred to unlife as an undead army rose.

39

Long ago, when Brota's tribe was slain by his enemies and he sought wisdom from the world around him, the beginnings of the first dance that ever graced the land of Rusk, it was often said that the sun had advised him to smite Garrok for killing his brethren.

The wind had disagreed with the sun, saying that violence led only to more bloodshed. When provoked by another, the wind advised, it was best to flow around the threats of the world, to peacefully forgive and live another day.

And yet, among the warring words of nature, no voice spoke louder to Brota than the plateau he danced upon.

"Move by no will but your own," the stone had said with simple finality. "Do not be conquered by another."

In this moment, as I stared up at this creature, I felt conquered. To see the beautiful face of my Lydia leer down at me, the creature mocking me with its sick parody, I felt a familiar anger sink into my limbs.

An anger that I had left my homeland with and carried with me for years.

The blood and viscera around us began to moan and groan, forming horrid mouths in its congealed undead body as coagulated tendrils began to writhe in the air.

"Gravebody!" Shawn's sword sliced one of the tendrils, cutting down one of the stray zombies rising from the grave alongside it. "Keep your center!"

"Ulric, don't leave a trace of it behind!" Penelope was already blasting various corpses trying to pick themselves up, dodging the stray tendrils.

The chaos around me, the shattering of the rising undead army, faded to the background as my grip tightened around Crow.

I had come expecting many things, but the mocking homage to my late love? This disrespect to her image? Her voice? Her eyes? The things she had passed down to our children with love had been stolen by this creature.

The creature giggled at my gaze, as if I were a suitor across the ballroom preparing to introduce myself.

It was too much.

I was suddenly leaping through the air, bringing Crow down in an overhand **Heavy Strike Technique** on its head.

The creature exploded into shadows, my attack failing to connect with anything solid. Instantly, I threw a murder of axes at the various slivers of shadows moving around the banister, each one cutting off tiny bits of slivers that continued to skitter about across the walls.

"You can't catch me!" The creature's voice echoed down one of the upper hallways of the keep. A coward unwilling to fight me head-on after provoking my hatred?

Vibrating my Vitae, I flexed my feet and legs into the familiar motions of the **Great Wind Sprint Technique** and followed.

"Wait, Rak— Fuck!" Shawn's voice and the distant sounds of combat, of shattering undead, became lost in the echoes of the distant halls and the solid stone of the keep's walls.

Every shadow was pierced by an axe; every giggle garnered my heated gaze. I felt like I was going mad as I felt my anger puppet me through the halls, chasing after this mockery.

"You know, I've been thinking a lot about you recently." The creature's whispers were met with another axe, my mind searching for an answer to this problem, a way to kill this thing as painfully as possible.

A monster that could not be attacked physically could often be attacked mentally, but I had no abilities to do so. However, an explosion or energy-charged attack could do it . . .

The shadows suddenly congealed into a wide grin on a nearby wall. "Ever since I met you, looking for answers, I couldn't stop."

Another axe cut through the stone that shadow had rested itself on, tearing into the stone and breaking the grin into pieces. I didn't want to waste my Vitae, so I had to keep myself under control.

Lydia's face emerged from another wall of shadows, an elongated tongue licking her lips. "I was stuck in this half-life—" An axe cut her off.

"—robbed of the power that Zactrik had promised me—" Another axe.

"—until I had a taste of your sweet—" I twisted around, channeling Vitae into my leg as I kicked the wall beside me, breaking through it with ease.

A pair of arms wrapped around my shoulders with a gentleness that belied the extreme speed it took to catch me off guard, accompanied by a disturbingly familiar whisper of affection. "Sweet Vitae. You were trying to kill me, of course, but . . . what is murder if not an expression of love?"

Her long and horrid tongue licked the entire side of my face.

I dashed away, breaking from her grip, but I could feel the grimy, shadowy essence on my clothes now. It felt unpleasant, somewhat abrasive on the skin.

"Stop talking," I said, stoking my Vitae, "with her voice."

And even here, in the middle of the large, spacious hallway, I moved with the errant wind, felt the spirit of the stone within the construction of the keep, the humidity in the air and tension of thunder that built between my fingers.

For that was the way of the **First Dance Stance**.

"Oh, I've waited so long to feel this, Rakta, dear." The creature licked her lips, looking positively exuberant. "Feed me everything you have and more."

She stepped out of the inky-black shadows, tendrils of her essence becoming spiked as they began to bloom throughout the hallway between us.

Each one looked nastier and more jagged than the last.

"First Dance Technique: Twister Through the Valley." Stone and shadows were suddenly torn asunder by the storm that gathered around me, my arms and legs surged by the eye of the storm.

"Yes, yes! **Black Art: Rose Garden!**" The creature's form rippled, and I felt a distinct wrongness in the air as I shot forward, the tendrils I rushed toward becoming spiked and barbed and set on stopping my advance.

My form rocketed through the dark barricades, feeling the tips and thorns ripping and tearing my clothes and skin through the blistering armor of wind around me. My blood rained across the stone, but I forged ahead, uncaring for anything but this thing's death.

I crashed into the creature, my hand wrapping around her neck, feeling a solidness to her form with my Vitae coursing through my entire body so heavily.

Crushing her neck, I stared down at her, emotions building up in my heart. I wanted to watch her die, but could I bear to watch life fade from Lydia's eyes again?

"Oh my," the creature spoke, her voice unimpeded by my grip. "What a brilliant flavor you have, dear."

I felt it then. The feeling of my Vitae pouring into her. I threw her aside, bringing out Crow again. "What are you?"

"Esmeralda." The creature's form cracked and shook as she stood up from the ground, looking positively ecstatic. "That's what, or rather, who I am. Strange, I'd thought you'd ask sooner."

A monster that absorbed Vitae. There were creatures who did that, monsters that absorbed Mana and Vitae from the area around them, but one that drained it from the source? I'd never heard of such a thing before in my entire life, not even by way of rumor.

And what had that technique of hers been? I could feel the world flinch at it, disturbed by the grotesque . . . technique? Spell? What was I dealing with here? How did I kill this thing?

I needed the others. The realization hit me like a stampeding horse. How far had I gone from the others? How many hallways? It'd been hard to keep track . . . I'd gotten so angry . . .

Shawn's advice from before bit into me like a viper. I'd let myself get swayed, had let myself get carried away. Were the others okay? Were they even still alive?

"Oh, what a nice look on your face, Rakta." Esmeralda licked her stolen lips, her teeth looking more and more sharklike. "Let's continue, alright? I'm finished with my appetizer."

With the roaring of a twister around me, I pumped my Vitae as fiercely as I could, empowering the blistering force into a truly powerful one that began to rip at the foundations around me.

"Yes! Look upon me with your beloved's face, feel that anger mixed with guilt and love! Look at me! Me!" The dark essence was practically oozing from her lips, pooling down her chin like a horrid drool.

Could I destroy her? I wanted to. I wanted to toss my concerns for my friends away and deal with this creature here and now. Rip her arms and legs off and let her suffer the cruel fate of her entire existence being snuffed out. I wanted to tear Lydia's face off of it.

I wanted Lydia.

But I needed to do what was right.

Twisting my body away from her, I pushed off from the ground, letting the force of the twister move beneath my limbs as I rushed back for my companions.

"No!" The sound echoed over my twister, a deep, disturbing echo of a voice that stretched and twisted into something monstrous, something that wasn't Lydia.

I wondered if it had ever been anyone.

I felt the keep shake on its foundation as I came crashing back through the hallway, sensing the growing wrongness behind me as Esmeralda followed me.

"Ulric, stop! You're going to bring everything down!" Shawn's call greeted me as I surged back into the larger conflict, breathing heavily with the twister around my form.

I couldn't have reached them at a better time. Necromancy was not an inherently evil magic, but the products of its forbidden and corrupted rituals could never be considered benign and their lack of fear and self-preservation made them the perfect weapons.

Ulric and Penelope were covered in quickly rotting wounds, the cuts and scrapes festering through the infected swipes by the gravebody that Shawn continued to do battle with as they recovered.

Ulric drank a potion, his wounds beginning to purge the horrid filth of the enemy and reknit. "That fuckin' thing almost got me!"

The gravebody was still swirling around them, a horrific thing born of necromantic rituals and special reagents tangled within the remains of the recently dead.

A mockery of more natural, primordial oozes, the gravebody was hard to injure, even harder to kill, and its attacks left injuries infected with deathly rot. Not to mention, its screams and guttural cries could send a lesser man into insanity.

Blurring with the wind, I swiped at a tendril that had been shooting toward one of Shawn's blind spots, heading straight for his neck. The visceral tendril splotched onto the ground, crying out as it tried to crawl away.

"Rakta! You're back!" Shawn cut another tendril of blood as it came for him, smiling at me in relief.

Penelope grunted, rolling to dodge a larger tendril of blood, before shooting and vaporizing it. "About fucking time, Lord Velbrun!"

I shook my head, throwing Crows at the larger parts of the gravebody and dodging its tendrils. "I lost my head; it wanted me alone."

"Didja fuckin' kill it!?" Ulric gripped the air in front of him as a tendril shot, a cube of space in front of him suddenly shattering and sending portions of the gravebody splattering against the wall.

A voice echoed throughout the keep.

"Oh, Rakta! I don't like being abandoned on the dance floor!" The singsong voice of Esmeralda echoed from up the stairs where I'd descended from.

The others shot me a look, and I frowned, explaining myself. "It's nothing like I've seen before. It was absorbing my Vitae and didn't seem injured at all."

Shawn cut down another large chunk of gravebody that had lashed out at him, frowning. "Absorbing your Vitae? Like a vampire?"

We all took a moment to look at him.

"A what?" Penelope shot another tendril, the piece of gravebody screaming with a new mouth moments before it sizzled out and went inert.

"Nothing, nothing." Shawn got into his **Valiant Hero Stance**, a stance of his own personal creation, **"Valiant Strike Technique!"**

His sword glowed brilliantly with burning energy, and Shawn dashed forward, ripping into the larger chunks of the creature and searing the gravebody with one of his more powerful techniques, cauterizing and purifying the undead monster with every swing.

Not letting the thing recover, I dove into it myself, the twister around me slicing into the monster with reckless abandon, my hands tearing it apart into smaller pieces that slowly rotted away.

Now on the defensive, the gravebody squealed with its horrific mouths and tried to back away and flee, but a sudden shattering of force behind it sent its largest portion straight at us, straight at Penelope.

Penelope seamlessly kneeled down and pulled a large cylinder-shaped weapon from her small belt bag, an impossible feat of space, and settled it on her shoulder. "Activate!"

The device hummed with energy, a glow building up at the end of the barrel of the heavy magical weapon.

From the tip, a blistering glow of energy suddenly fired, an explosion of rainbow Mana that hit the flying chunk of the gravebody and engulfed its form in a display of fire, electricity, and ice.

Panting, my twister fading, I watched as the remnants of the gravebody squealed before the Mana keeping its form intact faded and it was rendered inert.

Shawn flicked the blood from his blade, looking a little exhausted as well. "And that's, ha, why we do stuff as a team."

Ulric chuckled, and I smiled. It'd certainly been easy to slip back into formation even after so much time apart.

"There you are, Rakta! Come down to play with our friends, have we?" Lydia's stolen voice crept over the banister of the stairs, a dark cloud of shadows pouring around her as she crept into view.

We readied ourselves, my heart pounding with the fresh wounds of seeing the parody of Lydia. I had to keep my center, not allow myself to be conquered again.

I had to face this creature with my friends. The way it always should have been.

"Hey, Shawn." Penelope pulled out her Blaster 7, the weapon brightening up as she channeled her Mana through it. "Mind telling us what the fuck a vampire is?"

Shawn's sword glowed, his mouth set in a deep frown. "Like, I can, but I really don't know if this is, uh, the same thing."

"I don't care what it is," Ulric said, the world rumbling dangerously around his hands. "It picked the wrong face to steal."

I wholeheartedly agreed, settling back into the **First Dance Stance**.

40

The room filled with darkness as we all tensed, Esmeralda's eyes on me and me alone. She crept forward, almost tiptoeing down the stairs toward us, each step followed by a slight widening of her perverse smile.

"Don't underestimate her," I said, my Vitae vibrating. "She's fas—"

Esmeralda blurred, suddenly in front of me with her horrifying mouth wide-open in a smile that was too large for her face and filled to the brim with teeth. "Rakta!"

I dashed to the side, dodging her draining grip, before skipping backward, my speed picking up as my **Great Wind Sprint Technique** and **Skip Dash Technique** began working together.

The world around her suddenly shattered with explosive force, Ulric's eyes trained on her, but she was already moving, dodging the shock waves and heading straight toward . . . Penelope.

"This is a private affair!" She stabbed out with her hands at Penelope's neck, her nails becoming elongated spikes that spiraled out toward my friend like blackened knives.

There was little I could do but watch as the knives neared her skin.

Penelope's form glowed, flashing a bright-white light that suddenly winked out of existence as the hand speared her form. A few paces away behind the monster, Penelope blinked back into existence, her Blaster 7 raised.

"Missed." Penelope's taunt was followed by her weapon surging with energy, blasting out at the back of Esmeralda. The wicked creature was rocketed away from the force of the blow toward the wall of the keep, drenching it in more of her inky-black ooze.

Shawn, still settled in his **Valiant Hero Stance**, came up to Penelope's side with his sword glowing. "You got her?"

"No." I glared at the downed form, no doubt in my mind that my friend's attack had done nothing to the creature.

The body on the ground suddenly melted into inky-black shadows, before dollops of Esmeralda's essence pooled back together, a wheezy giggle echoing through the room.

"Mm, Mana doesn't taste so bad either." Two misshapen eyes lazily opened in the inky blackness, the insane cerulean pupils alight with excitement and hunger. "Very pure."

Another shock wave surged as the air behind Esmeralda's growing form shattered, the creature blurring away from the force of the blow, leaving a trail of dark essence behind.

"Ulric!" I grabbed my weapon firmly as I saw his eyes widen.

With the blinding speed of a **Swift Throw Technique**, I sent Crow out at the tendril of dark essence that had darted behind Ulric, ready to stab into him.

The tendril melted from the blow, sliced off by the cutting edge of a duplicated Crow, and Esmeralda's giggles echoed throughout the welcoming battlefield. This was no life-and-death struggle for her, I could tell.

It was just a game to this thing.

"Regroup! Back-to-back!" Shawn called, getting us back into formation. I fell back, feeling my heart ache at the sounds of my beloved's stolen voice.

Penelope charged her weapon up with some of her Mana. "So, she soaks up Mana and Vitae like it's nothing. And she's too tough to take out with mundane means."

"Anyone got any ideas?" Shawn's sword glowed. I could hear the frustration in his voice. He disliked complicated fights as much as the rest of us.

Ulric frowned, shaking his head. "She's too fast, and I can't go all out."

"Not that your magic would do anything," Penelope pointed out, but I could hear thoughtful doubt in her voice.

I glanced around the room, watching as the roiling, inky essence of our opponent rolled in and out of the normal shadows around the room. It was hard to tell, for certain, where the hazards were.

And even if Ulric could hurt her, she'd just dodge it.

But then a thought struck me. If she absorbed Mana, why was she dodging Ulric's attacks at all? If she were going for quantity, Ulric's spells should be a feast with how much Mana they required. She'd want to get hit by them.

I glanced at Penelope, and her eyes met mine. The recognition in her gaze resonated with my own sudden revelation.

The shock waves created by Ulric's shatter magic weren't magical. They were a natural by-product.

"Penelope, I trust you," I said. "I'll keep her busy."

Shawn nodded. "Whatever you two figured out, I'm down with it. Let's go, Rakta."

I smiled slightly, feeling my Vitae blend with the air of the blood-soaked battlefield and move with the tension in the air.

"First Dance Technique: Twister Through the Valley!" I felt the force of the air surge around my limbs, my body lifting off the ground as I became one with the storm I had called within the keep.

Shawn's entire body glowed, as he called out, **"Valiant Body Technique!"**

Empowered by his own heroic Vitae, primed to protect and vanquish the evil of his foes, Shawn smiled at me before looking at the shadows around us.

"You both smell delicious!" Esmeralda surged from the essence around the room, but we blurred straight past her, beginning a dance between her, Shawn, and me.

It was hard to tell time as I dashed across the air of the large welcoming hall of the keep, slicing tendrils of dark essence, throwing Esmeralda away from Ulric and Penelope when she got too close to them.

Shawn was burning away the tendrils as best he could, slamming into Esmeralda along with me, and keeping her attention on us.

"Ha ha! Such delicious Vitae!" Esmeralda danced through the air, her form distending and pulsing with the energy she'd absorbed from us. "Now for some Mana to wash it down! **Black Art: Rose Garden!**"

Suddenly the dark essence of the room became barbed and arced through the air, like jet-black lightning bolts, heading straight toward Penelope and Ulric.

In a dash, I strangled some of them in a grip, feeling my Vitae pouring into them as they tore through my skin and left my palms bleeding, but I couldn't stop them all by myself.

Ulric turned away from Penelope, his eyes shining as he saw the black streaks of death, but as his magic began to rumble, Shawn's voice called out.

"Hey, over here!" Shawn's form glowed with the brilliant light of his **True Opponent Technique**, his Vitae soaking the entire room, but most importantly, Esmeralda.

Her eyes shined as she turned sharply toward him, drawn to him like a moth to a flame, the sharp barbed slivers of her essence suddenly whirling around at him. "Tasty!"

And he became her target midattack, the dark essence shooting straight toward him as he began darting away, the essence chasing after him like a bloodhound through the air, right on his tail, eager to take a bite out of him.

"Rakta! Grab her!" Penelope called out, stopping me as I moved to help Shawn, but I trusted Penelope's plan above my own instincts.

I dashed for Esmeralda, her body barely resisting as I grabbed ahold of her and took her to the ground with me. I locked my limbs around her, holding her around her smaller form with my large frame.

"Oh, Rakta, dear! I'm loving these mixed messages." Her long tongue licked up and down my arm around her. "You're definitely my favorite flavor, dear!"

I felt a familiar rumbling above me, the rumbling of a world crying out in pain as a tension built inside of it. "Savor it. It'll be your last."

I was running low on Vitae, my reserves draining as Esmeralda seemed to eat every last speck of it through my grip on her, but I had enough for one last technique.

"First Dance Technique." I felt the twister around me fade, the wind leaving as I called upon the plateau. **"The Stand of the Unconquered Plateau."**

"Ulric, now!" Penelope yelled, the Fjordic man beside her suddenly grinning as he gripped the air in front of him, an incarnation on his lips.

"Rakta, that's adorable." The creature in my arms giggled. "I've already died once. Do you really think I can die again? From a hug I can easily get out of?"

She tried to wiggle from my grip, but my Vitae had become adamant. My body had become unmovable, unconquered by the world around me, by the horrid witch within my arms. There was no escape, there was no release.

No release except for the coming death.

The rumble above me became audible, Esmeralda's insane eyes suddenly flickering with fear and the glimmers of sanity, "R-rakta, dear? I, um, I can't get out, and . . . and that sounds . . . Rakta! Let me go! Please! Don't let me die again! Please, it's me. You love me!"

She wiggled in my arms, tried to ooze from my grip, but so long as my Vitae stood its ground, nothing could escape me. Not even this horrid monster.

"Let . . . go!" She began feasting on my Vitae even more ravenously, biting into my reserves like a starving dog as she bit at my ironlike neck and arms. Streaks of black tears began to fall from her eyes. "You're . . . you're going to let me die again, Rakta?"

I frowned, feeling the last vestiges of my Vitae resist her gluttony. "I'm sorry that no one will tell your story after this day, Esmeralda."

She screamed at me with a primal anger, bit at me and tried to claw my eyes out, but the rumble above me suddenly reached a crescendo, and I was engulfed by the destructive force of Ulric's shock waves.

And Lydia's screams of pain echoed in my heart until they were snuffed out.

I stared up at the sky hours later, my heart still heavy and my body exhausted. The surviving villagers had been rescued; the remnants of Esmeralda's undead had been slain.

The calker hive below the village would be dealt with by a specialized extermination squad before the week was out if Penelope's message reached the right person soon enough.

It was over.

"Hey, Rakta." I looked over at Shawn as he came to sit beside me on the steps of the keep.

I nodded. "Shawn. Is everything sorted?"

After all the fighting had been taken care of, I'd been too exhausted to be of any help. I'd had to depend on Penelope's potion supply to heal my wounds. Even now, my muscles were sore and cried out if I moved too much.

Getting home like this was not going to be the easiest task.

Shawn nodded, but he didn't look particularly happy. "We found Lord Taine of Crest, or, well, what remained of him. Seems like Esmeralda didn't try very hard to keep him alive when she started rounding up the villagers."

I closed my eyes at the mention of that wicked thing. I didn't want to hear her name, see her face. Lydia's face.

"Anyway," Shawn continued, sensing my displeasure. "We did find some of his letters. It seems like the late lord had some unsavory connections, and we have a few more leads now . . . and it seems like this wasn't supposed to happen."

"What do you mean?"

"This." Shawn gestured out to the remnants of blood and battle inside the keep. "Esmeralda isn't mentioned in any of the letters or anything. She just came here, sped up the plans, got the calkers stirred up . . ."

I considered that for a moment. Esmeralda wasn't even supposed to be here? Then why had she come? For me? Had she learned of my intentions to accompany my group? How?

"She mentioned Zactrik," I said, "said he'd promised her things."

My friend grimaced. "Yeah, we've heard his name thrown around a bit among the lord's letters. Penelope thinks he's a bigger part of this than Esmeralda ever was."

It had been far too hopeful for me to think that all of this would end with the death of that wretched thing, but I had hoped nonetheless.

"And whatever she was," I said solemnly, still unsure exactly of what the ritual had done to her, "he'll be something even more dangerous."

Whatever Esmeralda was, it was incomplete. Penelope had said so, all those months ago while examining the journal. Zactrik had used a sacrifice, actually performing the ritual as intended. We'd have to deal with him one day.

Shawn said nothing. I didn't blame him; it wasn't a pleasant thought.

The silver lining to this, at least, was that we had more leads to pursue now, well, they did. I had done my part hadn't I? I could leave to return to my children?

Or did I still have a responsibility? If I did not make a stand against this Zactrik with my friends, then I was at fault for every death I could have prevented, wasn't I?

"Don't do that," Shawn said.

A tad surprised at the interjection, I looked over. "I'm sorry?"

"That look," he said, frowning and biting at his lip. "You're trying to convince yourself to stick with us, see this through. Don't do that."

"If I don't accompany you, if I abandon you all again . . ." I couldn't even bear finishing the thought of how I'd feel if one of them got hurt.

"You have children, Rakta. You're a father. There are other capable people out there, people we can call on now that we have more proof." He smiled.

There was truth to that. CADs from across Derra could be asked to come and deal with such a strange and esoteric threat, and, well, the empire could not ignore such a conspiracy within its noble lines.

Putting a hand on my shoulder, Shawn squeezed firmly. "Go be a good dad. You've got enough on your plate, alright? Sometimes saving the world starts at home."

Even without his Vitae, Shawn glowed, and his words felt heavy with meaning. Nothing was empty in his genuine suggestion.

"Thank you, Shawn." I'd been moments from risking my life, leaving my children alone for weeks on end, but he was right.

I was no longer an adventurer. I was a father.

And I needed to go home.

41

The sun was rising just above the horizon as I reached Gelvurt a few days later. Recovered from the fight with Esmeralda, I was not.

And yet, I had managed to make it back at a decent pace, pushed onward by my relief that I was still alive and my children waiting for me to get home.

The local farmers were out in force by the time I arrived, and the village center was crawling with the morning merchantry of traveling peddlers.

Not wanting to make a scene of arriving back into the village, I gave the center a wide berth, breathing a sigh of relief as I reached the open archway of Velbrun Keep without interruption.

"It's good to be home." I looked around, walking across the courtyard to the door and pushing it open, stepping inside.

Feeling my bones ache and my muscles relax as I entered, I kept my gait gentle. My recovery was not going to be swift, it seemed. Beyond the Vitae I'd expended in the fight, the life energy that Esmeralda had drained from me . . .

It was not coming back quickly. A permanent mark upon my life? I hoped not, but such scars had been overcome before in the stories of my people. All that mattered was that I was alive enough to come home in one piece.

Shaking my head, I called out through the keep, "I'm home!"

My voice echoed through the keep, hopefully giving Doh enough time to put on clothes if she had, well, decided to take my absence as a chance to invite Dresden over.

A few moments later, I heard the rumbling of steps, before Doh came down, Dresden at her side, both of them grinning.

"Rakta! You're finally back!" Doh sat on the banister of the stairs and rode it down to the floor, before jumping off of it. "How did it go? What did you do?"

Before I could answer, she surprised me with a hug, one she quickly released as she came back to her senses. She looked as surprised as I felt at the sudden gesture.

"Doh, Doh." I calmed her with a hand, touched by the warm welcome. "I have much to tell, but please, how are my children doing?"

Dresden jogged down the steps as I spoke, not quite as willing to follow Doh's immature lead, but quickly gave me a respectful nod as he joined us.

"Well, fine." Doh looked uncomfortable. "They definitely missed you, uh, Daka cried a lot. Natakia's eating even less."

I was already moving up the stairs, both of them following. "And Dalton?"

To hear that Natakia had been eating even less, and that Daka had been crying for me to come home, I was almost disgusted with myself for having taken so long to return.

"Oh, he's fine." Doh shrugged, a smirk pulling at the edges of her lips. "I mean, nothing's changed with him. Maybe a bit richer?"

She giggled, looking over at a flustered Dresden. I gave them both looks. I liked straightforward, clear answers when it came to the well-being of my younglings.

Dresden coughed. "I let him play with some of my sils. I never got them back."

One of my village guards had their coin stolen by an infant. Truly, my children were exceptional. I would need to find those coins, of course.

I did not want to raise a cutpurse.

Stepping as silently as I could into the nursery, I found my three pairs of eyes staring at me. I stilled, before my body relaxed and I smiled, feeling a burden lift from my shoulders.

"I'm home." This time, the words felt truer.

Daka's gaze suddenly wettened, and her wailing cries broke the silence of the room at my words, her arms up and flailing toward me.

"Dah," she cried, "Dah dah."

Dah dah? Dad? Her first words? They made every tribulation of the past year worth it.

I picked her up, gathering Natakia and Dalton into my arms, as well, and gently settled into the rocking chair in the corner. "I'm sorry for being gone so long, my younglings."

Daka's grip was tight for a child of her age, her crying muffled into the robe on my chest. I gave her a gentle kiss on the forehead as I spoke to them.

"The Velbruns will not bother us, not for some time." I said, hoping my words were true. If they hadn't attempted anything bold while I was absent from Gelvurt, then perhaps they had taken my words seriously.

Daka continued to cry, and I let her, noticing Natakia's own wails beginning to harmonize with her sister's. Dalton's gaze was clear of tears, but I could feel his attention on me.

I spoke to him specifically. "Thank you, Dalton, for being strong for your sisters while I was gone."

He turned away, no longer looking me in the eye. That was fine; there was a glimmer of care in his eyes that I was sure would grow stronger and stronger every day.

Dalton would be a good brother.

I smiled, resting back with my children. I felt a peace within me, an inner contentedness that grew in the presence of my children in my arms. They were safe and sound.

Eventually, Daka and Natakia tired from their crying and sleepily looked up at me. The gurgles of Natakia's rumbling stomach made me smile down at her.

"We'll need to get all of you fed and ready for a nap, won't we?" I gave Natakia and Dalton a kiss on the head.

Daka squawked, slapping a hand on my chest. I'd already given her a kiss on the head, but I did so again, feeling unfettered with my love.

"Guh!" Natakia tangled with Daka as the babies tousled, but the conflict quickly drained from them as hunger and sleepiness crept in.

Doh crept in, peeking through the door. "Need help with that?"

Still feeling the drain from my last fight, I smiled at her. "I'd welcome it."

An hour later, as the children had their nap, I explained what I'd experienced in Crest, from the calkers to Esmeralda.

Orion, who had visited upon hearing of my return, looked gray. "To think that such a beast was within our village. She is well and truly killed, yes?"

"As killed as anything can be." I'd kept my minor doubts close to my chest, for anything was possible, but I'd heard the screams fade, the genuine loss of life within its crumbling pitch.

Doh frowned, Dresden's arms casually around her. "Taking the form of the dead, she has some fucking nerve. That shit doesn't fly!"

"It wasn't pleasant," I muttered, deeply frowning at the memories of the fight. "To hear her voice again . . . I . . ."

"Are you okay?" Dresden had been quiet, watching me as I told my story.

"Not really," I said, honestly. "Coming back, being with my children, it's what I need right now. It's what I'll need for a long time."

My wounded heart had been weak even before Crest, but to experience Lydia's death a second time so viscerally was the final nail in the coffin of my adventuring days.

Rakta the Dancer could finally sleep.

"Good," Dresden said with finality. "You're a good father. No need for you to go out and get yourself killed before your kids will even remember you."

Doh smirked. "Iunno, those kids are smart. I bet Dalton will have a list of complaints a mile long as soon as he learns to write, if he hasn't already."

She was joking, but I wasn't quite so irreverent of the thought. My children were prophesied; there was no telling what the next few years would hold for them.

"In any case, it sounds like we should celebrate the return of our Lord Velbrun," Orion said, smiling good-naturedly at the others. "Marisha and I have been saving some nicely aged wine for a special occasion."

He glanced at me, as if asking whether or not his suggestion was appropriate, but the fierce look Doh was giving me was daring me to deny such a treat.

"Very well," I chuckled. "Let's celebrate."

Doh cheered, Dresden clapped happily alongside her, and Orion seemed to begin reconsidering his offer.

The sky was beautiful in the morning. The greenery behind the keep was exceptionally vibrant, and the sounds of birds chirping in the distance encouraged me to smile.

It had been a few days since I'd arrived back in Gelvurt, my recovery increasing as I kept to my daily duties as the local lord and father to my children.

And yet, a kernel of unrest had kept me from sleeping well.

My childrens' noises as they sat in my lap, resting their backs against my stomach as they squirmed against one another, calmed me as I stared at the tombstone in front of me.

"Guh." Natakia knocked against Dalton. He gave her a look, a frown tugging at his lips.

Daka pulled at her awkwardly, her limbs not quite ready for such a movement. "Nuh!"

They were more beautiful than anything around me. The morning sun, the trees, and even the clouds could not even begin to compare to my youthful sparks.

"Children," I said, "I wanted to wait until you were older to tell certain stories."

They quieted at my words, Daka looking up at me with her bright-blue eyes as Natakia and Dalton gazed at the tombstone in front of us.

I rubbed Daka's head softly. "And yet, I believe that even if you do not carry this story with you in the future, even if I have to tell you it again, I think . . . I may need the practice, to be quite honest."

Lydia Velbrun. A name that had become my life for years. Did I truly understand the woman? Was every truth I knew about her only a fog to hide the lies? The unspoken realities of our relationship?

"It's hard to speak of those who have passed because we have only their stories to remember them by," I said. "And stories, well, often change depending on who tells them."

For every tribe that spoke of Brota as a hero, like mine had, there were those that instead looked up to Garrok as the true pinnacle of the Ruskan ideals.

Garrok, a Storyteller that slayed armies through his powerful words, was as much a part of our heritage as any other. A man who had given Brota's tribe every chance to surrender peacefully in his quest to unite the nation.

"So, listen well, my younglings, as I tell a story close to my heart, but one that is as true as any other." I thought of Lydia's sparkling blue eyes, her silvery hair, and the moon-touched skin that warmed at my touch.

"It was a star that began her journey. A young girl, barely into adulthood, looked up into the sky and found her future beyond the walls of her royal family . . ."

And so went the story of Lydia Velbrun, a story that went on and on as the sun rose into the sky.

FROM DAWN TO NOON
INTERLUDE:
DRESDEN BOOKER

And then, with a final slash, I speared the bandit duster with my sword!" Dad roared victoriously, gathering me up into his arms and holding me aloft in the air.

I cheered with him. "And Gelvurt was safe again!"

Dad sat me on his shoulders, pointing his blade into the sky. "Yes, boy! Gelvurt was safe again!"

"I wanna hear another one! Tell me about the merchants that were carrying wyvern eggs!" I kicked my feet, bumping my heels against Dad's chest.

Dad nodded, always happy to tell another story, and began to wave his sword expertly in the air. "There I was, training into the later afternoon, when I heard a distant call for help—"

"Dinner's ready!" Mom called out from the house.

Dad grinned up at me, a deal in his eyes. "Eat your corn and I'll finish the story."

I pouted fiercely. I hated corn.

I glared at the cob of corn on my plate, idly chewing on some of the meat Mom had gotten from the market this morning.

I didn't always eat lunch with Mom, so why did she always serve corn when I came around? I've hated it since I was a kid. I wasn't subtle about it either.

"So, dear," Mom got my attention. "How've things been?"

"Things have been fine." I shrugged. "Rakta has been dealing with a lot of the increased trade through the area, you know?"

Mom shook her head, giggling. "Dresden, I'll never get used to you being so casual to the local lord. When did you get so close to nobility?"

When the nobility turned out to be a decent guy that took the time out of his busy day to train me? When he managed to actually put Gelvurt on the map with that academy of his?

It had only been a year since Rakta had arrived in Gelvurt, but the village had gone through a lot of changes. Agriculture was still huge, of course, but there were a lot more buildings and merchants around.

I'd heard from Rakta that Niers and Alwur were improving, as well, but I never paid too much attention to what that really entailed.

I sighed, realizing I actually needed to answer. "Just done a lot of bodyguard work for him. Someone needs to protect his kids when he steps out of Gelvurt."

"Ah yes." Mom smiled fondly. "Those children of his are adorable. Martha and I were just talking about how precious that one girl, Natakia, looks in her dresses."

Yeah, Natakia was a cute kid, and no one knew it better than Natakia herself. I didn't really talk to the kids much, except Daka, but I definitely got weird vibes from them.

Learning to talk early was one thing, but they always seemed so . . . developed? Like, yeah, they acted like kids sometimes, they cried and fought over stupid stuff, but they just felt oddly mature.

Especially Dalton. Toddlers weren't supposed to talk in such complete sentences, right?

"Yeah, yeah, they're great." I shrugged, taking a scornful bite of corn. I'd protect them, no matter how odd they seemed.

"So, speaking of children, any word on Doh?"

I coughed, suddenly choking. I beat my chest, taking a big swig of water as Mom rushed around the table to make sure I was okay, but I caught the glint of amusement in her eyes.

"What, uh, Mom!" I tried to clear my throat again, mostly dislodging the corn. "Are you trying to kill me, Mom? Is feeding me corn not enough?"

"You have to eat your corn," Mom said, "but don't dodge the question, dear. Doh seems like a sweet girl! And I know you've got your eye on her; you've got the same look as your father did."

I scratched the back of my head, frowning. Mom knew Doh and I were close, but, uh, she didn't know how close we'd gotten or how shy Doh could sometimes get about . . . well, our relationship.

"Doh and I, well, I don't know . . ."

"I'm sorry to interrupt your meal, Bonnabel." The captain of the guard looked grim as he spoke to Mom. "It's about Lionel."

I stared up at the captain, feeling a tightness in my chest that I didn't understand. "What happened to Dad?"

"Dresden, dear, go to your room for a moment." Mom's voice was hard. I didn't want to, but I didn't have it in me to argue.

An hour later, Mom came into my room with red eyes and took me into her arms, holding me like I'd slip away if she didn't hold me tight enough.

"M-mom." My voice shook, my grip on her tightening as well. "Where, uh, where's Dad?"

"Dad's not coming back, dear." Mom sniffled. "Dad is, uh, Dad got very hurt protecting . . . protecting the village. Um, uh, like a hero."

My eyes burned. "W-what?"

With heavy slashes, I tore at the training dummy, feeling sweat pour down my forehead and neck, my muscles aching as I pushed them.

I had to keep my posture solid, defendable, to keep my **Iron Knight Stance** from slipping. It took only a second of losing my concentration, an attack from my blind spot, and I'd . . .

I swallowed, keeping my posture as I swung even harder into the dummy, beating it with the heavy training sword in my grip. I couldn't let myself get complacent, couldn't falter where others had. Dying wouldn't make me a hero.

"Wow." A familiar voice cooed from the edge of the training field. "What did that hunk of straw and leather do to such a fine, muscular man of Gelvurt?"

My blow lost its strength, my stance faltering as I blushed, turning over to look at Doh. "Hey."

She smiled, my face burning even more at the playfulness in her eyes. "Hey yourself."

I scratched the back of my head and wandered over to her, putting my sword back on the nearby table. "Nap time?"

Doh nodded, sighing as she sprawled out onto the fence, giving me a dramatic look of exhaustion. "The kids used to love nap time, you know? Now they complain, saying it's a waste of time! Can you believe it?"

"They don't know what they're missing. I love nap time," I said, leaning up against the fence next to her, idly playing with her hair.

"Oh yeah?" Doh leaned into my idle touch. "And why's that?"

I tried to think of something proper to say, but my tongue became heavy at the tension in the air. "Well, uh, I get to see you during nap time."

Doh sprung up, wrapping her arm around my neck and giving me a kiss on the lips. "You charmer."

I licked my lips. "I, uh, try." I just wasn't usually successful.

My lover giggled, but then I saw something about her change. Not like usual, with her body and skin shifting into a new form, but rather, a sudden change in her demeanor. She seemed nervous, uncertain.

I climbed over the fence to get closer to her. "Hey, what's wrong?"

Doh put her head onto my chest and was quiet for a time. I let her talk at her own pace, content with comforting her while she figured out her words.

"Who, uh, am I to you, Dresden?" Her eventual words were soft, uncertain.

I paused, taken off guard. "Doh?"

She looked up at me, biting her lip. There was a scared look in her eye, her question still standing in the air. This was important to her, even if I didn't understand it.

"I guess"—I felt a strange warmth in my stomach—"you're probably my favorite person. My exciting, always-changing girl? I don't . . . know what to say."

The earlier talk with Mom was echoing in the back of my head.

"I'm pregnant." Doh said the words like she was stabbing me in the back against her will, like she was trying to hurt me as quickly as possible to get it over with.

I blinked, feeling the world begin to spin. She was . . . pregnant? But how? We'd been careful, right? She was always so good about protecting herself from that, she had a spell and everything for it . . .

Oh.

"The solstice?" I looked at her. "When we snuck away from Rakta's speech with some of his wine?"

"Uh, yeah. I, well, I forgot . . . I'm sorry," she blubbered, beginning to become undone. "I'm so sorry, I do that sometimes, and, uh, it's a big thing that happens, and I barely remembered the night afterward and, um, uh . . ."

She was babbling, and the real fear I felt in her words dislodged something in the back of my throat. "I love you, Doh."

Doh blinked, stunned. I'd never said the words when I wasn't drunk or in the midst of, well, intimacy.

"I love you so much, and it's really scary that . . . that this happened by accident." I tried to find the right way to say things. "Are you . . . okay with a child? I know you . . ."

The last thing I wanted to do was force a kid onto Doh, even if I'd support her all the way. She never wanted kids, always seemed to be against the idea of having her own.

She'd told me months ago about her doppelgänger issues with memories. I wasn't sure how to help her with that, except starting writing in a journal I kept everything in now.

"I just . . . if they're like me . . ." Doh's eyes looked lost in horrible thoughts.

I held her tight. "You can teach them, Doh. Help them with their memories. And I, well, I'll help you. No matter what, no matter what you decide."

Doh sniffled, tears streaming down her cheeks. "I love you too."

The funeral was a quiet affair. Attended by a lot of faces I didn't recognize and the local lord. I knew the other guards, though, but I almost didn't recognize them either.

They were usually a lot louder.

Lord Velbrun said some words, coughing between his condolences, before he finally gave the local men the signal to lower Dad's casket into the ground, the local grave keeper ready to fill the hole up.

I hadn't gotten to see Dad's body. Mom said he'd been . . . that I couldn't see him. The dire wolf that had killed him had been slain in revenge by the local guards.

As the funeral came to an end, Lord Velbrun came to me, looking down at me with sad, old eyes. "Your father was a hero, young child."

I stared down at the slowly filling hole. "I don't want a hero, my lord. I want my dad."

I stared down at the bundle of cloth in my arms, the beautiful sleeping face of my newly born daughter. "She looks a lot like you."

Doh sleepily blinked, before looking at me with a furrowed gaze. "Very funny."

She might've sounded annoyed, but I knew how happy she was. After months and months of mood swings, complaining, keeping herself from shifting because we didn't know what would happen to the baby, and so much more, it was finally over.

Rakta had been kind to our hardships, keeping Doh cared for as her pregnancy became more and more pronounced. Honestly, I think he had been more worried than I had been when Doh went into labor, which was saying something because I wasn't exactly calm about it.

I heard the door behind me squeak open. Looking over, I saw Rakta peeking in, a worried glint in his eyes that melted into relief as he saw Doh looking back at him.

"Everything . . . went well?" he asked, sounding nervous. An odd sound coming from such a powerful man.

I nodded, smiling. "Want to hold her?"

He came over, his large build belying the grace within his gait. "I'd be honored."

Glancing at Doh, and getting a nod from her, Rakta took my daughter from my arms and held her gently, like the experienced father that he was. I was almost daunted at being compared to him one day.

"She's beautiful," Rakta said with finality. "What is her name, if I might ask?"

I turned to my wife. "Doh?"

She smiled, snuggling into her pillow after the strenuous labor. "Macy. 'Twas the first name that came to mind."

"It's a beautiful name." Rakta handed Macy back to me, and I passed her back over to Doh, who gently took her, like the experienced care-giver she was.

Man, I was really going to have to bust my ass to be a parent that rivaled either of these two. It really wasn't fair, was it?

Rakta stepped out of the room, giving us privacy, and I sat next to Doh, idly tending to her raven locks and looking down at our daughter. I didn't know if I'd ever be a hero like Rakta was, but that didn't matter to me.

All that mattered was that I was a father for this little girl for the rest of her life.

"I'm so glad I get to drink again." Doh snuggled into my side, shedding a few more tears of joy, our little Macy peacefully sleeping between us.

I combed my fingers through her hair, shedding a tear of my own. "Me too."

FROM DAWN TO NOON
INTERLUDE:
ESMERALDA ZEHR

I don't think they're coming back, dear." Charlotte was one of the kindest and most polite women in the entire village, but I hated when she called me dear.

I wasn't a dear. I wasn't a sweetheart. I was broke and alone, but I still deserved better than a fucking pet name that let people think they could cheat their way into my graces.

My annoyance didn't pull my gaze away from the trail though. "They'll be back. They promised they would be back today."

"Dear." I wanted to punch something. "That was two months ago."

I knew it was two months ago. I'd kept track of the time. So, I'd known it was two months ago. Did she think I didn't know it was two months ago?

Did she think I was stupid? I wasn't stupid. I was hungry.

"Uncle just has a lot of responsibilities in the capital," I explained to her like I would a child. "Things get turned around, and sorting them out takes time. They promised they would be back today."

She should know this. The entire village should know this. Had the shock of that troll coming into the village center and killing everyone it could get its hands on made them dumb?

Charlotte was quiet for a moment, before she sighed. "You don't need to starve yourself, Esme. I'm sorry about your grandfather, but he would not have wanted you to go hungry."

She had no idea what she was talking about. I'd been weak my entire life, a frail body after getting sick when I was young.

I hadn't even gotten to know my parents before they were dead, so Grandfather was all I had. And he'd made it very clear, no matter how sick I got, if I did not work, I did not eat.

After he'd died pushing me away from the troll's claws, I'd gone home and gorged myself on every bit of foodstuff he'd had in the cellars. I'd been stupid. I wasn't stupid anymore.

"Uncle promised me he would take me with him to the capital the next time he visited," I said. "I can make money and eat there."

I was good with words and numbers. I could make money in the capital.

I was scattered into little, tiny, itty-bitty shards of myself. And every little speck of my delightful form was filled to the brim of its very small cup with rage.

"He killed me," I muttered disbelievingly to my many selves. I had to be quiet so the world didn't hear me. "I'm dead now. I can't believe it. What will our children think? Their father is a murderer."

It was all a hilarious misunderstanding. I should kill Rakta. The handsome and heroic Rakta who had charmed me the day we'd met. I should kill him.

And then we could get back together! And be the best parents to our little kids! I should learn their names one day.

Maybe if I'd had a chance to really digest all of that delicious Vitae Rakta had given me I'd have a better grasp on the specifics, but I was getting the impression of the letter D when I thought of my kids.

Yeah, my kids struck me as the type to have D names.

"Any trace?" One of the metal men, the grand, useless guards of Cerula, spoke as they passed by my hiding spot.

His friend, or maybe lover, grunted. "Nothing. Not even sure what we're looking for; we cleaned the undead out of here a while ago."

Me, I wanted to scream at him. That'd ruin the game though. I was playing the hiding game. No one could find me because I was very good at the hiding game.

So good, even, that I had been hiding ever since Rakta had killed me. Mostly killed me. It was fine, probably, since he'd done it out of love.

I'd mostly kill him back later.

For now, I slithered away through a tiny crack that I'd been working on for a while, skittering my broken form into the narrow passage and out of the keep.

Ah, it was a beautiful night. A beauty that I was delighted to take advantage of to get away from this horrid place.

My uncle never came for me. Another merchant, some nameless soul, had come by and told me that he'd gotten a big trade deal that'd take him over Crest Sea somewhere with his family.

I guess I wasn't family anymore? Otherwise, I probably wouldn't still be in the empire, would I?

The merchant hadn't had an answer for me when I asked him that same question, but he'd given me a ride to the next village over.

A place called Niers.

"I can't believe someone is giving the Hadleys such a hard time." Some woman spoke to her friend as they walked past me. "They work hard to bake that bread every morning."

I munched on my breakfast while the two canaries continued down the street toward the tavern. In my opinion, the Hadleys should work harder at keeping their bread safe.

It was too good for how easy it was to steal.

Thievery hadn't been my first choice, I'd admit gladly. Unfortunately, for all it boasted to be a growing trade town, Niers had little place for a sickly rat who could read like me.

And those few who did weren't giving me a job because of what I could do. They were giving it to me because of how hungry I looked, how lonely I must be entering adulthood without my parents to guide me. Pitying the rat because she had nothing to give back.

Well, years of staying quiet and unseen had given me plenty of prac- tice getting into and out of places without being noticed.

Sucking at my fingers for the last crumbs of my breakfast, I decided I'd had enough of the streets and returned to my home.

The attic of the local keep.

After eating a few grazing cows from the villages I had passed by, I was beginning to feel a lot more like me. Which was good because there was no one I'd rather be!

I was still so broken, though, parts that I used to have not really coming back. I was looking more bovine than I had before, or at least, from what I remembered.

Rakta would kill me if he saw me looking like a cow! I had to look like me again to even have a chance for his love!

Unfortunately, it was kinda hard to remember exactly what I looked like! I got some of the arms and legs right, but I definitely hadn't had hooves before. And was my height a little off?

"Moo." The mournful noise echoed through the forest I was shambling through. Walking was harder with hooves. Maybe I needed a tail!

Wait, did I have a tail before? If I didn't have a tail, I probably didn't have hooves. Or maybe the fact that I have hooves now just proved that I used to have a tail for balance?

I was so hungry. Hungry for Vitae that wasn't a fucking cow. And no, that didn't mean I wanted to eat a pig or a chicken, I assured myself.

Where was a sorcerer or vanguard when you needed one? Some sweet, delicious, refined nectar for me to rebuild myself with! That's what I needed. Oh, I would give my left hoof to have some of Rakta's sweet Vitae right now.

I could almost taste the pleasant warmth.

"Excuse me." A man suddenly poked his head around the tree I'd rested up against after stumbling. "Do you happen to be the young lass that goes by Esmeralda?"

I blinked, looking around the entire forest for the punch line to this joke that I was missing.

"That's me," I said, before I realized I was talking to a piece of food. "I'm going to eat you now."

Like Grandfather always said, politeness is something, something time to eat! I rushed at him, my jaw unhinging as I let my teeth sharpen into sharp, thin needles, ready to rip into and tear!

Then I was on the ground, my face stuck in this annoying hole in the ground that I struggled to get out of. A pressure on the back of my neck—it felt like a foot—pushed me harder and harder into the sediment.

I collapsed my form and dashed away, my body reforming a few feet away as I rubbed my neck. "Ow. Is this about the cows?"

The man chuckled, but it sounded weird. Like someone had just been instructed to chuckle and so they had. I didn't like it, but I didn't like a lot of things.

I wondered what Rakta was doing right now. I liked Rakta.

"Cows? No, no." The man approached, and in the moonlight I saw that he walked with a large coat across his frame, coming down to his knees, and a wooden cane in his hand. He didn't limp, though; in fact, something about how easily he walked terrified me.

Suddenly I was flying backward through the air, only stopping as I crashed into a large oak that cracked in two as I hit, my entire body on fire from the blow.

Not because of the tree, fuck trees, but the burning hole in my gut as I looked down and saw a part of myself, a part of the inky blackness that was me, had just disappeared. Like it was nothing, like I was nothing.

The man was approaching me again, walking casually as if he hadn't just blown a hole in my newly formed gut. "I'd heard about what happened in Crest, but I couldn't quite believe it."

I made to move, but the tip of his cane was suddenly pressed up against my throat, faster than I could even register him moving, the threat pushing back up against the bark of the broken oak.

"To think, throwing out an old journal actually bore fruit." His eyes were bright in the dark night, shining with something that wasn't Vitae or Mana, but I wanted it. I wanted it so badly. "Too bad the fruit went rotten."

Something deep inside me was screaming to run away.

A noble was coming through the village today; everyone was talking about it. Not that it was all that special for a noble to come through the town, but apparently he was a lord.

A new Lord Velbrun heading over to the next village over, Gelvurt. I hadn't heard much about it beyond the rumors spreading around the village center, but I'd thought it was an opportunity to see what I could nick from the royal soul.

Even better, he was distracting Jorge.

"Come, have a pint on me, my lord!" That fat piece of lard was quick to get friendly with any pretty face that came through Niers. For once, I'd agree with him on that though.

The new Lord Velbrun of Gelvurt was very attractive. Tall, muscular, and he even had kids! A quality parent that actually stuck by his children.

I could appreciate that. In a detached way that wouldn't keep me from stealing from the rich man. One quick, subtle glance into his wagon, however, revealed a damning fact.

This guy had nothing but hay and a few chests. Nothing valuable at all!

Damn, maybe this guy was a fake noble. I'd heard about that happening before, some nobody getting ahold of a writ of royalty or whatever. Never actually seen it happen though.

I'd take one of those chests to make sure, but they looked heavy. I doubted I'd get very far, and the risk of being discovered was too dangerous.

No, no. It seemed that today was an ask-Quentin-for-food day. I had had a lot more of those kinds of days recently. It'd been harder and harder getting out of bed.

And I'd coughed yesterday, a nasty thing. It gave me a bad feeling.

A rattling spray of ooze burst from my mouth as I dragged my aching, broken body, or, at least, the tiny bit that was left of it, to the only safety I knew, the only safety I could remember clearly enough.

Zactrik, for all his promises of immortality and breaking the mortal coil, had certainly tried his very best to end me for good. Wasn't that kind of hypocritical?

I'd like to think that I was as immortal as he was! I was still alive right now, wasn't I? I spewed more of my black ichor onto the forest floor, soaking it back up to keep my strength up.

Days. It'd been days, or maybe weeks or months, since that horrid freak found me and tried to end me. Ever since, I'd been in unending pain and terrified of being discovered again. It was no longer a game; none of this was fun. I wanted Rakta.

I wasn't even sure how he found me, really, but by some stroke of luck, he hadn't tried again. Maybe I'd killed him? I didn't remember doing that. Although, I could barely remember anything at all except for pain and hunger.

I remembered Rakta, my love. My face. And my brother.

All the way from the Taines' lands to the Velbrun border, I kept those three things as close to my chest as possible. I didn't know what would happen to me without them.

Truly, those were the only things I kept as I cannibalized the parts of my form I didn't need for a little more energy as I reached the walls of the city. The cobblestone streets were nice, novel, and easy to slowly drag myself over to reach my destination.

A nice manor with nice windows that I made a nice little hole in for myself to squeeze my way through, flopping onto the ground with a hissing gurgle of pain.

"What was that?" I could hear my brother's voice in the next room over.

I gurgled loudly, trying to form words.

Footsteps approached. "Who's there? Show yourself or I'll call the guards."

I fashioned my face as well as I could, letting my inky-black goo become solid and formable, alongside making sure my voice was intact.

"Brother, help me."

He stared down at me, remnants of fear and anger bleeding out from his eyes as he recognized me, recognized who I was. Who I was and always would be.

Rakta would look at me like that one day. I knew he would.

FROM DAWN TO NOON
INTERLUDE:
SHAWN HANCHETT

"Congratulations to the graduating class of 2022!" President Wayne Carvajal smiled, his pearly teeth shining as the world erupted into noise.

Cheering, clapping, tears being shed, the world around me was alight with victorious success! I raised my own hands, whooping with my buddies as we danced around in our seats.

"Oh my god." Ricky wiped her eyes, her rarely combed brown hair in a ponytail. "I can't believe this is actually finally happening. Fuck you, Dad!"

She'd been fighting hard against him for a long time. This graduation was just one more step to never seeing him again.

I jostled her a bit, playfully. "It's super happening!"

Winfred joined in as he always did, clapping loudly but smiling softly. He'd never been much of a talker, but I was sure he was pretty overwhelmed by this huge crowd. I'd get him somewhere real quiet to properly celebrate.

I liked it when he opened up in private.

I shook hands with all the amazing people around, some of them I barely knew, others I'd spent the last four years in the same classes with. My bachelor's in English wasn't super crazy like some of the people here celebrating their first steps into law, but everyone here had reason to celebrate.

"Hey." I gathered up my friends. "Let's go bowling!"

Winfred and Ricky cheered, both of them in the same situation as me. No real family to go celebrate with. We still had one another though.

* * *

I woke to the shrill wail of my son with weary familiarity. I loved him, yeah? Like a whole bunch, but Daddy needed to sleep.

Tracy stirred awake beside me long enough to sleepily mutter, "Go be a hero."

Tempted to shake her awake and go deal with the little guy as a team, I gently pushed myself out of bed and let her rest. She'd been under a lot more stress than me during the pregnancy, so I could take a few bullets for her.

Tiptoeing my way into the nursery, I found my son with his blanket over his head, crying and wiggling and trying to get the heavy cloth off of him.

"Hey, hey." I gently picked the blanket off of him, his crying eyes looking up at me with fear and confusion. "Daddy's here now. You're okay; Daddy's here."

Winfred, my son, slowly began to stop crying as I rocked him back to sleep, his face breaking from the storm and falling back into a cute, peaceful slumber.

"What am I gonna do with you, boy?" I shook my head, continuing to rock him as I sat down, taking the lonely early-morning hours to really think about things.

It was hard to get introspective these days. It'd been, what, almost five years since I'd come to Derra? I wasn't attached to modern society, not really, but my friends . . . I always hoped they were doing okay. When I was tasked with helping out by Overseer, they had promised my friends were okay, but I was still worried.

I mean, the way I'd been brought into this world . . . I hope they weren't traumatized. I'd never thought I'd be away for this long, not years. Months, maybe, but . . . did I truly regret having come to Derra? I thought about that for a while.

"No," I muttered, caressing my son's cheeks. "If I had a choice, I know which one I'd take."

Here, I'd met amazing new people and helped others with problems that I never thought I'd have the ability to solve. Fighting the Warlock King, marrying the princess of an entire empire . . .

I was still getting used to my new titles, as was Tracy's father. He'd certainly not approved of me, but he'd said that he doubted anyone else came as close to his approval as I did.

Kind of backhanded, but it was as close as you got to a compliment from King Certimov.

[The king most likely has a lot of pressures, but is most likely overall benevolent for his position. Aging and with Zactrik's plans developing, he may be at a growing risk of harm.]

I breathed deeply, "Thanks, Oracle."

It was one thing to have an idea of how fantasy stories like these usually went, but Oracle, my gift from god, had kept me updated on a lot of angles that I didn't always consider. It didn't always help, but when it did, I listened.

For a long time I distrusted it, wary of being deceived or manipulated through its insight, but it had saved my life so many times, saved my friends and family so many times.

How else would I have known that Tracy had been possessed by that spirit when we'd first met? Or that Penelope was growing dangerously bored with her mundane magical devices?

I'd been able to save Tracy and give Penelope new ideas, uh, well, ideas I'd scraped from my old world. Although, with the rise in recreations of Penelope's magitech out in the public, I was beginning to doubt if that had been the best answer. The weapons had been useful, yeah, but it'd been a nasty surprise to have one of them used against me by that one noble.

"Sometimes, you just gotta live with these things." I put Winfred back down into his cradle.

Watching my son sleep, my mind wandered to other children out in the world. Specifically, the triplets of my good friend Rakta. He reminded me of Winfred sometimes, with how quiet he could be.

And yet, everyone listened to him when he spoke. I could see what Lydia liked about him, even if Oracle hadn't always had the best things to say about her.

His children, though, were going to be a handful. Three more souls from Earth? All children and at the center of a prophecy?

I'd been given a mission from Overseer to make things better in Derra, specifically the Certillian Empire, but not a prophecy. Lydia always said prophecies were serious business.

Wrapping my son up to keep him warm, I smiled. Rakta could handle it. He was a good guy, but that didn't mean I couldn't help out in my own ways.

* * *

"So, Shawn, you're really going to Mongolia?" Ricky chewed on her greasy pizza, watched Winfred get another strike. He was way too good at bowling for us to actually compete with him seriously.

He wiggled his eyebrows as he strutted back over, grinning goofily in the relatively empty bowling alley. *"Strike for me."*

I gave him a thumbs-up. *"Nice job, buddy. And yeah, the placement officer at the Peace Corps said that with my qualifications, Mongolia could really use someone like me teaching English."*

I already knew Mandarin, but I had to take a few courses on Mongolian in preparation for my trip. It'd help with the locals.

Winfred looked uncomfortable. *"When are you leaving?"*

"A couple months," I comforted him. *"More than enough time to party like rock stars, yeah? I'll need to keep working at Mr. Chick's to pay my part of the rent until I go."*

Ricky rolled her head side to side. *"God, next semester is gonna be a bitch without you. Graduate school would be so much better with both of my sidekicks."*

"I could, uh." Winfred tapped his knees. *"I could pay your part of the rent for you, these last months. I . . . if you only have these months to prepare, you shouldn't be worrying about that."*

Warmth swelled up in my heart toward both of them. My friends were great.

"That's real sweet, Winfred, but—"

"Holy shit, Allassandra Heatherton died!" Ricky interrupted me, her phone lighting up her shocked look. I wanted to continue reassuring Winfred, but . . . a death? Was it someone she knew?

"Who?" Winfred tilted his head.

"This big model, huge on Instagram and stuff. Says she got into a car wreck, but reports aren't out on what actually happened." She shook her head, before instantly moving on. *"Hey, we should go bungee jumping."*

I choked. *"Uh, what!? That sounds super dangerous!"*

Winfred nodded. *"I don't know . . ."*

"Stop being babies." Ricky smiled good-naturedly. *"My aunt does it all the time, and she's super safe about it! I'll call her up and get something scheduled."*

Breathing out air fondly at the casual commands, I shrugged. "Alright, I guess. How bad can it be?"

Hmm, I probably shouldn't say stuff like that. People in movies died after saying that kind of stuff.

I sliced another dire wolf out of the air, the local population of monstrous animals having become stirred up by one of Zactrik's schemes, I was sure. He wasn't like the Warlock King, deciding to wage a huge war.

No, Zactrik had a thousand different plays he was making from the shadows. I'd never even seen the man, but it was all I could do, with the help of CAD and my friends, to stop what we could.

Breathing heavily, I watched the royal guards around me deal with the remnants of the fanged beasts, splattering the ground with blood and gore.

"Alright," I called out, "I think that's all of them."

The guards relaxed, but only slightly. I appreciated their caution, but this didn't feel like a situation where we'd be ambushed once we lowered our guard. For one thing, there'd be no reason for it. We didn't have anything we were protecting, no escorts they could strike out at.

Wiping my sword off with a rag, I sheathed Road Less Traveled, my own little acknowledgment of my obscure origins, before approaching the captain of the platoon. "Back to the capital?"

He nodded. "Yes, Prince Certimov."

Yeah, that was strange. I didn't mind taking the Certimov name, but I'd appreciate it if people remembered I was technically Shawn Certimov-Hanchett.

As we began to regroup, a messenger eagle suddenly broke through the clearing, the symbol of the capital emblazoned on the silken bandana around its neck.

The captain called for the bird, the taloned messenger landing on his outstretched, armored arm. "Thank you, Hawks."

I wasn't sure how the captain remembered all the messenger birds' names, but I was distracted by a funny feeling in my stomach. A funny feeling that never meant good things for me or Derra.

"By the gods." The captain seemed to still as he read the message.

My stomach rumbled with dread. "Oh no, what does it say?"

"King Certimov has passed away."

Shit.

"Shawn! Wake up!" Ricky tapped on the glass window. "We're finally here!"

I opened my eyes from my nap, used to sudden awakenings, and pushed my comic book to the side. Just waking up, it was kinda hard to remember where I left off.

Something about a prophecy being revealed? This issue of the Warrior's adventure was getting a little convoluted, and I was pretty sure that his sister had been possessed by something in the last issue.

Writers usually don't focus on a character's face that creepily for no reason, yeah?

Another tap came at my window, "Wakey wakey! Starla's here!"

I groaned, getting my butt in gear. If Ricky's girlfriend was here, then I was in actual danger of being left behind in the car.

"Okay, I'm up, I'm up." I stepped out of Winfred's car, joining the others as we stood outside Rocky's Entertainment Park, a big industrial park that had a big bungee jump installation.

Starla was playing with Ricky's hair, being affectionate like she always was when the two were together. Winfred seemed a little uncomfortable, but he had to get used to Starla at some point.

I had a good feeling she'd be sticking around.

I wanted to apologize to and burn every story I'd read where the greatest hero in the world dipped their toes into actual authority and ended up as a pencil pusher king.

"Are you alright, Shawn?" Tracy was at my side, rubbing my shoulders.

I shook my head. "It's just been a tough few years since your father died. I mean, he wasn't, gah, I just underestimated how little time I'd have that wasn't spent dealing with . . ."

How did I even put it? Skeezy nobles? Centuries of tradition? The pedestal I stood on that seemed to wobble every time I stuttered over a word during a speech? I thanked the high heavens that I'd taken that public speaking class years ago.

Sometimes I just considered stepping down and getting a democratic government formed, but honestly, I wasn't sure how to even go about that with all the red tape around my position. Being a hero was one thing, but Tracy and Oracle were the only reason I'd even managed to find good, less corrupt advisers.

And Oracle had been quiet these last few months . . .

"I know it's hard, dear." Tracy kissed my cheek. "But you can't let them get to you, can't let this position get to you. Winfred's worried, you know?"

I thought about my son, whom I'd been so concerned about recently. Being the son of a hero was one thing, but the sons of nobility were always . . . complicated. How did I make sure he turned out right? How did I stop him from being some footnote villain that got in trouble with some mysterious hero in the future?

"I just . . . I want to do so much," I opened up. "Zactrik's still moving out there, and even though we've stopped him time and time again, he's playing the long game. He's waiting for something, and I'm not sure what."

That didn't change that there had been sightings of Zactrik in other nations now. His plans were happening here in the Certillian Empire while the man, or monster, himself seemed content to travel to the Mana Wastes of all things, among other concerning places.

"And," I continued, "it all feels impersonal now, Tracy. I used to lead my men, fight alongside them, but now my greatest strength is influence, and . . . I'm not used to that game."

My queen sweetly wrapped me up in her arms. "Don't forget about your friends, Shawn. Penelope and Ulric are still fighting the good fight, as you put it. And not to mention all those amazing souls you've trained."

She wasn't wrong. As king, I'd been quick to make my own personal squadron of heroes, trained by me personally between court and galas.

"I just hope it'll be enough." My thoughts went to Rakta and his children. Maybe they would be the game changers to finally pull the rug out from under Zactrik?

She kissed me on the lips. "It will be. I promise."

I believed her.

"Alright, your turn." Ricky nudged me as Winfred recovered from his turn a few paces away. The poor guy really wasn't too excited about this to begin with, but he seemed to be doing okay for right now.

I just wish he didn't need to feel like he had to push himself to do things he didn't want to do just to hang out with us. He could've chilled and watched . . . but I wasn't gonna stop him.

Although, I kinda wished someone would stop me.

I smiled nervously, "Really, uh, I'm sure Starla probably wants to go, yeah?"

Starla and Ricky shared a look, before smiling at me with matching glints of mischief in their eyes. In tandem, they started counting, "Three . . . two . . ."

I held up a hand, "Okay! Whoa, whoa! I do not want to be pushed, okay?"

Peering over to the edge of the jumping dock, I looked down at the water below us. The bungee jumping company that worked with Rocky's Entertainment Park was reputable, but accidents happened.

Tugging at my cord to make sure it wasn't loose, I nodded. "See you guys on the other si—"

Two pairs of hands suddenly pushed me off the jumping ledge.

"Aaaah!" I fell down, my eyes wildly looking around, just barely catching the looks of amusement, before I refocused on the fact that I was falling.

And the water was getting close, really close! Super, way too close, close! I continued to scream, throwing up my arms to protect myself, when a bright light suddenly flashed around.

"What's going o—!" And suddenly everything became too bright to speak.

"Father, good morning."

I smiled warmly at my son. "Good morning, Winfred. Did you sleep well?"

He nodded, his strawberry blond hair shaking. "Yes, Father! I had this amazing dream that I was a great hero like you! Killing monsters and taking names!"

"Oh really?" I almost blushed at his one-liner that he'd grown attached to from my stories. Rakta wasn't the only storyteller in the empire anymore. "Well, I'm sure that won't always be just a dream, will it?"

Winfred sat himself down as Tracy came in, a comb in hand and her eyes set on our son's unruly locks of hair.

"Winfred Certimov-Hanchett! I've told you about that hair of yours; now hold still!" She approached with iron in her eyes.

Winfred whined, "Mother! I'm hungry! Can't we eat first?"

He looked at me for help, but I casually looked away and didn't let him make eye contact. I wasn't going to go into the lion's den for the sake of his hair.

"No way, mister." She began to tug the comb through his tangled knots. "I swear, did a goose lay an egg on your head last night? Why is it always so messy?"

Winfred wiggled. "I want shorter hair! Like Father!"

I ran a hand through my short hair, closer to my scalp these days. Traditionally, a Certimov was expected to grow out their hair, for some ceremonial reason, but I'd managed to get by due to having married into the family.

My son, well, I hadn't fought against that tradition just yet.

"One day, maybe," my wife allowed. "Until then, you need to take better care of it! I'm sure I got you special herbal lotion to treat it with before going to bed!"

It was a nice morning spent listening to the heartwarming clamoring of my family. Being king had been hard, and would certainly be so for a long time, but even if I hadn't heard from Oracle in . . . years, I had managed.

Even if Zactrik's shadow was still creeping around, staying all but invisible to any investigation we had, we'd managed to find some nobles in his employ, rescued kidnapped children, and had made sure that none of his schemes truly came to fruition.

"Father! Tell Mother that I should be able to have my own sword!"

"A wooden sword is perfectly fine for a child your age!"

I chuckled, beginning to speak when an old familiar voice stopped me, one that resounded in the back of my head.

[Darkness rises. A heartwarming prelude to dark machinations hid within machinations. Prepare your nation, Shawn, for your red flag has been firmly planted.]

Winfred and Tracy both looked at me, suddenly worried. He pulled himself away from his mother. "Dad? Are you alright?"

My mouth was far too dry to even begin to respond.

REFERENCE NOTES

Vitae and Techniques

Vitae is physical energy, born from the heart and the tangible within the human body. All living beings have a base amount of physical energy inside of them, but it takes time, skill, and inherent potential to broaden this physical energy into a true resource to channel into techniques.

Techniques often require an act of word or movement to activate, but training out of the need for these concentration aids are rites of passage in mastering specific techniques. Those who use techniques are often referred to as martials, fighters, brawlers, cultivators, vitaecians, and vanguards, although other terminology exists, such as the academic title Vitae-Versed.

Stances are an integral aspect of using techniques, as they prime the user's Vitae to be more receptive to certain techniques. A stance that primes the Vitae to be more defensive will boost the effects of a technique's defensive aspects. Some techniques require a specific type of primed Vitae to be used at all.

Vitae is also used in channeling. A foundational base for techniques, channeling allows physical energy to be worked into the weapon the user is holding, enhancing its durability, sharpening its blade, and giving it resistance to magical effects and other benefits.

In-Text Techniques

Air Dance Technique: A technique that sends Vitae into the air underneath the user's feet, solidifying it into a small platform, allowing the user to run and walk through the air while they maintain concentration.

Air Slice Technique: This technique has the user enhance their weapon with a Vitae tinged for war, making wounds inflicted by the weapon harder to heal and recover from.

Colossal Might Technique: This technique allows the user to grow their physical form to a more formidable size, increasing muscle strength in return for slower speeds. Overuse of this technique can cause skeletal strain.

Counterstrike Technique: A technique that allows the user, when injured, to empower their next strike against their attacker. The strike is empowered based on the severity of the triggering injury and is drawn to the attacker, even if they are unseen.

Deep Blue Technique: A technique that allows the user to send Vitae into their eyes, tinting the physical world in a blue hue that reveals all living creatures and moving objects in a red light. Overuse of this technique leads to blindness.

First Dance Technique: Sunrise over the Mesa: A technique that requires the **First Dance Stance**. The user enhances the ambient heat in the environment around them, before collecting and pushing it all into one area, creating an area of bright light and heat that burns everything within it.

First Dance Technique: Twister Through the Valley: A technique that requires the **First Dance Stance**. The user manipulates the wind and air into a twister that moves with the user, amplifying their speed and strength with the force of a natural disaster.

First Dance Technique: The Stand of the Unconquered Plateau: A technique that requires the **First Dance Stance**. The user imbues their limbs and the air around them with the crushing weight and immovability of stone, immobilizing themselves, but granting them increased physical and magical resistances. The technique also allows them to solidify any hold they have on another, making the grapple inescapable.

Grasshopper Leap Technique: A simple technique that swiftly propels the user high into the sky, dependent on how much Vitae the user pumped into the technique.

Great Wind Sprint Technique: A technique that requires the user to circulate their Vitae into the air around them as they move, subtly manipulating it to push them forward and with less resistance. Allows for vastly increased speed and easier vertical movement.

Guard Periculum Technique: This technique, which requires high amounts of concentration and calm, allows the user to sense active danger to their person in a larger perimeter around them. The larger the perimeter, the more concentration required.

Healing Flesh Technique: A technique highly strenuous on the user, whereupon they direct their Vitae into their wounds and injuries, enhancing the healing process and allowing rapid regeneration. Requires high concentration and large amounts of Vitae.

Heavy Strike Technique: A simple, yet powerful technique that charges the user's weapon with an unwieldy amount of Vitae, increasing the power behind the blow at the cost of accuracy.

Horizon Throw Technique: Similar to the **Wide Cleave Technique**, this technique massively amplifies the edge of the user's weapon beyond the physical blade, creating a more far-reaching, deadlier projectile. The technique also increases the speed of the thrown object, making it somewhat frictionless to air.

Instinctive Reflex Technique: A technique that enhances the reflexes of the user, heightening their instinctive reactions to danger and allowing their body to move out of the way of attacks before their mind catches up.

Iron Skin Technique: A technique that enhances the skin of the user, imbuing the defensive power of iron across their body in specific areas. Higher proficiencies of the technique allow for full-body enhancement.

Nightingale Shift Technique: This technique allows the user to become unseen to the naked eye for a short period of time, with any act of aggression breaking this invisibility.

Redirecting Hand Technique: This technique allows the user to coat their hands in Vitae, allowing them to absorb harmful energies with one of their hands, before redirecting the absorbed energy out of their other hand.

Scourger Bloodhound Technique: This technique allows the user to pull the ambient Vitae from their five senses and collect it into their sense of smell, vastly enhancing the sole sense in return for rendering their other senses useless for a time.

Skip Dash Technique: A technique that allows the user to enhance their speed exponentially in one small moment, granting them incredible evasive ability. Highly Vitae intensive and control of movement requires intense training.

Stomping Leap Technique: A technique that sends the user into the sky, whereupon they come down with a crushing force on the area below them, bolstered by the height they managed to reach before coming down.

Swift Throw Technique: A technique that allows the user to accelerate the act of retrieving and throwing an object to superhuman levels, thereby allowing multiple objects to be thrown in a short time.

Swordspear Technique: A technique that channels Vitae into a straight-bladed weapon, amplifying the sharp tip of the blade beyond the physical edge for one short moment.

True Opponent Technique: A technique that requires the **Valiant Hero Stance.** Empowering the user's Vitae with a challenge to anyone the user considers a foe, the user is capable of forcing combatants to focus their offensive techniques and spells toward the user alone for a short time.

Valiant Body Technique: A technique that requires the **Valiant Hero Stance.** Upon use, the body of the user is coated in a brilliant golden light and all physical capabilities of the user are momentarily multiplied.

Valiant Strike Technique: A technique that requires the **Valiant Hero Stance.** Upon use, the weapon of the user is coated in a brilliant golden light that extends from the blade and momentarily multiplies the power behind each blow.

Wide Cleave Technique: A simple-to-learn-but-difficult-to-master technique that amplifies the edge of the user's weapon beyond the physical blade, giving it a larger, somewhat-difficult-to-notice attack range.

Wind Axe Technique: A technique that allows the user to solidify the air using Vitae into the form of a simple throwing axe, which can be thrown and used in combat for a short time.

In-Text Stances

Dancing Star Stance: A stance that primes the user's Vitae to be more conductive and long-lasting outside the user's body. Allows the user to manipulate objects, commonly weapons, they've recently imbued their Vitae into.

First Dance Stance: An ancient stance from the land of Rusk. Few are given the right to learn it; even fewer manage to master it. This stance primes the user's Vitae to saturate the environment around the user, moving with the primal energies of the weather.

Grace Stance: A stance that primes the user's Vitae for rapid reactions, increasing their reaction time and overall speed.

Iron Knight Stance: A stance that primes the user's Vitae to be more defensive and increases their endurance and resistance to injury. A common stance taught to the guards of the Certillian Empire.

Valiant Hero Stance: A unique stance created by Shawn Hanchett, it empowers the user's Vitae, increasing physical ability and resistance to bodily harm and mental influence. Rumor has it that the stance requires the user to be fighting a "true foe" to be properly used.

Mana and Spells

Mana is spiritual energy, born from the mind and the ethereal within the human body. Like Vitae, all creatures have a base amount of spiritual energy inside of them, but it takes time, skill, and inherent potential to hone that speck of spiritual energy into a true well of Mana to cast spells from.

Spells require incantations, longer ritualistic acts of spoken word and other foci (sometimes involving certain materials) that help concentrate Mana into the grooves of the spell. Those who cast spells are often referred to as sorcerers, magicians, wizards, warlocks, and bards, although other terminology exists, such as the academic title Mana-Versed.

Shortening incantations, or learning to no longer require certain foci for a spell, requires tremendous skill and time. Silent spells are considered a far bigger accomplishment than silent techniques due to the larger investment required to achieve such a mastery with Mana, it being a hard to grasp energy that requires tremendous focus.

Additionally, whereas techniques have stances to prime Vitae, Mana instead has rituals. Rituals are longer castings of spells, often requiring days to months to cast larger, more powerful spells. Often, multiple magicians of different or similar studies work together on rituals, making them complex projects that produce far-reaching effects.

Another key aspect of Mana is enchantment. Mana is capable of imbuing objects over long periods of time with complex magical abilities, with enchanters and artificers, creators of magical devices composed of multiple magical components, being in high demand throughout Derra.

In-Text Spells

Clear River of Memories (*"From a foggy torrent, from a cracked mirror, ordain this one with insight of yesteryear, of that which has passed and become dormant. Brush away the dust."*): A spell of memory magic. This spell causes the target to fall into a coma as they vividly remember their life. The user cannot direct the target to specific memories, with such a responsibility falling to the target. The target can get lost in their memories if they do not stay focused and can remain in the coma for a long period of time.

Map of Consciousness (*"Memories of memories, mind eye awakening."*): A spell of memory magic. This spell outlines the impacts on the target's memory, from trauma to magical tempering. The user is able to identify the general details of when, where, and why a memory was forgotten if they are strong enough.

Palace of Memories (*"My House of Yesterday, open to me."*): A spell of memory magic. This spell allows the user to protect their memories from degradation over time or by supernatural influence.

Shatter Thy Sight (---): A spell of shatter magic. This spell breaks and crushes an object or area within the user's sight, but has little direct effect on living creatures. The explosive shock waves of the spell, however, can be weaponized.

Shatter Thy World (*"Derra, I demolish."*): A spell of shatter magic. This spell breaks and crushes the area around the user, including above and below. Far more destructive than **Shatter Thy Sight**, this spell can cause great harm to those beyond the user, and the explosive shock waves of the spell are considerably more dangerous as well.

Strike of Lightning (*"Lord of Thunder, grant me nimbus strength, inner energy."*): A spell of lightning magic. This spell shoots a fierce bolt of lightning from the hand of the user at the target. Its true equivalency to a lightning bolt is contested, but it is hard to dodge and can be devastating in the hands of a master magician.

ABOUT THE AUTHOR

Payton Fletcher is the author of My Children from Another World, a slice-of-life reverse-Isekai trilogy, as well as a small-town journalist. Also known as _Glasses, Fletcher first fell for the stories of his great-grandfather and the rest of his family. When he became a journalist and began to hear even more people's stories, he decided to finally put his own ideas down on paper for the world to read. In addition to writing, he spends his time walking around his downtown area, researching new ideas, reading new books, and trying to put his glasses back together whenever they fall apart. Fletcher lives in southern Georgia.

Podium
DISCOVER
STORIES UNBOUND
PodiumAudio.com